DAVID
COPPERFIELD

CHARLES DICKENS'
DAVID
COPPERFIELD

ILLUSTRATED BY EVERETT SHINN

THE LITERARY GUILD OF AMERICA, INC.
Garden City, New York

Charles Dickens - from an old etching

CHAPTER 1   I AM BORN ◆ ◆ ◆

WHETHER I shall turn out to be the hero of my own life, or whether that station will be held by anybody else, these pages must show. To begin my life with the beginning of my life, I record that I was born (as I have been informed and believe) on a Friday, at twelve o'clock at night. It was remarked that the clock began to strike, and I began to cry, simultaneously.

In consideration of the day and hour of my birth, it was declared by the nurse, and by some sage women in the neighborhood, first, that I was destined to be unlucky in life; and secondly, that I was privileged to see ghosts and spirits: both these gifts inevitably attaching, as they believed, to all unlucky infants of either gender born towards the small hours on a Friday night.

I was born at Blunderstone, in Suffolk, a posthumous child. My father's eyes had closed upon the light of this world six months when mine opened on it. There is something strange to me, even now, in the reflection that he never saw me.

An aunt of my father's, and consequently a great-aunt of mine, was the principal magnate of our family. Miss Trotwood, or Miss Betsey, as my poor mother always called her when she sufficiently overcame her dread of this formidable personage to mention her at all (which was seldom), had been married to a husband younger than herself, who was very handsome, except in the sense of the homely adage, "handsome is, that handsome does"; for he was strongly suspected of having beaten Miss Betsey, and even of having once made some hasty but determined arrangements to throw her out of a two-pair-of-stairs window. These evidences of an incompatibility of temper induced Miss Betsey to pay him off, and effect a separation by mutual consent. He went to India with his capital, and there, according to a wild legend in our family, he was once seen riding on an elephant, in company with a Baboon; but I think it must have been a Baboo—or a Begum. Anyhow, from India tidings of his death reached home, within ten years. How they affected my aunt, nobody knew; for immediately upon the separation she took her maiden name again, bought a cottage in a hamlet on the seacoast a long way off, established herself there as a single woman with one servant, and was understood to live secluded, ever afterwards, in an inflexible retirement.

My father had once been a favorite of hers, I believe; but she was mortally affronted by his marriage, on the ground that my mother was "a wax doll." She had never seen my mother, but she knew her to be not yet twenty. My father and Miss Betsey never met again. He was double my mother's age when he married, and of but a delicate constitution. He died a year afterwards, and, as I have said, six months before I came into the world.

This was the state of matters on the afternoon of, what I may be excused for calling, that eventful and important Friday. My mother was sitting by the fire, that bright, windy March afternoon, very timid and sad, and very doubtful of ever coming alive out of the trial that was before her, when, lifting her eyes to the window opposite, she saw a strange lady coming up the garden.

My mother had a sure foreboding at the second glance that it was Miss Betsey. The setting sun was glowing on the strange lady, over the garden fence; and she came walking up to the door with a fell rigidity of figure and composure of countenance that could have belonged to nobody else.

When she reached the house, she gave another proof of her identity. My father had often hinted that she seldom conducted herself like any ordinary Christian; and now, instead of ringing the bell, she came and looked in at that identical window, pressing the end of her nose against the glass to that extent that my poor dear mother used to say it became perfectly flat and white in a moment.

She gave my mother such a turn that I have always been convinced I am indebted to Miss Betsey for having been born on a Friday.

My mother had left her chair in her agitation, and gone behind it in the corner. Miss Betsey, looking round the room, slowly and inquiringly, began on the other side, and carried her eyes on, like a Saracen's Head in a Dutch clock, until they reached my mother. Then she made a frown and a gesture to my mother, like one who was accustomed to be obeyed, to come and open the door. My mother went.

"Mrs. David Copperfield, I *think*," said Miss Betsey.

"Yes," said my mother faintly.

"Miss Trotwood," said the visitor. "You have heard of her, I dare say?"

My mother answered she had had that pleasure. And she had a disagreeable consciousness of not appearing to imply that it had been an overpowering pleasure.

"Now you see her," said Miss Betsey. My mother bent her head, and begged her to walk in. When they were both seated, and Miss Betsey said nothing, my mother, after vainly trying to restrain herself, began to cry.

"Oh, tut, tut, tut!" said Miss Betsey, in a hurry. "Don't do that! Come, come."

My mother couldn't help it notwithstanding, so she cried until she had had her cry out.

"Take off your cap, child," said Miss Betsey, "and let me see you."

My mother was too much afraid of her to refuse compliance with this odd request, if she had any disposition to do so. Therefore she did as she was told, and did it with such nervous hands that her hair (which was luxuriant and beautiful) fell all about her face.

"Why, bless my heart!" exclaimed Miss Betsey, "you are a very Baby!"

My mother was, no doubt, unusually youthful in appearance even for her years. She hung her head, as if it were her fault, poor thing, and said, sobbing, that indeed she was afraid she was but a childish widow, and would be but a childish mother if she lived. In a short pause which ensued she had a fancy that she felt Miss Betsey touch her hair, and that with no ungentle hand; but, looking at her, in her timid hope, she found that lady sitting with the skirt of her dress tucked up, her hands folded on one knee, and her feet upon the fender, frowning at the fire.

3

"In the name of Heaven," said Miss Betsey suddenly, "why Rookery?"

"The name was Mr. Copperfield's choice," returned my mother. "When he bought the house, he liked to think that there were rooks about it."

"David Copperfield all over!" cried Miss Betsey. "David Copperfield from head to foot! Calls a house a rookery when there's not a rook near it!"

"Mr. Copperfield," returned my mother, "is dead, and if you dare to speak unkindly of him to me——"

My poor dear mother, I suppose, had some momentary intention of committing an assault and battery upon my aunt, who could easily have settled her with one hand, even if my mother had been in far better training for such an encounter than she was that evening. But it passed with the action of rising from her chair, and she sat down again very meekly, and fainted.

When she came to herself, or when Miss Betsey had restored her, whichever it was, she found the latter standing at the window. The twilight was by this time shading down into darkness, and dimly as they saw each other, they could not have done that without the aid of the fire.

"I am all in a tremble," faltered my mother. "I don't know what's the matter. I shall die, I am sure!"

"No, no, no," said Miss Betsey. "Have some tea."

"Oh, dear me, dear me, do you think it will do me any good?" cried my mother in a helpless manner.

"Of course it will," said Miss Betsey. "It's nothing but fancy. What do you call your girl?"

"I don't know that it will be a girl, yet, ma'am," said my mother innocently.

"Bless the Baby!" exclaimed Miss Betsey. "I don't mean that. I mean your servant-girl."

"Peggotty," said my mother.

"Peggotty!" repeated Miss Betsey, with some indignation. "Do you mean to say, child, that any human being has gone into a Christian church and got herself named Peggotty?"

"It's her surname," said my mother faintly. "Mr. Copperfield called her by it, because her Christian name was the same as mine."

"Here, Peggotty!" cried Miss Betsey, opening the parlor door. "Tea. Your mistress is a little unwell. Don't dawdle."

Having issued this mandate with as much potentiality as if she had been a recognized authority in the house, Miss Betsey shut the door again, and sat down as before, with her feet on the fender, the skirt of her dress tucked up, and her hands folded on one knee.

"You were speaking about its being a girl," said Miss Betsey. "I have no doubt it will be a girl. I have a presentiment that it must be a girl. Now, child, from the moment of the birth of this girl——"

"Perhaps boy," my mother took the liberty of putting in.

"I tell you I have a presentiment that it must be a girl," returned Miss Betsey. "Don't contradict. From the moment of this girl's birth, child, I intend to be her friend. I intend to be her godmother, and I beg you'll call her Betsey Trotwood Copperfield. There must be no mistakes in life with *this* Betsey Trotwood. There must be no trifling with *her* affections, poor dear. She must be well brought up, and well guarded from reposing any foolish confidences where they are not deserved. I must make that *my* care."

There was a twitch of Miss Betsey's head, after each of these sentences, as if her own old wrongs were working within her, and she repressed any plainer reference to them by strong constraint.

"And was David good to you, child?" asked Miss Betsey, when she had been silent for a little while, and these motions of her head had gradually ceased. "Were you comfortable together?"

"We were very happy," said my mother. "Mr. Copperfield was only too good to me."

"What! He spoilt you, I suppose?" returned Miss Betsey.

"For being quite alone and dependent on myself in this rough world again, yes, I fear he did indeed," sobbed my mother.

"Well, don't cry!" said Miss Betsey. "You were not equally matched, child—if any two people *can* be equally matched—and so I asked the question. You were an orphan, weren't you?"

"Yes."

"And a governess?"

"I was nursery-governess in a family where Mr. Copperfield came to visit. Mr. Copperfield was very kind to me, and took a great deal of notice of me, and paid me a good deal of attention, and at last proposed to me. And I accepted him. And so we were married," said my mother simply.

"Ha! Poor baby!" mused Miss Betsey, with her frown still bent upon the fire. "Do you know anything?"

"I beg you pardon, ma'am," faltered my mother.

"About keeping house, for instance," said Miss Betsey.

5

"Not much, I fear," returned my mother. "Not so much as I could wish. But Mr. Copperfield was teaching me——"

"Much he knew about it himself!" said Miss Betsey in a parenthesis.

"I kept my housekeeping book regularly, and balanced it with Mr. Copperfield every night," cried my mother in another burst of distress, and breaking down again.

"Well, well!" said Miss Betsey. "Don't cry any more."

"And I am sure we never had a word of difference respecting it, except when Mr. Copperfield objected to my threes and fives being too much like each other, or to my putting curly tails to my sevens and nines," resumed my mother in another burst, and breaking down again.

"You'll make yourself ill," said Miss Betsey, "and you know that will not be good either for you or for my goddaughter. Come! you mustn't do it!"

This argument had some share in quieting my mother, though her increasing indisposition perhaps had a larger one. There was an interval of silence, only broken by Miss Betsey's occasionally ejaculating "Ha!" as she sat with her feet upon the fender.

"David had bought an annuity for himself with his money, I know," said she by-and-by. "What did he do for you?"

"Mr. Copperfield," said my mother, answering with some difficulty, "was so considerate and good as to secure the reversion of a part of it to me."

"How much?" asked Miss Betsey.

"A hundred and five pounds a year," said my mother.

"He might have done worse," said my aunt.

The word was appropriate to the moment. My mother was so much worse that Peggotty, coming in with the tea-board and candles, and seeing at a glance how ill she was, conveyed her upstairs to her own room with all speed; and immediately dispatched Ham Peggotty, her nephew, who had been for some days past secreted in the house, unknown to my mother, as a special messenger in case of emergency, to fetch the nurse and doctor.

Those allied powers were considerably astonished, when they arrived within a few minutes of each other, to find an unknown lady of portentous appearance sitting before the fire, with her bonnet tied over her left arm, stopping her ears with jewelers' cotton. Peggotty knowing nothing about her, and my mother saying nothing about her, she was quite a mystery in the parlor.

The doctor having been upstairs and come down again, and having satisfied himself, I suppose, that there was a probability of this unknown lady and himself having to sit there, face to face, for some hours, laid himself out to be polite and social. He was the meekest of his sex, the mildest of little men. He sidled in and out of a room, to take up the less space. It is nothing to say that he hadn't a word to throw at a dog. He couldn't have *thrown* a word at a mad dog. He might have offered him one gently, or half a one, or a fragment of one—for he spoke as slowly as he walked; but he wouldn't have been rude to him, and he couldn't have been quick with him, for any earthly consideration.

Mr. Chillip, looking mildly at my aunt, with his head on one side, and making her a little bow, said, in allusion to the jewelers' cotton, as he softly touched his left ear,

"Some local irritation, ma'am?"

"What?" replied my aunt, pulling the cotton out of one ear like a cork.

Mr. Chillip was so alarmed by her abruptness—as he told my mother afterwards—that it was a mercy he didn't lose his presence of mind. But he repeated sweetly,

"Some local irritation, ma'am?"

"Nonsense!" replied my aunt, and corked herself again, at one blow.

Mr. Chillip could do nothing after this but sit and look at her feebly, as she sat and looked at the fire, until he was called upstairs again. After some quarter of an hour's absence he returned.

"Well?" said my aunt, taking the cotton out of the ear nearest to him.

"Well, ma'am," returned Mr. Chillip, "we are—we are progressing slowly, ma'am."

"Ba—a—ah!" said my aunt, with a perfect shake on the contemptuous interjection, and corked herself as before.

Really—really—as Mr. Chillip told my mother, he was almost shocked. But he sat and looked at her, notwithstanding, for nearly two hours, as she sat looking at the fire, until he was again called out. After another absence, he again returned.

"Well?" said my aunt, taking out the cotton on that side again.

"Well, ma'am," returned Mr. Chillip, "we are—we are progressing slowly, ma'am."

"Ya—a—ah!" said my aunt, with such a snarl at him, that Mr. Chillip absolutely could not bear it. It was really calculated to break

7

his spirit, he said afterwards. He preferred to go and sit upon the stairs, in the dark and a strong draft, until he was again sent for.

The mild Mr. Chillip could not possibly bear malice at such a time, if at any time. He sidled into the parlor as soon as he was at liberty, and said to my aunt in his meekest manner,

"Well, ma'am, I am happy to congratulate you."

"What upon?" said my aunt sharply.

Mr. Chillip was fluttered again by the extreme severity of my aunt's manner; so he made her a little bow, and gave her a little smile, to mollify her.

"Mercy on the man, what's he doing!" cried my aunt impatiently. "Can't he speak?"

"Be calm, my dear ma'am," said Mr. Chillip in his softest accents. "There is no longer any occasion for uneasiness, ma'am. Be calm."

It has since been considered almost a miracle that my aunt didn't shake him, and shake what he had to say out of him. She only shook her own head at him, but in a way that made him quail.

"Well, ma'am," resumed Mr. Chillip, as soon as he had courage, "I am happy to congratulate you. All is now over, ma'am, and well over."

During the five minutes or so that Mr. Chillip devoted to the delivery of this oration my aunt eyed him narrowly.

"How is she?" said my aunt, folding her arms, with her bonnet still tied on one of them.

"Well, ma'am, she will soon be quite comfortable, I hope," returned Mr. Chillip—"quite as comfortable as we can expect a young mother to be, under these melancholy domestic circumstances. There cannot be any objection to your seeing her presently, ma'am. It may do her good."

"And *she*—how is *she*?" said my aunt sharply.

Mr. Chillip laid his head a little more on one side, and looked at my aunt like an amiable bird.

"The baby," said my aunt—"how is she?"

"Ma'am," returned Mr. Chillip, "I apprehended you had known. It's a boy."

My aunt said never a word, but took her bonnet by the strings, in the manner of a sling, aimed a blow at Mr. Chillip's head with it, put it on bent, walked out, and never came back.

"I am indebted to Aunt Betsey for having been born on a Friday."

CHAPTER 2 🍃 I OBSERVE ✦ ✦ ✦

THE first objects that assume a distinct presence before me, as I look far back into the blank of my infancy, are my mother with her pretty hair and youthful shape, and Peggotty, with no shape at all, and eyes so dark that they seemed to darken their whole neighborhood in her face, and cheeks so hard and red that I wondered the birds didn't peck her in preference to apples.

Peggotty and I were sitting one night by the parlor fire, alone. I had been reading to Peggotty about crocodiles. I must have read very perspicuously, or the poor soul must have been deeply interested, for I remember she had a cloudy impression, after I had done, that they were a sort of vegetable. I was tired of reading, and dead sleepy; but having leave, as a high treat, to sit up until my mother came home from spending the evening at a neighbor's, I would rather have died upon my post (of course) than have gone to bed.

"Peggotty," says I suddenly, "were you ever married?"

"Lord, Master Davy," replied Peggotty. "What's put marriage in your head?"

She answered with such a start that it quite awoke me. And then she stopped in her work, and looked at me, with her needle drawn out to its thread's length.

"But *were* you ever married, Peggotty?" says I. "You are a very handsome woman, an't you?"

"Me handsome, Davy!" said Peggotty. "Lawk, no, my dear!"

"You an't cross, I suppose, Peggotty, are you?" said I.

She laid aside her work and opening her arms wide, took my curly head within them, and gave it a good squeeze. I know it was a good squeeze, because, being very plump, whenever she made any little exertion after she was dressed, some of the buttons on the back of her gown flew off. And I recollect two bursting to the opposite side of the parlor while she was hugging me.

"Now let me hear some more about the crorkindills," said Peggotty, who was not quite right in the name yet.

We had exhausted the crocodiles, and begun with the alligators, when the garden-bell rang. We went out to the door, and there was my mother, looking unusually pretty, I thought, and with her a gentleman with beautiful black hair and whiskers, who had walked home with us from church last Sunday.

As my mother stooped down on the threshold to take me in her arms and kiss me, the gentleman said I was a more highly privileged little fellow than a monarch—or something like that; for my later understanding comes, I am sensible, to my aid here.

"What does that mean?" I asked him, over her shoulder.

He patted me on the head; but somehow, I didn't like him or his deep voice, and I was jealous that his hand should touch my mother's in touching me—which it did. I put it away as well as I could.

"Oh, Davy!" remonstrated my mother.

"Dear boy!" said the gentleman. "I cannot wonder at his devotion!"

I never saw such a beautiful color on my mother's face before. She gently chid me for being rude; and, keeping me close to her shawl, turned to thank the gentleman for taking so much trouble as to bring her home. She put out her hand to him as she spoke, and, as he met it with his own, she glanced, I thought, at me.

"Let us say 'good-night,' my fine boy," said the gentleman, when he had bent his head—*I* saw him!—over my mother's little glove.

"Good-night!" said I.

"Come! let us be the best friends in the world!" said the gentleman, laughing. "Shake hands!"

My right hand was in my mother's left, so I gave him the other.

"Why, that's the wrong hand, Davy!" laughed the gentleman.

My mother drew my right hand forward; but I was resolved, for my former reason, not to give it him, and I did not. I gave him the other, and he shook it heartily, and said I was a brave fellow, and went away.

Peggotty, who had not said a word or moved a finger, secured the fastenings instantly, and we all went into the parlor. My mother, contrary to her usual habit, instead of coming to the elbow-chair by the fire, remained at the other end of the room, and sat singing to herself. I fell asleep. When I half awoke, I found Peggotty and my mother both in tears, and both talking.

"Not such a one as this, Mr. Copperfield wouldn't have liked," said Peggotty. "That I say, and that I swear!"

"Good heavens!" cried my mother, "you'll drive me mad! Was ever any poor girl so ill-used by her servants as I am? Why do I do myself the injustice of calling myself a girl? Have I never been married, Peggotty?"

"God knows you have, ma'am," returned Peggotty.

"Then, how can you dare," said my mother—"you know I don't mean how can you dare, Peggotty, but how can you have the heart —to make me so uncomfortable and say such bitter things to me, when you are well aware that I haven't, out of this place, a single friend to turn to?"

"The more's the reason," returned Peggotty, "for saying that it won't do. No! That it won't do. No! No price could make it do. No!"—I thought Peggotty would have thrown the candlestick away, she was so emphatic with it.

"And my dear boy," cried my mother, coming to the elbow-chair in which I was, and caressing me—"my own little Davy! You know as well as I do, that on his account only last quarter I wouldn't buy myself a new parasol, though that old green one is frayed the whole way up, and the fringe is perfectly mangy? You know it is, Peggotty; you can't deny it." Then, turning affectionately to me, with her cheek against mine, "Am I a naughty mamma to you, Davy? Am I a nasty, cruel, selfish, bad mamma? Say I am, my child—say 'yes,' dear boy, and Peggotty will love you; and Peggotty's love is a great deal better than mine, Davy. I don't love you at all, do I?"

At this we all fell a-crying together. I think I was the loudest of the party, but I am sure we were all sincere about it. We went to bed greatly dejected.

Whether it was the following Sunday when I saw the gentleman again, or whether there was any greater lapse of time before he reappeared, there he was, in church, and he walked home with us afterwards. He came in, too, to look at a famous geranium we had, in the parlor-window. It did not appear to me that he took much notice of it, but before he went he asked my mother to give him a bit of the blossom. She begged him to choose it for himself, but he refused to do that—I could not understand why—so she plucked it for him, and gave it into his hand. He said he would never, never part with it any more; and I thought he must be quite a fool not to know that it would fall to pieces in a day or two.

Gradually, I became used to seeing the gentleman with the black whiskers. I liked him no better than at first, and had the same uneasy jealousy of him. He had that kind of shallow black eye—I want a better word to express an eye that has no depth in it to be looked into—which seems, from some peculiarity of light, to be disfigured, for a moment at a time, by a cast. A squareness about the lower part of his face, and the dotted indication of the strong black beard he shaved close every day, reminded me of the wax-work that had traveled into our neighborhood some half a year before. This, his regular eyebrows, and the rich white, and black, and brown of his complexion—confound his complexion, and his memory!—made me think him, in spite of my misgivings, a very handsome man. I have no doubt that my poor dear mother thought him so too.

One evening (when my mother was out as before), Peggotty, after looking at me several times, and opening her mouth as if she were going to speak, without doing it—which I thought was merely gaping, or I should have been rather alarmed—said coaxingly,

"Master Davy, how should you like to go along with me and spend a fortnight at my brother's at Yarmouth? Wouldn't *that* be a treat?"

"Is your brother an agreeable man, Peggotty?" I inquired provisionally.

"Oh, what an agreeable man he is!" cried Peggotty, holding up her hands. "Then there's the sea; and the boats and ships; and the fishermen; and the beach; and Am to play with——"

Peggotty meant her nephew Ham, mentioned in my first chapter; but she spoke of him as a morsel of English Grammar.

The day soon came for our going. It touches me nearly now, although I tell it lightly, to recollect how eager I was to leave my happy home; to think how little I suspected what I did leave forever.

12

THE carrier's horse was the laziest horse in the world, I should hope, and shuffled along, with his head down, as if he liked to keep the people waiting to whom the packages were directed. The carrier had a way of keeping his head down, like his horse, and of drooping sleepily forward as he drove, with one of his arms on each of his knees. I say "drove," but it struck me that the cart would have gone to Yarmouth quite as well without him, for the horse did all that. And as to conversation, he had no idea of it but whistling. I was quite tired, and very glad, when we saw Yarmouth.

When we got into the street (which was strange enough to me), and smelt the fish, and pitch, and oakum, and tar, and saw the sailors walking about, and the carts jingling up and down over the stones, I felt that Yarmouth was, upon the whole, the finest place in the universe.

"Here's my Am!" screamed Peggotty, "growed out of knowl-edge!"

He was now a huge, strong fellow of six feet high, broad in pro-portion, and round-shouldered; but with a simpering boy's face and curly light hair that gave him quite a sheepish look. He was dressed in a canvas jacket, and a pair of such very stiff trousers that they would have stood quite as well alone, without any legs in them. And you couldn't so properly have said he wore a hat, as that he was covered in a-top, like an old building, with something pitchy.

Ham carrying me on his back and a small box of ours under his arm, and Peggotty carrying another small box of ours, we turned down lanes bestrewn with bits of chips and little hillocks of sand, and went past gas-works, rope-walks, boat-builders' yards, ship-wrights' yards, ship-breakers' yards, calkers' yards, riggers' lofts, smiths' forges, and a great litter of such places, until Ham said,

"Yon's our house, Mas'r Davy!"

I looked in all directions, as far as I could stare over the wilderness, and away at the sea, and away at the river, but no house could *I* make out. There was a black barge, or some other kind of superannuated boat, not far off, high and dry on the ground, with an iron funnel sticking out of it for a chimney and smoking very cosily; but nothing else in the way of a habitation that was visible to *me*.

"That's not it," said I—"that ship-looking thing?"

"That's it, Mas'r Davy," returned Ham.

If it had been Aladdin's palace, roc's egg and all, I suppose I could not have been more charmed with the romantic idea of living in it. There was a delightful door cut in the side, and it was roofed in, and there were little windows in it; but the wonderful charm of it was, that it was a real boat, which had no doubt been upon the water hundreds of times, and which had never been intended to be lived in, on dry land.

It was beautifully clean inside, and as tidy as possible. There was a table, and a Dutch clock, and a chest of drawers, and on the chest of drawers there was a tea-tray with a painting on it of a lady with a parasol, taking a walk with a military-looking child who was trundling a hoop. The tray was kept from tumbling down by a Bible; and the tray, if it had tumbled down, would have smashed a quantity of cups and saucers and a teapot that were grouped around the book. On the walls there were some common colored pictures, framed and glazed, of Scripture subjects.

Peggotty opened a little door and showed me my bedroom. It was the completest and most desirable bedroom ever seen—in the stern of the vessel; with a little window, where the rudder used to go through; a little looking-glass, just the right height for me, nailed against the wall, and framed with oyster-shells; a little bed, which there was just room enough to get into; and a nosegay of seaweed in a blue mug on the table. One thing I particularly noticed in this delightful house was the smell of fish. On my imparting this discovery in confidence to Peggotty, she informed me that her brother dealt in lobsters, crabs, and crawfish.

We were welcomed by a very civil woman in a white apron, whom I had seen curtsying at the door when I was on Ham's back, about a quarter of a mile off. Likewise by a most beautiful little girl (or I thought her so), with a necklace of blue beads on, who wouldn't let me kiss her when I offered to, but ran away and hid herself. By-and-by, when we had dined in a sumptuous manner off boiled dabs, melted butter, and potatoes, with a chop for me, a hairy man with a very good-natured face came home. As he called Peggotty "Lass," and gave her a hearty smack on the cheek, I had no doubt, from the general propriety of her conduct, that he was her brother; and so he turned out—being presently introduced to me as Mr. Peggotty, the master of the house.

"Glad to see you, sir," said Mr. Peggotty. "You'll find us rough, sir, but you'll find us ready."

I thanked him, and replied that I was sure I should be happy in such a delightful place.

"I'm much obleeged, I'm sure," said Mr. Peggotty. "Well, sir, if you can make out here, for a fortnut, 'long wi' her," nodding at his sister, "and Ham, and little Em'ly, we shall be proud of your company."

Having done the honors of his house in this hospitable manner, Mr. Peggotty went out to wash himself in a kettleful of hot water, remarking that "cold would never get *his* muck off." He soon returned, greatly improved in appearance; but so rubicund, that I couldn't help thinking his face had this in common with the lobsters, crabs, and crawfish—that it went into the hot water very black and came out very red.

After tea, when the door was shut and all was made snug (the nights being cold and misty now), it seemed to me the most delicious retreat that the imagination of man could conceive. Little Em'ly had overcome her shyness, and was sitting by my side upon the lowest and least of the lockers, which was just large enough for us two, and just fitted into the chimney corner. Mr. Peggotty was smoking his pipe. I felt it was time for conversation and confidence.

"Mr. Peggotty," says I.

"Sir," says he.

"Did you give your son the name of Ham because you lived in a sort of ark?"

Mr. Peggotty seemed to think it a deep idea, but answered, "No, sir. I never giv him no name."

"Who gave him that name, then?" said I, putting question number two of the catechism to Mr. Peggotty.

"Why, sir, his father giv it him," said Mr. Peggotty.

"I thought you were his father!"

"My brother Joe was *his* father," said Mr. Peggotty.

"Dead, Mr. Peggotty?" I hinted, after a respectful pause.

"Drowndead," said Mr. Peggotty.

I was very much surprised that Mr. Peggotty was not Ham's father, and began to wonder whether I was mistaken about his relationship to anybody else there. I was so curious to know, that I made up my mind to have it out with Mr. Peggotty.

"Little Em'ly," I said, glancing at her—"she is your daughter, isn't she, Mr. Peggotty?"

"No, sir. My brother-in-law, Tom, was *her* father."

I couldn't help it. "Dead, Mr. Peggotty?" I hinted, after another respectful silence.

"Drowndead," said Mr. Peggotty.

I felt the difficulty of resuming the subject, but had not got to the bottom of it yet, and must get to the bottom somehow. So I said, "Haven't you *any* children, Mr. Peggotty?"

"No, master," he answered, with a short laugh. "I'm a bacheldore."

"A bachelor!" I said, astonished. "Why, who's that, Mr. Peggotty?" pointing to the person in the apron who was knitting.

"That's Missis Gummidge," said Mr. Peggotty.

"Gummidge, Mr. Peggotty?"

But at this point Peggotty—I mean my own peculiar Peggotty— made such impressive motions to me not to ask any more questions, that I could only sit and look at all the silent company, until it was time to go to bed. Then, in the privacy of my own little cabin, she informed me that Ham and Em'ly were an orphan nephew and niece, whom my host had at different times adopted in their childhood, when they were left destitute; and that Mrs. Gummidge was the widow of his partner in a boat, who had died very poor. He was but a poor man himself, said Peggotty, but as good as gold and as true as steel—those were her similes. The only subject, she informed me, on which he ever showed a violent temper or swore an oath, was this generosity of his; and if it were ever referred to by any one of them, he struck the table a heavy blow with his right hand (had split it on one such occasion), and swore a dreadful oath that

16

he would be "Gormed" if he didn't cut and run for good, if it was ever mentioned again. It appeared, in answer to my inquiries, that nobody had the least idea of the etymology of this terrible verb passive to be gormed, but that they all regarded it as constituting a most solemn imprecation.

As slumber gradually stole upon me, I heard the wind howling out at sea and coming on across the flat so fiercely, that I had a lazy apprehension of the great deep rising in the night. Nothing happened, however, worse than morning. Almost as soon as it shone upon the oyster-shell frame of my mirror I was out of bed, and out with little Em'ly, picking up stones upon the beach.

"You're quite a sailor, I suppose?" I said to Em'ly.

"No," replied Em'ly, shaking her head; "I'm afraid of the sea."

"Afraid!" I said, with a becoming air of boldness, and looking very big at the mighty ocean. "*I* an't!"

"Ah! but it's cruel," said Em'ly. "I have seen it very cruel to some of our men. I have seen it tear a boat as big as our house all to pieces."

"I hope it wasn't the boat that——"

"That father was drownded in?" said Em'ly. "No; not that one. I never see that boat."

"Nor him?" I asked her.

Little Em'ly shook her head. "Not to remember."

Here was a coincidence! I immediately went into an explanation how I had never seen my own father. But there were some differences between Em'ly's orphanhood and mine, it appeared. She had lost her mother before her father; and where her father's grave was no one knew, except that it was somewhere in the depths of the sea.

"Besides," said Em'ly, as she looked about for shells and pebbles, "your father was a gentleman, and your mother is a lady; and my father was a fisherman, and my mother was a fisherman's daughter, and my uncle Dan is a fisherman."

"Dan is Mr. Peggotty, is he?" said I.

"Uncle Dan—yonder," answered Em'ly, nodding at the boat.

"Yes; I mean him. He must be very good, I should think?"

"Good?" said Em'ly. "If I was ever to be a lady, I'd give him a sky-blue coat with diamond buttons, nankeen trousers, a red velvet waistcoat, a cocked hat, a large gold watch, a silver pipe, and a box of money."

"You would like to be a lady?" I said.

Em'ly looked at me, and laughed and nodded "Yes."

17

"I should like it very much. We would all be gentlefolks together then—me, and uncle, and Ham, and Mrs. Gummidge. We wouldn't mind then when there come stormy weather—not for our own sakes, I mean. We would for the poor fishermen's, to be sure, and we'd help 'em with money when they come to any hurt."

We strolled a long way, and loaded ourselves with things that we thought curious, and then made our way home to Mr. Peggotty's dwelling. We stopped under the lee of the lobster outhouse to exchange an innocent kiss, and went in to breakfast glowing with health and pleasure.

Of course I was in love with little Em'ly. I am sure I loved that baby quite as truly, quite as tenderly, with greater purity and more disinterestedness, than can enter into the best love of a later time of life, high and ennobling as it is. I am sure my fancy raised up something round that blue-eyed mite of a child which etherealized, and made a very angel of her.

We used to walk about that dim old flat at Yarmouth in a loving manner, hours and hours. The days sported by us, as if Time had not grown up himself yet, but were a child too, and always at play. I told Em'ly I adored her, and that unless she confessed she adored me I should be reduced to the necessity of killing myself with a sword. She said she did, and I have no doubt she did.

So the fortnight slipped away, varied by nothing but the variation of the tide, which altered Mr. Peggotty's times of going out and coming in, and altered Ham's engagements also. At last the day came for going home.

Now, all the time I had been on my visit, I had been ungrateful to my home again, and had thought little or nothing about it. But I was no sooner turned toward it than my reproachful young conscience seemed to point that way with a steady finger; and I felt, all the more for the sinking of my spirits, that it was my nest, and that my mother was my comforter and friend.

The door opened, and I looked, half laughing and half crying in my pleasant agitation, for my mother. It was not she, but a strange servant.

"Why, Peggotty!" I said ruefully, "isn't she come home?"

"Yes, yes, Master Davy," said Peggotty. "She's come home. Wait a bit, Master Davy, and I'll—I'll tell you something." She took me by the hand; led me, wondering, into the kitchen; and shut the door.

"Peggotty!" said I, quite frightened, "what's the matter?"

"Nothing's the matter, bless you, Master Davy dear!" she answered, assuming an air of sprightliness.

"Something's the matter, I'm sure. Where's mamma?"

"Where's mamma, Master Davy?" repeated Peggotty.

"Yes. Why hasn't she come out to the gate, and what have we come in here for? Oh, she's not dead, Peggotty?"

Peggotty cried out No! with an astonishing volume of voice; and then sat down, and began to pant, and said I had given her a turn.

I gave her a hug to take away the turn, or to give her another turn in the right direction, and then stood before her, looking at her in anxious inquiry.

"You see, dear, I should have told you before now," said Peggotty, "but I hadn't an opportunity. I ought to have made it, perhaps, but I couldn't azackly"—that was always the substitute for exactly, in Peggotty's militia of words—"bring my mind to it."

"Go on, Peggotty," said I, more frightened than before.

"Master Davy," said Peggotty, untying her bonnet with a shaking hand, and speaking in a breathless sort of way, "what do you think? You have got a pa!"

I trembled, and turned white. Peggotty gave a gasp, as if she were swallowing something that was very hard, and, putting out her hand, said,

"Come and see him."

"I don't want to see him."

"And your mamma," said Peggotty.

I ceased to draw back, and we went straight to the best parlor, where she left me. On one side of the fire sat my mother; on the other, Mr. Murdstone. My mother dropped her work, and arose hurriedly, but timidly I thought.

"Now, Clara my dear," said Mr. Murdstone, "recollect! Control yourself, always control yourself!—Davy boy, how do you do?"

I gave him my hand. After a moment of suspense, I went and kissed my mother. She kissed me, patted me gently on the shoulder, and sat down again to her work.

As soon as I could creep away, I crept upstairs. My old dear bedroom was changed, and I was to lie a long way off. I rambled downstairs to find anything that was like itself, so altered it all seemed, and roamed into the yard. I very soon started back from there, for the empty dog-kennel was filled up with a great dog—deep-mouthed and black-haired like Him—and he was very angry at the sight of me, and sprang out to get at me.

19

I WAS awakened by somebody saying, "Here he is!" and uncovering my hot head. My mother and Peggotty had come to look for me, and it was one of them who had done it.

"Davy," said my mother, "what's the matter?"

I thought it was very strange that she should ask me, and answered, "Nothing." I turned over on my face, I recollect, to hide my trembling lip, which answered her with greater truth.

"Davy," said my mother. "Davy, my child!"

I dare say no words she could have uttered would have affected me so much, then, as her calling me her child. I hid my tears in the bedclothes, and pressed her from me with my hand, when she would have raised me up.

"This is your doing, Peggotty, you cruel thing!" said my mother. "I have no doubt at all about it. How can you reconcile it to your conscience, I wonder, to prejudice my own boy against me? What do you mean by it, Peggotty?"

Poor Peggotty lifted up her hands and eyes, and only answered, in a sort of paraphrase of the grace I usually repeated after dinner, "Lord forgive you, Mrs. Copperfield; and for what you have said this minute, may you never be truly sorry!"

"It's enough to distract me," cried my mother. "On my honeymoon, too, when my most inveterate enemy might relent, one would think, and not envy me a little peace of mind and happiness. Davy, you naughty boy! Peggotty, you savage creature!"

I felt the touch of a hand that I knew was neither hers nor Peggotty's, and slipped to my feet at the bedside. It was Mr. Murdstone's hand, and he kept it on my arm as he said,

"What's this? Clara, my love, have you forgotten?—Firmness, my dear!"

"I am very sorry, Edward," said my mother. "I meant to be very good, but I am so uncomfortable."

"Indeed!" he answered. "That's a bad hearing, so soon, Clara."

"I say it's very hard I should be made so now," returned my mother, pouting; "and it is—very hard—isn't it?"

He drew her to him, whispered in her ear, and kissed her. I knew as well, when I saw my mother's head lean down upon his shoulder, and her arm touch his neck—I knew as well that he could mold her pliant nature into any form he chose, as I know, now, that he did it.

"Go you below, my love," said Mr. Murdstone. "David and I will come down together. My friend," turning a darkening face on Peggotty, when he had watched my mother out, and dismissed her with a nod and a smile, "do you know your mistress' name?"

"She has been my mistress a long time, sir," answered Peggotty. "I ought to it."

"That's true," he answered. "But I thought I heard you, as I came upstairs, address her by a name that is not hers. She has taken mine, you know. Will you remember that?"

Peggotty, with some uneasy glances at me, curtsied herself out of the room without replying, seeing, I suppose, that she was expected to go, and had no excuse for remaining. When we two were left alone, he shut the door, and sitting on a chair, and holding me standing before him, looked steadily into my eyes. I felt my own attracted, no less steadily, to his. My heart beat fast and high.

"David," he said, making his lips thin by pressing them together, "if I have an obstinate horse or dog to deal with, what do you think I do?"

"I don't know."

"I beat him."

I had answered in a kind of breathless whisper, but I felt, in my silence, that my breath was shorter now.

"I make him wince, and smart. I say to myself, 'I'll conquer that fellow'; and if it were to cost him all the blood he had, I should do it. What is that upon your face?"

"Dirt," I said.

He knew it was the mark of tears as well as I. But if he had asked the question twenty times, each time with twenty blows, I believe my baby heart would have burst before I would have told him so.

"You have a good deal of intelligence for a little fellow," he said, with a grave smile that belonged to him, "and you understood me very well, I see. Wash that face, sir, and come down with me."

He pointed to the washing-stand and motioned me with his head to obey him directly. I had little doubt then, and I have less doubt now, that he would have knocked me down without the least compunction if I had hesitated.

"Clara, my dear," he said, when I had done his bidding, and he walked me into the parlor, with his hand still on my arm, "you will not be made uncomfortable any more, I hope. We shall soon improve our youthful humors."

God help me, I might have been improved for my whole life, I might have been made another creature perhaps, for life, by a kind word at that season. I thought my mother was sorry to see me standing in the room so scared and strange. But the word was not spoken, and the time for it was gone.

After dinner, when we were sitting by the fire, and I was meditating an escape to Peggotty without having the hardihood to slip away, lest it should offend the master of the house, a coach drove up to the garden-gate, and he went out to receive the visitor. My mother followed him. I was timidly following her, when she turned round at the parlor door, in the dusk, and taking me in her embrace as she had been used to do, whispered me to love my new father and be obedient to him. She did this hurriedly and secretly, as if it were wrong, but tenderly; and, putting out her hand behind her, held mine in it, until we came near to where he was standing in the garden, where she let mine go, and drew hers through his arm.

It was Miss Murdstone who was arrived, and a gloomy-looking lady she was; dark, like her brother, whom she greatly resembled in face and voice, and with very heavy eyebrows, nearly meeting over her large nose, as if, being disabled by the wrongs of her sex from wearing whiskers, she had carried them to that account. She brought with her two uncompromising hard black boxes, with her initials on the lids in hard brass nails. When she paid the coachman she took

22

her money out of a hard steel purse, and she kept the purse in a very jail of a bag which hung upon her arm by a heavy chain, and shut up like a bite. I had never, at that time, seen such a metallic lady altogether as Miss Murdstone was.

She was brought into the parlor with many tokens of welcome, and there formally recognized my mother as a new and near relation. Then she looked at me, and said,

"Is that your boy, sister-in-law?"

My mother acknowledged me.

"Generally speaking," said Miss Murdstone, "I don't like boys.— How d'ye do, boy?"

Under these encouraging circumstances, I replied that I was very well, and that I hoped she was the same, with such an indifferent grace that Miss Murdstone disposed of me in two words—

"Wants manner!"

Having uttered which with great distinctness, she begged the favor of being shown to her room, which became to me from that time forth a place of awe and dread.

As well as I could make out, she had come for good, and had no intention of ever going again. On the very first morning after her arrival she was up and ringing her bell at cock-crow. When my mother came down to breakfast, and was going to make the tea, Miss Murdstone gave her a kind of peck on the cheek, which was her nearest approach to a kiss, and said,

"Now, Clara, my dear, I am come here, you know, to relieve you of all the trouble I can. You're much too pretty and thoughtless"— my mother blushed but laughed, and seemed not to dislike this character—"to have any duties imposed upon you that can be undertaken by me. If you'll be so good as give me your keys, my dear, I'll attend to all this sort of thing in future."

From that time Miss Murdstone kept the keys in her own little pail all day, and under her pillow all night, and my mother had no more to do with them than I had.

My mother did not suffer her authority to pass from her without a shadow of protest. One night, when Miss Murdstone had been developing certain household plans to her brother, of which he signified his approbation, my mother suddenly began to cry, and said she thought she might have been consulted.

"Clara!" said Mr. Murdstone sternly. "Clara! I wonder at you."

"It's very hard," said my mother, "that in my own house——"

"*My* own house?" repeated Mr. Murdstone. "Clara!"

"*Our* own house, I mean," faltered my mother, evidently frightened—"I hope you must know what I mean, Edward—it's very hard that in *your* own house I may not have a word to say about domestic matters. I am sure I managed very well before we were married. There's evidence," said my mother, sobbing; "ask Peggotty if I didn't do very well when I wasn't interfered with."

"Edward," said Miss Murdstone, "let there be an end of this. I go tomorrow."

"Jane Murdstone," said her brother, "be silent! How dare you to insinuate that you don't know my character better than your words imply?"

"I am sure," my poor mother went on, at a grievous disadvantage, and with many tears, "I don't want anybody to go. I should be very miserable and unhappy if anybody was to go. I don't ask much. I am not unreasonable. I only want to be consulted sometimes. I am very much obliged to anybody who assists me, and I only want to be consulted as a mere form, sometimes. I thought you were pleased, once, with my being a little inexperienced and girlish, Edward—but you seem to hate me for it now, you are so severe."

"Edward," said Miss Murdstone again, "let there be an end of this. I go tomorrow."

"Jane Murdstone," thundered Mr. Murdstone, "will you be silent? How dare you?"

Miss Murdstone made a jail-delivery of her pocket-handkerchief, and held it before her eyes.

"Clara," he continued, looking at my mother, "you surprise me! you astound me! Yes, I had a satisfaction in the thought of marrying an inexperienced and artless person, and forming her character, and infusing into it some amount of that firmness and decision of which it stood in need. But when Jane Murdstone is kind enough to come to my assistance in this endeavor, and to assume, for my sake, a condition something like a housekeeper's, and when she meets with a base return——"

"Oh, pray, pray, Edward," cried my mother, "don't accuse me of being ungrateful. I am sure I am not ungrateful. No one ever said I was before. I have many faults, but not that. Oh, don't, my dear!"

"When Jane Murdstone meets, I say," he went on, after waiting until my mother was silent, "with a base return, that feeling of mine is chilled and altered."

"Don't, my love, say that!" implored my mother very piteously. "Oh, don't, Edward! I can't bear to hear it. Whatever I am, I am

24

affectionate. I know I am affectionate. Ask Peggotty. I am sure she'll tell you I'm affectionate."

"There is no extent of mere weakness, Clara," said Mr. Murdstone in reply, "that can have the least weight with me. You lose breath."

"Pray let us be friends," said my mother; "I couldn't live under coldness or unkindness. I am so sorry. I have a great many defects, I know, and it's very good of you, Edward, with your strength of mind, to endeavor to correct them for me.—Jane, I don't object to anything. I should be quite broken-hearted if you thought of leaving——" My mother was too much overcome to go on.

"Jane Murdstone," said Mr. Murdstone to his sister, "any harsh words between us are, I hope, uncommon. It is not my fault that so unusual an occurrence has taken place tonight. I was betrayed into it by another. Nor is it your fault. You were betrayed into it by another. Let us both try to forget it. And as this," he added, after these magnanimous words, "is not a fit scene for the boy— David, go to bed!"

I could hardly find the door, through the tears that stood in my eyes.

Going down next morning rather earlier than usual, I paused outside the parlor door, on hearing my mother's voice. She was very earnestly and humbly entreating Miss Murdstone's pardon, which that lady granted, and a perfect reconciliation took place. I never knew my mother afterwards to give an opinion on any matter, without first appealing to Miss Murdstone.

There had been some talk on occasions of my going to boarding-school. Mr. and Miss Murdstone had originated it, and my mother had of course agreed with them. Nothing, however, was concluded on the subject yet. In the meantime I learnt lessons at home.

Shall I ever forget those lessons? They were presided over nominally by my mother, but really by Mr. Murdstone and his sister, who were always present, and found them a favorable occasion for giving my mother lessons in that miscalled firmness which was the bane of both our lives.

Let me remember how it used to be, and bring one morning back again.

I come into the second-best parlor after breakfast, with my books, and an exercise book, and a slate. My mother is ready for me at her writing-desk, but not half so ready as Mr. Murdstone in his easy-chair by the window (though he pretends to be reading a book), or as Miss Murdstone, sitting near my mother stringing steel beads.

I hand the first book to my mother. Perhaps it is a grammar, perhaps a history or geography. I take a last drowning look at the page as I give it into her hand, and start off aloud at a racing pace while I have got it fresh. I trip over a word. Mr. Murdstone looks up. I trip over another word. Miss Murdstone looks up. I redden, tumble over half a dozen words, and stop. I think my mother would show me the book if she dared, but she does not dare, and she says softly,

"Oh, Davy, Davy!"

"Now, Clara," says Mr. Murdstone, "be firm with the boy. Don't say, 'Oh, Davy, Davy!' That's childish. He knows his lesson, or he does not know it."

"He does *not* know it," Miss Murdstone interposes awfully.

"I am really afraid he does not," says my mother.

"Then, you see, Clara," returned Miss Murdstone, "you should just give him the book back, and make him know it."

"Yes, certainly," says my mother; "that is what I intend to do, my dear Jane.—Now, Davy, try once more, and don't be stupid."

I obey the first clause of the injunction of trying once more, but am not so successful with the second, for I am very stupid. I tumble down before I get to the old place, at a point where I was all right before. But the greatest effect in these miserable lessons is when my mother (thinking nobody is observing her) tries to give me the cue by the motion of her lips. At that instant, Miss Murdstone, who has been lying in wait for nothing else all along, says in a deep warning voice, "Clara!"

My mother starts, colors, and smiles faintly. Mr. Murdstone comes out of his chair, takes the book, throws it at me or boxes my ears with it, and turns me out of the room by the shoulders.

The natural result of this treatment, continued, I suppose, for some six months or more, was to make me sullen, dull, and dogged. I believe I should have been almost stupefied but for one circumstance.

It was this. My father had left a small collection of books in a little room upstairs. From that blessed little room, Roderick Random, Peregrine Pickle, Humphrey Clinker, Tom Jones, the Vicar of Wakefield, Don Quixote, Gil Blas, and Robinson Crusoe, came out, a glorious host, to keep me company. I consoled myself under my small troubles (which were great troubles to me), by impersonating my favorite characters in them—as I did—and by putting Mr. and Miss Murdstone into all the bad ones—which I did too. This was my only and my constant comfort.

One morning when I went into the parlor with my books, I found my mother looking anxious, Miss Murdstone looking firm, and Mr. Murdstone binding something round the bottom of a cane—a lithe and limber cane, which he left off binding when I came in, and poised and switched in the air.

"I tell you, Clara," said Mr. Murdstone, "I have been often flogged myself."

"To be sure; of course," said Miss Murdstone.

"Certainly, my dear Jane," faltered my mother meekly. "But—but do you think it did Edward good?"

"Do you think it did Edward harm, Clara?" asked Mr. Murdstone gravely.

"That's the point," said his sister.

To this my mother returned, "Certainly, my dear Jane," and said no more. I felt apprehensive that I was personally interested in this dialogue, and sought Mr. Murdstone's eye as it lighted on mine.

"Now, David," he said—and I saw that cast again as he said it—"you must be far more careful today than usual." He gave the cane another poise and another switch; and having finished his preparation of it, laid it down beside him with an expressive look, and took up his book.

We began badly, and went on worse. I had come in with an idea of distinguishing myself rather, conceiving that I was very well prepared; but it turned out to be quite a mistake. Book after book was added to the heap of failures, Miss Murdstone being firmly watchful of us all the time. And at last my mother burst out crying.

"Clara!" said Miss Murdstone in her warning voice.

"I am not quite well, my dear Jane, I think," said my mother.

I saw him wink solemnly at his sister, as he rose and said, taking up the cane,

"Why, Jane, we can hardly expect Clara to bear, with perfect firmness, the worry and torment that David has occasioned her today. That would be stoical. Clara is greatly strengthened and improved, but we can hardly expect so much from her.—David, you and I will go upstairs, boy."

As he took me out at the door my mother ran toward us. Miss Murdstone said, "Clara! are you a perfect fool?" and interfered. I saw my mother stop her ears then, and I heard her crying.

He walked me up to my room slowly and gravely (I am certain he had a delight in that formal parade of executing justice), and when we got there, suddenly twisted my head under his arm.

27

"Mr. Murdstone! sir!" I cried to him; "don't! pray don't beat me! I have tried to learn, sir; but I can't learn while you and Miss Murdstone are by. I can't, indeed!"

"Can't you, indeed, David?" he said. "We'll try that."

He had my head as in a vice; but I twined round him somehow, and stopped him for a moment, entreating him not to beat me. It was only for a moment that I stopped him, for he cut me heavily an instant afterwards; and in the same instant I caught the hand with which he held me in my mouth, between my teeth, and bit it through. It sets my teeth on edge to think of it.

He beat me then as if he would have beaten me to death. Above all the noise we made, I heard them running up the stairs, and crying out. I heard my mother crying out, and Peggotty. Then he was gone, and the door was locked outside; and I was lying, fevered and hot, and torn and sore, and raging in my puny way, upon the floor.

I sat listening for a long while, but there was not a sound. I crawled up from the floor, and saw my face in the glass, so swollen, red, and ugly that it almost frightened me. My stripes were sore and stiff, and made me cry afresh, when I moved; but they were nothing to the guilt I felt. It lay heavier on my breast than if I had been a most atrocious criminal, I dare say.

It had begun to grow dark, when the key was turned, and Miss Murdstone came in with some bread, and meat, and milk. These she put down upon the table without a word, glaring at me the while with exemplary firmness, and then retired, locking the door.

My imprisonment lasted five days. On the last night of my restraint I was awakened by hearing my own name spoken in a whisper. I groped my way to the door, and putting my own lips to the keyhole, whispered, "Is that you, Peggotty dear?"

"Yes, my own precious Davy," she replied. "Be as soft as a mouse, or the Cat'll hear us."

I understood this to mean Miss Murdstone, and was sensible of the urgency of the case, her room being close by.

"How's mamma, dear Peggotty? Is she very angry with me?"

I could hear Peggotty crying softly on her side of the keyhole, as I was doing on mine, before she answered, "No; not very."

"What is going to be done with me, Peggotty dear? Do you know?"

"School—near London," was Peggotty's answer.

Then Peggotty fitted her mouth close to the keyhole and delivered these words through it with as much feeling and earnestness as a keyhole has ever been the medium of communicating, I will venture to assert—shooting in each broken little sentence in a convulsive little burst of its own—

"Davy, dear. If I ain't been azackly as intimate with you. Lately, as I used to be. It ain't because I don't love you. Just as well and more, my pretty poppet. It's because I thought it better for you. And for someone else besides. Davy, my darling, are you listening? Can you hear?"

"Ye—ye—ye—yes, Peggotty!" I sobbed.

"My own!" said Peggotty, with infinite compassion. "What I want to say, is. That you must never forget me. For I'll never forget you. And I'll take as much care of your mamma, Davy. As ever I took of you. And I won't leave her. The day may come when she'll be glad to lay her poor head. On her stupid, cross, old Peggotty's arm again. And I'll write to you, my dear. Though I ain't no scholar. And I'll—I'll——" Peggotty fell to kissing the keyhole, as she couldn't kiss me. We both of us kissed the keyhole with the greatest affection (I patted it with my hand, I recollect, as if it had been her honest face), and parted.

In the morning, I found my mother, very pale and with red eyes, into whose arms I ran, and begged her pardon from my suffering soul.

"Oh, Davy!" she said, "that you could hurt anyone I love! Try to be better, pray to be better! I forgive you; but I am so grieved, Davy, that you should have such bad passions in your heart."

They had persuaded her that I was a wicked fellow, and she was more sorry for that than for my going away. I looked for Peggotty, but neither she nor Mr. Murdstone appeared. My former acquaintance, the carrier, was at the door.

"Clara!" said Miss Murdstone, in her warning note.

"Ready, my dear Jane," returned my mother. "Good-bye, Davy. You are going for your own good. Good-bye, my child. You will come home in the holidays, and be a better boy."

"Clara!" Miss Murdstone repeated.

"Certainly, my dear Jane," replied my mother, who was holding me.—"I forgive you, my dear boy. God bless you!"

"Clara!" Miss Murdstone repeated.

Miss Murdstone was good enough to take me out to the cart, and to say on the way that she hoped I would repent before I came to a bad end; and then I got into the cart, and the lazy horse walked off with it.

CHAPTER 5 ❧ I AM SENT AWAY FROM HOME • • •

We might have gone about half a mile, and my pocket-handkerchief was quite wet through, when the carrier stopped short.

Looking out to ascertain for what, I saw, to my amazement, Peggotty burst from a hedge and climb into the cart. She took me in both her arms, and squeezed me to her stays until the pressure on my nose was extremely painful, though I never thought of that till afterwards, when I found it very tender. Not a single word did Peggotty speak. Releasing one of her arms, she put it down in her pocket to the elbow, and brought out some paper bags of cakes, which she crammed into my pockets, and a purse, which she put into my hand; but not one word did she say. After another and a final squeeze with both arms, she got down from the cart and ran away, and my belief is, and has always been, without a solitary button on her gown. I picked up one of several that were rolling about, and treasured it as a keepsake for a long time.

The carrier looked at me, as if to inquire if she were coming back. I shook my head, and said I thought not. "Then, come up!" said the carrier to the lazy horse, who came up accordingly.

I had now leisure to examine the purse. It was a stiff leather purse,

30

with a snap, and had three bright shillings in it, which Peggotty had evidently polished up with whitening for my greater delight. But its most precious contents were two half-crowns folded together in a bit of paper, on which was written, in my mother's hand, "For Davy. With my love."

After we had jogged on for some little time, I asked the carrier if he was going all the way?

"All the way where?" inquired the carrier.

"There," I said.

"Where's there?" inquired the carrier.

"Near London," I said.

"Why, that horse," said the carrier, jerking the rein to point him out, "would be deader than pork afore he got over half the ground."

"Are you only going to Yarmouth, then?" I asked.

"That's about it," said the carrier. "And there I shall take you to the stage-cutch, the stage-cutch'll take you to—wherever it is."

As this was a great deal for the carrier (whose name was Mr. Barkis) to say—he being, as I observed in a former chapter, of a phlegmatic temperament, and not at all conversational—I offered him a cake as a mark of attention, which he ate at one gulp, exactly like an elephant, and which made no more impression on his big face than it would have done on an elephant's.

"Did *she* make 'em, now?" said Mr. Barkis, always leaning forward, in his slouching way, on the footboard of the cart, with an arm on each knee.

"Peggotty, do you mean, sir?"

"Ah!" said Mr. Barkis. "Her."

"Yes; she makes all our pastry and does all our cooking."

"Do she though?" said Mr. Barkis.

He made up his mouth as if to whistle, but he didn't whistle. He sat looking at the horse's ears, as if he saw something new there; and sat so for a considerable time. By-and-by he said,

"No sweethearts, I b'lieve?"

"Sweetmeats did you say, Mr. Barkis?" For I thought he wanted something else to eat, and had pointedly alluded to that description of refreshment.

"Hearts," said Mr. Barkis. "Sweethearts; no person walks with her?"

"With Peggotty?"

"Ah!" he said. "Her."

"Oh, no. She never had a sweetheart."

"Didn't she though?" said Mr. Barkis.

Again he made up his mouth to whistle, and again he didn't whistle, but sat looking at the horse's ears.

"So she makes," said Mr. Barkis, after a long interval of reflection, "all the apple parsties, and doos all the cooking, do she?"

I replied that such was the fact.

"Well, I'll tell you what," said Mr. Barkis. "P'raps you might be writin' to her?"

"I shall certainly write to her," I rejoined.

"Ah!" he said, slowly turning his eyes toward me. "Well, if you was writin' to her, p'raps you'd recollect to say that Barkis was willin'; would you?"

"That Barkis is willing," I replied. "Is that all the message?"

"Ye—es," he said, considering. "Ye—es; Barkis is willin'."

"But you will be at Blunderstone again tomorrow, Mr. Barkis," I said, faltering a little at the idea of my being far away from it then, "and could give your own message so much better."

As he repudiated this suggestion, however, with a jerk of his head, and once more confirmed his previous request by saying, with profound gravity, "Barkis is willin'. That's the message," I readily undertook its transmission. (While I was waiting for the coach in the hotel at Yarmouth that very afternoon, I procured a sheet of paper and an inkstand and wrote a note to Peggotty, which ran thus:— "My dear Peggotty. I have come here safe. Barkis is willing. My love to mamma. Yours affectionately. P.S.—He says he particularly wants you to know—*Barkis is willing*.")

We started from Yarmouth at three o'clock in the afternoon, and we were due in London about eight next morning. We approached it by degrees, and got, in due time, to the inn in the Whitechapel district for which we were bound. The guard's eye lighted on me as he was getting down, and he said at the booking-office door,

"Is there anybody here for a yoongster booked in the name of Murdstone, from Bloonderstone, Sooffolk, to be left till called for?"

Nobody answered.

"Try Copperfield, if you please, sir," said I, looking helplessly down.

"Is there anybody here for a yoongster, booked in the name of Murdstone, from Bloonderstone, Sooffolk, but owning to the name of Copperfield, to be left till called for?" said the guard. "Come! *is* there anybody?"

No; there was nobody. A procession of most tremendous considerations began to march through my mind. Supposing nobody should ever fetch me, how long would they consent to keep me there? Supposing there was no mistake in the case, and Mr. Murdstone had devised this plan to get rid of me, what should I do? If I started off at once, and tried to walk back home, how could I ever find my way, how could I ever hope to walk so far, how could I make sure of anyone but Peggotty, even if I got back? If I found out the nearest proper authorities, and offered myself to go for a soldier, or a sailor, I was such a little fellow that it was most likely they wouldn't take me in. These thoughts, and a hundred other such thoughts, turned me burning hot, and made me giddy with apprehension and dismay. I was in the height of my fever when a man entered and whispered to the clerk, who pushed me over to him, as if I were weighed, bought, delivered, and paid for.

As I went out of the office, hand in hand with this new acquaintance, I stole a look at him. He was a gaunt, sallow young man, with hollow cheeks, and a chin almost as black as Mr. Murdstone's; but there the likeness ended, for his whiskers were shaved off, and his hair, instead of being glossy, was rusty and dry. He was dressed in a suit of black clothes which were rather rusty and dry too, and rather short in the sleeves and legs; and he had a white neckerchief on, that was not over clean. I did not, and do not, suppose that this neckerchief was all the linen he wore, but it was all he showed or gave any hint of.

"You're the new boy?" he said.

"Yes, sir," I said. I supposed I was. I didn't know.

"I'm one of the masters at Salem House," *he* said.

I made him a bow, and felt very much overawed. I was so ashamed to allude to a commonplace thing like my box, to a scholar and a master at Salem House, that we had gone some little distance from the yard before I had the hardihood to mention it. We turned back, on my humbly insinuating that it might be useful to me hereafter; and he told the clerk that the carrier had instructions to call for it at noon.

"If you please, sir," I said, when we had accomplished about the same distance as before. "is it far?"

"It's down by Blackheath," he said.

"Is *that* far, sir?" I diffidently asked.

"It's a good step," he said. "We shall go by the stage-coach. It's about six miles."

33

We found the coach very near at hand, and got upon the roof; but I was so dead sleepy, that when we stopped on the road to take up somebody else, they put me inside where there were no passengers, and where I slept profoundly, until I found the coach going at a footpace up a steep hill among green leaves. Presently it stopped, and had come to its destination.

A short walk brought us—I mean the Master and me—to Salem House, which was inclosed with a high brick wall, and looked very dull. Over a door in this wall was a board with SALEM HOUSE upon it; and through a grating in this door we were surveyed, when we rang the bell, by a surly face, which I found, on the door being opened, belonged to a stout man with a bull-neck, a wooden leg, overhanging temples, and his hair cut close all round his head.

"The new boy," said the Master.

The man with the wooden leg eyed me all over—it didn't take long, for there was not much of me—and locked the gate behind us, and took out the key. We were going up to the house, among some dark, heavy trees, when he called after my conductor,

"Hallo!"

We looked back, and he was standing at the door of a little lodge, where he lived, with a pair of boots in his hand.

"Here! The cobbler's been," he said, "since you've been out, Mr. Mell, and he says he can't mend 'em any more. He says there ain't a bit of the original boot left, and he wonders you expect it."

With these words he threw the boots towards Mr. Mell, who went back a few paces to pick them up, and looked at them (very disconsolately, I was afraid) as we went on together. I observed then, for the first time, that the boots he had on were a good deal the worse for wear, and that his stocking was just breaking out in one place, like a bud.

Salem House was a square brick building with wings, of a bare and unfurnished appearance. All about it was so very quiet, that I said to Mr. Mell I supposed the boys were out. But he seemed surprised at my not knowing that it was holiday-time; that all the boys were at their several homes; that Mr. Creakle, the proprietor, was down by the seaside with Mrs. and Miss Creakle; and that I was sent in holiday-time as a punishment for my misdoing—all of which he explained to me as we went along.

I gazed upon the schoolroom into which he took me as the most forlorn and desolate place I had ever seen—a long room, with three long rows of desks and six of forms, and bristling all round with

34

pegs for hats and slates. Scraps of old copy-books and exercises litter the dirty floor. Mr. Mell having left me while he took his irreparable boots upstairs, I went softly to the upper end of the room, observing all this as I crept along. Suddenly I came upon a pasteboard placard, beautifully written, which was lying on the desk, and bore these words, "*Take care of him. He bites.*"

I got upon the desk immediately, apprehensive of at least a great dog underneath; but, though I looked all round with anxious eyes, I could see nothing of him. I was still engaged in peering about when Mr. Mell came back, and asked me what I did up there.

"I beg your pardon, sir," says I; "if you please, I'm looking for the dog."

"Dog?" says he. "What dog?"

"That's to be taken care of, sir—that bites?"

"No, Copperfield," says he gravely, "that's not a dog. That's a boy. My instructions are, Copperfield, to put this placard on your back. I am sorry to make such a beginning, but I must do it."

With that he took me down, and tied the placard, which was neatly constructed for the purpose, on my shoulders like a knapsack; and wherever I went, afterwards, I had the consolation of carrying it.

What I suffered from that placard nobody can imagine. There was an old door in the playground, on which the boys had a custom of carving their names. It was completely covered with such inscriptions. I could not read a boy's name without inquiring in what tone and with what emphasis *he* would read, "Take care of him. He bites." There was one boy—a certain J. Steerforth—who cut his name very deep and very often, who, I conceived, would read it in a rather strong voice, and afterwards pull my hair. There was another boy, one Tommy Traddles, who I dreaded would make game of it, and pretend to be dreadfully frightened of me. There was a third, George Demple, who I fancied would sing it. I have looked, a little shrinking creature, at that door, until the owners of all the names—there were five-and-forty of them in the school then, Mr. Mell said—seemed to cry out, each in his own way, "Take care of him. He bites!"

I had long tasks every day to do with Mr. Mell; but I did them, there being no Mr. and Miss Murdstone here, and got through them without disgrace. Mr. Mell never said much to me, but he was never harsh to me. I suppose we were company to each other, without talking.

35

CHAPTER 6 ❦ I ENLARGE MY CIRCLE OF ACQUAINTANCE ◆ ◆ ◆

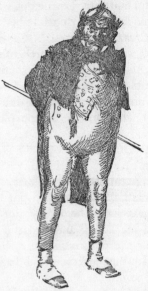

I HAD led this life about a month, when I was informed by Mr. Mell that Mr. Creakle would be home that evening. Before bed-time I was fetched by the man with the wooden leg to appear before him.

I went on my way, trembling, to Mr. Creakle's presence; which so abashed me when I was ushered into it, that I hardly saw Mrs. Creakle or Miss Creakle (who were both there), or anything but Mr. Creakle, a stout gentleman with a bunch of watch-chain and seals, in an armchair, with a tumbler and bottle beside him.

"So," said Mr. Creakle, "this is the young gentleman whose teeth are to be filed! Turn him round."

The wooden-legged man turned me about so as to exhibit the placard; and having afforded time for a full survey of it, turned me about again, with my face to Mr. Creakle, and posted himself at Mr. Creakle's side. Mr. Creakle's face was fiery, and his eyes were small and deep in his head; he had thick veins in his forehead, a little nose, and a large chin. He was bald on the top of his head, and had some thin, wet-looking hair, that was just turning gray, brushed across each temple, so that the two sides interlaced on his forehead. But the circumstance about him which impressed me most was that he had no voice, but spoke in a whisper. The exertion this cost him, or the consciousness of talking in that feeble way, made his angry face so much more angry, and his thick veins so much thicker, when he spoke, that I am not surprised, on looking back, at this peculiarity striking me as his chief one.

"Now," said Mr. Creakle, "what's the report of this boy?"

"There's nothing against him yet," returned the man with the wooden leg. "There has been no opportunity."

I thought Mr. Creakle was disappointed. I thought Mrs. and Miss Creakle (at whom I now glanced for the first time, and who were, both, thin and quiet) were not disappointed.

"Come here, sir," said Mr. Creakle, beckoning to me.

"Come here," said the man with the wooden leg, repeating the gesture.

"I have the happiness of knowing your father-in-law," whispered Mr. Creakle, taking me by the ear; "and a worthy man he is, and a man of a strong character. He knows me, and I know him. Do *you* know me, hey?" said Mr. Creakle, pinching my ear with ferocious playfulness.

"Not yet, sir," I said, flinching with the pain.

"Not yet, hey?" repeated Mr. Creakle; "but you will soon, hey?"

"You will soon, hey?" repeated the man with the wooden leg. I afterwards found that he generally acted, with his strong voice, as Mr. Creakle's interpreter to the boys.

I was very much frightened, and said I hoped so, if he pleased. I felt, all this while, as if my ear were blazing; he pinched it so hard.

"I'll tell you what I am," whispered Mr. Creakle, letting it go at last with a screw at parting that brought the water into my eyes; "I'm a Tartar."

"A Tartar," said the man with the wooden leg.

"When I say I'll do a thing, I do it," said Mr. Creakle; "and when I say I will have a thing done, I will have it done."

"—Will have a thing done, I will have it done," repeated the man with the wooden leg.

"I am a determined character," said Mr. Creakle; "that's what I am. I do my duty; that's what *I* do. My flesh and blood"—he looked at Mrs. Creakle as he said this—"when it rises against me, is not my flesh and blood. I discard it.—Now you have begun to know me, my young friend, and you may go.—Take him away." I went to bed, as it was time, and lay quaking for a couple of hours.

Next morning Mr. Sharp came back. Mr. Sharp was the first

master, and superior to Mr. Mell. Mr. Mell took his meals with the boys, but Mr. Sharp dined and supped at Mr. Creakle's table. He was a limp, delicate-looking gentleman, I thought, with a good deal of nose, and a way of carrying his head on one side as if it were a little too heavy for him. His hair was very smooth and wavy; but I was informed by the very first boy who came back that it was a wig (a second-hand one, *he* said), and that Mr. Sharp went out every Saturday afternoon to get it curled.

It was no other than Tommy Traddles who gave me this piece of intelligence. He was the first boy who returned. He introduced himself by informing me that I should find his name on the right-hand corner of the gate, over the topbolt. Upon that I said, "Traddles?" to which he replied, "The same"; and then he asked me for a full account of myself and family.

It was a happy circumstance for me that Traddles came back first. He enjoyed my placard so much, that he saved me from the embarrassment of either disclosure or concealment, by presenting me to every other boy who came back, great or small, immediately on his arrival, in this form of introduction, "Look here! Here's a game!" The greater part could not resist the temptation of pretending that I was a dog, and patting and smoothing me, lest I should bite, and saying, "Lie down, sir!" and calling me Towzer; but on the whole it was much better than I had anticipated.

I was not considered as being formally received into the school, however, until J. Steerforth arrived. Before this boy, who was reputed to be a great scholar, and was very good-looking, and at least half a dozen years my senior, I was carried as before a magistrate. He inquired, under a shed in the playground, into the particulars of my punishment, and was pleased to express his opinion that it was "a jolly shame"; for which I became bound to him ever afterwards.

"What money have you got, Copperfield?" he said, walking aside with me when he had disposed of my affair in these terms.

I told him seven shillings.

"You had better give it to me to take care of," he said. "At least you can, if you like. You needn't, if you don't like."

I hastened to comply with his friendly suggestion, and opening Peggotty's purse, turned it upside down into his hand.

"Do you want to spend anything now?" he asked me.

"No, thank you," I replied.

"You can, if you like, you know," said Steerforth. "Say the word."

"No, thank you, sir," I repeated.

"Perhaps you'd like to spend a couple of shillings or so in a bottle of currant wine by-and-by, up in the bedroom?" said Steerforth. "You belong to my bedroom, I find."

It certainly had not occurred to me before, but I said, Yes, I should like that.

"Very good," said Steerforth. "You'll be glad to spend another shilling or so in almond cakes, I dare say?"

I said, Yes, I should like that, too.

"And another shilling or so in biscuits, and another in fruit, eh?" said Steerforth. "I say, young Copperfield, you're going it!"

I smiled because he smiled, but I was a little troubled in my mind, too.

"Well," said Steerforth, "we must make it stretch as far as we can, that's all. I'll do the best in my power for you. I can go out when I like, and I'll smuggle the prog in."

He was as good as his word. When we went upstairs to bed, he produced the whole seven shillings' worth, and laid it out on my bed in the moonlight, saying,

"There you are, young Copperfield, and a royal spread you've got."

I couldn't think of doing the honors of the feast at my time of life while he was by; my hand shook at the very thought of it. I begged him to do me the favor of presiding; and my request being seconded by the other boys who were in that room, he acceded to it, and sat upon my pillow, handing round the viands—with perfect fairness, I must say—and dispensing the currant wine in a little glass without a foot, which was his own property.

How well I recollect our sitting there, talking in whispers—or their talking, and my respectfully listening, I ought rather to say. I heard all kinds of things about the school and all belonging to it. I heard that Mr. Creakle was the sternest and most severe of masters; that he laid about him, right and left, every day of his life, charging in among the boys like a trooper, and slashing away unmercifully; that he knew nothing himself but the art of slashing, being more ignorant (J. Steerforth said) than the lowest boy in the school.

But the greatest wonder that I heard of Mr. Creakle was, there being one boy in the school on whom he never ventured to lay a hand, and that boy being J. Steerforth. Steerforth himself confirmed this when it was stated, and said that he should like to begin to see him do it. On being asked by a mild boy (not me) how he would proceed if he did begin to see him do it, he said he would commence by knocking him down with a blow on the forehead from the seven-and-sixpenny ink-bottle that was always on the mantelpiece. We sat in the dark for some time, breathless.

I heard that Mr. Sharp and Mr. Mell were both supposed to be wretchedly paid; and that when there was hot and cold meat for dinner at Mr. Creakle's table, Mr. Sharp was always expected to say he preferred cold—which was again corroborated by J. Steerforth, the only parlor-boarder. I heard that the table-beer was a robbery of parents, and the pudding an imposition. I heard that Miss Creakle was regarded by the school in general as being in love with Steerforth; and I am sure, as I sat in the dark, thinking of his nice voice, and his fine face, and his easy manner, and his curling hair, I thought it very likely.

David meets a friendly waiter on his journey to London.

CHAPTER 7 ❧ MY "FIRST HALF" AT SALEM HOUSE ◆ ◆ ◆

SCHOOL began in earnest next day. A profound impression was made upon me, I remember, by the roar of voices in the schoolroom suddenly becoming hushed as death when Mr. Creakle entered after breakfast, and stood in the doorway looking round upon us like a giant in a story-book surveying his captives.

Tungay stood at Mr. Creakle's elbow. He had no occasion, I thought, to cry out "Silence!" so ferociously, for the boys were all struck speechless and motionless.

Mr. Creakle was seen to speak, and Tungay was heard, to this effect:

"Now, boys, this is a new half. Take care what you're about in this new half. Come fresh up to the lessons, I advise you, for I come fresh up to the punishment. I won't flinch. It will be of no use your rubbing yourselves; you won't rub the marks out that I shall give you. Now get to work, every boy!"

When this dreadful exordium was over, and Tungay had stumped out again, Mr. Creakle came to where I sat, and told me that if I were famous for biting, he was famous for biting too. He then

41

showed me the cane, and asked me what I thought of *that* for a tooth? Was it a sharp tooth, hey? Was it a double tooth, hey? Had it a deep prong, hey? Did it bite, hey? Did it bite? At every question he gave me a fleshy cut with it that made me writhe; so I was very soon made free of Salem House (as Steerforth said), and was very soon in tears also.

I should think there never can have been a man who enjoyed his profession more than Mr. Creakle did. He had a delight in cutting at the boys, which was like the satisfaction of a craving appetite. I am confident that he couldn't resist a chubby boy especially; that there was a fascination in such a subject, which made him restless in his mind until he had scored and marked him for the day. I was chubby myself, and ought to know.

Poor Traddles! In a tight sky-blue suit that made his arms and legs like German sausages, or roly-poly puddings, he was the merriest and most miserable of all the boys. He was always being caned —I think he was caned every day that half-year, except one holiday Monday when he was only ruler'd on both hands—and was always going to write to his uncle about it, and never did. After laying his head on the desk for a little while, he would cheer up somehow, begin to laugh again, and draw skeletons all over his slate, before his eyes were dry. I used at first to wonder what comfort Traddles found in drawing skeletons; I believe he only did it because they were easy, and didn't want any features.

There was one advantage, and only one that I know of, in Mr. Creakle's severity. He found my placard in his way when he came up or down behind the form on which I sat, and wanted to make a cut at me in passing. For this reason it was soon taken off.

An accidental circumstance cemented the intimacy between Steerforth and me. It happened on one occasion, when he was doing me the honor of talking to me in the playground, that I hazarded the observation that something or somebody—I forget what now—was like something or somebody in "Peregrine Pickle." He said nothing at the time; but when I was going to bed at night, asked me if I had got that book.

I told him no, and explained how it was that I had read it, and all those other books of which I have made mention.

"And do you recollect them?" Steerforth said.

Oh, yes, I replied; and I believed I recollected them very well.

"Then I tell you what, young Copperfield," said Steerforth, "you shall tell 'em to me. I can't get to sleep very early at night, and I generally wake rather early in the morning. We'll go over 'em one after another. We'll make some regular Arabian Nights of it."

I felt extremely flattered by this arrangement, and we commenced carrying it into execution that very evening. The drawback was, that I was often sleepy at night, and then it was rather hard work, and it must be done; for to disappoint or displease Steerforth was of course out of the question. In the morning too, it was a tiresome thing to be roused, like the Sultana Scheherazade, and forced into a long story before the getting-up bell rang. But Steerforth was resolute; and as he explained to me, in return, my sums and exercises and anything in my tasks that was too hard for me, I was no loser by the transaction.

I was much assisted by Mr. Mell, who had a liking for me that I am grateful to remember. It always gave me pain to observe that Steerforth treated him with systematic disparagement, and seldom lost an occasion of wounding his feelings, or inducing others to do so.

One day when Mr. Creakle kept the house from indisposition, which naturally diffused a lively joy through the school, there was a good deal of noise in the course of the morning's work. It was the day of the week on which Mr. Sharp went out to get his wig curled; so Mr. Mell, who always did the drudgery, whatever it was, kept school by himself. If I could associate the idea of a bull or a bear with anyone so mild as Mr. Mell, I should think of him, in connection with that afternoon when the uproar was at its height, as of one of those animals baited by a thousand dogs. Boys started in and out of their places, playing at puss-in-the-corner with other boys; there were laughing boys, singing boys, talking boys, dancing boys, howling boys; boys shuffled with their feet, boys whirled about him, grinning, making faces, mimicking him behind his back and before his eyes.

"Silence!" cried Mr. Mell, suddenly rising up and striking his desk with the book. "What does this mean? It's impossible to bear it. It's maddening. How can you do it to me, boys?"

It was my book that he struck his desk with; and as I stood beside him, following his eye as it glanced round the room, I saw the boys all stop, some suddenly surprised, some half afraid, and some sorry perhaps.

Steerforth's place was at the bottom of the school, at the opposite end of the long room. He was lounging with his back against the wall, and his hands in his pockets, and looked at Mr. Mell with his

mouth shut up as if he were whistling, when Mr. Mell looked at
him.

"Silence, Mr. Steerforth!" said Mr. Mell.

"Silence yourself," said Steerforth, turning red. "Whom are you
talking to?"

"Sit down," said Mr. Mell.

"Sit down yourself," said Steerforth, "and mind your business."

There was a titter, and some applause. But Mr. Mell was so white
that silence immediately succeeded.

"If you think, Steerforth," said Mr. Mell, "that I am not acquainted with the power you can establish over any mind here"—
he laid his hand, without considering what he did (as I supposed),
upon my head—"or that I have not observed you urging your jun-
iors on to every sort of outrage against me, you are mistaken."

"I don't give myself the trouble of thinking at all about you," said
Steerforth coolly; "so I'm not mistaken, as it happens."

"And when you make use of your position of favoritism here,
sir," pursued Mr. Mell, with his lip trembling very much, "to insult
a gentleman——"

"A what?—where is he?" said Steerforth.

Here somebody cried out, "Shame, J. Steerforth! Too bad!" It
was Traddles, whom Mr. Mell instantly discomfited by bidding him
hold his tongue.

"To insult one who is not fortunate in life, sir, and who never
gave you the least offense, and the many reasons for not insulting
whom you are old enough and wise enough to understand," said
Mr. Mell, with his lip trembling more and more, "you commit a
mean and base action. You can sit down or stand up as you please,
sir.—Copperfield, go on."

"Young Copperfield," said Steerforth, coming forward up the
room, "stop a bit. I tell you what, Mr. Mell, once for all: when you
take the liberty of calling me mean or base, or anything of that sort,
you are an impudent beggar. You are always a beggar, you know;
but when you do that, you are an impudent beggar."

I am not clear whether he was going to strike Mr. Mell, or Mr.
Mell was going to strike him, or if there was any such intention on
either side. I saw a rigidity come upon the whole school as if they
had been turned into stone, and found Mr. Creakle in the midst of
us, with Tungay at his side, and Mrs. and Miss Creakle looking in
at the door as if they were frightened. Mr. Mell, with his elbows on
his desk and his face in his hands, sat for some moments quite still.

"Mr. Mell," said Mr. Creakle, shaking him by the arm—and his whisper was so audible now that Tungay felt it unnecessary to repeat his words—"you have not forgotten yourself, I hope?"

"No, sir, no," returned the Master, showing his face, and shaking his head, and rubbing his hands in great agitation. "No, sir, no. I have remembered myself; I—no, Mr. Creakle, I have not forgotten myself; I—I have remembered myself, sir. I—I—could wish you had remembered me a little sooner, Mr. Creakle. It—it—would have been more kind, sir, more just, sir. It would have saved me something, sir."

Mr. Creakle, looking hard at Mr. Mell, put his hand on Tungay's shoulder, and got his feet upon the form close by, and sat upon the desk. After still looking hard at Mr. Mell from this throne, as he shook his head and rubbed his hands, and remained in the same state of agitation, Mr. Creakle turned to Steerforth, and said,

"Now, sir, as he don't condescend to tell me, what *is* this?"

Steerforth evaded the question for a little while, looking in scorn and anger on his opponent, and remaining silent. I could not help thinking even in that interval, I remember, what a noble fellow he was in appearance, and how homely and plain Mr. Mell looked opposed to him.

"What did he mean by talking about favorites, then?" said Steerforth at length.

"Favorites?" repeated Mr. Creakle, with the veins in his forehead swelling quickly. "Who talked about favorites?"

"He did," said Steerforth.

"And pray, what did you mean by that, sir?" demanded Mr. Creakle, turning angrily on his assistant.

"I meant, Mr. Creakle," he returned in a low voice, "as I said—that no pupil had a right to avail himself of his position of favoritism to degrade me."

"To degrade *you?*" said Mr. Creakle. "My stars! But give me leave to ask you, Mr. What's-your-name" (and here Mr. Creakle folded his arms, cane and all, upon his chest, and made such a knot of his brows that his little eyes were hardly visible below them), "whether, when you talk about favorites, you showed proper respect to me? To me, sir," said Mr. Creakle, darting his head at him suddenly, and drawing it back again, "the principal of this establishment, and your employer."

"It was not judicious, sir, I am willing to admit," said Mr. Mell. "I should not have done so if I had been cool."

Here Steerforth struck in.

"Then he said I was mean, and then he said I was base; and then I called him a beggar. If I had been cool, perhaps I shouldn't have called him a beggar; but I did, and I am ready to take the consequences of it."

Without considering, perhaps, whether there were any consequences to be taken, I felt quite in a glow at this gallant speech. It made an impression on the boys too, for there was a low stir among them, though no one spoke a word.

"I am surprised, Steerforth—although your candor does you honor," said Mr. Creakle, "does you honor, certainly—I am surprised, Steerforth, I must say, that you should attach such an epithet to any person employed and paid in Salem House, sir."

Steerforth gave a short laugh.

"That's not an answer, sir," said Mr. Creakle, "to my remark. I expect more than that from you, Steerforth."

If Mr. Mell looked homely in my eyes before the handsome boy, it would be quite impossible to say how homely Mr. Creakle looked.

"Let him deny it," said Steerforth.

"Deny that he is a beggar, Steerforth?" cried Mr. Creakle. "Why, where does he go a-begging?"

"If he is not a beggar himself, his near relation's one," said Steerforth. "What I have to say is, that his mother lives on charity in an alms-house."

Mr. Creakle turned to his assistant with a severe frown and labored politeness:

"Now you hear what this gentleman says, Mr. Mell. Have the goodness, if you please, to set him right before the assembled school."

"He is right, sir, without correction," returned Mr. Mell, in the midst of a dead silence; "what he has said is true."

"Be so good, then, as declare publicly, will you," said Mr. Creakle, putting his head on one side, and rolling his eyes round the school, "whether it ever came to my knowledge until this moment?"

"I believe not directly," he returned.

"Why, you know not," said Mr. Creakle. "Don't you, man?"

"I apprehend you never supposed my worldly circumstances to be very good," replied the assistant. "You know what my position is, and always has been, here."

"I apprehend, if you come to that," said Mr. Creakle, with his veins swelling again bigger than ever, "that you've been in a wrong position altogether, and mistook this for a charity school. Mr. Mell, we'll part, if you please. The sooner the better."

"There is no time," answered Mr. Mell, rising, "like the present."

"Sir, to you!" said Mr. Creakle.

"I take my leave of you, Mr. Creakle, and all of you," said Mr. Mell, glancing round the room. "James Steerforth, the best wish I can leave you is that you may come to be ashamed of what you have done today."

Taking a few books from his desk, and leaving the key in it for his successor, he went out of the school with his property under his arm. Mr. Creakle then made a speech, through Tungay, in which he thanked Steerforth for asserting (though perhaps too warmly) the independence and respectability of Salem House, and which he wound up by shaking hands with Steerforth; while we gave three cheers—I did not quite know what for, but I supposed for Steerforth, and so joined in them ardently, though I felt miserable. Mr. Creakle then caned Tommy Traddles for being discovered in tears instead of cheers, on account of Mr. Mell's departure; and went back to his sofa, or his bed, or wherever he had come from.

The rest of the half-year is a jumble in my recollection of the daily strife and struggle of our lives; of the waning summer and the changing season; of the frosty mornings when we were rung out of bed, and the cold, cold smell of the dark nights when we were rung into bed again; of the evening schoolroom dimly lighted and indifferently warmed, and the morning schoolroom which was nothing but a great shivering-machine; of the alternation of boiled beef with roast beef, and boiled mutton with roast mutton; of clods of bread-and-butter, dog-eared lesson-books, cracked slates, tear-blotted copy-books, canings, rulerings, hair-cuttings, rainy Sundays, suet-puddings, and a dirty atmosphere of ink surrounding all.

I well remember, though, how the distant idea of the holidays, after seeming for an immense time to be a stationary speck, began to come toward us, and to grow and grow. How, from counting months, we came to weeks, and then to days; and how I then began to be afraid that I should not be sent for; and when I learned from Steerforth that I *had* been sent for, and was certainly to go home, had dim forebodings that I might break my leg first. How the breaking-up day changed its place fast, at last, from the week after next to next week, this week, the day after tomorrow, tomorrow, today, tonight—when I was inside the Yarmouth mail, and going home.

WHEN we arrived before day at the inn where the mail stopped, I was shown up to a nice little bedroom, with DOLPHIN painted on the door. Very cold I was, I know, notwithstanding the hot tea they had given me before a large fire downstairs; and very glad I was to turn into the Dolphin's bed, pull the Dolphin's blankets round my head, and go to sleep.

Mr. Barkis, the carrier, was to call for me in the morning at nine o'clock. I got up at eight, a little giddy from the shortness of my night's rest, and was ready for him before the appointed time. He received me exactly as if not five minutes had elapsed since we were last together, and I had only been into the hotel to get change for sixpence, or something of that sort.

As soon as I and my box were in the cart, and the carrier was seated, the lazy horse walked away with us all at his accustomed pace.

"You look very well, Mr. Barkis," I said, thinking he would like to know it.

Mr. Barkis rubbed his cheek with his cuff, and then looked at his cuff as if he expected to find some of the bloom upon it; but made no other acknowledgment of the compliment.

"I gave your message, Mr. Barkis," I said; "I wrote to Peggotty."

"Ah!" said Mr. Barkis.

Mr. Barkis seemed gruff, and answered dryly.

"Wasn't it right, Mr. Barkis?" I asked, after a little hesitation.

"Why, no," said Mr. Barkis.

"Not the message?"

"The message was right enough, perhaps," said Mr. Barkis; "but it come to an end there."

Not understanding what he meant, I repeated inquisitively, "Came to an end, Mr. Barkis?"

"Nothing come of it," he explained, looking at me sideways. "No answer."

"There was an answer expected, was there, Mr. Barkis?" said I, opening my eyes; for this was a new light to me.

"When a man says he's willin'," said Mr. Barkis, turning his glance slowly on me again, "it's as much as to say, that man's a-waitin' for a answer."

"Well, Mr. Barkis?"

"Well," said Mr. Barkis, carrying his eyes back to his horse's ears, "that man's been a-waitin' for a answer ever since."

"Have you told her so, Mr. Barkis?"

"N—no," growled Mr. Barkis, reflecting about it. "I ain't got no call to go and tell her so. I never said six words to her myself. I ain't a-goin' to tell her so."

"Would you like me to do it, Mr. Barkis?" said I doubtfully.

"You might tell her, if you would," said Mr. Barkis, with another slow look at me, "that Barkis was a-waitin' for a answer. Says you—what name is it?"

"Her name?"

"Ah!" said Mr. Barkis, with a nod of his head.

"Peggotty."

"Chrisen name? or nat'ral name?" said Mr. Barkis.

"Oh, it's not her Christian name. Her Christian name is Clara."

"Is it though?" said Mr. Barkis.

He seemed to find an immense fund of reflection in this circumstance, and sat pondering and inwardly whistling for some time.

"Well!" he resumed at length. "Says you, 'Peggotty! Barkis is a-waitin' for a answer.' Says she, perhaps, 'Answer to what?' Says you, 'To what I told you.' 'What is that?' says she. 'Barkis is willin',' says you."

This extremely artful suggestion, Mr. Barkis accompanied with a nudge of his elbow that gave me quite a stitch in my side. After that, he slouched over his horse in his usual manner, and made no other reference to the subject except, half an hour afterwards, taking a piece of chalk from his pocket, and writing up, inside the tilt of the cart, "Clara Peggotty,"—apparently as a private memorandum.

God knows how infantine the memory may have been that was awakened within me by the sound of my mother's voice in the old parlor, when I set foot in the hall. She was singing in a low tone. I think I must have lain in her arms and heard her singing so to me when I was but a baby.

I believed, from the solitary and thoughtful way in which my mother murmured her song, that she was alone. And I went softly into the room. She was sitting by the fire, suckling an infant, whose tiny hand she held against her neck.

I spoke to her, and she started, and cried out. But seeing me, she called me her dear Davy, her own boy! and coming half across the room to meet me, kneeled down upon the ground and kissed me, and laid my head down on her bosom near the little creature that was nestling there, and put its hand up to my lips.

I wish I had died. I wish I had died then, with that feeling in my heart! I should have been more fit for heaven than I ever have been since.

"He is your brother," said my mother, fondling me. "Davy, my pretty boy! My poor child!" Then she kissed me more and more, and clasped me round the neck. This she was doing when Peggotty came running in, and bounced down on the ground beside us, and went mad about us both for a quarter of an hour.

It seemed that Mr. and Miss Murdstone had gone out upon a visit in the neighborhood, and would not return before night. I had never hoped for this. I had never thought it possible that we three could be together, undisturbed, once more; and I felt, for the time, as if the old days were come back.

We dined together by the fireside. Peggotty was in attendance to wait upon us, but my mother wouldn't let her do it, and made her dine with us. While we were at table, I thought it a favorable occasion to tell Peggotty about Mr. Barkis, who, before I had finished what I had to tell her, began to laugh, and throw her apron over her face.

"Peggotty," said my mother, "what's the matter?"

Peggotty only laughed the more, and held her apron tight over her face when my mother tried to pull it away, and sat as if her head were in a bag.

"What are you doing, you stupid creature?" said my mother, laughing.

"Oh, drat the man!" cried Peggotty. "He wants to marry me."

"It would be a very good match for you, wouldn't it?" said my mother.

"Oh! I don't know," said Peggotty. "Don't ask me. I wouldn't have him if he was made of gold. Nor I wouldn't have anybody."

"Then why don't you tell him so, you ridiculous thing?" said my mother.

"Tell him so," retorted Peggotty, looking out of her apron. "He has never said a word to me about it. He knows better. If he was to make so bold as say a word to me, I should slap his face."

I remarked that my mother, though she smiled when Peggotty looked at her, became more serious and thoughtful. I had seen at first that she was changed. Her face was very pretty still, but it looked careworn, and too delicate; and her hand was so thin and white that it seemed to me to be almost transparent. But the change to which I now refer was superadded to this: it was in her manner, which became anxious and fluttered. At last she said, putting out her hand, and laying it affectionately on the hand of her old servant,

"Peggotty dear, you are not going to be married?"

"Me, ma'am?" returned Peggotty, staring. "Lord bless you, no!"

"Not just yet?" said my mother tenderly.

"Never!" cried Peggotty.

My mother took her hand, and said,

"Don't leave me, Peggotty. Stay with me. It will not be for long, perhaps. What should I ever do without you?"

"Me leave you, my precious!" cried Peggotty. "Not for all the world and his wife. Why, what's put that in your silly little head?" For Peggotty had been used of old to talk to my mother sometimes like a child.

We sat round the fire, and talked delightfully. I almost believed that I had never been away; that Mr. and Miss Murdstone were pictures, and would vanish when the fire got low; and that there was nothing real in all that I remembered, save my mother, Peggotty, and I.

It was almost ten o'clock before we heard the sound of wheels. We all got up then; and my mother said hurriedly that, as it was so late, and Mr. and Miss Murdstone approved of early hours for young people, perhaps I had better go to bed. I kissed her, and went upstairs with my candle directly, before they came in. It appeared to my childish fancy, as I ascended to the bedroom where I had been imprisoned, that they brought a cold blast of air into the house which blew away the old familiar feeling like a feather.

I felt uncomfortable about going down to breakfast in the morning, as I had never set eyes on Mr. Murdstone since the day when I committed my memorable offense. However, as it must be done, I went down, after two or three false starts halfway, and as many runs back on tiptoe to my own room, and presented myself in the parlor.

He was standing before the fire with his back to it, while Miss Murdstone made the tea. He looked at me steadily as I entered, but made no sign of recognition whatever.

I went up to him, after a moment of confusion, and said, "I beg your pardon, sir. I am very sorry for what I did, and I hope you will forgive me."

"I am glad to hear you are sorry, David," he replied.

The hand he gave me was the hand I had bitten. I could not restrain my eye from resting for an instant on a red spot upon it; but it was not so red as I turned, when I met that sinister expression in his face.

"How do you do, ma'am?" I said to Miss Murdstone.

"Ah, dear me!" sighed Miss Murdstone, giving me the tea-caddy scoop instead of her fingers. "How long are the holidays?"

"A month, ma'am."

"Counting from when?"

"From today, ma'am."

"Oh!" said Miss Murdstone. "Then here's *one* day off."

She kept a calendar of the holidays in this way, and every morning checked a day off in exactly the same manner. She did it gloomily until she came to ten; but when she got into two figures she became more hopeful, and, as the time advanced, even jocular.

I felt that I made them as uncomfortable as they made me. If I came into the room where they were, and they were talking together, and my mother seemed cheerful, an anxious cloud would steal over her face from the moment of my entrance. If Mr. Murdstone were in his best humor, I checked him. If Miss Murdstone were in her worst, I intensified it. Therefore I resolved to keep myself as much out of their way as I could.

In the evening, sometimes, I went and sat with Peggotty in the kitchen. There I was comfortable, and not afraid of being myself. But neither of these resources was approved of in the parlor. I was still held to be necessary to my poor mother's training, and, as one of her trials, could not be suffered to absent myself.

"David," said Mr. Murdstone, one day after dinner when I was going to leave the room as usual, "I am sorry to observe that you are of a sullen disposition."

"As sulky as a bear!" said Miss Murdstone.

I stood still, and hung my head.

"Now, David," said Mr. Murdstone, "a sullen, obdurate disposition is, of all tempers, the worst."

"And the boy's is, of all such dispositions that ever I have seen," remarked his sister, "the most confirmed and stubborn. I think, my dear Clara, even you must observe it?"

"I beg your pardon, my dear Jane," said my mother, "but are you quite sure—I am certain you'll excuse me, my dear Jane—that you understand Davy?"

"We'll say I don't understand the boy, Clara," returned Miss Murdstone, arranging the little fetters on her wrists. "We'll agree, if you please, that I don't understand him at all. He is much too deep for me. But perhaps my brother's penetration may enable him to have some insight into his character. And I believe my brother was speaking on the subject when we—not very decently—interrupted him."

"I think, Clara," said Mr. Murdstone, in a low grave voice, "that there may be better and more dispassionate judges of such a question than you."

"Edward," replied my mother timidly, "you are a far better judge of all questions than I pretend to be. Both you and Jane. I only said——"

"You only said something weak and inconsiderate," he replied. "Try not do it again, my dear Clara, and keep a watch upon yourself."

My mother's lips moved, as if she answered, "Yes, my dear Edward," but she said nothing aloud.

"I was sorry, David, I remarked," said Mr. Murdstone, turning his head and his eyes stiffly toward me, "to observe that you are of a sullen disposition. This is not a character that I can suffer to develop itself beneath my eyes without an effort at improvement. You must endeavor, sir, to change it. We must endeavor to change it for you."

"I beg your pardon, sir," I faltered. "I have never meant to be sullen since I came back."

"Don't take refuge in a lie, sir!" he returned so fiercely that I saw my mother involuntarily put out her trembling hand as if to interpose between us. "You have withdrawn yourself in your sullenness to your own room. I will not have this room shunned as if it were infected, at the pleasure of a child. Sit down."

He ordered me like a dog, and I obeyed like a dog.

"One thing more," he said. "I observe that you have an attachment to low and common company. You are not to associate with servants. The kitchen will not improve you, in the many respects in which you need improvement. Now, David, you understand me, and you know what will be the consequence if you fail to obey me to the letter."

I knew well—better perhaps than he thought, as far as my poor mother was concerned—and I obeyed him to the letter. I retreated to my own room no more; I took refuge with Peggotty no more; but sat wearily in the parlor day after day, looking forward to night, and bedtime.

Thus the holidays lagged away, until the morning came when Miss Murdstone said, "Here's the last day off!" and gave me the closing cup of tea of the vacation.

I was not sorry to go. I had lapsed into a stupid state; but I was recovering a little, and looking forward to Steerforth, albeit Mr. Creakle loomed behind him. Again Mr. Barkis appeared at the gate, and again Miss Murdstone in her warning voice said, "Clara!" when my mother bent over me to bid me farewell.

I kissed her and my baby brother, and was very sorry then; but not sorry to go away, for the gulf between us was there, and the parting was there, every day. And it is not so much the embrace she gave me that lives in my mind, though it was as fervent as could be, as what followed the embrace.

I was in the carrier's cart when I heard her calling to me. I looked out, and she stood at the garden gate alone, holding her baby up in her arms for me to see. It was cold, still weather, and not a hair of her head or a fold of her dress was stirred, as she looked intently at me, holding up her child.

So I lost her. So I saw her afterwards, in my sleep at school—a silent presence near my bed—looking at me with the same intent face—holding up her baby in her arms.

I PASS over all that happened at school, until the anniversary of
my birthday came round in March. It was after breakfast, and
we had been summoned in from the playground, when Mr.
Sharp entered and said,

"David Copperfield is to go into the parlor."

I expected a hamper from Peggotty, and brightened at the order.
Some of the boys about me put in their claim not to be forgotten in
the distribution of the good things, as I got out of my seat with
great alacrity.

"Don't hurry, David," said Mr. Sharp. "There's time enough, my
boy; don't hurry."

I might have been surprised by the feeling tone in which he spoke,
if I had given it a thought; but I gave it none until afterwards. I
hurried away to the parlor; and there I found Mr. Creakle, sitting
at his breakfast with the cane and a newspaper before him, and Mrs.
Creakle with an opened letter in her hand. But no hamper.

"David Copperfield," said Mrs. Creakle, leading me to a sofa, and
sitting down beside me, "I want to speak to you very particularly.
I have something to tell you, my child."

Mr. Creakle, at whom of course I looked, shook his head without

55

looking at me, and stopped up a sigh with a very large piece of buttered toast.

"You are too young to know how the world changes every day," said Mrs. Creakle, "and how the people in it pass away. But we all have to learn it, David; some of us when we are young, some of us when we are old, some of us at all times of our lives."

I looked at her earnestly.

"When you came away from home at the end of the vacation," said Mrs. Creakle, after a pause, "were they all well?" After another pause, "Was your mamma well?"

I trembled without distinctly knowing why, and still looked at her earnestly, making no attempt to answer.

"Because," said she, "I grieve to tell you that I hear this morning your mamma is very ill."

A mist rose between Mrs. Creakle and me, and her figure seemed to move in it for an instant. Then I felt the burning tears run down my face, and it was steady again.

"She is very dangerously ill," she added.

I knew all now.

"She is dead."

There was no need to tell me so. I had already broken out into a desolate cry, and felt an orphan in the wide world.

She was very kind to me. She kept me there all day, and left me alone sometimes; and I cried, and wore myself to sleep, and awoke and cried again. When I could cry no more, I began to think; and then the oppression on my breast was heaviest, and my grief a dull pain that there was no ease for.

I left Salem House upon the morrow afternoon. I little thought then that I left it never to return. We traveled very slowly all night, and did not get into Yarmouth before nine or ten o'clock in the morning. I looked out for Barkis, but he was not there; and instead of him a fat, short-winded, merry-looking little old man in black, with rusty little bunches of ribbons at the knees of his breeches, black stockings, and a broad-brimmed hat, came puffing up to the coach-window, and said,

"Master Copperfield?"

"Yes, sir."

"Will you come with me, young sir, if you please," he said, opening the door, "and I shall have the pleasure of taking you home?"

I put my hand in his, wondering who he was, and we walked away to a shop in a narrow street, on which was written OMER,

DRAPER, TAILOR, HABERDASHER, FUNERAL FURNISHER, etc. It was a close and stifling little shop, full of all sorts of clothing, made and unmade, including one window full of beaver-hats and bonnets. We went into a little back-parlor behind the shop, where we found three young women at work on a quantity of black materials, which were heaped upon the table, and little bits and cuttings of which were littered all over the floor. There was a good fire in the room, and a breathless smell of warm black crêpe. I did not know what the smell was then, but I know now.

The three young women, who appeared to be very industrious and comfortable, raised their heads to look at me, and then went on with their work. Stitch, stitch, stitch. At the same time there came from a workshop across a little yard outside the window a regular sound of hammering that kept a kind of tune: RAT—tat-tat, RAT—tat-tat, RAT—tat-tat, without any variation.

"Well," said my conductor to one of the three young women, "how do you get on, Minnie?"

"We shall be ready by the trying-on time," she replied gaily, without looking up. "Don't you be afraid, father."

Mr. Omer took off his broad-brimmed hat, and sat down and panted. He was so fat that he was obliged to pant some time before he could say,

"That's right."

"Father!" said Minnie playfully, "what a porpoise you do grow!"

"Well, I don't know how it is, my dear," he replied, considering about it. "I *am* rather so."

"You are such a comfortable man, you see," said Minnie. "You take things so easy."

"No use taking 'em otherwise, my dear," said Mr. Omer. "As I have got my breath now, I think I'll measure this young scholar.— Would you walk into the shop, Master Copperfield?"

I preceded Mr. Omer, in compliance with his request; and after showing me a roll of cloth which he said was extra super, and too good mourning for anything short of parents, he took my various dimensions, and put them down in a book.

"I have been acquainted with you," said Mr. Omer, "I have been acquainted with you a long time, my young friend."

"Have you, sir?"

"All your life," said Mr. Omer. "I may say before it. I knew your father before you. He was five foot nine and a half, and he lays in five and twen-ty foot of ground."

"RAT—tat-tat, RAT—tat-tat, RAT—tat-tat," across the yard.

"He lays in five and twen-ty foot of ground, if he lays in a fraction," said Mr. Omer pleasantly. "It was either his request or her direction—I forget which."

"Do you know how my little brother is, sir?" I inquired.

Mr. Omer shook his head.

"RAT—tat-tat, RAT—tat-tat, RAT—tat-tat."

"He is in his mother's arms," said he.

"Oh, poor little fellow! Is he dead?"

"Don't mind it more than you can help," said Mr. Omer. "Yes; the baby's dead."

Presently the tune left off, and a good-looking young fellow came across the yard into the room. He had a hammer in his hand, and his mouth was full of little nails, which he was obliged to take out before he could speak.

"Well, Joram!" said Mr. Omer, "how do *you* get on?"

"All right," said Joram. "Done, sir. Will you give me your opinion of it?"

"I will," said Mr. Omer, rising. "My dear"—and he stopped and turned to me—"would you like to see your——"

"No, father," Minnie interposed.

"I thought it might be agreeable, my dear," said Mr. Omer. "But perhaps you're right."

I can't say how I knew it was my dear, dear mother's coffin that they went to look at. I had never heard one making; I had never seen one that I know of; but it came into my mind what the noise was, while it was going on, and when the young man entered, I am sure I knew what he had been doing.

The chaise soon came round to the front of the shop. I remember it as a kind of half chaise-cart, half pianoforte van, painted of a somber color, and drawn by a black horse with a long tail. When we reached home, I dropped out of the chaise behind, as quickly as possible.

I was in Peggotty's arms before I got to the door, and she took me into the house. Her grief burst out when she first saw me; but she controlled it soon, and spoke in whispers, and walked softly, as if the dead could be disturbed. She had not been in bed, I found, for a long time. She sat up at night still, and watched. As long as her poor dear pretty was above the ground, she said, she would never desert her.

Mr. Murdstone took no heed of me when I went into the parlor, where he was, but sat by the fireside, weeping silently, and pondering in his elbow-chair. Miss Murdstone, who was busy at her writing-desk, which was covered with letters and papers, gave me her cold finger-nails, and asked me, in an iron whisper, if I had been measured for my mourning.

I said, "Yes."

"And your shirts," said Miss Murdstone—"have you brought 'em home?"

"Yes, ma'am. I have brought home all my clothes."

This was all the consolation that her firmness administered to me. I do not doubt that she had a choice pleasure in exhibiting what she called her self-command, and her firmness, and her strength of mind, and her common sense and the whole diabolical catalogue of her unamiable qualities, on such an occasion.

If the funeral had been yesterday, I could not recollect it better— the very air of the best parlor, when I went in at the door, the bright condition of the fire, the shining of the wine in the decanters, the patterns of the glasses and plates, the faint sweet smell of cake, the odor of Miss Murdstone's dress, and our black clothes. When we go out to the door, the bearers and their load are in the garden; and they move before us down the path, and past the elms, and through the gate, and into the churchyard, where I have so often heard the birds sing on a summer morning.

We stand around the grave. The day seems different to me from every other day, and the light not of the same color—of a sadder color. Now there is a solemn hush, which we have brought from home with what is resting in the mold; and while we stand bareheaded, I hear the voice of the clergyman, sounding remote in the open air, and yet distinct and plain, saying, "I am the Resurrection and the Life, saith the Lord!" Then I hear sobs; and, standing apart among the lookers-on, I see that good and faithful servant, whom of all the people upon earth I love the best, and unto whom my childish heart is certain that the Lord will one day say, "Well done."

It is over, and the earth is filled in, and we turn to come away. Before us stands our house, so pretty and unchanged, so linked in my mind with the young idea of what is gone, that all my sorrow has been nothing to the sorrow it calls forth.

THE first act of business Miss Murdstone performed when the
day of the solemnity was over, and light was freely admitted
into the house, was to give Peggotty a month's warning. Much
as Peggotty would have disliked such a service, I believe she would
have retained it, for my sake, in preference to the best upon earth.
She told me we must part, and told me why; and we condoled with
one another, in all sincerity.

Peggotty went on to say,

"I'm a-going, Davy, you see, to my brother's first for another
fortnight's visit—just till I have had time to look about me, and get
to be something like myself again. Now, I have been thinking that
perhaps, as they don't want you here at present, you might be let to
go along with me."

The idea of being again surrounded by those honest faces made a
calm in my heart. It was ruffled next moment, to be sure, by a doubt
of Miss Murdstone giving her consent; and even that was set at rest
soon, for she came out to take an evening grope in the store-closet
while we were yet in conversation, and Peggotty, with a boldness
that amazed me, broached the topic on the spot.

"The boy will be idle there," said Miss Murdstone, looking into a pickle-jar, "and idleness is the root of all evil. But, to be sure, he would be idle here—or anywhere, in my opinion."

Peggotty had an angry answer ready, I could see; but she swallowed it for my sake, and remained silent.

"Humph!" said Miss Murdstone, still keeping her eye on the pickles; "it is of more importance than anything else—it is of paramount importance—that my brother should not be disturbed or made uncomfortable. I suppose I had better say yes."

I thanked her, without making any demonstration of joy, lest it should induce her to withdraw her assent. However, the permission was given, and was never retracted; for when the month was out, Peggotty and I were ready to depart.

Mr. Barkis came into the house for Peggotty's boxes. Peggotty was naturally in low spirits at leaving what had been her home so many years, and where the two strong attachments of her life—for my mother and myself—had been formed; and she got into the cart, and sat in it with her handkerchief at her eyes.

So long as she remained in this condition, Mr. Barkis gave no sign of life whatever. He sat in his usual place and attitude, like a great stuffed figure. But when she began to look about her, and to speak to me, he nodded his head and grinned several times. I have not the least notion at whom, or what he meant by it.

"It's a beautiful day, Mr. Barkis!" I said, as an act of politeness.

"It ain't bad," said Mr. Barkis, who generally qualified his speech, and rarely committed himself.

"Peggotty is quite comfortable now, Mr. Barkis," I remarked, for his satisfaction.

"Is she, though?" said Mr. Barkis.

After reflecting about it, with a sagacious air, Mr. Barkis eyed her, and said,

"*Are* you pretty comfortable?"

Peggotty laughed, and answered in the affirmative.

"But really and truly, you know. Are you?" growled Mr. Barkis, sliding nearer to her on the seat, and nudging her with his elbow. "Are you? Really and truly, pretty comfortable? Are you? Eh?" At each of these inquiries Mr. Barkis shuffled nearer to her, and gave her another nudge; so that at last we were all crowded together in the left-hand corner of the cart, and I was so squeezed that I could hardly bear it.

Peggotty calling his attention to my sufferings, Mr. Barkis gave me a little more room at once, and got away by degrees. But I could not help observing that he seemed to think he had hit upon a wonderful expedient for expressing himself in a neat, agreeable, and pointed manner, without the inconvenience of inventing conversation. He manifestly chuckled over it for some time. By-and-by he turned to Peggotty again, and repeating, "Are you pretty comfortable, though?" bore down upon us as before, until the breath was nearly wedged out of my body.

Mr. Peggotty and Ham waited for us at the old place. They received me and Peggotty in an affectionate manner, and shook hands with Mr. Barkis, who, with his hat on the very back of his head, and a shamefaced leer upon his countenance, and pervading his very legs, presented but a vacant appearance, I thought. They each took one of Peggotty's trunks, and we were going away, when Mr. Barkis solemnly made a sign to me with his forefinger to come under an archway.

"I say," growled Mr. Barkis, "it was all right."

I looked up into his face, and answered, with an attempt to be very profound, "Oh!"

"It didn't come to a end there," said Mr. Barkis, nodding confidentially. "It was all right."

Again I answered, "Oh!"

"You know who was willin'," said my friend. "It was Barkis, and Barkis only."

I nodded assent.

"It's all right," said Mr. Barkis, shaking hands; "I'm a friend of yourn. You made it all right, first. It's all right."

In his attempts to be particularly lucid, Mr. Barkis was so extremely mysterious that I might have stood looking in his face for an hour, and most assuredly should have got as much information out of it as out of the face of a clock that had stopped, but for Peggotty's calling me away.

Mrs. Gummidge was waiting at the door as if she had stood there ever since. But there was no little Em'ly to be seen, so I asked Mr. Peggotty where she was.

"She's at school, sir," said Mr. Peggotty, wiping the heat consequent on the porterage of Peggotty's box from his forehead; "she'll be home," looking at the Dutch clock, "in from twenty minutes to half an hour's time. We all on us feel the loss of her, bless ye!"

A figure appeared in the distance before long, and I soon knew it to be Em'ly, who was a little creature still in stature, though she was grown. But when she drew nearer, and I saw her blue eyes looking bluer, and her dimpled face looking brighter, and her whole self prettier and gayer, a curious feeling came over me that made me pretend not to know her, and pass by as if I were looking at something a long way off. I have never done such a thing since in later life, or I am mistaken.

Little Em'ly didn't care a bit. She saw me well enough; but instead of turning round and calling after me, ran away laughing. This obliged me to run after her, and she ran so fast that we were very near the cottage before I caught her.

"Oh, it's you, is it?" said little Em'ly.

"Why, you knew who it was, Em'ly," said I.

"And didn't *you* know who it was?" said Em'ly. I was going to kiss her, but she covered her cherry lips with her hands, and said she wasn't a baby now, and ran away, laughing more than ever, into the house.

She seemed to delight in teasing me, which was a change in her I wondered at very much. The tea-table was ready and our little locker was put out in its old place; but instead of coming to sit by me, she went and bestowed her company upon that grumbling Mrs. Gummidge, and on Mr. Peggotty's inquiring why, rumpled her hair all over her face to hide it, and would do nothing but laugh.

On the very first evening after our arrival, Mr. Barkis appeared in an exceedingly vacant and awkward condition, and with a bundle of oranges tied up in a handkerchief. As he made no allusion of any kind to this property, he was supposed to have left it behind him by accident when he went away; until Ham, running after him to restore it, came back with the information that it was intended for Peggotty. After that occasion he appeared every evening at exactly the same hour, and always with a little bundle, to which he never alluded, and which he regularly put behind the door, and left there. These offerings of affection were of a most various and eccentric description. Among them I remember a double set of pigs' trotters, a huge pin cushion, half a bushel or so of apples, a pair of jet earrings, some Spanish onions, a box of dominoes, a canary bird and cage, and a leg of pickled pork.

Mr. Barkis' wooing, as I remember it, was altogether of a peculiar kind. He very seldom said anything, but would sit by the fire in much the same attitude as he sat in his cart, and stare heavily at Peggotty, who was opposite. He seemed to enjoy himself very much, and not to feel at all called upon to talk.

At length, when the term of my visit was nearly expired, it was given out that Peggotty and Mr. Barkis were going to make a day's holiday together, and that little Em'ly and I were to accompany them. I had but a broken sleep the night before, in anticipation of the pleasure of a whole day with Em'ly. We were all astir betimes in the morning; and while we were yet at breakfast, Mr. Barkis appeared in the distance, driving a chaise-cart towards the object of his affections.

Peggotty was dressed as usual, in her neat and quiet mourning; but Mr. Barkis bloomed in a new blue coat, of which the tailor had given him such good measure, that the cuffs would have rendered gloves unnecessary in the coldest weather, while the collar was so high that it pushed his hair up on end on the top of his head. His bright buttons, too, were of the largest size. Rendered complete by drab pantaloons and a buff waistcoat, I thought Mr. Barkis a phenomenon of respectability.

When we were all in a bustle outside the door, I found that Mr. Peggotty was prepared with an old shoe, which was to be thrown after us for luck, and which he offered to Mrs. Gummidge for that purpose.

"No. It had better be done by somebody else, Dan'l," said Mrs. Gummidge. "I'm a lone lorn creetur' myself, and everythink that reminds me of creetur's that ain't lone and lorn, goes contrairy with me."

"Come, old gal!" cried Mr. Peggotty. "Take and heave it."

"No, Dan'l," returned Mrs. Gummidge, whimpering and shaking her head. "If I felt less, I could do more. You don't feel like me, Dan'l; thinks don't go contrairy with you, nor you with them. You had better do it yourself."

But here Peggotty, who had been going about from one to another in a hurried way, kissing everybody, called out from the cart, in which we all were by this time (Em'ly and I on two little chairs, side by side), that Mrs. Gummidge must do it. So Mrs. Gummidge did it; and, I am sorry to relate, cast a damp upon the festive character of our departure, by immediately bursting into tears, and sinking subdued into the arms of Ham, with the declaration that she knowed she was a burden, and had better be carried to the house at once.

Away we went, however, on our holiday excursion; and the first thing we did was to stop at a church, where Mr. Barkis tied the horse to some rails, and went in with Peggotty, leaving little Em'ly and me alone in the chaise. I took that occasion to put my arm round Em'ly's waist, and propose that as I was going away so very soon now, we should determine to be very affectionate to one another, and very happy, all day. Little Em'ly consenting, and allowing me to kiss her, I became desperate; informing her, I recollect, that I never could love another, and that I was prepared to shed the blood of anybody who should aspire to her affections.

How merry little Em'ly made herself about it! With what a demure assumption of being immensely older and wiser than I, the fairy little woman said I was "a silly boy"; and then laughed so charmingly that I forgot the pain of being called by this disparaging name, in the pleasure of looking at her.

Mr. Barkis and Peggotty were a good while in the church, but came out at last; and then we drove away into the country. As we were going along, Mr. Barkis turned to me, and said, with a wink—by-the-by, I should hardly have thought before that he *could* wink,

"What name was it as I wrote up in the cart?"

"Clara Peggotty," I answered.

"What name would it be as I should write up now?"

"Clara Peggotty again?" I suggested.

"Clara Peggotty BARKIS!" he returned, and burst into a roar of laughter that shook the chaise.

In a word, they were married, and had gone into the church for no other purpose. We drove to a little inn in a by-road, where we were expected, and where we had a very comfortable dinner, and passed the day with great satisfaction.

Well, we came to the old boat again in good time at night, and there Mr. and Mrs. Barkis bade us good-bye, and drove away snugly to their own home.

A beautiful little home it was; and a little room in the roof (with the crocodile book on a shelf by the bed's head) was to be always mine, Peggotty said, and should always be kept for me in exactly the same state.

"Young or old, Davy dear, as long as I am alive and have this house over my head," said Peggotty, "you shall find it as if I expected you here directly minute. I shall keep it every day as I used to keep your old little room, my darling; and if you was to go to China, you might think of it as being kept just the same all the time you were away."

I went home in the morning, with herself and Mr. Barkis in the cart. They left me at the gate, not easily or lightly; and it was a strange sight to me to see the cart go on, taking Peggotty away, and leaving me under the old elm trees looking at the house in which there was no face to look on mine with love or liking any more.

I fell into a state of neglect, which I cannot look back upon without compassion. I was not actively ill-used. I was not beaten, or starved; but the wrong that was done to me had no intervals of relenting, and was done in a systematic, passionless manner. Day after day, week after week, month after month, I was coldly neglected. I wonder sometimes, when I think of it, what they would have done if I had been taken with an illness; whether I should have lain down in my lonely room, and languished through it in my usual solitary way, or whether anybody would have helped me out.

I now approach a period of my life which I can never lose the remembrance of while I remember anything, and the recollection of which has often, without my invocation, come before me like a ghost, and haunted happier times.

I had been out one day, loitering somewhere, in the listless meditative manner that my way of life engendered, when, turning the corner of a lane near our house, I came upon Mr. Murdstone walking with a gentleman. I knew him to be Mr. Quinion, whom I had seen before—it is no matter—I need not recall when.

Mr. Quinion lay at our house that night. After breakfast the next morning, I had put my chair away, and was going out of the room, when Mr. Murdstone called me back. He then gravely repaired to another table, where his sister sat herself at her desk. Mr. Quinion, with his hands in his pockets, stood looking out of window; and I stood looking at them all.

"David," said Mr. Murdstone, "to the young this is a world for action, not for moping and droning in."

"As you do," added his sister.

"Jane Murdstone, leave it to me, if you please. I say, David, to the young this is a world for action, and not for moping and droning in. It is especially so for a young boy of your disposition, which requires a great deal of correcting, and to which no greater service can be done than to force it to conform to the ways of the working world, and to bend it and break it."

"For stubbornness won't do here," said his sister. "What it wants is to be crushed. And crushed it must be—shall be, too!"

He gave her a look, half in remonstrance, half in approval, and went on,

"I suppose you know, David, that I am not rich. At any rate, you know it now. You have received some considerable education already. Education is costly; and even if it were not, and I could afford it, I am of opinion that it would not be at all advantageous to you to be kept at a school. What is before you is a fight with the world; and the sooner you begin it, the better."

I think it occurred to me that I had already begun it, in my poor way; but it occurs to me now, whether or no.

"You have heard the 'counting-house' mentioned sometimes," said Mr. Murdstone.

"The counting-house, sir?" I repeated.

"Of Murdstone and Grinby, in the wine trade," he replied.

I suppose I looked uncertain, for he went on hastily,

"You have heard the 'counting-house' mentioned, or the business, or the cellars, or the wharf, or something about it."

"I think I have heard the business mentioned, sir," I said, remembering what I vaguely knew of his and his sister's resources. "But I don't know when."

"It does not matter when," he returned. "Mr. Quinion manages that business."

I glanced at the latter deferentially as he stood looking out of window.

"Mr. Quinion suggests that it gives employment to some other boys, and that he sees no reason why it shouldn't, on the same terms, give employment to you."

"He having," Mr. Quinion observed in a low voice, and half turning round, "no other prospect, Murdstone."

Mr. Murdstone, with an impatient, even an angry gesture, resumed, without noticing what he had said,

"So you are now going to London, David, with Mr. Quinion, to begin the world on your own account."

"In short, you are provided for," observed his sister; "and will please to do your duty."

Though I quite understood that the purpose of this announcement was to get rid of me, I have no distinct remembrance whether it pleased or frightened me. My impression is, that I was in a state of confusion about it, and, oscillating between the two points, touched neither.

CHAPTER 11 ❦ I BEGIN LIFE ON MY OWN ACCOUNT, AND DON'T LIKE IT ✦ ✦ ✦

Murdstone and Grinby's warehouse was at the water side. It was a crazy old house with a wharf of its own, abutting on the water when the tide was in, and on the mud when the tide was out, and literally overrun with rats. Its paneled rooms, discolored with the dirt and smoke of a hundred years, I dare say, its decaying floors and staircases, the squeaking and scuffing of the old grey rats down in the cellars, and the dirt and rottenness of the place, are all before me, just as they were in the evil hour when I went among them for the first time, with my trembling hand in Mr. Quinion's.

Murdstone and Grinby's trade was the supply of wines and spirits. A great many empty bottles were one of the consequences of this traffic, and certain men and boys were employed to examine them against the light, and reject those that were flawed, and to rinse and wash them. When the empty bottles ran short, there were labels to be pasted on full ones, or corks to be fitted to them, or seals to be put upon the corks, or finished bottles to be packed in casks. All this work was my work.

The oldest of the regular boys was summoned to show me my business. His name was Mick Walker, and he wore a ragged apron and a paper cap. He informed me that his father was a bargeman, and walked, in a black velvet head-dress, in the Lord Mayor's Show. He also informed me that our principal associate would be another boy whom he introduced by the—to me—extraordinary name of Mealy Potatoes. I discovered, however, that this youth had not been christened by that name, but that it had been bestowed upon him in the warehouse, on account of his complexion, which was pale or mealy. Mealy's father was a waterman.

No words can express the secret agony of my soul as I sunk into this companionship. The deep remembrance of the sense I had of being utterly without hope now—of the shame I felt in my position —cannot be written. As often as Mick Walker went away in the course of that forenoon, I mingled my tears with the water in which I was washing the bottles, and sobbed as if there were a flaw in my own breast, and it were in danger of bursting.

The counting-house clock was at half-past twelve, and there was general preparation of going to dinner, when Mr. Quinion tapped at the counting-house window, and beckoned to me to go in. I went in, and found there a stoutish, middle-aged person, in a brown surtout and black tights and shoes, with no more hair upon his head (which was a large one, and very shining) than there is upon an egg, and with a very extensive face, which he turned full upon me. His clothes were shabby, but he had an imposing shirt-collar on. He carried a jaunty sort of a stick, with a large pair of rusty tassels to it; and a quizzing-glass hung outside his coat—for ornament, I afterwards found, as he very seldom looked through it, and couldn't see anything when he did.

"This," said Mr. Quinion, in allusion to myself, "is he."

"This," said the stranger, with a certain condescending roll in his voice, and a certain indescribable air of doing something genteel, which impressed me very much, "is Master Copperfield. I hope I see you well, sir?"

I said I was very well, and hoped he was. I was sufficiently ill at ease, Heaven knows; but it was not in my nature to complain much at that time of my life, so I said I was very well, and hoped he was.

"I am," said the stranger, "thank Heaven, quite well. I have received a letter from Mr. Murdstone, in which he mentions that he would desire me to receive into an apartment in the rear of my house, which is at present unoccupied—and is, in short, to be let as a—in short," said the stranger with a smile, and in a burst of confidence, "as a bedroom—the young beginner whom I have now the pleasure to—" and the stranger waved his hand, and settled his chin in his shirt-collar.

"This is Mr. Micawber," said Mr. Quinion to me.

"Ahem!" said the stranger, "that is my name."

"Mr. Micawber," said Mr. Quinion, "is known to Mr. Murdstone. He takes orders for us on commission, when he can get any. He has been written to by Mr. Murdstone on the subject of your lodgings, and he will receive you as a lodger."

"My address," said Mr. Micawber, "is Windsor Terrace, City Road. I—in short," said Mr. Micawber, with the same genteel air, and in another burst of confidence—"I live there."

I made him a bow.

"Under the impression," said Mr. Micawber, "that your peregrinations in this metropolis have not as yet been extensive, and that you might have some difficulty in penetrating the arcana of the Modern Babylon in the direction of the City Road—in short," said Mr. Micawber, in another burst of confidence, "that you might lose yourself—I shall be happy to call this evening, and install you in the knowledge of the nearest way."

I thanked him with all my heart, for it was friendly in him to offer to take that trouble. He put on his hat, and went out with his cane under his arm—very upright, and humming a tune.

Mr. Quinion then formally engaged me to be as useful as I could in the warehouse of Murdstone and Grinby, at a salary, I think, of six shillings a week. He paid me a week down and I gave Mealy sixpence out of it to get my trunk carried to Windsor Terrace at night—it being too heavy for my strength, small as it was. I paid sixpence more for my dinner.

At the appointed time in the evening, Mr. Micawber reappeared. I washed my hands and face, to do the greater honor to his gentility, and we walked to our house, as I suppose I must now call it, together.

Arrived at his house in Windsor Terrace (which I noticed was shabby like himself, but also, like himself, made all the show it could), he presented me to Mrs. Micawber, a thin and faded lady, not at all young, who was sitting in the parlor (the first floor was altogether unfurnished, and the blinds were kept down to delude the neighbors), with a baby at her breast. This baby was one of twins; and I may remark here that I hardly ever, in all my experience of the family, saw both the twins detached from Mrs. Micawber at the same time.

There were two other children—Master Micawber, aged about four, and Miss Micawber, aged about three. These, and a dark-complexioned young woman, with a habit of snorting (who was servant to the family, and informed me, before half an hour had expired, that she was "a orfling," and came from St. Luke's Work-house, in the neighborhood), completed the establishment.

"I never thought," said Mrs. Micawber, "before I was married, when I lived with papa and mamma, that I should ever find it neces-sary to take a lodger. But Mr. Micawber being in difficulties, all considerations of private feeling must give way."

I said, "Yes, ma'am."

"If Mr. Micawber's creditors *will not* give him time," said Mrs. Micawber, "they must take the consequences; blood cannot be ob-tained from a stone; neither can anything on account be obtained at present from Mr. Micawber."

Poor Mrs. Micawber! She said she had tried to exert herself; and so, I have no doubt, she had. The center of the street door was perfectly covered with a great brass-plate, on which was engraved, "Mrs. Micawber's Boarding Establishment for Young Ladies"; but I never found that any young lady had ever been to school there, or that any young lady ever came or proposed to come, or that the least preparation was ever made to receive any young lady. The only visitors I ever saw or heard of were creditors. *They* used to come at all hours, and some of them were quite ferocious. One dirty-faced man (I think he was a bootmaker) used to edge himself into the passage as early as seven o'clock in the morning, and call up the stairs to Mr. Micawber: "Come! you ain't out yet, you know. Pay us, will you? Don't hide, you know; that's mean. I wouldn't be mean, if I was you. Pay us, will you? You just pay us, d'ye hear? Come!" Receiving no answer to these taunts, he would mount in his wrath to the words "swindlers" and "robbers"; and these being in-effectual too, would sometimes go to the extremity of crossing the street, and roaring up at the windows of the second floor, where he knew Mr. Micawber was. At these times, Mr. Micawber would be transported with grief and mortification, even to the length (as I was once made aware by a scream from his wife) of making motions at himself with a razor; but within half an hour afterwards he would polish up his shoes with extraordinary pains, and go out, humming a tune with a greater air of gentility than ever. Mrs. Micawber was quite as elastic. I have known her to be thrown into fainting fits by the king's taxes at three o'clock, and to eat lamb-chops breaded, and drink warm ale (paid for with two teaspoons that had gone to the pawnbroker's), at four. On one occasion, when an execution had just been put in, coming home through some chance as early as six o'clock, I saw her lying (of course, with a twin) under the grate in a swoon, with her hair all torn about her face; but I never knew her more cheerful than she was, that very same night, over a veal-cutlet before the kitchen fire, telling me stories about her papa and mamma, and the company they used to keep.

In this house, and with this family, I passed my leisure time. My own exclusive breakfast of a penny loaf and a pennyworth of milk, I provided myself. I kept another small loaf, and a modicum of cheese, on a particular shelf of a particular cupboard, to make my supper on when I came back at night. I worked from morning until night, with common men and boys, a shabby child. I lounged about the streets, insufficiently and unsatisfactorily fed. I know that, but for the mercy of God, I might easily have been, for any care that was taken of me, a little robber or a little vagabond.

Mr. Micawber's difficulties were an addition to the distressed state of my mind. In my forlorn state, I became quite attached to the family, and used to walk about, busy with Mrs. Micawber's calculations of ways and means, and heavy with the weight of Mr. Micawber's debts. On a Saturday night, which was my grand treat (partly because it was a great thing to walk home with six or seven shillings in my pocket, looking into the shops and thinking what such a sum would buy, and partly because I went home early), Mrs. Micawber would make the most heartrending confidences to me. It was nothing at all unusual for Mr. Micawber to sob violently at the beginning of one of these Saturday-night conversations, and sing about Jack's delight being his lovely Nan toward the end of it. I have known him come home to supper with a flood of tears, and a declaration that nothing was now left but a jail; and go to bed making a calculation of the expense of putting bow-windows to the house, "in case anything turned up," which was his favorite expression.

A curious equality of friendship, originating, I suppose, in our respective circumstances, sprung up between me and these people, notwithstanding the ludicrous disparity in our years. But I never allowed myself to be prevailed upon to accept any invitation to eat and drink with them, until Mrs. Micawber took me into her entire confidence. This she did one evening as follows:

"Master Copperfield," said Mrs. Micawber, "I make no stranger of you, and therefore do not hesitate to say that Mr. Micawber's difficulties are coming to a crisis. With the exception of the heel of a Dutch cheese, there is really not a scrap of anything in the larder."

"Dear me," I said, in great concern.

I had two or three shillings of my week's money in my pocket—from which I presume that it must have been on a Wednesday night when we held this conversation— and I hastily produced them, and with heartfelt emotion begged Mrs. Micawber to accept of them as a loan. But that lady, kissing me, and making me put them back in my pocket, replied that she couldn't think of it.

"No, my dear Master Copperfield," said she, "far be it from my thoughts! But you have a discretion beyond your years, and can render me another kind of service, if you will, and a service I will thankfully accept of."

I begged Mrs. Micawber to name it.

"I have parted with the plate myself," said Mrs. Micawber. "But there are still a few trifles that we could part with. Mr. Micawber's feelings would never allow *him* to dispose of them; and Clickett"— this was the girl from the workhouse—"being of a vulgar mind, would take painful liberties if so much confidence was reposed in her. Master Copperfield, if I might ask you——"

I understood Mrs. Micawber now, and begged her to make use of me to any extent. I began to dispose of the more portable articles of property that very evening; and went out on a similar expedition almost every morning, before I went to Murdstone and Grinby's.

At last Mr. Micawber's difficulties came to a crisis, and he was arrested early one morning, and carried over to the King's Bench Prison, in the Borough. He told me, as he went out of the house, that the god of day had now gone down upon him; and I really thought his heart was broken, and mine too. But I heard, afterwards, that he was seen to play a lively game of skittles before noon.

On the first Sunday after he was taken there, I was to go and see him, and have dinner with him. Mr. Micawber was waiting for me within the gate, and we went up to his room (top story but one), and cried very much. He solemnly conjured me, I remember, to take warning by his fate, and to observe that if a man had twenty pounds a year for his income, and spent nineteen pounds nineteen shillings and sixpence, he would be happy, but that if he spent twenty pounds one he would be miserable. After which he borrowed a shilling of me for porter, gave me a written order on Mrs. Micawber for the amount, and put away his pocket-handkerchief, and cheered up.

We sat before a little fire, with two bricks put within the rusted grate, one on each side, to prevent its burning too many coals; until another debtor, who shared the room with Mr. Micawber, came in from the bakehouse with the loin of mutton which was our joint-stock repast. Then I was sent up to "Captain Hopkins" in the room overhead, with Mr. Micawber's compliments, and I was his young friend, and would Captain Hopkins lend me a knife and fork.

There was something gipsy-like and agreeable in the dinner, after all. I took back Captain Hopkins's knife and fork early in the afternoon, and went home to comfort Mrs. Micawber with an account of my visit. She fainted when she saw me return, and made a little jug of egg-hot afterwards to console us while we talked it over.

I don't know how the household furniture came to be sold for the family benefit, or who sold it, except that *I* did not. Sold it was, however, and carried away in a van—except the bed, a few chairs, and the kitchen-table. With these possessions we encamped, as it were, in the two parlors of the emptied house in Windsor Terrace —Mrs. Micawber, the children, the Orfling, and myself—and lived in those rooms night and day. I have no idea for how long, though it seems to me for a long time. At last Mrs. Micawber resolved to move into the prison, where Mr. Micawber had now secured a room to himself. So I took the key of the house to the landlord, who was very glad to get it; and the beds were sent over to the King's Bench, except mine, for which a little room was hired outside the walls in the neighborhood of that Institution, very much to my satisfaction, since the Micawbers and I had become too used to one another, in our troubles, to part.

I led the same secretly unhappy life; but I led it in the same lonely, self-reliant manner. The only changes I am conscious of are, first, that I had grown more shabby; and secondly, that I was now relieved of much of the weight of Mr. and Mrs. Micawber's cares, for some relatives or friends had engaged to help them at their present pass, and they lived more comfortably in the prison than they had lived for a long while out of it. Mrs. Micawber informed me that "her family" had decided that Mr. Micawber should apply for his release under the Insolvent Debtors' Act, which would set him free, she expected, in about six weeks.

"And then," said Mr. Micawber, who was present, "I have no doubt I shall, please Heaven, begin to be beforehand with the world, and to live in a perfectly new manner, if—in short, if anything turns up."

I N DUE time Mr. Micawber's petition was ripe for hearing, and that gentleman was ordered to be discharged under the Act, to my great joy.

"On such an occasion I will give you, Master Copperfield," said Mrs. Micawber, "in a little more flip"—for we had been having some already—"the memory of my papa and mamma."

"Are they dead, ma'am?" I inquired, after drinking the toast in a wine-glass.

"My mamma departed this life," said Mrs. Micawber, "before Mr. Micawber's difficulties commenced—or at least before they became pressing. My papa lived to bail Mr. Micawber several times, and then expired, regretted by a numerous circle."

Mrs. Micawber shook her head, and dropped a pious tear upon the twin who happened to be in hand.

As I could hardly hope for more favorable opportunity of putting a question in which I had a near interest, I said to Mrs. Micawber,

"May I ask, ma'am, what you and Mr. Micawber intend to do, now that Mr. Micawber is out of difficulties, and at liberty? Have you settled yet?"

75

"My family," said Mrs. Micawber, who always said those two words with an air, though I never could discover who came under the denomination—"my family are of opinion that Mr. Micawber should quit London, and exert his talents in the country. Mr. Micawber is a man of great talent, Master Copperfield."

I said I was sure of that.

"Of great talent," repeated Mrs. Micawber. "My family are of opinion that, with a little interest, something might be done for a man of his ability in the Custom House. The influence of my family being local, it is their wish that Mr. Micawber should go down to Plymouth. They think it indispensable that he should be upon the spot."

"That he may be ready?" I suggested.

"Exactly," returned Mrs. Micawber. "That he may be ready, in case of anything turning up."

"And do you go too, ma'am?"

The events of the day, in combination with the twins, if not with the flip, had made Mrs. Micawber hysterical, as she replied,

"I never will desert Mr. Micawber. Mr. Micawber may have concealed his difficulties from me in the first instance, but his sanguine temper may have led him to expect that he would overcome them. The pearl necklace and bracelets, which I inherited from mamma, have been disposed of for less than half their value, and the set of coral, which was the wedding gift of my papa, has been actually thrown away for nothing. But I never will desert Mr. Micawber. No!" cried Mrs. Micawber, more affected than before, "I never will do it! It's of no use asking me!"

I felt quite uncomfortable—as if Mrs. Micawber supposed I had asked her to do anything of the sort!—and sat looking at her in alarm.

"He is the parent of my children! He is the father of my twins! He is the husband of my affections," cried Mrs. Micawber, "and I ne—ver—will—desert Mr. Micawber!"

Mr. Micawber was so deeply affected by this proof of her devotion (as to me, I was dissolved in tears), that he hung over her in a passionate manner, imploring her to look up, and to be calm. But the more he asked Mrs. Micawber to look up, the more she fixed her eyes on nothing; and the more he asked her to compose herself, the more she wouldn't. Consequently Mr. Micawber was soon so overcome, that he mingled his tears with hers and mine; until he begged me to do him the favor of taking a chair on the staircase, while he got her into bed.

The very next day showed me that Mrs. Micawber had not spoken of their going away without warrant. They took a lodging in the house where I lived, for a week, at the expiration of which time they were to start for Plymouth. I think we became fonder of one another as the time went on. On the last Sunday they invited me to dinner, and we had a loin of pork and apple-sauce and a pudding.

"I shall never, Master Copperfield," said Mrs. Micawber, "revert to the period when Mr. Micawber was in difficulties, without thinking of you. Your conduct has always been of the most delicate and obliging description. You have never been a lodger; you have been a friend."

I expressed my sense of this commendation, and said I was very sorry we were going to lose one another.

"My dear young friend," said Mr. Micawber, "I am older than you; a man of some experience in life, and—and of some experience, in short, in difficulties, generally speaking. At present, and until something turns up (which I am, I may say, hourly expecting), I have nothing to bestow but advice. Still my advice is so far worth taking that—in short, that I have never taken it myself, and am the" —here Mr. Micawber, who had been beaming and smiling all over his head and face up to the present moment, checked himself and frowned—"the miserable wretch you behold."

"My dear Micawber!" urged his wife.

"I say," returned Mr. Micawber, quite forgetting himself, and smiling again, "the miserable wretch you behold. My advice is, never to do tomorrow what you can do today. Procrastination is the thief of time. Collar him!"

"My other piece of advice, Copperfield," said Mr. Micawber, "you know. Annual income twenty pounds, annual expenditure nineteen nineteen six, result happiness. Annual income twenty pounds, annual expenditure twenty pounds ought and six, result misery. The blossom is blighted, the leaf is withered, the god of day goes down upon the dreary scene, and—and, in short, you are forever floored. As I am!"

To make his example the more impressive, Mr. Micawber drank a glass of punch with an air of great enjoyment and satisfaction, and whistled the College Hornpipe.

Next morning I met the whole family at the coach office, and saw them, with a desolate heart, take their places outside, at the back.

I think, as Mrs. Micawber sat at the back of the coach with the children, and I stood in the road looking wistfully at them, a mist cleared from her eyes, and she saw what a little creature I really was, I think so, because she beckoned to me to climb up, with quite a new and motherly expression in her face, and put her arm round my neck, and gave me just such a kiss as she might have given to her own boy. I had barely time to get down again before the coach started, and I could hardly see the family for the handkerchiefs they waved. It was gone in a minute. I went to begin my weary day at Murdstone and Grinby's.

But with no intention of passing many more weary days there. No. I had resolved to run away—to go, by some means or other, down into the country, to the only relation I had in the world, and tell my story to my aunt, Miss Betsey.

I don't know how this desperate idea came into my brain. But, once there, it remained there, and hardened into a purpose than which I have never entertained a more determined purpose in my life. I am far from sure that I believed there was anything hopeful in it, but my mind was thoroughly made up that it must be carried into execution.

As I did not even know where Miss Betsey lived, I wrote a long letter to Peggotty, and asked her, incidentally, if she remembered; pretending that I had heard of such a lady living at a certain place I named at random, and had a curiosity to know if it were the same. In the course of that letter I told Peggotty that I had a particular occasion for half a guinea; and that if she could lend me that sum until I could repay it, I should be very much obliged to her, and would tell her afterwards what I had wanted it for.

Peggotty's answer soon arrived, and was, as usual, full of affectionate devotion. She enclosed the half-guinea and told me that Miss Betsey lived near Dover, but whether at Dover itself, at Hythe, Sandgate, or Folkestone, she could not say. One of our men, however, informing me that they were all close together, I resolved to set out at the end of that week.

Being a very honest little creature, and unwilling to disgrace the memory I was going to leave behind me at Murdstone and Grinby's, I considered myself bound to remain until Saturday night; and, as I had been paid a week's wages in advance when I first came there, not to present myself in the counting-house at the usual hour to receive my stipend. For this reason I had borrowed the half-guinea, that I might not be without a fund for my traveling expenses. Accordingly, when the Saturday night came, I shook Mick Walker by the hand; asked him, when it came to his turn to be paid, to say to Mr. Quinion that I had gone to move my box to Tipp's; and, bidding a last good-night to Mealy Potatoes, ran away.

My box was at my old lodging over the water, and I had written a direction for it on the back of one of our address cards that we nailed on the casks: "Master David, to be left till called for at the Coach Office, Dover." This I had in my pocket ready to put on the box, after I should have got it out of the house; and as I went toward my lodging, I looked about me for someone who would help me to carry it to the booking-office.

There was a long-legged young man, with a very little empty donkey-cart, whose eye I caught as I was going by, and who, addressing me as "Sixpenn'orth of bad ha'pence," hoped "I should know him agin to swear to"—in allusion, I have no doubt, to my staring at him. I stopped to assure him that I had not done so in bad manners, but uncertain whether he might or might not like a job.

"Wot job?" said the long-legged young man.

"To move a box," I answered.

"Wot box?" said the long-legged young man.

I told him mine, which was down that street there, and which I wanted him to take to the Dover coach office for sixpence.

"Done with you for a tanner!" said the long-legged young man, and directly got upon his cart, which was nothing but a large wooden tray on wheels, and rattled away at such a rate that it was as much as I could do to keep pace with the donkey.

There was a defiant manner about this young man, and particularly about the way in which he chewed straw as he spoke to me, that I did not much like. As the bargain was made, however, I took him upstairs to the room I was leaving, and we brought the box down, and put it on his cart. Now, I was unwilling to put the direction card on there, lest any of my landlord's family should fathom what I was doing, and detain me; so I said to the young man that I would be glad if he would stop for a minute when he came to the dead-wall of the King's Bench prison. The words were no sooner out of my mouth, than he rattled away as if he, my box, the cart, and the donkey, were all equally mad; and I was quite out of breath with running and calling after him, when I caught him at the place appointed.

Being much flushed and excited, I tumbled my half-guinea out of my pocket in pulling the card out. I put it in my mouth for safety, and though my hands trembled a good deal, had just tied the card on very much to my satisfaction, when I felt myself violently chucked under the chin by the long-legged young man, and saw my half-guinea fly out of my mouth into his hand.

"Wot!" said the young man, seizing me by my jacket collar, with a frightful grin. "This is a pollis case, is it? You're a-going to bolt, are you? Come to the pollis, you young warmin; come to the pollis!"

"You give me my money back, if you please," said I, very much frightened, "and leave me alone."

"Come to the pollis!" said the young man. "You shall prove it yourn to the pollis."

"Give me my box and money, will you?" I cried, bursting into tears.

The young man still replied, "Come to the pollis!" and was dragging me against the donkey in a violent manner, as if there were any affinity between that animal and a magistrate, when he changed his mind, jumped into the cart, sat upon my box, and exclaiming that he would drive to the pollis straight, rattled away harder than ever.

I ran after him as fast as I could, but I had no breath to call out with, and should not have dared to call out now if I had. I narrowly escaped being run over, twenty times at least, in a half mile. Now I lost him, now I saw him, now I lost him, now I was cut at with a whip, now shouted at, now down in the mud, now up again, now running into somebody's arms, now running headlong at a post. At length, confused by fright and heat, and doubting whether half London might not by this time be turning out for my apprehension, I left the young man to go where he would with my box and money; and, panting and crying, but never stopping, faced about for Greenwich, which I had understood was on the Dover Road— taking very little more out of the world, toward the retreat of my aunt, Miss Betsey, than I had brought into it, on the night when my arrival gave her so much umbrage.

CHAPTER 13 ✤ THE SEQUEL OF MY RESOLUTION ✦ ✦ ✦

I SAT down on a doorstep, quite spent and exhausted, and with hardly breath enough to cry for the loss of my box and half-guinea.

It was by this time dark; I heard the clocks strike ten as I sat resting. But it was a summer night, fortunately, and fine weather. When I had recovered my breath, and had got rid of a stifling sensation in my throat, I rose up and went on. I trudged on miserably, though as fast as I could, until I happened to pass a little shop, where it was written up that ladies' and gentlemen's wardrobes were bought, and that the best price was given for rags, bones, and kitchen-stuff. The master of this shop was sitting at the door in his shirt sleeves, smoking; and as there were a great many coats and pairs of trousers dangling from the low ceiling, and only two feeble candles burning inside to show what they were, I fancied that he looked like a man of a revengeful disposition, who had hung all his enemies, and was enjoying himself.

My late experiences with Mr. and Mrs. Micawber suggested to me that here might be a means of keeping off the wolf for a little while. I went up the next by-street, took off my waistcoat, rolled it neatly under my arm, and came back to the shop-door. "If you please, sir," I said, "I am to sell this for a fair price."

Mr. Dolloby—Dolloby was the name over the shop-door, at least—took the waistcoat, stood his pipe on its head against the doorpost, went into the shop, followed by me, snuffed the two candles with his fingers, spread the waistcoat on the counter, and looked at it there, held it up against the light, and looked at it there, and ultimately said,

"What do you call a price, now, for this here little weskit?"

"Oh! you know best, sir," I returned modestly.

"I can't be buyer and seller too," said Mr. Dolloby. "Put a price on this here little weskit."

"Would eighteenpence be?" I hinted, after some hesitation.

Mr. Dolloby rolled it up again, and gave it me back. "I should rob my family," he said, "if I was to offer ninepence for it."

This was a disagreeable way of putting the business, because it imposed upon me, a perfect stranger, the unpleasantness of asking Mr. Dolloby to rob his family on my account. My circumstances being so very pressing, however, I said I would take ninepence for it, if he pleased. Mr. Dolloby, not without some grumbling, gave ninepence. I wished him good-night, and walked out of the shop, the richer by that sum, and the poorer by a waistcoat.

I had had a hard day's work, and was pretty well jaded when I came climbing out at last upon the level of Blackheath. I found a haystack, and I lay down by it. Never shall I forget the lonely sensation of first lying down without a roof above my head!

Sleep came upon me as it came on many other outcasts, against whom house-doors were locked and house-dogs barked that night—until the warm beams of the sun awoke me. I crept away and struck into the long dusty track which I had first known to be the Dover Road when I little expected that any eyes would ever see me the wayfarer I was now upon it.

I got that Sunday through three-and-twenty miles on the straight road, though not very easily, for I was new to that kind of toil. I see myself, as evening closes in, coming over the bridge at Rochester, footsore and tired, and eating bread that I had bought for supper. One or two little houses with the notice, "Lodgings for Travelers," hanging out had tempted me; but I was afraid of spending the few pence I had, and was even more afraid of the vicious looks of the trampers I had met or overtaken. I sought no shelter, therefore, but the sky; and toiling into Chatham, upon a sort of grass-grown battery overhanging a lane, slept soundly until morning. Feeling that I could go but a very little way that day, I resolved to make the sale of my jacket its principal business. Accordingly, I took the jacket off, that I might learn to do without it; and carrying it under my arm, began a tour of inspection of the various slop-shops.

It was a likely place to sell a jacket in, for the dealers in second-hand clothes were numerous, and were, generally speaking, on the look-out for customers at their shop-doors. At last I found one that I thought looked promising, at the corner of a dirty lane.

Into this shop, which was low and small, and which was darkened rather than lighted by a little window overhung with clothes, and was descended into by some steps, I went with a palpitating heart, which was not relieved when an ugly old man, with the lower part of his face all covered with a stubby grey beard, rushed out of a dirty den behind it, and seized me by the hair of my head. He was a dreadful old man to look at, in a filthy flannel waistcoat, and smelling terribly of rum. His bedstead, covered with a tumbled and ragged piece of patchwork, was in the den he had come from, where another little window showed a prospect of more stinging-nettles and a lame donkey.

"Oh, what do you want?" grinned this old man, in a fierce, monotonous whine. "Oh, my eyes and limbs, what do you want? Oh, my lungs and liver, what do you want? Oh, goroo, goroo!"

I was so much dismayed by these words, and particularly by the repetition of the last unknown one, which was a kind of rattle in his throat, that I could make no answer; hereupon the old man, still holding me by the hair, repeated,

"Oh, what do you want? Oh, my eyes and limbs, what do you want? Oh, my lungs and liver, what do you want? Oh, goroo!"— which he screwed out of himself with an energy that made his eyes start in his head.

"I wanted to know," I said, trembling, "if you would buy a jacket."

"Oh, let's see the jacket!" cried the old man. "Oh, my heart on fire, show the jacket to us! Oh, my eyes and limbs, bring the jacket out!"

With that he took his trembling hands, which were like the claws of a great bird, out of my hair, and put on a pair of spectacles, not at all ornamental to his inflamed eyes.

"Oh, how much for the jacket?" cried the old man, after examining it. "Oh—goroo!—how much for the jacket?"

"Half a crown," I answered, recovering myself.

"Oh, my lungs and liver," cried the old man, "no! Oh, my eyes, no! Oh, my limbs, no! Eighteenpence. Goroo!"

Every time he uttered this ejaculation his eyes seemed to be in danger of starting out; and every sentence he spoke he delivered in a sort of tune, always exactly the same, and more like a gust of wind which begins low, mounts up high, and falls again, than any other comparison I can find for it.

"Well," said I, glad to have closed the bargain, "I'll take eighteenpence."

"Oh, my liver!" cried the old man, throwing the jacket on a shelf, "get out of the shop! Oh, my lungs, get out of the shop! Oh, my eyes and limbs—goroo!—don't ask for money; make it an exchange."

I never was so frightened in my life, before or since; but I told him humbly that I wanted money, and that nothing else was of any use to me, but that I would wait for it, as he desired, outside, and had no wish to hurry him. So I went outside, and sat down in the shade in a corner. And I sat there so many hours, that the shade became sunlight, and the sunlight became shade again, and still I sat there waiting for the money.

There never was such another drunken madman in that line of business, I hope. That he was well known in the neighborhood, and enjoyed the reputation of having sold himself to the devil, I soon understood from the visits he received from the boys, who continually came skirmishing about the shop, shouting that legend, and calling to him to bring out his gold. "You ain't poor, you know, Charley, as you pretend. Bring out your gold. Bring out some of the gold you sold yourself to the devil for. Come! It's in the lining of the mattress, Charley. Rip it open, and let's have some!" This, and many offers to lend him a knife for the purpose, exasperated him to such a degree, that the whole day was a succession of rushes on his part and flights on the part of the boys.

He made many attempts to induce me to consent to exchange—at one time coming out with a fishing-rod, at another with a fiddle, at another with a cocked hat, at another with a flute. But I resisted all these overtures, and sat there in desperation, each time asking him, with tears in my eyes, for the money or my jacket. At last he began to pay me in halfpence at a time, and was full two hours getting by easy stages to a shilling.

"Oh, my eyes and limbs!" he then cried, peeping hideously out of the shop, after a long pause, "will you go for twopence more?"

"I can't," I said; "I shall be starved."

"Oh, my lungs and liver, will you go for threepence?"

"I would go for nothing, if I could," I said, "but I want the money badly."

"Oh, go—roo!" (it is really impossible to express how he twisted this ejaculation out of himself, as he peeped round the doorpost at me, showing nothing but his crafty old head), "will you go for fourpence?"

I was so faint and weary that I closed with this offer; and taking the money out of his claw, not without trembling, went away more hungry and thirsty than I had ever been, a little before sunset. But at an expense of threepence I soon refreshed myself completely; and, being in better spirits then, limped seven miles upon my road.

My bed at night was under another haystack, where I rested comfortably, after having washed my blistered feet in a stream, and dressed them as well as I was able with some cool leaves. I took the road again next morning, through a succession of hop-grounds and orchards.

The trampers were worse than ever that day, and inspired me with a dread that is yet quite fresh in my mind. Some of them were most ferocious-looking ruffians, who stared at me as I went by; and stopped, perhaps, and called after me to come back and speak to them, and when I took to my heels, stoned me. I recollect one young fellow—a tinker, I suppose, from his wallet and brazier—who had a woman with him, and who faced about and stared at me thus, and then roared to me in such a tremendous voice to come back, that I halted and looked round.

"Come here, when you're called," said the tinker, "or I'll rip your young body open."

I thought it best to go back. As I drew nearer to them, trying to propitiate the tinker by my looks, I observed that the woman had a black eye.

"Where are you going?" said the tinker, gripping the bosom of my shirt with his blackened hand.

"I am going to Dover," I said.

"Where do you come from?" asked the tinker, giving his hand another turn in my shirt, to hold me more securely.

"I come from London," I said.

With his disengaged hand he made a menace of striking me, and then looked at me from head to foot.

"Have you got the price of a pint of beer about you?" said the tinker. "If you have, out with it, afore I take it away!"

I should certainly have produced it, but that I met the woman's look, and saw her very slightly shake her head, and form "No!" with her lips.

"I am very poor," I said, attempting to smile, "and have got no money."

"Why, what do you mean?" said the tinker, looking so sternly at me that I almost feared he saw the money in my pocket.

"Sir!" I stammered.

"What do you mean," said the tinker, "by wearing my brother's silk handkerchief? Give it over here!" And he had mine off my neck in a moment, and tossed it to the woman.

The woman burst into a fit of laughter, as if she thought this a joke, and tossed it back to me, nodded once, as slightly as before, and made the word "Go!" with her lips. Before I could obey, however, the tinker seized the handkerchief out of my hand with a roughness that threw me away like a feather, and putting it loosely round his own neck, turned upon the woman with an oath, and knocked her down. I never shall forget seeing her fall backward on the hard road, and lie there with her bonnet tumbled off, and her hair all whitened in the dust; nor, when I looked back from a distance, seeing her sitting on the pathway (which was a bank by the roadside), wiping the blood from her face with a corner of her shawl, while he went on ahead.

This adventure frightened me so, that, afterwards, when I saw any of these people coming, I turned back until I could find a hiding-place, where I remained until they had gone out of sight; which happened so often that I was very seriously delayed. I came, at last, upon the bare, wide downs near Dover; and I actually set foot in the town itself, on the sixth day of my flight.

I inquired about my aunt among the boatmen first, and received various answers. One said she lived in the South Foreland Light, and had singed her whiskers by doing so; another, that she was made fast to the great buoy outside the harbor, and could only be visited at half-tide; a third, that she was locked up in Maidstone Jail for child-stealing; a fourth, that she was seen to mount a broom, in the last high wind, and make direct for Calais. The shopkeepers generally replied, without hearing what I had to say, that they had got nothing for me. I felt more miserable and destitute than I had done at any period of my running away. My money was all gone; I had nothing left to dispose of; I was hungry, thirsty, and worn out; and seemed as distant from my end as if I had remained in London.

At length I went into a little shop and inquired if they could have the goodness to tell me where Miss Trotwood lived. I addressed myself to a man behind the counter, who was weighing some rice for a young woman; but the latter, taking the inquiry to herself, turned round quickly.

"My mistress?" she said. "What do you want with her, boy?"

"I want," I replied, "to speak to her, if you please."

"To beg of her, you mean," retorted the damsel.

"No," I said, "indeed." But suddenly remembering that in truth I came for no other purpose, I held my peace in confusion, and felt my face burn.

My aunt's handmaid, as I supposed she was from what she had said, put her rice in a little basket and walked out of the shop, telling me that I could follow her, if I wanted to know where Miss Trotwood lived. We soon came to a very neat little cottage with cheerful bow-windows—in front of it, a small square graveled court or garden full of flowers, carefully tended, and smelling deliciously.

"This is Miss Trotwood's," said the young woman. "Now you know; and that's all I have got to say." With which words she hurried into the house, as if to shake off the responsibility of my appearance; and left me standing at the garden gate, looking disconsolately over the top of it toward the parlor window.

My shoes were by this time in a woeful condition. The soles had shed themselves bit by bit, and the upper leathers had broken and burst until the very shape and form of shoes had departed from them. My hat (which had served me for a nightcap, too) was so crushed and bent, that no old battered handleless saucepan on a dunghill need have been ashamed to vie with it. My shirt and trousers, stained with heat, dew, grass, and the Kentish soil on which I had slept—and torn besides—might have frightened the birds from my aunt's garden, as I stood at the gate. My hair had known no comb or brush since I left London. My face, neck, and hands, from unaccustomed exposure to the air and sun, were burnt to a berry-brown. From head to foot I was powdered almost as white with chalk and dust, as if I had come out of a limekiln. In this plight, and with a strong consciousness of it, I waited to introduce myself to, and make my first impression on, my formidable aunt.

The unbroken stillness of the parlor window leading me to infer, after a while, that she was not there, I lifted up my eyes to the window above it, where I saw a florid, pleasant looking gentleman, with a grey head, who shut up one eye in a grotesque manner, nodded his head at me several times, shook it at me as often, laughed, and went away.

I had been discomposed enough before; but I was so much the more discomposed by this unexpected behavior, that I was on the point of slinking off, to think how I had best proceed, when there came out of the house a lady with her handkerchief tied over her cap, and a pair of gardening gloves on her hands, wearing a gardening pocket like a tollman's apron, and carrying a great knife. I knew her immediately to be Miss Betsey.

"Go away!" said Miss Betsey, shaking her head, and making a distant chop in the air with her knife. "Go along! No boys here!"

I watched her, with my heart at my lips, as she marched to a corner of her garden, and stooped to dig up some little root there. Then, without a scrap of courage, but with a great deal of desperation, I went softly in and stood beside her, touching her with my finger.

"If you please, ma'am," I began.

She started and looked up.

"If you please, aunt."

"Eh?" exclaimed Miss Betsey, in a tone of amazement I have never heard approached.

"If you please, aunt, I am your nephew."

"Oh, Lord!" said my aunt, and sat flat down in the garden-path.

"I am David Copperfield, of Blunderstone, in Suffolk—where you came, on the night when I was born, and saw my dear mamma. I have been very unhappy since she died. I have been slighted, and taught nothing, and thrown upon myself, and put to work not fit for me. It made me run away to you. I was robbed at first setting out, and have walked all the way, and never slept in a bed since I began the journey." Here my self-support gave all at once, and with a movement of my hands, intended to show her my ragged state, and call it to witness that I had suffered something, I broke into a passion of crying, which I suppose had been pent up within me all the week.

My aunt, with every sort of expression but wonder discharged from her countenance, sat on the gravel, staring at me, until I began to cry; when she got up in a hurry, collared me, and took me into the parlor. Her first proceeding there was to unlock a tall press, bring out several bottles, and pour some of the contents of each into my mouth. I think they must have been taken out at random, for I am sure I tasted aniseed water, anchovy sauce, and salad dressing. When she had administered these restoratives, as I was still quite hysterical, and unable to control my sobs, she put me on the sofa, with a shawl under my head, and the handkerchief from her own head under my feet, lest I should sully the cover; and ejaculated at intervals, "Mercy on us!" letting those exclamations off like minute-guns.

After a time she rang the bell. "Janet," said my aunt, when her servant came in, "go upstairs, give my compliments to Mr. Dick, and say I wish to speak to him."

Janet looked a little surprised to see me lying stiffly on the sofa (I was afraid to move lest it should be displeasing to my aunt), but went on her errand. My aunt, with her hands behind her, walked up and down the room, until the gentleman who had squinted at me from the upper window came in laughing.

"Mr. Dick," said my aunt, "don't be a fool, because nobody can be more discreet than you can when you choose. We all know that. So don't be a fool, whatever you are."

The gentleman was serious immediately, and looked at me, I thought, as if he would entreat me to say nothing about the window.

"Mr. Dick," said my aunt, "you have heard me mention David Copperfield? Now don't pretend not to have a memory, because you and I know better."

"David Copperfield?" said Mr. Dick, who did not appear to me to remember much about it. "*David* Copperfield? Oh, yes, to be sure. David, certainly."

"Well," said my aunt, "this is his boy, his son. He would be as like his father as it's possible to be, if he was not so like his mother, too."

"His son?" said Mr. Dick. "David's son? Indeed!"

"Yes," pursued my aunt; "and he has done a pretty piece of business. He has run away. Ah! his sister, Betsey Trotwood, never would have run away." My aunt shook her head firmly, confident in the character and behavior of the girl who never was born. "Now here you see young David Copperfield, and the question I put to you is, what shall I do with him?"

"What shall you do with him?" said Mr. Dick feebly, scratching his head. "Oh! do with him?"

"Yes," said my aunt, with a grave look, and her forefinger held up. "Come! I want some very sound advice."

"Why, if I was you," said Mr. Dick, considering, and looking vacantly at me, "I should—" The contemplation of me seemed to inspire him with a sudden idea, and he added briskly, "I should wash him!"

"Janet," said my aunt, turning round with a quiet triumph, which I did not then understand, "Mr. Dick sets us all right. Heat the bath!"

Although I was deeply interested in this dialogue, I could not help observing my aunt, Mr. Dick, and Janet, while it was in progress, and completing a survey I had already been engaged in making of the room.

My aunt was a tall, hard-featured lady, but by no means ill-looking. There was an inflexibility in her face, in her voice, in her gait and carriage, amply sufficient to account for the effect she had made upon a gentle creature like my mother; but her features were rather handsome than otherwise, though unbending and austere. I particularly noticed that she had a very quick bright eye. Her hair, which was grey, was arranged in two plain divisions, under what I believe would be called a mob-cap—I mean a cap, much more common then than now, with side-pieces fastening under the chin. Her dress was of a lavender color, and perfectly neat; but scantily made, as if she desired to be as little encumbered as possible. She wore at her side a gentleman's gold watch, if I might judge from its size and make, with an appropriate chain and seals. She had some linen at her throat not unlike a short-collar, and things at her wrists like little shirt-wristbands.

Janet had gone away to get the bath ready, when my aunt, to my great alarm, became in one moment rigid with indignation, and had hardly voice to cry out, "Janet! donkeys!"

Upon which Janet came running up the stairs as if the house were in flames, darted out on a little piece of green in front, and warned off two saddle-donkeys, lady-ridden, that had presumed to set hoof upon it.

To this hour I don't know whether my aunt had any lawful right of way over that patch of green; but in whatever occupation she was engaged, a donkey turned the current of her ideas in a moment, and she was upon him straight. There were three alarms before the bath was ready; and on the occasion of the last and most desperate of all, I saw my aunt engage, single-handed, with a sandy-headed lad of fifteen, and bump his sandy head against her own gate, before he seemed to comprehend what was the matter.

When I had bathed, they (I mean my aunt and Janet) enrobed me in a shirt and a pair of trousers belonging to Mr. Dick, and tied me up in two or three great shawls. What sort of bundle I looked like, I don't know, but I felt a very hot one. Feeling also very faint and drowsy, I soon lay down on the sofa again and fell asleep.

After tea, we sat at the window—on the look-out, as I imagined, from my aunt's sharp expression of face, for more invaders—until dusk, when Janet set candles, and a backgammon board, on the table, and pulled down the blinds.

"Now, Mr. Dick," said my aunt, with her grave look, and her forefinger up as before, "I am going to ask you another question. Look at this child."

"David's son?" said Mr. Dick, with an attentive, puzzled face.

"Exactly so," returned my aunt. "What would you do with him now?"

"Do with David's son?" said Mr. Dick.

"Ay," replied my aunt, "with David's son."

"Oh!" said Mr. Dick. "Yes. Do with—I should put him to bed."

"Janet!" cried my aunt, with the same complacent triumph that I had remarked before, "Mr. Dick sets us all right. If the bed is ready, we'll take him up to it."

Janet reporting it to be quite ready, I was taken up to it; kindly, but in some sort like a prisoner—my aunt going in front, and Janet bringing up the rear. The only circumstance which gave me any new hope, was my aunt's stopping on the stairs to inquire about a smell of fire that was prevalent there; and Janet's replying that she had been making tinder down in the kitchen of my old shirt.

CHAPTER 14  MY AUNT MAKES UP HER MIND ABOUT ME• •

N GOING down in the morning, I found my aunt musing so profoundly over the breakfast-table, with her elbow on the tray, that the contents of the urn had overflowed the teapot, and were laying the whole table-cloth under water, when my entrance put her meditations to flight. I felt sure that I had been the subject of her reflections, and was more than ever anxious to know her intentions toward me. Yet I dared not express my anxiety, lest it should give her offense.

"Hallo!" said my aunt, after a long time.

I looked up, and met her sharp bright glance respectfully.

"I have written to him," said my aunt.

"To ——?"

"To your father-in-law," said my aunt. "I have sent him a letter that I'll trouble him to attend to, or he and I will fall out, I can tell him!"

"Does he know where I am, aunt?" I inquired, alarmed.

"I have told him," said my aunt, with a nod.

"Shall I—be—given up to him?" I faltered.

"I don't know," said my aunt. "We shall see."

"Oh! I can't think what I shall do," I exclaimed, "if I have to go back to Mr. Murdstone!"

"I don't know anything about it," said my aunt, shaking her head. "I can't say, I am sure. We shall see."

My spirits sank under these words, and I became very downcast and heavy of heart. My aunt, without appearing to take much heed of me, put on a coarse apron with a bib, which she took out of the press; washed up the teacups with her own hands; and, when everything was washed and set in the tray again, and the cloth folded and put on the top of the whole, rang for Janet to remove it. She next swept up the crumbs with a little broom (putting on a pair of gloves first), until there did not appear to be one microscopic speck left on the carpet; next dusted and arranged the room, which was dusted and arranged to a hair's-breadth already. When all these tasks were performed to her satisfaction, she took off the gloves and apron, folded them up, put them in the particular corner of the press from which they had been taken, brought out her workbox to her own table in the open window, and sat down to work.

"I wish you'd go upstairs," said my aunt, as she threaded her needle, "and give my compliments to Mr. Dick, and I'll be glad to know how he gets on with his Memorial."

I rose with all alacrity, to acquit myself of this commission.

"I suppose," said my aunt, eyeing me as narrowly as she had eyed the needle in threading it, "you think Mr. Dick a short name, eh?"

"I thought it was rather a short name, yesterday," I confessed.

"You are not to suppose that he hasn't got a longer name, if he chose to use it," said my aunt, with a loftier air. "Babley—Mr. Richard Babley—that's the gentleman's true name."

I was going to suggest, with a modest sense of my youth and the familiarity I had been already guilty of, that I had better give him the full benefit of that name, when my aunt went on to say,

"But don't you call him by it, whatever you do. He can't bear his name. That's a peculiarity of his. So take care, child, you don't call him anything *but* Mr. Dick."

I promised to obey, and went upstairs with my message, thinking, as I went, that if Mr. Dick had been working at his Memorial long, at the same rate as I had seen him working at it, through the open door, when I came down, he was probably getting on very well indeed. I found him still driving at it with a long pen, and his head almost laid upon the paper. He was so intent upon it, that I had ample leisure to observe the large paper kite in a corner, the confusion of bundles of manuscript, the number of pens, and, above all, the quantity of ink (which he seemed to have in, in half-gallon jars by the dozen), before he observed my being present.

"Ha! Phœbus!" said Mr. Dick, laying down his pen. "How does the world go? I'll tell you what," he added, in a lower tone, "I shouldn't wish it to be mentioned, but it's a"—here he beckoned to me, and put his lips close to my ear—"it's a mad world. Mad as Bedlam, boy!" said Mr. Dick, taking snuff from a round box on the table, and laughing heartily.

Without presuming to give my opinion on this question, I delivered my message.

"Well," said Mr. Dick, in answer, "my compliments to her, and I—I believe I have made a start. I think I have made a start," said Mr. Dick, passing his hand among his grey hair, and casting anything but a confident look at his manuscript. "You have been to school?"

"Yes, sir," I answered; "for a short time."

"Do you recollect the date," said Mr. Dick, looking earnestly at me, and taking up his pen to note it down, "when King Charles the First had his head cut off?"

I said I believed it happened in the year sixteen hundred and forty-nine.

"Well," returned Mr. Dick, scratching his ear with his pen, and looking dubiously at me, "so the books say; but I don't see how that can be. Because, if it was so long ago, how could the people about him have made that mistake of putting some of the trouble out of *his* head, after it was taken off, into *mine?*"

I was very much surprised by the inquiry, but could give no information on this point.

"It's very strange," said Mr. Dick, with a despondent look upon his papers, and with his hand among his hair again, "that I never can get that quite right; I never can make that perfectly clear. But no matter, no matter!" he said cheerfully, and rousing himself; "there's time enough! My compliments to Miss Trotwood—I am getting on very well indeed."

I was going away, when he directed my attention to the kite.

"What do you think of that for a kite?" he said.

I answered that it was a beautiful one. I should think it must have been as much as seven feet high.

"I made it. We'll go and fly it, you and I," said Mr. Dick. "Do you see this?"

He showed me that it was covered with manuscript, very closely and laboriously written; but so plainly that, as I looked along the lines, I thought I saw some allusion to King Charles the First's head again in one or two places.

"There's plenty of string," said Mr. Dick; "and when it flies high, it takes the facts a long way. That's my manner of diffusing 'em. I don't know where they may come down. It's according to circumstances, and the wind, and so forth; but I take my chance of that."

His face was so very mild and pleasant, and had something so reverend in it, though it was hale and hearty, that I was not sure but that he was having a good-humored jest with me. So I laughed, and he laughed, and we parted the best friends possible.

"Well, child," said my aunt, when I went downstairs. "And what of Mr. Dick this morning?"

I informed her that he sent his compliments, and was getting on very well indeed.

"What do you think of him?" said my aunt.

"Is he—is Mr. Dick—I ask because I don't know, aunt—is he at all out of his mind then?" I stammered, for I felt I was on dangerous ground.

"Not a morsel," said my aunt.

"Oh, indeed!" I observed faintly.

"He has been *called* mad," said my aunt. "I have a selfish pleasure in saying he has been called mad, or I should not have had the benefit of his society and advice for these last ten years and upwards— in fact, ever since your sister, Betsey Trotwood, disappointed me."

"So long as that?" I said.

"And nice people they were who had the audacity to call him mad," pursued my aunt. "Mr. Dick is a sort of distant connection of mine; it doesn't matter how; I needn't enter into that. If it hadn't been for me, his own brother would have shut him up for life— that's all."

I found out afterwards that Mr. Dick had been for upwards of ten years endeavoring to keep King Charles the First out of the Memorial; but he had been constantly getting into it, and was there now.

"I say again," said my aunt, "nobody knows what that man's mind is except myself; and he's the most amenable and friendly creature in existence. If he likes to fly a kite sometimes, what of that? Franklin used to fly a kite."

At length the reply from Mr. Murdstone came, and my aunt informed me, to my infinite terror, that he was coming to speak to her himself on the next day. I sat with my thoughts running astray on all possible and impossible results of Mr. Murdstone's visit, until I beheld Miss Murdstone, on a side-saddle, ride deliberately over the sacred piece of green, and stop in front of the house, looking about her.

"Go along with you!" cried my aunt, shaking her head and her fist at the window. "You have no business there. How dare you trespass? Go along! Oh, you bold-faced thing!"

My aunt was so exasperated by the coolness with which Miss Murdstone looked about her, that I really believe she was motionless, and unable for the moment to dart out according to custom. I seized the opportunity to inform her who it was, and that the gentleman now coming near the offender (for the way up was very steep, and he had dropped behind) was Mr. Murdstone himself.

"Shall I go away, aunt?" I asked, trembling.

"No, sir," said my aunt; "certainly not!" With which she pushed me into a corner near her, and fenced me in with a chair, as if it were a prison or a bar of justice. This position I continued to occupy during the whole interview, and from it I now saw Mr. and Miss Murdstone enter the room.

"Oh!" said my aunt, "I was not aware at first to whom I had the pleasure of objecting. But I don't allow anybody to ride over that turf."

"Your regulation is rather awkward to strangers," said Miss Murdstone.

"Is it?" said my aunt.

Mr. Murdstone seemed afraid of a renewal of hostilities, and interposing began,

"Miss Trotwood!"

"I beg your pardon," observed my aunt, with a keen look. "You are the Mr. Murdstone who married the widow of my late nephew, David Copperfield, of Blunderstone Rookery?—Though why Rookery, *I* don't know!"

"I am," said Mr. Murdstone.

"You'll excuse my saying, sir," returned my aunt, "that I think it would have been a much better and happier thing if you had left that poor child alone."

"I so far agree with what Miss Trotwood has remarked," observed Miss Murdstone, bridling, "that I consider our lamented Clara to have been, in all essential respects, a mere child."

"It is a comfort to you and me, ma'am," said my aunt, "who are getting on in life, and are not likely to be made unhappy by our personal attractions, that nobody can say the same of us."

"No doubt!" returned Miss Murdstone, though, I thought, not with a very ready or gracious assent. "And it certainly might have been, as you say, a better and happier thing for my brother if he had never entered into such a marriage. I have always been of that opinion."

"I have no doubt you have," said my aunt—"Janet," ringing the bell, "my compliments to Mr. Dick, and beg him to come down."

Until he came, my aunt sat perfectly upright and stiff, frowning at the wall. When he came, my aunt performed the ceremony of introduction.

"Mr. Dick—an old and intimate friend, on whose judgment," said my aunt, with emphasis, as an admonition to Mr. Dick, who was biting his forefinger and looking rather foolish, "I rely."

Mr. Dick took his finger out of his mouth on this hint, and stood among the group with a grave and attentive expression of face. My aunt inclined her head to Mr. Murdstone, who went on,

"Miss Trotwood, on the receipt of your letter, I considered it an act of greater justice to myself, and perhaps of more respect to you——"

"Thank you," said my aunt, still eyeing him keenly; "you needn't mind me."

"To answer it in person, however inconvenient the journey," pursued Mr. Murdstone, "rather than by letter. This unhappy boy, who has run away from his friends and his occupation——"

"And whose appearance," interposed his sister, directing general attention to me in my indefinable costume, "is perfectly scandalous and disgraceful."

"Jane Murdstone," said her brother, "have the goodness not to interrupt me. This unhappy boy, Miss Trotwood, has been the occasion of much domestic trouble and uneasiness, both during the lifetime of my late dear wife, and since. He has a sullen, rebellious spirit, a violent temper, and an untoward, intractable disposition. Both my sister and myself have endeavored to correct his vices, but ineffectually."

"It can hardly be necessary for me to confirm anything stated by my brother," said Miss Murdstone, "but I beg to observe that, of all the boys in the world, I believe this is the worst boy."

"Strong!" said my aunt shortly.

"But not at all too strong for the facts," returned Miss Murdstone.

"Ha!" said my aunt. "Well, sir?"

"I have my own opinions," resumed Mr. Murdstone, whose face darkened more and more, the more he and my aunt observed each other, which they did very narrowly, "as to the best mode of bringing him up. It is enough that I place this boy under the eye of a friend of my own, in a respectable business; that it does not please him; that he runs away from it, makes himself a common vagabond about the country, and comes here, in rags, to appeal to you, Miss Trotwood."

"But about the respectable business first," said my aunt. "If he had been your own boy, you would have put him to it, just the same, I suppose?"

"If he had been my brother's own boy," returned Miss Murdstone, striking in, "his character, I trust, would have been altogether different."

"Or if the poor child, his mother, had been alive, he would still have gone into the respectable business, would he?" said my aunt.

"I believe," said Mr. Murdstone, with an inclination of his head, "that Clara would have disputed nothing which myself and my sister, Jane Murdstone, were agreed was for the best."

Miss Murdstone confirmed this with an audible murmur.

"Your late wife, sir, was a most unworldly, most unhappy, most unfortunate Baby," returned my aunt, shaking her head at him. "That's what *she* was. And now, what have you got to say next?"

"Merely this, Miss Trotwood," he returned. "I am here to take David back; to take him back unconditionally, to dispose of him as I think proper, and to deal with him as I think right. I am not here to make any promise, or give any pledge to anybody. Now I must caution you that if you step in between him and me now, you must step in, Miss Trotwood, forever. I cannot trifle or be trifled with. Is he ready to go? If he is not, my doors are shut against him henceforth."

To this address my aunt had listened with the closest attention, sitting perfectly upright, with her hands folded on one knee, and looking grimly on the speaker.

"And what does the boy say?" said my aunt. "Are you ready to go, David?"

I answered no, and entreated her not to let me go. And I begged and prayed my aunt to befriend and protect me, for my father's sake.

"Mr. Dick," said my aunt, "what shall I do with this child?"

Mr. Dick considered, hesitated, brightened, and rejoined, "Have him measured for a suit of clothes directly."

"Mr. Dick," said my aunt triumphantly, "give me your hand, for your common sense is invaluable." Having shaken it with great cordiality, she pulled me toward her, and said to Mr. Murdstone,

"You can go when you like; I'll take my chance with the boy. If he's all you say he is, at least I can do as much for him then as you have done. But I don't believe a word of it."

"Miss Trotwood," rejoined Mr. Murdstone, shrugging his shoulders as he rose, "if you were a gentleman——"

"Bah! Stuff and nonsense!" said my aunt. "Don't talk to me!"

"How exquisitely polite!" exclaimed Miss Murdstone, rising. "Overpowering, really!"

"Do you think I don't know," said my aunt, turning a deaf ear to the sister, and continuing to address the brother, and to shake her head at him with infinite expression, "what kind of life you must have led that poor, unhappy, misdirected Baby? Do you think I don't know what a woeful day it was for the soft little creature when *you* first came in her way—smirking and making great eyes at her, I'll be bound, as if you couldn't say 'boh!' to a goose! The poor, benighted innocent had never seen such a man. He was made of sweetness. He worshiped her. He doted on her boy—tenderly doted on him! He was to be another father to him, and they were all to live together in a garden of roses, weren't they? Ugh! Get along with you, do!" said my aunt.

"I never heard anything like this person in my life!" exclaimed Miss Murdstone.

Miss Betsey, without taking the least notice of the interruption, continued to address herself to Mr. Murdstone.

"Mr. Murdstone," she said, shaking her finger at him, "you were a tyrant to the simple Baby, and through the best part of her weakness you gave her the wounds she died of. There is the truth for your comfort, however you like it. And you and your instruments may make the most of it."

"Allow me to inquire, Miss Trotwood," interposed Miss Murdstone, "whom you are pleased to call, in a choice of words in which I am not experienced, my brother's instruments?"

Still stone-deaf to the voice, and utterly unmoved by it, Miss Betsy pursued her discourse.

"Good-day, sir," said my aunt, "and good-bye! Good-day to you, too, ma'am," said my aunt, turning suddenly upon his sister. "Let me see you ride a donkey over *my* green again, and as sure as you have a head upon your shoulders, I'll knock your bonnet off, and tread upon it!"

It would require a painter, and no common painter too, to depict my aunt's face as she delivered herself of this very unexpected sentiment, and Miss Murdstone's face as she heard it. But the manner of the speech, no less than the matter, was so fiery that Miss Murdstone, without a word in answer, discreetly put her arm through her brother's, and walked haughtily out of the cottage; my aunt remaining in the window looking after them—prepared, I have no doubt, in case of the donkey's reappearance, to carry her threat into instant execution.

No attempt at defiance being made, however, her face gradually relaxed, and became so pleasant that I was emboldened to kiss and thank her, which I did with great heartiness, and with both my arms clasped around her neck. I then shook hands with Mr. Dick, who shook hands with me a great many times, and hailed this happy close of the proceedings with repeated bursts of laughter.

"You'll consider yourself guardian, jointly with me, of this child, Mr. Dick," said my aunt.

"I shall be delighted," said Mr. Dick, "to be the guardian of David's son."

"Very good," returned my aunt; "*that's* settled. I have been thinking, do you know, Mr. Dick, that I might call him Trotwood?"

"Certainly, certainly. Call him Trotwood, certainly," said Mr. Dick. "David's son's Trotwood."

"Trotwood Copperfield, you mean," returned my aunt.

"Yes, to be sure. Yes. Trotwood Copperfield," said Mr. Dick, a little abashed.

Thus I began my new life, in a new name, and with everything new about me. A curtain had forever fallen on my life at Murdstone and Grinby's. No one has ever raised that curtain since. I have lifted it for a moment, even in this narrative, with a reluctant hand, and dropped it gladly. The remembrance of that life is fraught with so much pain to me, with so much mental suffering and want of hope, that I have never had the courage even to examine how long I was doomed to lead it. Whether it lasted for a year, or more or less, I do not know. I only know that it was, and ceased to be; and that I have written, and there I leave it.

MR. DICK and I soon became the best of friends, and very often, when his day's work was done, went out together to fly the great kite. Every day of his life he had a long sitting at the Memorial, which never made the least progress, however hard he labored; for King Charles the First always strayed into it, sooner or later, and then it was thrown aside, and another one begun. What Mr. Dick supposed would come of the Memorial, if it were completed, he knew no more than anybody else, I believe. Nor was it at all necessary that he should trouble himself with such questions; for if anything were certain under the sun, it was certain that the Memorial never would be finished.

While I advanced in friendship and intimacy with Mr. Dick, I did not go backward in favor of his staunch friend, my aunt. She took so kindly to me that, in the course of a few weeks, she shortened my adopted name of Trotwood into Trot; and even encouraged me to hope that, if I went on as I had begun, I might take equal rank in her affections with my sister Betsey Trotwood.

"Trot," said my aunt one evening, when the backgammon board was placed as usual for herself and Mr. Dick, "we must not forget your education."

This was my only subject of anxiety, and I felt quite delighted by her referring to it.

"Should you like to go to school at Canterbury?" said my aunt.

I replied that I should like it very much, as it was so near her.

"Good," said my aunt. "Should you like to go tomorrow?"

Being already no stranger to the general rapidity of my aunt's evolutions, I was not surprised by the suddenness of the proposal, and said, "Yes."

"Good," said my aunt again.—"Janet, hire the grey pony and chaise tomorrow morning at ten o'clock, and pack up Master Trotwood's clothes tonight."

My aunt, who was perfectly indifferent to public opinion, drove the grey pony through Dover in a masterly manner, sitting high and stiff like a state coachman. We came to Canterbury and at length stopped before a very old house bulging out over the road —a house with long low lattice-windows bulging out still farther, and beams with carved heads on the ends bulging out too, so that I fancied the whole house was leaning forward, trying to see who was passing on the narrow pavement below.

When the pony-chaise stopped at the door, I saw a cadaverous face appear at a small window on the ground-floor (in a little round tower that formed one side of the house), and quickly disappear. The low arched door then opened, and the face came out. It was quite as cadaverous as it had looked in the window, though in the grain of it there was that tinge of red which is sometimes to be observed in the skins of red-haired people. It belonged to a red-haired person—a youth of fifteen, as I take it now, but looking much older—whose hair was cropped as close as the closest stubble, who had hardly any eyebrows and no eyelashes, and eyes of a red-brown, so unsheltered and unshaded, that I remember wondering how he went to sleep. He was high-shouldered and bony; dressed in decent black, with a white wisp of a neckcloth; buttoned up to the throat; and had a long, lank, skeleton hand, which particularly attracted my attention, as he stood at the pony's head, rubbing his chin with it, and looking up at us in the chaise.

"Is Mr. Wickfield at home, Uriah Heep?" said my aunt.

"Mr. Wickfield's at home, ma'am," said Uriah Heep, "if you'll please to walk in there," pointing with his long hand.

We got out, and leaving him to hold the pony, went into a long low parlor looking toward the street. A door at the farther end of the room opening, a gentleman entered.

"Well, Miss Trotwood," said Mr. Wickfield—for I soon found that it was he, and that he was a lawyer, and steward of the estates of a rich gentleman of the county—"what wind blows you here? Not an ill wind, I hope?"

"No," replied my aunt, "I have not come for any law."

"That's right, ma'am," said Mr. Wickfield. "You had better come for anything else."

His hair was quite white now, though his eyebrows were still black. He had a very agreeable face, and, I thought, was handsome. There was a certain richness in his complexion which I had been long accustomed, under Peggotty's tuition, to connect with port wine; and I fancied it was in his voice too, and referred his growing corpulency to the same cause.

"This is my nephew," said my aunt.

"Wasn't aware you had one, Miss Trotwood," said Mr. Wickfield.

"My grand-nephew, that is to say," observed my aunt.

"Wasn't aware you had a grand-nephew, I give you my word," said Mr. Wickfield.

"I have adopted him," said my aunt, with a wave of her hand, importing that his knowledge and his ignorance were all one to her, "and I have brought him here, to put him to a school where he may be thoroughly well taught and well treated. Now tell me where that school is, and what it is, and all about it."

"At the best we have," said Mr. Wickfield, considering, "your nephew couldn't board just now."

"But he could board somewhere else, I suppose?" suggested my aunt.

Mr. Wickfield thought I could. After a little discussion, he proposed to take my aunt to the school, that she might see it and judge for herself; also, to take her, with the same object, to two or three houses where he thought I could be boarded. I said I would gladly remain behind, and returned into Mr. Wickfield's office.

It so happened that this was opposite a narrow passage, which ended in the little circular room where I had seen Uriah Heep's pale face looking out of window. Uriah, having taken the pony to a neighboring stable, was at work at a desk in this room, which had a brass frame on the top to hang papers upon, and on which the writing he was making a copy of was then hanging. It made me uncomfortable to observe that, every now and then, his sleepless eyes would come below the writing, like two red suns, and stealthily stare at me for I dare say a whole minute at a time.

At length, much to my relief, my aunt and Mr. Wickfield came back, after a pretty long absence. They were not so successful as I could have wished; for though the advantages of the school were undeniable, my aunt had not approved of any of the boarding-houses proposed for me.

"It's very unfortunate," said my aunt. "I don't know what to do."

"It *does* happen unfortunately," said Mr. Wickfield. "But I'll tell you what you can do, Miss Trotwood."

"What's that?" inquired my aunt.

"Leave your nephew here for the present. He's a quiet fellow. He won't disturb me at all. It's a capital house for study—as quiet as a monastery, and almost as roomy. Leave him here."

"I am very much obliged to you," said my aunt, "and so is he, I see; but——"

"Come! I know what you mean," cried Mr. Wickfield. "You shall not be oppressed by the receipt of favors, Miss Trotwood. You may pay for him, if you like. We won't be hard about terms, but you shall pay if you will."

"On that understanding," said my aunt, "though it doesn't lessen the real obligation, I shall be very glad to leave him."

"Then come and see my little housekeeper," said Mr. Wickfield.

We accordingly went up a wonderful old staircase, with a balustrade so broad that we might have gone up that almost as easily, and into a shady old drawing-room, lighted by some three or four of the quaint windows I had looked up at from the street.

Mr. Wickfield tapped at a door in a corner of the paneled wall, and a girl of about my own age came quickly out and kissed him. Although her face was quite bright and happy, there was a tranquillity about it, and about her—a quiet, good, calm spirit—that I never have forgotten—that I never shall forget.

This was his little housekeeper, his daughter Agnes, Mr. Wickfield said. She had a little basket-trifle hanging at her side with keys in it, and she looked as staid and as discreet a housekeeper as the old house could have. She listened to her father, as he told her about me, with a pleasant face; and when he had concluded, proposed to my aunt that we should go upstairs and see my room. We all went together, she before us; and a glorious old room it was, with oak beams and diamond panes, and the broad balustrade going all the way up to it.

"I'm one of the masters at Salem House."

My aunt was as happy as I was, in the arrangement made for me, and we went down to the drawing-room, well pleased and gratified. Agnes went back to her governess, and Mr. Wickfield to his office.

"Trot," said my aunt, "be a credit to yourself, to me, and Mr. Dick, and Heaven be with you!"

I was greatly overcome, and could only thank her, again and again, and send my love to Mr. Dick.

"Never," said my aunt, "be mean in anything; never be false; never be cruel. Avoid those three vices, Trot, and I can always be hopeful of you."

I promised, as well as I could, that I would not abuse her kindness or forget her admonition.

"The pony's at the door," said my aunt, "and I am off! Stay here."

With these words she embraced me hastily, and went out of the room, shutting the door after her. At first I was startled by so abrupt a departure, and almost feared I had displeased her; but when I looked into the street, and saw how dejectedly she got into the chaise, and drove away without looking up, I understood her better, and did not do her that injustice.

By five o'clock, which was Mr. Wickfield's dinner-hour, I had mustered up my spirits again, and was ready for my knife and fork. The cloth was only laid for us two; but Agnes was waiting in the drawing-room before dinner, went down with her father, and sat opposite to him at table. I doubted whether he could have dined without her.

We did not stay there after dinner, but came upstairs into the drawing-room again, in one snug corner of which Agnes set glasses for her father, and a decanter of port wine. I thought he would have missed its usual flavor, if it had been put there for him by any other hands. There he sat, taking his wine, and taking a good deal of it, for two hours, while Agnes played on the piano, worked, and talked to him and me.

Agnes made the tea, and presided over it; and the time passed away after it as after dinner, until she went to bed, when her father took her in his arms and kissed her, and, she being gone, ordered candles in his office. Then I went to bed too.

But in the course of the evening I saw Uriah Heep shutting up the office, and feeling friendly toward everybody, went in and spoke to him, and at parting gave him my hand. But oh, what a clammy hand his was! as ghostly to the touch as to the sight! I rubbed mine afterwards to warm it, *and to rub his off*.

NEXT morning, after breakfast, I entered on school life again. I went, accompanied by Mr. Wickfield, to the scene of my future studies—a grave building in a courtyard, with a learned air about it—and was introduced to my new master.

Doctor Strong looked almost as rusty, to my thinking, as the tall iron rails and gates outside the house. He was in his library, with his clothes not particularly well brushed, and his hair not particularly well combed, his knee-smalls unbraced, his long black gaiters unbuttoned, and his shoes yawning like two caverns on the hearthrug. Turning upon me a lusterless eye, that reminded me of a long-forgotten blind old horse who once used to crop the grass, and tumble over the graves, in Blunderstone churchyard, he said he was glad to see me.

But, sitting at work, not far off from Doctor Strong, was a very pretty young lady—whom he called Annie, and who was his daughter, I supposed—who got me out of my difficulty by kneeling down to put Doctor Strong's shoes on, and button his gaiters, which she did with great cheerfulness and quickness. When she had finished, and we were going out to the schoolroom, I was much surprised to hear Mr. Wickfield, in bidding her good-morning, address her as "Mrs. Strong."

The schoolroom was a pretty large hall on the quietest side of the house. About five-and-twenty boys were studiously engaged at their books when we went in; but they rose to give the Doctor good-morning,

"A new boy, young gentlemen," said the Doctor: "Trotwood Copperfield."

One Adams, who was the head-boy, then stepped out of his place and welcomed me. He looked like a young clergyman, in his white cravat; but he was very affable and good-humored, and he showed me my place, and presented me to the masters, in a gentlemanly way that would have put me at my ease, if anything could.

As I went to my airy old room at Wickfield's, the grave shadow of the staircase seemed to fall upon my doubts and fears, and to make the past more indistinct. I sat there, sturdily conning my books, until dinner-time (we were out of school for good at three), and went down, hopeful of becoming a passable sort of boy yet.

When we had dined we went upstairs again, where everything went on exactly as on the previous day. Mr. Wickfield sat down to drink, and drank a good deal. Agnes played the piano to him, sat by him, and worked and talked, and played some games at dominoes with me. The time having come for her withdrawal for the night, and she having left us, I gave Mr. Wickfield my hand, preparatory to going away myself. But he checked me and said, "Should you like to stay with us, Trotwood, or to go elsewhere?"

"To stay," I answered quickly.

"Stay with us, Trotwood, eh?" he said. "I am glad of it. You are company to us both. It is wholesome to have you here—wholesome for me, wholesome for Agnes, wholesome perhaps for all of us."

"I am sure it is for me, sir," I said. "I am so glad to be here."

"That's a fine fellow!" said Mr. Wickfield. "As long as you are glad to be here, you shall stay here." I thanked him for his consideration; and he went down soon afterwards.

Seeing a light in the little round office, and immediately feeling myself attracted toward Uriah Heep, who had a sort of fascination for me, I went in there. I found Uriah reading a great fat book, with such demonstrative attention that his lank forefinger followed up every line as he read, and made clammy tracks along the page (or so I fully believed) like a snail.

"You are working late tonight, Uriah," says I.

"Yes, Master Copperfield," says Uriah.

As I was getting on the stool opposite, to talk to him more conveniently, I observed that he had not such a thing as a smile about him, and that he could only widen his mouth and make two hard creases down his cheeks, one on each side, to stand for one.

"I am not doing office-work, Master Copperfield," said Uriah.

"What work, then?" I asked.

"I am improving my legal knowledge, Master Copperfield," said Uriah. "I am going through *Tidd's Practice*. Oh, what a writer Mr. Tidd is, Master Copperfield!"

I observed that his nostrils, which were thin and pointed, with sharp dints in them, had a singular and most uncomfortable way of expanding and contracting themselves—that they seemed to twinkle instead of his eyes, which hardly ever twinkled at all.

"I suppose you are quite a great lawyer?" I said, after looking at him for some time.

"Me, Master Copperfield?" said Uriah. "Oh, no! I'm a very umble person."

It was no fancy of mine about his hands, I observed; for he frequently ground the palms against each other, as if to squeeze them dry and warm, besides often wiping them, in a stealthy way, on his pocket-handkerchief.

"I am well aware that I am the umblest person going," said Uriah Heep modestly, "let the other be where he may. My mother is likewise a very umble person. We live in an umble abode, Master Copperfield, but have much to be thankful for. My father's former calling was umble; he was a sexton."

"What is he now?" I asked.

"He is a partaker of glory at present, Master Copperfield," said Uriah Heep. "But we have much to be thankful for. How much have I to be thankful for in living with Mr. Wickfield!"

I asked Uriah if he had been with Mr. Wickfield long.

"I have been with him going on four year, Master Copperfield," said Uriah, shutting up his book, after carefully marking the place where he had left off—"since a year after my father's death. How much have I to be thankful for in that! How much have I to be thankful for in Mr. Wickfield's kind intention to give me my articles, which would otherwise not lay within the umble means of mother and self!"

"Then, when your articled time is over, you'll be a regular lawyer, I suppose?" said I.

"With the blessing of Providence, Master Copperfield," returned Uriah.

"Perhaps you'll be a partner in Mr. Wickfield's business one of these days," I said, to make myself agreeable; "and it will be Wickfield and Heep, or Heep, late Wickfield."

"Oh, no, Master Copperfield," returned Uriah, shaking his head; "I am much too umble for that!"

He certainly did look uncommonly like the carved face on the beam outside my window, as he sat, in his humility, eyeing me sideways, with his mouth widened, and the creases in his cheeks.

"Mr. Wickfield is a most excellent man, Master Copperfield," said Uriah. "If you have known him long, you know it, I am sure, much better than I can inform you."

I replied that I was certain he was; but that I had not known him long myself, though he was a friend of my aunt's.

"Oh, indeed, Master Copperfield," said Uriah. "Your aunt is a sweet lady, Master Copperfield!"

He had a way of writhing, when he wanted to express enthusiasm, which diverted my attention from the compliment he had paid my relation to the snaky twistings of his throat and body.

"A sweet lady, Master Copperfield!" said Uriah Heep. "She has a great admiration for Miss Agnes, Master Copperfield, I believe?"

"Everybody must have," I returned.

"Oh, thank you, Master Copperfield," said Uriah Heep, "for that remark! It is so true! Umble as I am, I know it is *so* true! Oh, thank you, Master Copperfield!"

He writhed himself quite off his stool in the excitement of his feelings, and, being off, began to make arrangements for going home.

"Mother will be expecting me," he said, referring to a pale, inexpressive-faced watch in his pocket, "and getting uneasy; for though we are very umble, Master Copperfield, we are much attached to one another. If you would come and see us any afternoon, and take a cup of tea at our lowly dwelling, mother would be as proud of your company as I should be."

I said I should be glad to come.

"Thank you, Master Copperfield," returned Uriah, putting his book away upon the shelf. "I suppose you stop here some time, Master Copperfield?"

I said I was going to be brought up there, I believed, as long as I remained at school.

"Oh, indeed!" exclaimed Uriah. "I should think *you* would come into the business at last, Master Copperfield!"

I protested that I had no views of that sort, and that no such scheme was entertained in my behalf by anybody; but Uriah insisted on blandly replying to all my assurances, "Oh, yes, Master Copperfield, I should think you would, indeed!" and, "Oh, indeed, Master Copperfield, I should think you would, certainly!" over and over again. Being at last ready to leave the office for the night, he asked me if it would suit my convenience to have the light put out; and on my answering "Yes," instantly extinguished it. After shaking hands with me—his hand felt like a fish in the dark—he opened the door into the street a very little, and crept out, and shut it, leaving me to grope my way back into the house, which cost me some trouble and a fall over his stool.

In less than a fortnight I was quite at home, and happy, among my new companions.

Doctor Strong's was an excellent school, as different from Mr. Creakle's as good is from evil. It was on a sound system, with an appeal, in everything, to the honor and good faith of the boys, which worked wonders. We all felt that we had a part in the management of the place, and in sustaining its character and dignity. We had noble games out of hours, and plenty of liberty; but even then, as I remember, we were well spoken of in the town, and rarely did any disgrace, by our appearance or manner, to the reputation of Doctor Strong and Doctor Strong's boys.

Some of the higher scholars boarded in the Doctor's house, and through them I learned, at second hand, some particulars of the Doctor's history—as, how he had not yet been married twelve months to the beautiful young lady I had seen in the study. Also, how the Doctor's cogitating manner was attributable to his being always engaged in looking out for Greek roots, which, in my innocence and ignorance, I supposed to be a botanical furor on the Doctor's part, especially as he always looked at the ground when he walked about, until I understood that they were roots of words, with a view to a new Dictionary which he had in contemplation. Adams, our head-boy, who had a turn for mathematics, had made a calculation, I was informed, of the time this Dictionary would take in completing, on the Doctor's plan, and at the Doctor's rate of going. He considered that it might be done in one thousand six hundred and forty-nine years, counting from the Doctor's last, or sixty-second, birthday.

I T HAD not occurred to me to mention Peggotty since I ran away; but, of course, I wrote her a letter almost as soon as I was housed at Dover, and another and a longer letter containing all particulars fully related, when my aunt took me formally under her protection. On my being settled at Doctor Strong's, I wrote to her again, detailing my happy condition and prospects.

To these communications Peggotty replied as promptly, if not as concisely, as a merchant's clerk. Mr. Barkis was an excellent husband, she said, though still a little near; but we all had our faults, and she had plenty (though I am sure I don't know what they were); and he sent his duty, and my little bedroom was always ready for me. Mr. Peggotty was well, and Ham was well, and Mrs. Gummidge was but poorly, and little Em'ly wouldn't send her love, but said that Peggotty might send it, if she liked.

My aunt made several excursions over to Canterbury to see me, and always at unseasonable hours—with the view, I suppose, of taking me by surprise. But finding me well employed, and bearing a good character, and hearing on all hands that I rose fast in the school, she soon discontinued these visits. I saw her every third or fourth week, when I went over to Dover for a treat; and I saw Mr. Dick every alternate Wednesday, when he arrived by stage-coach at noon, to stay until next morning.

"Trotwood," said Mr. Dick, with an air of mystery, one Wednesday, "who's the man that hides near our house and frightens her?"

"Frightens my aunt, sir?"

"I can't make it out," said Mr. Dick, shaking his head. "There's something wrong, somewhere. I was walking out with Miss Trotwood after tea, just at dark, and there he was, close to our house."

"Walking about?" I inquired.

"Walking about?" repeated Mr. Dick. "Let me see. I must recollect a bit. N—no, no; he was not walking about."

I asked, as the shortest way to get at it, what he *was* doing.

"Well, he wasn't there at all," said Mr. Dick, "until he came up behind her and whispered. Then she turned round and fainted, and I stood still and looked at him, and he walked away; but that he should have been hiding ever since (in the ground or somewhere) is the most extraordinary thing!"

"*Has* he been hiding ever since?" I asked.

"To be sure he has," retorted Mr. Dick, nodding his head gravely. "Never came out till last night. We were walking last night, and he came up behind her again, and I knew him again."

"And did he frighten my aunt again?"

"All of a shiver," said Mr. Dick, counterfeiting that affection, and making his teeth chatter. "But, Trotwood, come here," getting me close to him, that he might whisper very softly: "Why did she give him money, boy, in the moonlight?"

"He was a beggar, perhaps."

Mr. Dick shook his head, as utterly renouncing the suggestion; and having replied a great many times, and with great confidence, "No beggar, no beggar, no beggar, sir!" went on to say, that from his window he had afterwards, and late at night, seen my aunt give this person money outside the garden rails in the moonlight.

I had not the least belief, in the outset of this story, that the unknown was anything but a delusion of Mr. Dick's, but after some reflection I began to entertain the question whether an attempt might have been twice made to take poor Mr. Dick himself from under my aunt's protection.

One Thursday morning, when I was about to walk with Mr. Dick from the hotel to the coach-office before going back to school (for we had an hour's school before breakfast), I met Uriah in the street, who reminded me of the promise I had made to take tea with himself and his mother, adding, with a writhe, "But I didn't expect you to keep it, Master Copperfield; we're so very umble."

I really had not yet been able to make up my mind whether I liked Uriah or detested him; but I felt it quite an affront to be supposed proud, and said I only wanted to be asked.

"Oh, if that's all, Master Copperfield," said Uriah, "and it really isn't our umbleness that prevents you, will you come this evening? But if it is our umbleness, I hope you won't mind owning to it, Master Copperfield, for we are all well aware of our condition."

I said I would mention it to Mr. Wickfield, and if he approved, as I had no doubt he would, I would come with pleasure. So, at six o'clock that evening, I announced myself as ready to Uriah.

"Mother will be proud, indeed," he said, as we walked away together. "Or she would be proud, if it wasn't sinful, Master Copperfield."

"Yet you didn't mind supposing *I* was proud," I returned.

"Oh dear, no, Master Copperfield!" returned Uriah. "Oh, believe me, no! I shouldn't have deemed it at all proud if you had thought *us* too umble for you; because we are so very umble."

"Have you been studying much law lately?" I asked, to change the subject.

"Oh, Master Copperfield," he said, with an air of self-denial, "my reading is hardly to be called study. I have passed an hour or two in the evening, sometimes, with Mr. Tidd."

"Rather hard, I suppose?" said I.

"He is hard to *me*, sometimes," returned Uriah. "But I don't know what he might be to a gifted person."

After beating a little tune on his chin as we walked on, with the two forefingers of his skeleton right hand, he added:

"There are expressions, you see, Master Copperfield—Latin words and terms—in Mr. Tidd, that are trying to a reader of my umble attainments."

"Would you like to be taught Latin?" I said briskly. "I will teach it you with pleasure, as I learn it."

"Oh, thank you, Master Copperfield," he answered, shaking his head. "I am sure it's very kind of you to make the offer, but I am much too umble to accept it."

"What nonsense, Uriah!"

"Oh, indeed you must excuse me, Master Copperfield! I am greatly obliged, and I should like it of all things, I assure you; but

I am far too umble. Learning ain't for me. A person like myself had better not aspire. If he is to get on in life, he must get on umbly, Master Copperfield."

I never saw his mouth so wide, or the creases in his cheeks so deep, as when he delivered himself of these sentiments—shaking his head all the time, and writhing modestly.

"I think you are wrong, Uriah," I said. "I dare say there are several things that I could teach you, if you would like to learn them."

"Oh, I don't doubt that, Master Copperfield," he answered, "not in the least. But not being umble yourself, you don't judge well, perhaps, for them that are. I won't provoke my betters with knowledge, thank you. I'm much too umble. Here is my umble dwelling, Master Copperfield!"

We entered a low, old-fashioned room, walked straight into from the street, and found there Mrs. Heep, who was the dead image of Uriah, only short. She received me with the utmost humility, and apologized to me for giving her son a kiss, observing that, lowly as they were, they had their natural affections, which they hoped would give no offense to anyone. It was a perfectly decent room, half-parlor and half-kitchen; there were the usual articles of furniture. I don't remember that any individual object had a bare, pinched, spare look, but I do remember that the whole place had.

It was perhaps a part of Mrs. Heep's humility that she still wore weeds. Notwithstanding the lapse of time that had occurred since Mr. Heep's decease, she still wore weeds. I think there was some compromise in the cap, but otherwise she was as weedy as in the early days of her mourning.

"This is a day to be remembered, my Uriah, I am sure," said Mrs. Heep, making the tea, "when Master Copperfield pays us a visit."

"I said you'd think so, mother," said Uriah.

"If I could have wished father to remain among us for any reason," said Mrs. Heep, "it would have been, that he might have known his company this afternoon."

I felt embarrassed by these compliments; but I was sensible, too, of being entertained as an honored guest, and I thought Mrs. Heep an agreeable woman.

"My Uriah," said Mrs. Heep, "has looked forward to this, sir, a long while. He had his fears that our umbleness stood in the way, and I joined in them myself. Umble we are, umble we have been, umble we shall ever be," said Mrs. Heep.

"I am sure you have no occasion to be so, ma'am," I said, "unless you like."

"Thank you, sir," retorted Mrs. Heep. "We know our station, and are thankful in it."

I found that Mrs. Heep gradually got nearer to me, and that Uriah gradually got opposite to me, and that they respectfully plied me with the choicest of the eatables on the table. There was nothing particularly choice there, to be sure; but I took the will for the deed, and felt that they were very attentive. Presently they began to talk about aunts, and then I told them about mine; and about fathers and mothers, and then I told them about mine; and then Mrs. Heep began to talk about fathers-in-law, and then I began to tell her about mine, but stopped, because my aunt had advised me to observe a silence on that subject. A tender young cork, however, would have had no more chance against a pair of corkscrews, or a tender young tooth against a pair of dentists, than I had against Uriah and Mrs. Heep. They wormed things out of me that I had no desire to tell, with a certainty I blush to think of.

The skill with which the one followed up whatever the other said, was a touch of art which I was still less proof against. Uriah threw the ball to Mrs. Heep; Mrs. Heep caught it, and threw it back to Uriah; Uriah kept it up a little while, then sent it back to Mrs. Heep; and so they went on tossing it about, until I had no idea who had got it, and was quite bewildered. The ball itself was always changing, too. Now it was Mr. Wickfield, now Agnes; now the excellence of Mr. Wickfield, now my admiration of Agnes; now the extent of Mr. Wickfield's business and resources, now our domestic life after dinner; now the wine that Mr. Wickfield took, the reason why he took it, and the pity that it was he took so much; now one thing, now another, then everything at once. And all the time, without appearing to speak very often, or to do anything but sometimes encourage them a little, for fear they should be overcome by their humility and the honor of my company, I found myself perpetually letting out something or other that I had no business to let out, and seeing the effect of it in the twinkling of Uriah's dinted nostrils.

I had begun to be a little uncomfortable, and to wish myself well out of the visit, when a figure coming down the street passed the door—it stood open, the weather being close for the time of year— came back again, looked in, and walked in, exclaiming loudly, "Copperfield! Is it possible?"

It was Mr. Micawber! It was Mr. Micawber, with his eyeglass, and his walking-stick, and his shirt-collar, and his genteel air, and the condescending roll in his voice, all complete!

"My dear Copperfield," said Mr. Micawber, putting out his hand, "this is indeed a meeting which is calculated to impress the mind with a sense of the instability and uncertainty of all human—in short, it is a most extraordinary meeting. Copperfield, my dear fellow, how do you do?"

I was glad to see him too, and shook hands with him heartily, inquiring how Mrs. Micawber was.

"Thank you," said Mr. Micawber, waving his hand as of old, and settling his chin in his shirt-collar, "she is tolerably convalescent. The twins no longer derive their sustenance from Nature's founts —in short," said Mr. Micawber, in one of his bursts of confidence, "they are weaned—and Mrs. Micawber is, at present, my traveling companion. She will be rejoiced, Copperfield, to renew her acquaintance with one who has proved himself in all respects a worthy minister at the sacred altar of friendship."

I said I should be delighted to see her.

"You are very good," said Mr. Micawber.

Mr. Micawber then smiled, settled his chin again, and looked about him.

"I have discovered my friend Copperfield," said Mr. Micawber genteelly, and without addressing himself particularly to any one, "not in solitude, but partaking of a social meal in company with a widow lady and one who is apparently her offspring—in short," said Mr. Micawber, in another of his bursts of confidence, "her son. I shall esteem it an honor to be presented."

I could do no less, under these circumstances, than make Mr. Micawber known to Uriah Heep and his mother, which I accordingly did. As they abased themselves before him, Mr. Micawber took a seat, and waved his hand in his most courtly manner.

"Any friend of my friend Copperfield's," said Mr. Micawber, "has a personal claim upon myself."

"We are too umble, sir," said Mrs. Heep, "my son and me, to be the friends of Master Copperfield. He has been so good as take his tea with us, and we are thankful to him for his company; also to you, sir, for your notice."

"Ma'am," returned Mr. Micawber, with a bow, "you are very obliging. And what are you doing, Copperfield? Still in the wine trade?"

I was excessively anxious to get Mr. Micawber away, and replied, with my hat in my hand, and a very red face, I have no doubt, that I was a pupil at Doctor Strong's.

"A pupil?" said Mr. Micawber, raising his eyebrows. "I am extremely happy to hear it. Although a mind like my friend Copperfield's"—to Uriah and Mrs. Heep—"does not require that cultivation which, without his knowledge of men and things, it would require, still it is a rich soil teeming with latent vegetation—in short," said Mr. Micawber, smiling, in another burst of confidence, "it is an intellect capable of getting up the classics to any extent."

Mr. Micawber closed this handsome tribute by saying, "Mr. Heep! good-evening. Mrs. Heep! your servant," and then walking out with me in his most fashionable manner, making a good deal of noise on the pavement with his shoes, and humming a tune.

It was a little inn where Mr. Micawber put up, and he occupied a little room in it, partitioned off from the commercial room, and strongly flavored with tobacco-smoke. Mrs. Micawber was amazed, but very glad to see me. I was very glad to see her too, and, after an affectionate greeting on both sides, sat down on the small sofa near her.

"My dear," said Mr. Micawber, "if you will mention to Copperfield what our present position is, which I have no doubt he will like to know, I will go and look at the paper the while, and see whether anything turns up among the advertisements."

"I thought you were at Plymouth, ma'am," I said to Mrs. Micawber, as he went out.

"My dear Master Copperfield," she replied, "we went to Plymouth."

"To be on the spot," I hinted.

"Just so," said Mrs. Micawber—"to be on the spot. But the truth is, talent is not wanted in the Custom House. The local influence of my family was quite unavailing to obtain any employment in that department for a man of Mr. Micawber's abilities. Apart from which," said Mrs. Micawber, lowering her voice—"this is between ourselves—our reception was cool."

I said, and thought, that they ought to be ashamed of themselves.

"Still, so it was," continued Mrs. Micawber. "Under such circumstances, what could a man of Mr. Micawber's spirit do? But one obvious course was left—to borrow of that branch of my family the money to return to London, and to return at any sacrifice."

"Then you all came back again, ma'am?" I said.

"We all came back again," replied Mrs. Micawber. "Since then, I have consulted other branches of my family on the course which it is most expedient for Mr. Micawber to take—for I maintain that he must take some course, Master Copperfield," said Mrs. Micawber argumentatively. "It is clear that a family of six, not including a domestic, cannot live upon air."

"Certainly, ma'am," said I.

"The opinion of those other branches of my family," pursued Mrs. Micawber, "is, that Mr. Micawber should immediately turn his attention to the coal trade. Mr. Micawber was induced to think, on inquiry, that there might be an opening for a man of his talent in the Medway coal trade. Then, as Mr. Micawber very properly said, the first step to be taken clearly was, to come and *see* the Medway. Which we came and saw. I say 'we,' Master Copperfield; for I never will," said Mrs. Micawber with emotion—"I never will desert Mr. Micawber."

I murmured my admiration and approbation.

"We have been here," said Mrs. Micawber, "three days. Nothing has, as yet, turned up; and we are at present waiting for a remittance from London to discharge our pecuniary obligations at this hotel."

I felt the utmost sympathy for Mr. and Mrs. Micawber in this anxious extremity, and said as much to Mr. Micawber, who now returned—adding that I only wished I had money enough to lend them the amount they needed. Mr. Micawber's answer expressed the disturbance of his mind. He said, shaking hands with me, "Copperfield, you are a true friend; but when the worst comes to the worst, no man is without a friend who is possessed of shaving materials." At this dreadful hint Mrs. Micawber threw her arms round Mr. Micawber's neck, and entreated him to be calm. He wept; but so far recovered, almost immediately, as to ring the bell for the waiter, and bespeak a hot kidney pudding and a plate of shrimps for breakfast in the morning.

When I took my leave of them, they both pressed me so much to come and dine before they went away that I could not refuse. We had a beautiful little dinner—quite an elegant dish of fish, the kidney-end of a loin of veal roasted, fried sausage-meat, a partridge, and a pudding. There was wine, and there was strong ale; and after dinner, Mrs. Micawber made us a bowl of hot punch with her own hands.

Mr. Micawber was uncommonly convivial. I never saw him such good company. He made his face shine with the punch, so that it looked as if it had been varnished all over. As the punch disappeared, Mr. Micawber became still more friendly and convivial. Mrs. Micawber's spirits becoming elevated, too. We sang "Auld Lang Syne." When we came to "Here's a hand, my trusty frere," we all joined hands round the table.

In a word, I never saw anybody so thoroughly jovial as Mr. Micawber was, down to the very last moment of the evening. Consequently, I was not prepared, at seven o'clock next morning, to receive the following communication, dated half-past nine in the evening, a quarter of an hour after I had left him:

"My dear Young Friend,
    "The die is cast—all is over. Hiding the ravages of care with a sickly mask of mirth, I have not informed you, this evening, that there is no hope of the remittance! Under these circumstances, alike humiliating to endure, humiliating to contemplate, and humiliating to relate, I have discharged the pecuniary liability contracted at this establishment by giving a note of hand, made payable fourteen days after date, at my residence, Pentonville, London. When it becomes due, it will not be taken up. The result is destruction. The bolt is impending, and the tree must fall.
    "Let the wretched man who now addresses you, my dear Copperfield, be a beacon to you through life. He writes with that intention, and in that hope. If he could think himself of so much use, one gleam of day might, by possibility, penetrate into the cheerless dungeon of his remaining existence—though his longevity is, at present (to say the least of it), extremely problematical.
    "This is the last communication, my dear Copperfield, you will ever receive

"From
"The
"Beggared Outcast,
"Wilkins Micawber."

I was so shocked by the contents of this heartrending letter that I ran off directly toward the little hotel, with the intention of trying to soothe Mr. Micawber with a word of comfort. But, halfway there, I met the London coach, with Mr. and Mrs. Micawber up behind; Mr. Micawber, the very picture of tranquil enjoyment, smiling at Mrs. Micawber's conversation, eating walnuts out of a paper bag, with a bottle sticking out of his breast pocket. As they did not see me, I thought it best, all things considered, not to see them. So, with a great weight taken off my mind, I turned into a by-street that was the nearest way to school, and felt, upon the whole, relieved that they were gone.

M<small>Y SCHOOL</small> days! The silent gliding on of my existence—the unseen, unfelt progress of my life—from childhood up to youth! Let me think, as I look back upon that flowing water, now a dry channel overgrown with leaves, whether there are any marks along its course by which I can remember how it ran.

I am not the last boy in the school. I have risen, in a few months, over several heads. But the first boy seems to me a mighty creature, dwelling afar off, whose giddy height is unattainable. Agnes says "No"; but I say "Yes"; I hold him in a reverential respect.

But who is this that breaks upon me? This is Miss Shepherd, whom I love.

Miss Shepherd is a boarder at the Misses Nettingalls' establishment. I adore Miss Shepherd. She is a little girl, in a spencer, with a round face and curly flaxen hair.

For some time I am doubtful of Miss Shepherd's feelings; but at length, Fate being propitious, we meet at the dancing-school. I have Miss Shepherd for my partner. I touch Miss Shepherd's glove, and feel a thrill go up the right arm of my jacket, and come out at my hair. I say nothing tender to Miss Shepherd, but we understand each other. Miss Shepherd and myself live but to be united.

Why do I secretly give Miss Shepherd twelve Brazil nuts for a present, I wonder? They are not expressive of affection; they are difficult to pack into a parcel of any regular shape; they are hard to crack, even in room doors, and they are oily when cracked. Yet I feel that they are appropriate to Miss Shepherd. Soft, seedy biscuits, also, I bestow upon Miss Shepherd; and oranges innumerable. Once, I kiss Miss Shepherd in the cloak-room. Ecstasy!

Miss Shepherd being the one pervading theme and vision of my life, how do I ever come to break with her? I can't conceive. And yet a coolness grows between Miss Shepherd and myself. Whispers reach me of Miss Shepherd having said she wished I wouldn't stare so, and having avowed a preference for Master Jones—for Jones! a boy of no merit whatever! The gulf between me and Miss Shepherd widens. At last, one day, I meet the Misses Nettingalls' establishment out walking. Miss Shepherd makes a face as she goes by, and laughs to her companion. All is over. The devotion of a life (it seems a life—it is all the same) is at an end.

I am higher in the school, and no one breaks my peace. I am not at all polite now to the Misses Nettingalls' young ladies. I think the dancing-school a tiresome affair, and wonder why the girls can't dance by themselves and leave us alone. I am growing great in Latin verses, and neglect the laces of my boots. Doctor Strong refers to me in public as a promising young scholar. Mr. Dick is wild with joy, and my aunt remits me a guinea by the next post.

The shade of a young butcher rises, like the apparition of an armed head in *Macbeth*. Who is this young butcher? He is the terror of the youth of Canterbury. There is a vague belief abroad that the beef-suet with which he anoints his hair gives him unnatural strength, and that he is a match for a man. He is a broad-faced, bull-necked young butcher, with rough red cheeks, and ill-conditioned mind, and an injurious tongue. His main use of this tongue is to disparage Doctor Strong's young gentlemen. He says, publicly, that if they want anything, he'll give it 'em. He names individuals among them (myself included) whom he could undertake to settle with one hand, and the other tied behind him. He waylays the smaller boys to punch their unprotected heads, and calls challenges after me in the open streets. For these sufficient reasons, I resolve to fight the butcher.

It is a summer evening, down in a green hollow, at the corner of a wall. I meet the butcher by appointment. I am attended by a select body of our boys; the butcher, by two other butchers, a young publican, and a sweep. The preliminaries are adjusted, and the butcher and myself stand face to face. In a moment, the butcher lights ten thousand candles out of my left eyebrow. In another moment, I don't know where the wall is, or where I am, or where anybody is.

I am taken home in a sad plight; and I have beef-steaks put on my eyes, and am rubbed with vinegar and brandy, and find a great white puffy place bursting out on my upper lip, which swells immoderately. Agnes is a sister to me, and condoles with me, and reads to me, and makes the time light and happy. She thinks I couldn't have done otherwise than fight the butcher, while she shrinks and trembles at my having fought him.

Time has stolen on unobserved; for Adams is not the head-boy in the days that are come now, nor has he been this many and many a day. Adams has left the school so long, that there are not many there, besides myself, who know him. *I* am the head-boy now! I look down on the line of boys below me, with a condescending interest in such of them as bring to my mind the boy I was myself when I first came there. That little fellow seems to be no part of me. I remember him as something left behind upon the road of life.

And the little girl I saw on that first day at Mr. Wickfield's, where is she? Gone also. In her stead, Agnes, my sweet sister (as I call her in my thoughts), my counselor and friend, the better angel of the lives of all who come within her calm, good, self-denying influence, is quite a woman.

What other changes have come upon me, besides the changes in my growth and looks, and in the knowledge I have garnered all this while? I wear a gold watch and chain, a ring upon my little finger, and a long-tailed coat; and I use a great deal of bear's-grease —which, taken in conjunction with the ring, looks bad. Am I in love again? I am. I worship the eldest Miss Larkins.

The eldest Miss Larkins is not a little girl. She is a tall, dark, black-eyed, fine figure of a woman. The eldest Miss Larkins is not a chicken; for the youngest Miss Larkins is not that, and the eldest must be three or four years older. Perhaps the eldest Miss Larkins may be about thirty. My passion for her is beyond all bounds.

The eldest Miss Larkins knows officers. It is an awful thing to bear. I see them speaking to her in the street. I see them cross the way to meet her, when her bonnet (she has a bright taste in bonnets) is seen coming down the pavement, accompanied by her sister's bonnet. She laughs and talks, and seems to like it. I spend a good deal of my own spare time in walking up and down to meet her. If I can bow to her once in the day (I know her to bow to, knowing Mr. Larkins), I am happier.

I think continually about my age. Say I am seventeen, and say that seventeen is young for the eldest Miss Larkins, what of that? Besides, I shall be one-and-twenty in no time almost. When I dress (the occupation of two hours) for a great ball given at the Larkins' (the anticipation of three weeks), I indulge my fancy with pleasing images. I picture myself taking courage to make a declaration to Miss Larkins. I picture Miss Larkins sinking her head upon my shoulder, and saying, "Oh, Mr. Copperfield, can I believe my ears?" I picture Mr. Larkins waiting on me next morning, and saying, "My dear Copperfield, my daughter has told me all. Youth is no objection. Here are twenty thousand pounds. Be happy!" I picture my aunt relenting, and blessing us; and Mr. Dick and Doctor Strong being present at the marriage ceremony. I am a sensible fellow, I believe—I believe, on looking back I mean—and modest, I am sure; but all this goes on notwithstanding.

I repair to the enchanted house, where there are lights, chattering, music, flowers, officers (I am sorry to see), and the eldest Miss Larkins, a blaze of beauty. She is dressed in blue, with blue flowers in her hair—forget-me-nots. As if *she* had any need to wear forget-me-nots! It is the first really grown-up party that I have ever been invited to, and I am a little uncomfortable; for I appear not to belong to anybody, and nobody appears to have anything to say to me, except Mr. Larkins, who asks me how my school-fellows are—which he needn't do, as I have not come there to be insulted.

But after I have stood in the doorway for some time, and feasted my eyes upon the goddess of my heart, she approaches me—she, the eldest Miss Larkins!—and asks me pleasantly if I dance.

I stammer, with a bow, "With you, Miss Larkins."

"With no one else?" inquires Miss Larkins.

"I should have no pleasure in dancing with anyone else."

Miss Larkins laughs and blushes (or I think she blushes), and says, "Next time but one, I shall be very glad."

The time arrives. "It is a waltz, I think," Miss Larkins doubtfully observes, when I present myself. "Do you waltz? If not, Captain Bailey——"

But I do waltz (pretty well, too, as it happens), and I take Miss Larkins out. I take her sternly from the side of Captain Bailey. He is wretched, I have no doubt; but he is nothing to me. I have been wretched too. I waltz with the eldest Miss Larkins! I don't know where, among whom, or how long; I only know that I swim about in space, with a blue angel, in a state of blissful delirium, until I find myself alone with her in a little room, resting on a sofa. She admires a flower (pink-camellia japonica, price half a crown) in my button-hole. I give it her, and say,

"I ask an inestimable price for it, Miss Larkins."

"Indeed! What is that?" returns Miss Larkins.

"A flower of yours, that I may treasure it as a miser does gold."

"You're a bold boy," says Miss Larkins. "There."

She gives it me, not displeased, and I put it to my lips, and then into my breast. Miss Larkins, laughing, draws her hand through my arm, and says, "Now take me back to Captain Bailey."

I am lost in the recollection of this delicious interview, and the waltz, when she comes to me again, with a plain elderly gentleman, who has been playing whist all night, upon her arm, and says,

"Oh! here is my bold friend!—Mr. Chestle wants to know you, Mr. Copperfield."

I feel at once that he is a friend of the family, and am much gratified.

"I admire your taste, sir," says Mr. Chestle. "It does you credit. I suppose you don't take much interest in hops; but I am a pretty large grower myself, and if you ever like to come over to our neighborhood and take a run about our place, we shall be glad for you to stop as long as you like."

I thank Mr. Chestle warmly, and shake hands. I think I am in a happy dream. I waltz with the eldest Miss Larkins once again. She says I waltz so well! I go home in a state of unspeakable bliss, and waltz in imagination, all night long, with my arm round the blue waist of my dear divinity.

"Trotwood," says Agnes, one day after dinner, "who do you think is going to be married tomorrow? Someone you admire."

"Not you, I suppose, Agnes?"

"Not me!" raising her cheerful face from the music she is copying. "Do you hear him, papa?—The eldest Miss Larkins."

"To—to Captain Bailey?" I have just enough power to ask.

"No; to no captain. To Mr. Chestle, a hop-grower."

I am terribly dejected for about a week or two. I frequently lament over the late Miss Larkins' faded flower. Being, by that time, rather tired of this kind of life, and having received new provocation from the butcher, I throw the flower away, go out with the butcher, and gloriously defeat him.

CHAPTER 19 ❧ I LOOK ABOUT ME, AND MAKE A DISCOVERY • • •

M Y AUNT and I had held many grave deliberations on the calling to which I should be devoted. For a year or more I had endeavored to find a satisfactory answer to her often-repeated question, "What I would like to be?" But I had no particular liking, that I could discover, for anything.

"Trot, I tell you what, my dear," said my aunt, one morning in the Christmas season when I left school: "a little change, and a glimpse of life out of doors, may be useful in helping you to know your own mind, and form a cooler judgment. Suppose you were to take a little journey now. Suppose you were to go down into the old part of the country again, for instance, and see that—that out-of-the-way woman with the savagest of name," said my aunt, for she could never thoroughly forgive Peggotty for being so called.

"Of all things in the world, aunt, I should like it best!"

"Well," said my aunt, "that's lucky, for I should like it too."

In pursuance of my aunt's kind scheme, I was shortly afterwards fitted out with a handsome purse of money and a portmanteau, and tenderly dismissed upon my expedition.

I went to Canterbury first, that I might take leave of Agnes and Mr. Wickfield. Agnes was very glad to see me, and told me that the house had not been like itself since I had left it.

"I am sure I am not like myself when I am away," said I. "I seem to want my right hand when I miss you—though that's not saying much, for there's no head in my right hand, and no heart. Everyone who knows you consults with you, and is guided by you, Agnes."

"Everyone who knows me spoils me," she answered, smiling.

"No. It's because you are like no one else. You are so good and so sweet-tempered. You have such a gentle nature, and you are always right."

"You talk," said Agnes, breaking into a pleasant laugh, as she sat at work, "as if I were the late Miss Larkins."

"Come! it's not fair to abuse my confidence," I answered, reddening at the recollection of my blue enslaver. "But I shall confide in you just the same, Agnes; I can never grow out of that. Whenever I fall into trouble, or fall in love, I shall always tell you, if you'll let me—even when I come to fall in love in earnest."

"Why, you have always been in earnest!" said Agnes, laughing again.

"Oh! that was as a child or a schoolboy," said I, laughing in my turn, not without being a little shamefaced. "Times are altering now and I suppose I shall be in a terrible state of earnestness one day or other. My wonder is, that you are not in earnest yourself by this time, Agnes."

Agnes laughed again, and shook her head.

"Oh, I know you are not!" said I; "because if you had been, you would have told me—or at least" (for I saw a faint blush in her face) "you would have let me find it out for myself. But there is no one that I know of who deserves to love *you*, Agnes. Someone of a nobler character, and more worthy altogether, than anyone I have ever seen here, must rise up before I give *my* consent."

We had gone on, so far, in a mixture of confidential jest and earnest, that had long grown naturally out of our familiar relations, begun as mere children. But Agnes, now suddenly lifting up her eyes to mine, and speaking in a different manner, said,

"Trotwood, have you observed any gradual alteration in papa?"

I had observed it, and had often wondered whether she had too. I must have shown as much now in my face.

"Tell me what it is," she said in a low voice.

"I think he does himself no good by the habit that has increased upon him since I first came here. He is often very nervous, or I fancy so."

"It is not fancy," said Agnes, shaking her head.

"His hand trembles, his speech is not plain, and his eyes look wild. I have remarked that, at those times, and when he is least like himself, he is most certain to be wanted on some business."

"By Uriah," said Agnes.

"Yes; and the sense of being unfit for it, or of not having understood it, or of having shown his condition in spite of himself, seems to make him so uneasy that next day he is worse."

Her hand passed softly before my lips while I was yet speaking, and in a moment she had met her father at the door of the room, and was hanging on his shoulder. The expression of her face, as they both looked toward me, I felt to be very touching. She was at once so proud of him and devoted to him, yet so compassionate and sorry, and so reliant upon me to be so too—that nothing she could have said would have expressed more to me, or moved me more.

I got away from Agnes and her father, somehow, with an indifferent show of being very manly, and took my seat upon the box of the London coach.

The main object on my mind, I remember, when we got fairly on the road, was to appear as old as possible to the coachman, and to speak extremely gruff.

"You are going through, sir?" said the coachman.

"Yes, William," I said condescendingly (I knew him); "I am going to London. I shall go down into Suffolk afterwards."

"Shooting, sir?" said the coachman.

He knew as well as I did that it was just as likely, at that time of year, I was going down there whaling; but I felt complimented too.

"I don't know," I said, pretending to be undecided, "whether I shall take a shot or not."

"Birds is got wery shy, I'm told," said William.

"So I understand," said I.

"Is Suffolk your county, sir?" asked William.

"Yes," I said, with some importance; "Suffolk's my county."

It was curious and interesting to be sitting up there, behind four horses—well educated, well dressed, and with plenty of money in my pocket—and to look out for the places where I had slept on my weary journey. When we came at last within a stage of London, and passed the veritable Salem House where Mr. Creakle had laid about him with a heavy hand, I would have given all I had for lawful permission to get down and thrash him, and let all the boys out like so many caged sparrows.

We went to the Golden Cross at Charing Cross, then a moldy sort of establishment in a close neighborhood. A waiter showed me into the coffee-room, and a chambermaid introduced me to my small bedchamber, which smelt like a hackney-coach, and was shut up like a family vault. I was still painfully conscious of my youth, for nobody stood in any awe of me at all.

"Well, now," said the waiter in a tone of confidence, "what would you like? Young gentlemen likes poultry in general: have a fowl?"

I told him, as majestically as I could, that I wasn't in the humor for a fowl.

"Ain't you?" said the waiter. "Young gentlemen is generally tired of beef and mutton: have a weal cutlet?"

I assented to this proposal, in default of being able to suggest anything else.

"Do you care for taters?" said the waiter, with an insinuating smile, and his head on one side. "Young gentlemen generally has been overdosed with taters."

I commanded him, in my deepest voice, to order a veal cutlet and potatoes, and all things fitting; and to inquire at the bar if there were any letters for Trotwood Copperfield, Esquire—which I knew there were not, and couldn't be, but thought it manly to appear to expect.

I don't know when the figure of a handsome, well-formed young man, dressed with a tasteful easy negligence which I have reason to remember very well, became a real presence to me. But I recollect being conscious of his company without having noticed his coming in. I went up to him at once, with a fast-beating heart, and said,

"Steerforth! won't you speak to me?"

He looked at me—just as he used to look sometimes—but I saw no recognition in his face.

"You don't remember me, I am afraid," said I.

"My God!" he suddenly exclaimed. "It's little Copperfield!"

I grasped him by both hands, and could not let them go. But for very shame, and the fear that it might displease him, I could have held him round the neck and cried.

"I never, never, never was so glad! My dear Steerforth, I am so overjoyed to see you!"

"And I am rejoiced to see you, too!" he said, shaking my hands heartily. "Why, Copperfield, old boy, don't be overpowered!" And yet he was glad, too, I thought, to see how the delight I had in meeting him affected me.

I brushed away the tears that my utmost resolution had not been

128

able to keep back, and I made a clumsy laugh of it, and we sat down together, side by side.

"Why, how do you come to be here?" said Steerforth, clapping me on the shoulder.

"I came here by the Canterbury coach today. How do *you* come to be here, Steerforth?"

"Well, I am what they call an Oxford man," he returned—"that is to say, I get bored to death down there periodically—and I am on my way now to my mother's. You're a devilish amiable-looking fellow, Copperfield. Just what you used to be, now I look at you. Not altered in the least."

"I knew *you* immediately," I said; "but you are more easily remembered."

He laughed as he ran his hand through the clustering curls of his hair.

"My dear young Davy," he said, clapping me on the shoulder again, "you are a very Daisy. The daisy of the field at sunrise is not fresher than you are.—Holloa, you, sir!"

This was addressed to the waiter, who had been very attentive to our recognition at a distance, and now came forward deferentially.

"Where have you put my friend, Mr. Copperfield?" said Steerforth.

"Beg your pardon, sir?"

"Where does he sleep? What's his number? You know what I mean," said Steerforth.

"Well, sir," said the waiter, with an apologetic air, "Mr. Copperfield is at present in forty-four, sir."

"And what the devil do you mean," retorted Steerforth, "by putting Mr. Copperfield into a little loft over a stable?"

"Why, you see, we wasn't aware, sir," returned the waiter, still apologetically, "as Mr. Copperfield was anyways particular. We can give Mr. Copperfield seventy-two, sir, if it would be preferred. Next you, sir."

"Of course it would be preferred," said Steerforth. "And do it at once."

The waiter immediately withdrew to make the exchange. Steerforth, very much amused at my having been put into forty-four, laughed again, and clapped me on the shoulder again, and invited me to breakfast with him next morning at ten o'clock, an invitation I was only too proud and happy to accept.

I FOUND Steerforth expecting me, but in a snug private apartment, red-curtained and Turkey-carpeted, where the fire burnt
bright, and a fine hot breakfast was set forth on a table covered
with a clean cloth; and a cheerful miniature of the room, the fire, the
breakfast, Steerforth, and all, was shining in the little round mirror
over the sideboard. I was rather bashful at first, Steerforth being so
self-possessed, and elegant, and superior to me in all respects (age
included); but his easy patronage soon put that to rights, and made
me quite at home. As to the waiter's familiarity, it was quenched as
if it had never been. He attended on us, as I may say, in sackcloth
and ashes.

"Now, Copperfield," said Steerforth, when we were alone, "I
should like to hear what you are doing, and where you are going,
and all about you. I feel as if you were my property."

Glowing with pleasure to find that he had still this interest in me,
I told him how my aunt had proposed the little expedition that I had
before me, and whither it tended.

"As you are in no hurry, then," said Steerforth, "come home with
me to Highgate, and stay a day or two. You will be pleased with my
mother—she is a little vain and prosy about me, but that you can
forgive her—and she will be pleased with you."

"I should like to be as sure of that as you are kind enough to say you are," I answered, smiling.

"Oh!" said Steerforth, "everyone who likes me has a claim on her that is sure to be acknowledged."

"Then I think I shall be a favorite," said I.

"Good!" said Steerforth. "Come and prove it."

It was dusk when the stage-coach stopped with us at an old brick house at Highgate, on the summit of the hill. An elderly lady, though not very far advanced in years, with a proud carriage and a handsome face, was in the doorway as we alighted, and greeting Steerforth as "My dearest James," folded him in her arms. To this lady he presented me as his mother, and she gave me a stately welcome.

It was a genteel, old-fashioned house, very quiet and orderly. From the windows of my room I saw all London lying in the distance like a great vapor, with here and there some lights twinkling through it. I had only time, in dressing, to glance at the solid furniture, the framed pieces of work (done, I supposed, by Steerforth's mother when she was a girl), and some pictures in crayons of ladies with powdered hair and bodices, coming and going on the walls, as the newly kindled fire crackled and sputtered, when I was called to dinner.

There was a second lady in the dining-room, of a slight short figure, dark, and not agreeable to look at, but with some appearance of good looks too. She had black hair and eager black eyes, and was thin, and had a scar upon her lip. It was an old scar—I should rather call it seam, for it was not discolored, and had healed years ago—which had once cut through her mouth, downward toward the chin, but was now barely visible across the table, except above and on her upper lip, the shape of which it had altered. I concluded in my own mind that she was about thirty years of age, and that she wished to be married. Her thinness seemed to be the effect of some wasting fire within her, which found a vent in her gaunt eyes.

She was introduced as Miss Dartle, and both Steerforth and his mother called her Rosa. I found that she lived there, and had been for a long time Mrs. Steerforth's companion. It appeared to me that she never said anything she wanted to say outright, but hinted it. For example, when Mrs. Steerforth observed, more in jest than earnest, that she feared her son led but a wild life at college, Miss Dartle put in thus:

"Oh, really? You know how ignorant I am, and that I only ask for information, but isn't it always so? I thought that kind of life was on all hands understood to be—eh?"

"It is education for a very grave profession, if you mean that, Rosa," Mrs. Steerforth answered, with some coldness.

"Oh! Yes! That's very true," returned Miss Dartle. "But isn't it, though?—I want to be put right, if I am wrong—isn't it, really?"

"Really what?" said Mrs. Steerforth.

"Oh! you mean it's *not!*" returned Miss Dartle. "Well, I'm very glad to hear it! Now, I know what to do! That's the advantage of asking. I shall never allow people to talk before me about wastefulness and profligacy, and so forth, in connection with that life, any more."

"And you will be right," said Mrs. Steerforth. "My son's tutor is a conscientious gentleman; and if I had not implicit reliance on my son, I should have reliance on him."

"Should you?" said Miss Dartle. "Dear me! Conscientious, is he? Really conscientious, now?"

"Yes, I am convinced of it," said Mrs. Steerforth.

"How very nice!" exclaimed Miss Dartle. "What a comfort! Really conscientious? Then he's not—but of course he can't be, if he's really conscientious. Well, I shall be quite happy in my opinion of him, from this time. You can't think how it elevates him in my opinion, to know for certain that he's really conscientious!"

Mrs. Steerforth speaking to me about my intention of going down to Suffolk, I said at hazard how glad I should be if Steerforth would only go there with me.

"Should I?" said Steerforth. "Well, I think I should. I must see what can be done. It would be worth a journey (not to mention the pleasure of a journey with you, Daisy), to see that sort of people together, and to make one of 'em."

Miss Dartle, whose sparkling eyes had been watchful of us, now broke in again.

"Oh, but, really! Do tell me. Are they, though?" she said.

"Are they what? And are who what?" said Steerforth.

"That sort of people. Are they really animals and clods, and beings of another order? I want to know *so* much."

"Why, there's a pretty wide separation between them and us," said Steerforth, with indifference. "They are not to be expected to be as sensitive as we are. Their delicacy is not to be shocked, or hurt very easily. They are wonderfully virtuous, I dare say."

"Really!" said Miss Dartle. "Well, I don't know, now, when I have been better pleased than to hear that. It's so consoling! It's such a delight to know that, when they suffer, they don't feel!"

I believed that Steerforth had said what he had in jest, or to draw Miss Dartle out; and I expected him to say as much when she was gone, and we two were sitting before the fire. But he merely asked me what I thought of her.

"She is very clever, is she not?" I asked.

"Clever! She brings everything to a grindstone," said Steerforth, "and sharpens it, as she has sharpened her own face and figure these years past. She has worn herself away by constant sharpening. She is all edge."

"What a remarkable scar that is upon her lip!" I said.

Steerforth's face fell, and he paused a moment.

"Why, the fact is," he returned, "*I* did that."

"By an unfortunate accident?"

"No. I was a young boy, and she exasperated me, and I threw a hammer at her. A promising young angel I must have been!"

I was deeply sorry to have touched on such a painful theme, but that was useless now.

"And I have no doubt she loves you like a brother?" said I.

"Humph!" retorted Steerforth, looking at the fire. "Some brothers are not loved overmuch; and some love—but help yourself, Copperfield!"

When the evening was pretty far spent, and a tray of glasses and decanters came in, Steerforth promised, over the fire, that he would seriously think of going down into the country with me. There was no hurry, he said—a week hence would do; and his mother hospitably said the same.

THERE was a servant in that house—a man who, I understood, was usually with Steerforth, and had come into his service at the University, who was in appearance a pattern of respectability. I believe there never existed in his station a more respectable-looking man. He was taciturn, soft-footed, very quiet in his manner, deferential, observant, always at hand when wanted, and never near when not wanted; but his great claim to consideration was his respectability. He had not a pliant face, he had rather a stiff neck, rather a tight smooth head with short hair clinging to it at the sides, a soft way of speaking, with a peculiar habit of whispering the letter *s* so distinctly that he seemed to use it oftener than any other man; but every peculiarity that he had he made respectable. If his nose had been upside down, he would have made that respectable. Even the fact that no one knew his Christian name seemed to form a part of his respectability. Nothing could be objected against his surname, Littimer, by which he was known. Peter might have been hanged, or Tom transported, but Littimer was perfectly respectable.

Littimer was in my room in the morning before I was up, to bring me that reproachful shaving-water, and to put out my clothes.

"Mr. Steerforth will be glad to hear how you have rested, sir."

"Thank you," said I, "very well indeed. Is Mr. Steerforth quite well?"

"Thank you, sir, Mr. Steerforth is tolerably well." Another of his characteristics. No use of superlatives. A cool calm medium always.

"Is there anything more I can have the honor of doing for you, sir? The warning-bell will ring at nine; the family take breakfast at half-past nine."

"Nothing, I thank you."

"I thank *you*, sir, if you please;" and with that, and with a little inclination of his head, as an apology for correcting me, he went out.

He got horses for us, and Steerforth, who knew everything, gave me lessons in riding. He provided foils for us, and Steerforth gave me lessons in fencing; gloves, and I began, of the same master, to improve in boxing. It gave me no manner of concern that Steerforth should find me a novice in these sciences; but I never could bear to show my want of skill before the respectable Littimer. I had no reason to believe that Littimer understood such arts himself—he never led me to suppose anything of the kind, by so much as the vibration of one of his respectable eyelashes—yet whenever he was by, while we were practicing, I felt myself the greenest and most inexperienced of mortals.

I am particular about this man, because he made a particular effect on me at that time, and because of what took place thereafter.

The week passed away in a most delightful manner. We bade adieu to Mrs. Steerforth and Miss Dartle, with many thanks on my part, and much kindness on the devoted mother's. The last thing I saw was Littimer's unruffled eye, fraught, as I fancied, with the silent conviction that I was very young indeed.

What I felt in returning so auspiciously to the old familiar places, I shall not endeavour to describe. We went down by the mail. I was so concerned, I recollect, even for the honor of Yarmouth, that when Steerforth said, as we drove through its dark streets to the inn, that, as well as he could make out, it was a good, queer, out-of-the-way kind of hole, I was highly pleased. We went to bed on our arrival and breakfasted late in the morning. Steerforth, who was in great spirits, had been strolling about the beach before I was up, and had made acquaintance, he said, with half the boatmen in the place. Moreover, he had seen in the distance what he was sure must be the identical house of Mr. Peggotty.

"When do you propose to introduce me there, Daisy?" he said. "I am at your disposal. Make your own arrangements."

"Why, I was thinking that this evening would be a good time, Steerforth, when they are all sitting round the fire. I must see Peggotty first of all."

"Well," replied Steerforth, looking at his watch, "suppose I deliver you up to be cried over for a couple of hours; is that long enough?"

I answered, laughing, that I thought we might get through it in that time, but that he must come also.

"I'll come anywhere you like," said Steerforth, "or do anything you like. Tell me where to come to, and in two hours I'll produce myself in any state you please, sentimental or comical."

I gave him minute directions for finding the residence of Mr. Barkis, carrier to Blunderstone and elsewhere; and, on this understanding, went out alone. I found nothing changed, until I came to Mr. Omer's shop. OMER AND JORAM was now written up, where OMER used to be; but the inscription, DRAPER, TAILOR, HABERDASHER, FUNERAL FURNISHER, etc., remained as it was.

My footsteps seemed to tend so naturally to the shopdoor that I went across the road and looked in. There was a pretty woman at the back of the shop, dancing a little child in her arms, while another little fellow clung to her apron. I had no difficulty in recognizing either Minnie or Minnie's children.

"Is Mr. Omer at home?" said I, entering. "I should like to see him, for a moment, if he is."

"Oh, yes, sir, he is at home," said Minnie; "Joe, call your grandfather."

The little fellow, who was holding her apron, gave a lusty shout, and soon Mr. Omer, shorter-winded than of yore, but not much older-looking, stood before me.

"Servant, sir," said Mr. Omer. "What can I do for you, sir?"

"You can shake hands with me, Mr. Omer, if you please," said I, putting out my own. "You were very good-natured to me once, when I am afraid I didn't show that I thought so."

"I think my memory has got as short as my breath," said Mr. Omer, looking at me, and shaking his head; "for I don't remember you."

"Don't you remember your coming to the coach to meet me, and

"If you please, aunt, I am your nephew."

EVERETT SHINN
1947

my having breakfast here, and our riding out to Blunderstone together?"

"To—be—sure," said Mr. Omer, touching my waistcoat with his
forefinger. "Barkis's the carrier's wife—Peggotty's the boatman's
sister—she had something to do with your family? She was in service
there, sure?"

My answering in the affirmative gave him great satisfaction.

"Well, sir, we've got a young relation of hers here, under articles
to us, that has as elegant a taste in the dressmaking business—I assure
you I don't believe there's a duchess in England can touch her."

"Not little Em'ly?" said I involuntarily.

"Em'ly's her name," said Mr. Omer, "and she's little too. But if
you'll believe me, she has such a face of her own that half the
women in this town are mad against her."

"Nonsense, father!" cried Minnie.

"My dear," said Mr. Omer, "I don't say it's the case with you,"
winking at me; "but I say that half the women in Yarmouth—ah!
and in five mile round, are mad against that girl."

"Then she should have kept to her own station in life, father,"
said Minnie, "and not have given them any hold to talk about
her."

"You see," he said, wiping his head, and breathing with difficulty,
"an ill-natured story got about that Em'ly wanted to be a lady.
Now, my opinion is, that it came into circulation principally on
account of her sometimes saying, at the school, that if she was a lady
she would like to do so-and-so for her uncle—don't you see?—and
buy him such-and-such fine things."

"I assure you, Mr. Omer, she has said so to me," I returned
eagerly, "when we were both children."

Mr. Omer nodded his head and rubbed his chin. As they had
spoken in a subdued tone while speaking of Em'ly, I had no doubt
that she was near. On my asking now if that were not so, Mr. Omer
nodded yes, and nodded toward the door of the parlor.

"Wouldn't you like to step in," said Mr. Omer, "and speak to
her? Walk in and speak to her, sir! Make yourself at home!"

I was too bashful to do so then. I was afraid of confusing her,
and I was no less afraid of confusing myself. But I informed myself
of the hour at which she left of an evening, in order that our visit
might be timed accordingly; and taking leave of Mr. Omer and his
pretty daughter, went away to my dear old Peggotty's.

Here she was, in the tiled kitchen, cooking dinner! The moment

I knocked at the door she opened it, and asked me what I pleased to want? I looked at her with a smile, but she gave me no smile in return. I had never ceased to write to her, but it must have been seven years since we had met.

"Is Mr. Barkis at home, ma'am?" I said, feigning to speak roughly to her.

"He's at home, sir," returned Peggotty; "but he's bad abed with the rheumatics."

"Don't he go over to Blunderstone now?" I asked.

"When he's well he do," she answered.

"Do *you* ever go there, Mrs. Barkis?"

She looked at me more attentively, and I noticed a quick movement of her hands toward each other.

"Because I want to ask a question about a house there that they call the—what is it?—the Rookery," said I.

She took a step backward, and put out her hands in an undecided, frightened way, as if to keep me off.

"Peggotty!" I cried to her. She cried, "My darling boy!" and we both burst into tears, and were locked in one another's arms.

I went upstairs with her; and having waited outside for a minute, while she said a word of preparation to Mr. Barkis, presented myself before that invalid.

He received me with absolute enthusiasm. He was too rheumatic to be shaken hands with; but he begged me to shake the tassel on the top of his nightcap, which I did most cordially. When I sat down by the side of the bed, he said that it did him a world of good to feel as if he was driving me on the Blunderstone road again. As he lay in bed, face upward, and so covered, with that exception, that he seemed to be nothing but a face—like a conventional cherubim—he looked the queerest object I ever beheld.

"What name was it as I wrote up in the cart, sir?" said Mr. Barkis, with a slow rheumatic smile.

"Ah! Mr. Barkis, we had some grave talks about that matter, hadn't we?"

"I was willin' a long time, sir?" said Mr. Barkis.

"A long time," said I.

"And I don't regret it," said Mr. Barkis. "Do you remember what you told me once, about her making all the apple-parsties and doing all the cooking?"

"Yes, very well," I returned.

"It was as true," said Mr. Barkis, "as turnips is. It was as true," said Mr. Barkis, nodding his nightcap, which was his only means of emphasis, "as taxes is; and nothing's truer than them."

Mr. Barkis turned his eyes upon me, as if for my assent to this result of his reflections in bed; and I gave it.

"Nothing's truer than them," repeated Mr. Barkis. "A man as poor as I am finds that out in his mind when he's laid up. I'm a very poor man, sir."

"I am sorry to hear it, Mr. Barkis."

"A very poor man, indeed, I am," said Mr. Barkis.

Here his right hand came slowly and feebly from under the bed-clothes, and with a purposeless uncertain grasp took hold of a stick which was loosely tied to the side of the bed. After some poking about with this instrument, in the course of which his face assumed a variety of distracted expressions, Mr. Barkis poked it against a box, an end of which had been visible to me all the time. Then his face became composed.

"Old clothes," said Mr. Barkis.

"Oh!" said I.

"I wish it was money, sir," said Mr. Barkis.

"I wish it was, indeed," said I.

"But it AIN'T," said Mr. Barkis, opening both his eyes as wide as he possibly could. I expressed myself quite sure of that; and Mr. Barkis, turning his eyes more gently to his wife, said,

"She's the usefullest and best of women, C. P. Barkis. All the praise that anyone can give to C. P. Barkis she deserves, and more! My dear, you'll get a dinner today for company—something good to eat and drink, will you?"

I should have protested against this unnecessary demonstration in my honor, but that I saw Peggotty, on the opposite side of the bed, extremely anxious I should not. So I held my peace.

"I have got a trifle of money somewhere about me, my dear," said Mr. Barkis; "but I'm a little tired. If you and Mr. David will leave me for a short nap, I'll try and find it when I wake."

We left the room, in compliance, with this request. When we got outside the door, Peggotty informed me that Mr. Barkis, being now a "little nearer" than he used to be, always resorted to this same device before producing a single coin from his store; and that he endured unheard-of agonies in crawling out of bed alone, and taking it from that unlucky box. In effect, we presently heard him uttering suppressed groans of the most dismal nature, until he had got into bed again, suffering, I have no doubt, a martyrdom; and then called us in, pretending to have just woke up from a refreshing sleep, and to produce a guinea from under his pillow.

I prepared Peggotty for Steerforth's arrival, and it was not long before he came. His easy, spirited good-humor, his genial manner, his handsome looks, his natural gift of adapting himself to whomsoever he pleased, and making direct, when he cared to do it, to the main point of interest in anybody's heart, bound her to him wholly in five minutes. I sincerely believe she had a kind of adoration for him before he left the house that night.

We started forth, at eight o'clock, for Mr. Peggotty's boat. I walked beside him, over the dark wintry sands, toward the old boat, the wind sighing around us even more mournfully than it had sighed and moaned upon the night when I first darkened Mr. Peggotty's door.

"This is a wild kind of place, Steerforth, is it not?"

"Dismal enough in the dark," he said; "and the sea roars as if it were hungry for us. Is that the boat, where I see a light yonder?"

"That's the boat," said I.

A murmur of voices had been audible on the outside, and, at the moment of our entrance, a clapping of hands, which latter noise, I was surprised to see, proceeded from the generally disconsolate Mrs. Gummidge. But Mrs. Gummidge was not the only person there who was unusually excited. Mr. Peggotty, his face lighted up with uncommon satisfaction, and laughing with all his might, held his rough arms wide open, as if for little Em'ly to run into them; Ham, with a mixed expression in his face of admiration, exultation, and a lumbering sort of bashfulness that sat upon him very well, held little Em'ly by the hand, as if he were presenting her to Mr. Peggotty; little Em'ly herself, blushing and shy, but delighted with Mr. Peggotty's delight, as her joyous eyes expressed, was stopped by our entrance (for she saw us first) in the very act of springing from Ham to nestle in Mr. Peggotty's embrace.

The little picture was so instantaneously dissolved by our going in, that one might have doubted whether it had ever been. I was in the midst of the astonished family, face to face with Mr. Peggotty, and holding out my hand to him, when Ham shouted,

"Mas'r Davy! It's Mas'r Davy!"

In a moment we were all shaking hands with one another, all talking at once.

"Why, that you two gentl'men should come to this here roof tonight, of all nights in my life," said Mr. Peggotty, "is such a thing as never happened afore, I do rightly believe!—Em'ly, my darling, come here! Come here, my little witch! There's Mas'r Davy's friend, my dear! He comes to see you, along with Mas'r Davy, on the brightest night of your uncle's life as ever was or will be, Gorm the t'other one, and horroar for it!"

After delivering this speech all in a breath, and with extraordinary animation and pleasure, Mr. Peggotty put one of his large hands rapturously on each side of his niece's face, and kissing it a dozen times, laid it with a gentle pride and love upon his broad chest, and patted it as if his hand had been a lady's. Then he let her go; and as she ran into the little chamber where I used to sleep, looked round upon us, quite hot and out of breath with his uncommon satisfaction.

"This here little Em'ly of ours," said Mr. Peggotty, "has been, in our house, what I suppose (I'm a ignorant man, but that's my belief) no one but a little bright-eyed creetur *can* be in a house. She ain't my child—I never had one; but I couldn't love her more. You understand! I couldn't do it!"

"I quite understand," said Steerforth.

Mr. Peggotty ruffled his hair again with both hands, as a further preparation for what he was going to say, and went on, with a hand upon each of his knees,

"There was a certain person as had know'd our Em'ly from the time when her father was drownded; as had seen her constant—when a babby, when a young gal, when a woman. Not much of a person to look at, he warn't," said Mr. Peggotty, "something o' my own build—rough—a good deal o' the sou'-wester in him—wery salt—but, on the whole, a honest sort of a chap, with his 'art in the right place."

I thought I had never seen Ham grin to anything like the extent to which he sat grinning at us now.

"What does this here blessed tarpaulin go and do," said Mr. Peggotty, with his face one high noon of enjoyment, "but he loses that there 'art of his to our little Em'ly. He follers her about, he makes hisself a sort o' sarvant to her, he loses in a great measure his relish for his wittles, and in the long-run he makes it clear to me wot's amiss."

Mr. Peggotty waved his right arm, and then, exchanging a nod with Ham, whose eye he caught, proceeded,

"Well, I counsels him to speak to Em'ly. He's big enough, but he's bashfuller than a little 'un, and he don't like. So *I* speak. 'What!

him!' says Em'ly. '*Him* that I've know'd so intimate so many years, and like so much! Oh, uncle, I never can have *him*. He's such a good fellow!' I gives her a kiss, and I says no more to her. Then I aways to him, and I says, 'I wish it could have been so, but it can't. But you can both be as you was; and wot I say to you is, Be as you was with her, like a man.' He says to me, a-shaking of my hand, 'I will!' he says. And he was—honorable and manful—for two year going on, and we was just the same at home here as afore."

Mr. Peggotty's face, which had varied in its expression with the various stages of his narrative, now resumed all its former triumphant delight, as he laid a hand upon my knee and a hand upon Steerforth's (previously wetting them both, for the greater emphasis of the action), and divided the following speech between us:

"All of a sudden, one evening—as it might be tonight—comes little Em'ly from her work, and him with her! He takes hold of her hand, and he cries out to me, joyful, 'Look here! This is to be my little wife!' And she says, half bold and half shy, and half a-laughing and half a-crying, 'Yes, uncle! If you please.'—If I please!" cried Mr. Peggotty, rolling his head in an ecstasy at the idea; "Lord, as if I should do anythink else!—Then Missis Gummidge, she claps her hands like a play, and you come in. Theer! the murder's out!" said Mr. Peggotty.

Ham staggered, as well he might, under the blow Mr. Peggotty dealt him in his unbounded joy, as a mark of confidence and friendship; but feeling called upon to say something to us, he said, with much faltering and great difficulty,

"She warn't no higher than you was, Mas'r Davy—when you first come—when I thought what she'd grow up to be. I see her grow up—gentl'men—like a flower. I'd lay down my life for her—Mas'r Davy—oh! most content and cheerful! She's more to me—gentl'men —than—she's all to me that ever I can want, and more than ever I— than ever I could say. I—I love her true. There ain't a gentl'man in all the land—nor yet sailing upon all the sea—that can love his lady more than I love her, though there's many a common man—would say better—what he meant."

If it had depended upon me to touch the prevailing chord among them with any skill, I should have made a poor hand of it. But it depended upon Steerforth; and he did it with such address, that in a few minutes we were all as easy and as happy as it was possible to be.

"Mr. Peggotty," he said, "you are a thoroughly good fellow, and deserve to be as happy as you are tonight. My hand upon it!—Ham, I give you joy, my boy. My hand upon that, too!—Daisy, stir the fire, and make it a brisk one!—And, Mr. Peggotty, unless you can induce your gentle niece to come back (for whom I vacate this seat in the corner), I shall go. Any gap at your fireside on such a night—such a gap least of all—I wouldn't make, for the wealth of the Indies!"

So Mr. Peggotty went into my old room to fetch little Em'ly. At first, little Em'ly didn't like to come, and then Ham went. Presently they brought her to the fireside, very much confused and very shy. But she soon became more assured when she found how gently and respectfully Steerforth spoke to her; how skilfully he avoided anything that would embarrass her; how he talked to Mr. Peggotty of boats, and ships, and tides, and fish; how delighted he was with the boat and all belonging to it; how lightly and easily he carried on, until he brought us, by degrees, into a charmed circle, and we were all talking away without any reserve.

As to Mrs. Gummidge, he roused that victim of despondency with a success never attained by anyone else (so Mr. Peggotty informed me), since the decease of the old one. He left her so little leisure for being miserable, that she said next day she thought she must have been bewitched.

We parted merrily; and as they all stood crowded round the door to light us as far as they could upon our road, I saw the sweet blue eyes of little Em'ly peeping after us, from behind Ham, and heard her soft voice calling to us to be careful how we went.

"A most engaging little beauty," said Steerforth, taking my arm. "That's rather a chuckle-headed fellow for the girl, isn't he?"

He had been so hearty with him, and with them all, that I felt a shock. But seeing a laugh in his eyes, I answered, much relieved,

"Ah, Steerforth! it's well for you to joke about the poor! You may skirmish with Miss Dartle, or try to hide your sympathies in jest from me, but I know better. When I see how perfectly you understand them, how exquisitely you can enter into happiness like this plain fisherman's, or humor a love like my old nurse's, I know that there is not a joy or sorrow, not an emotion, of such people, that can be indifferent to you. And I admire and love you for it, Steerforth, twenty times the more!"

He stopped, and looking in my face, said, "Daisy, I believe you are in earnest, and are good. I wish we all were!"

CHAPTER 22 ❧ SOME OLD SCENES, AND SOME NEW PEOPLE ◆ ◆ ◆

STEERFORTH and I stayed for more than a fortnight in that part of the country. We were very much together, I need not say, but occasionally we were asunder for some hours at a time. He was a good sailor, and I was but an indifferent one; and when he went out boating with Mr. Peggotty, which was a favorite amusement of his, I generally remained ashore. I heard of his being afloat, wrapped in fisherman's clothes, whole moonlight nights, and coming back when the morning tide was at flood. By this time, however, I knew that his restless nature and bold spirits delighted to find a vent in rough toil and hard weather, as in any other means of excitement that presented itself freshly to him; so none of his proceedings surprised me.

One dark evening, I found him alone in Mr. Peggotty's house, sitting thoughtfully before the fire. He was so intent upon his own reflections that he was quite unconscious of my approach. This, indeed, he might easily have been if he had been less absorbed, for footsteps fell noiselessly on the sandy ground outside; but even my entrance failed to rouse him. I was standing close to him, looking at him; and still, with a heavy brow, he was lost in his meditations.

He gave such a start when I put my hand upon his shoulder, that he made me start too.

"You come upon me," he said, almost angrily, "like a reproach-ful ghost!"

"I was obliged to announce myself somehow," I replied. "Have I called you down from the stars?"

"No," he answered; "no."

"Up from anywhere, then?" said I, taking my seat near him.

"I was looking at the pictures in the fire," he returned.

"But you are spoiling them for me," said I, as he stirred it quickly with a piece of burning wood, striking out of it a train of red-hot sparks that went careering up the little chimney and roaring out into the air.

"You would not have seen them," he returned. "I detest this mongrel time, neither day nor night. David, I wish to God I had had a judicious father these last twenty years!"

"My dear Steerforth, what is the matter?"

"I wish with all my soul I had been better guided!" he exclaimed. "I wish with all my soul I could guide myself better!"

There was a passionate dejection in his manner that quite amazed me. He was more unlike himself than I could have supposed possible. I begged him, with all the earnestness I felt, to tell me what had occurred to cross him so unusually, and to let me sympathize with him, if I could not hope to advise him. Before I had well concluded, he began to laugh, took my arm, and hurried me away.

"Tut, it's nothing, Daisy! nothing!" he replied. "I am never con-tented, except with your freshness, my gentle Daisy. As to fitfulness, I have never learned the art of binding myself to any of the wheels on which the Ixions of these days are turning round and round. I missed it somehow in a bad apprenticeship, and now don't care about it.—You know I have bought a boat down here?"

"What an extraordinary fellow you are, Steerforth!" I exclaimed, stopping—for this was the first I had heard of it—"when you may never care to come near the place again!"

"I don't know that," he returned. "I have taken a fancy to the place. At all events," walking me briskly on, "I have bought a boat that was for sale—a clipper, Mr. Peggotty says; and so she is—and Mr. Peggotty will be master of her in my absence."

"Now I understand you, Steerforth!" said I exultingly. "You pre-tend to have bought it for yourself, but you have really done so to confer a benefit on him. I might have known as much at first, know-ing you. My dear, kind Steerforth, how can I tell you what I think of your generosity?"

145

"Tush!" he answered, turning red; "the less said the better."

Afraid of offending him by pursuing the subject when he made so light of it, I only pursued it in my thoughts as we went on at even a quicker pace than before.

"She must be newly rigged," said Steerforth; "and I shall leave Littimer behind to see it done, that I may know she is quite complete. Did I tell you Littimer had come down?"

"The same as ever?" said I.

"The same as ever," said Steerforth. "Distant and quiet as the North Pole. He shall see to the boat being fresh named. She's the *Stormy Petrel* now. What does Mr. Peggotty care for stormy petrels? I'll have her christened again."

"By what name?" I asked.

"The *Little Em'ly*."

As he had continued to look steadily at me, I took it as a reminder that he objected to being extolled for his consideration. I could not help showing in my face how much it pleased me; but I said little, and he resumed his usual smile, and seemed relieved.

"But see here," he said, looking before us, "where the original little Em'ly comes! And that fellow with her, eh? Upon my soul, he's a true knight; he never leaves her!"

Ham was a boatbuilder in these days, having improved a natural ingenuity in that handicraft until he had become a skilled workman. He was in his working dress, and looked rugged enough, but manly withal, and a very fit protector for the blooming little creature at his side.

She withdrew her hand timidly from his arm as we stopped to speak to them, and blushed as she gave it to Steerforth and to me. When they passed on, after we had exchanged a few words, she did not like to replace that hand, but, still appearing timid and constrained, walked by herself.

Suddenly there passed us—evidently following them—a young woman, whose face I saw as she went by. She was lightly dressed, looked bold, and haggard, and flaunting, and poor; but seemed for the time to have given all that to the wind which was blowing, and to have nothing in her mind but going after them. As the dark distant level, absorbing their figures into itself, left but itself visible between us and the sea and clouds, her figure disappeared in like manner, still no nearer to them than before.

"That is a black shadow to be following the girl," said Steerforth, standing still; "what does it mean?"

He spoke in a low voice that sounded almost strange to me.

"She must have it in her mind to beg of them, I think," said I.

"A beggar would be no novelty," said Steerforth; "but it is a strange thing that the beggar should take that shape tonight."

"Why?" I asked him.

"For no better reason, truly, than because I was thinking," he said, after a pause, "of something like it when it came by. Where the Devil did it come from, I wonder?"

"From the shadow of this wall, I think," said I, as we emerged upon a road on which a wall abutted.

"It's gone!" he returned, looking over his shoulder. "And all ill go with it. Now for our dinner!"

But he looked again over his shoulder toward the sea-line glimmering afar off, and yet again. And he wondered about it, in some broken expressions, several times, in the short remainder of our walk; and only seemed to forget it when the light of fire and candle shone upon us, seated warm and merry, at table.

I was surprised, when I came to Mr. Barkis' house, to find Ham walking up and down in front of it, and still more surprised to learn from him that little Em'ly was inside. I naturally inquired why he was not there too, instead of pacing the streets by himself?

"Why, you see, Mas'r Davy," he rejoined, in a hesitating manner, "Em'ly she's talking to some 'un in here."

"I should have thought," said I, smiling, "that that was a reason for your being in here too, Ham."

"Well, Mas'r Davy, in a general way, so't would be," he returned; "but lookee here, Mas'r Davy," lowering his voice, and speaking very gravely. "It's a young woman, sir—a young woman that Em'ly knowed once, and doesn't ought to know no more."

When I heard these words, a light began to fall upon the figure I had seen following them some hours ago.

"It's a poor wurem, Mas'r Davy," said Ham, "as is trod under foot by all the town—up street and down street. The mowld o' the churchyard don't hold any that the folk shrink away from more."

"Did I see her tonight, Ham, after we met you?"

"Keeping us in sight?" said Ham. "It's like you did, Mas'r Davy. Not that I know'd then she was theer, sir, but along of her creeping soon arterwards under Em'ly's little winder, when she sees the light come, and whisp'ring 'Em'ly, Em'ly, for Christ's sake, have a woman's heart toward me. I was once like you!' Those was solemn words, Mas'r Davy, fur to hear!"

"They were indeed, Ham. What did Em'ly do?"

"Says Em'ly, 'Martha, is it you? Oh, Martha, can it be you?'—for they had sat at work together, many a day, at Mr. Omer's. Em'ly couldn't speak to her theer, for her loving uncle was come home, and he wouldn't—no, Mas'r Davy," said Ham, with great earnestness, "he couldn't, kind-natur'd, tender-hearted as he is, see them two together, side by side, for all the treasures that's wrecked in the sea."

I felt how true this was. I knew it, on the instant, quite as well as Ham.

"So Em'ly writes in pencil on a bit of paper," he pursued, "and gives it to her out o' window to bring here. 'Show that,' she says, 'to my aunt, Mrs. Barkis, and she'll set you down by her fire, for the love of me, till uncle is gone out, and I can come.' By-and-by she asks me to bring her."

We walked up and down for a minute or two, in silence. The door opened then, and Peggotty appeared, beckoning to Ham to come in. I would have kept away, but she came after me, entreating me to come in too. I found myself among them, before I considered whither I was going.

The girl—the same I had seen upon the sands—was near the fire. She was sitting on the ground, with her head and one arm lying on a chair. I fancied, from the disposition of her figure, that Em'ly had but newly risen from the chair, and that the forlorn head might perhaps have been lying on her lap. I saw but little of the girl's face, over which her hair fell loose and scattered, as if she had been disordering it with her own hands; but I saw that she was young, and of a fair complexion. Peggotty had been crying. So had little Em'ly. Not a word was spoken when we first went in, and the Dutch clock by the dresser seemed, in the silence, to tick twice as loud as usual.

Em'ly spoke first.

"Martha wants," she said to Ham, "to go to London."

"Why to London?" returned Ham.

He stood between them, looking on the prostrate girl with a mixture of compassion for her, and of jealousy of her holding any companionship with her whom he loved so well. They both spoke as if she were ill, in a soft, suppresed tone that was plainly heard, although it hardly rose above a whisper.

"Better there than here," said a third voice aloud—Martha's, though she did not move. "No one knows me there. Everybody knows me here."

"What will she do there?" inquired Ham.

"She will try to do well," said little Em'ly. "You don't know what she has said to us. Does he—do they—aunt?"

Peggotty shook her head compassionately.

"I'll try," said Martha, "if you'll help me away. I never can do worse than I have done here. I may do better. Oh!" with a dreadful shiver, "take me out of these streets, where the whole town knows me from a child!"

As Em'ly held out her hand to Ham, I saw him put in it a little canvas bag.

"It's all yourn, Em'ly," I could hear him say. "I haven't nowt in all the wureld that ain't yourn, my dear. It ain't of no delight to me, except for you!"

The tears rose freshly in her eyes, but she turned away and went to Martha. What she gave her I don't know. I saw her stooping over her, and putting money in her bosom. She whispered something, as she asked was that enough? "More than enough," the other said, and took her hand and kissed it.

Then Martha arose, and gathering her shawl about her, covering her face with it, and weeping aloud, went slowly to the door. She stopped a moment before going out, as if she would have uttered something, or turned back; but no word passed her lips. Making the same low, dreary, wretched moaning in her shawl, she went away.

As the door closed, little Em'ly looked at us three in a hurried manner, and then hid her face in her hands, and fell to sobbing.

"Doen't, Em'ly!" said Ham, tapping her gently on the shoulder. "Doen't, my dear! You doen't ought to cry so, pretty!"

"Oh, Ham!" she exclaimed, still weeping pitifully, "I am not as good a girl as I ought to be! I know I have not the thankful heart sometimes I ought to have!"

"Yes, yes, you have, I'm sure," said Ham.

"No! no! no!" cried little Em'ly, sobbing, and shaking her head. "I am not as good a girl as I ought to be. Not near! not near!"

And still she cried, as if her heart would break.

"I try your love too much. I know I do!" she sobbed. "I'm often cross to you, and changeable with you, when I ought to be far different. You are never so to me. Why am I ever so to you, when I should think of nothing but how to be grateful, and to make you happy!"

"You always make me so," said Ham, "my dear! I am happy in the sight of you. I am happy, all day long, in the thoughts of you."

"Ah! that's not enough!" she cried. "That is because you are good; not because I am."

"Poor little tender-heart!" said Ham, in a low voice. "Martha has overset her altogether."

"Please, aunt," sobbed Em'ly, "come here and let me lay my head upon you. Oh, I am very miserable tonight, aunt! Oh, I am not as good a girl as I ought to be! I am not, I know!"

She dropped her face on my old nurse's breast, and wept silently, while my old nurse hushed her like an infant.

I saw her do, that night, what I had never seen her do before—I saw her innocently kiss her chosen husband on the cheek, and creep close to his bluff form as if it were her best support. When they went away together in the waning moonlight, I saw that she held his arm with both her hands, and still kept close to him.

CHAPTER 23 ⚜ I CORROBORATE MR. DICK, AND CHOOSE A PROFESSION ♦ ♦ ♦

WHILE we were at breakfast, a letter was delivered to me from my aunt. As it contained matter on which I thought Steerforth could advise me as well as anyone, and on which I knew I should be delighted to consult him, I resolved to make it a subject of discussion on our journey home. For the present we had enough to do in taking leave of all our friends.

"Do you stay long here, Littimer?" said I, as he stood waiting to see the coach start.

"No, sir," he replied; "probably not very long, sir."

"He can hardly say just now," observed Steerforth carelessly. "He knows what he has to do, and he'll do it."

"That I am sure he will," said I.

Littimer touched his hat in acknowledgment of my good opinion, and I felt about eight years old. He touched it once more, wishing us a good journey; and we left him standing on the pavement, as respectable a mystery as any pyramid in Egypt.

For some little time we held no conversation. At length Steerforth, becoming gay and talkative in a moment, as he could become anything he liked at any moment, pulled me by the arm.

"Find a voice, David. What about the letter you were speaking of at breakfast?"

"Oh," said I, taking it out of my pocket, "it's from my aunt."

"And what does she say requiring consideration?"

"Why, she reminds me, Steerforth," said I, "that I came out on this expedition to look about me, and to think a little."

"Which, of course, you have done?"

"Indeed I can't say I have, particularly. To tell you the truth, I am afraid I had forgotten it."

"Well, look about you now, and make up for your negligence," said Steerforth. "Look to the right, and you'll see a flat country, with a good deal of marsh in it; look to the left, and you'll see the same. Look to the front, and you'll find no difference; look to the rear, and there it is still."

I laughed, and replied that I saw no suitable profession in the whole prospect, which was perhaps to be attributed to its flatness.

"What says our aunt on the subject?" inquired Steerforth, glancing at the letter in my hand. "Does she suggest anything?"

"Why, yes," said I. "She asks me here if I think I should like to be a proctor. What do you think of it?"

"Well, I don't know," replied Steerforth coolly. "You may as well do that as anything else, I suppose."

I could not help laughing again at his balancing all callings and professions so equally, and I told him so.

"What *is* a proctor, Steerforth?" said I.

"Why, he is a sort of monkish attorney," replied Steerforth. "He is, to some faded courts held in Doctors' Commons—a lazy old nook near St. Paul's Churchyard—what solicitors are to the courts of law and equity. He is a functionary whose existence, in the natural course of things, should have terminated about two hundred years ago. I can tell you best what he is by telling you what Doctors' Commons is. It's a little out-of-the-way place where they administer what is called ecclesiastical law, and play all kinds of tricks with obsolete old monsters of Acts of Parliament, which three-fourths of the world know nothing about, and the other fourth supposes to have been dug up, in a fossil state, in the days of the Edwards. It's a place that has an ancient monopoly in suits about people's wills and people's marriages, and disputes among ships and boats. I would recommend you to take to Doctors' Commons kindly, David. They plume themselves on their gentility there, I can tell you, if that's any satisfaction."

I quite made up my mind to do so. I then told Steerforth that my aunt was in town awaiting me (as I found from her letter), and that she had taken lodgings for a week at a kind of private hotel in Lincoln's Inn Fields, where there was a stone staircase, and a convenient door in the roof—my aunt being firmly persuaded that every house in London was going to be burnt down every night.

We achieved the rest of our journey pleasantly, sometimes recurring to Doctors' Commons, and anticipating the distant days when I should be a proctor there, which Steerforth pictured in a variety of humorous and whimsical lights, that made us both merry. When we came to our journey's end, he went home, and I drove to Lincoln's Inn Fields, where I found my aunt up, and waiting supper.

If I had been round the world since we parted, we could hardly have been better pleased to meet again. My aunt cried outright as she embraced me, and said, pretending to laugh, that if my poor mother had been alive, that silly little creature would have shed tears, she had no doubt.

"So you have left Mr. Dick behind, aunt?" said I. "I am sorry for that.—Ah, Janet, how do you do?"

As Janet curtsied, hoping I was well, I observed my aunt's visage lengthen very much.

"I am sorry for it, too," said my aunt, rubbing her nose. "I have had no peace of mind, Trot, since I have been here."

Before I could ask why, she told me.

"I am convinced," said my aunt, laying her hand with melancholy firmness on the table, "that Dick's character is not a character to keep the donkeys off. I am confident he wants strength of purpose. I ought to have left Janet at home instead, and then my mind might perhaps have been at ease. If ever there was a donkey trespassing on my green," said my aunt, with emphasis, "there was one this afternoon at four o'clock. A cold feeling came over me from head to foot, and I *know* it was a donkey!"

I tried to comfort her on this point, but she rejected consolation.

"It was a donkey," said my aunt; "and it was the one with the stumpy tail which that Murdering sister of a woman rode when she came to my house." This had been, ever since, the only name my aunt knew for Miss Murdstone.

Supper was comfortably served and hot. When the table was cleared, Janet assisted her to arrange her hair, to put on her nightcap, which was of a smarter construction than usual ("in case of fire," my aunt said), and to fold her gown back over her knees—these being her usual preparations for warming herself before going to bed. I then made her, according to certain established regulations from which no deviation, however slight, could ever be permitted, a glass of hot white wine and water, and a slice of toast cut into long thin strips. With these accompaniments we were left alone to finish the evening, my aunt sitting opposite to me drinking her wine and water—soaking her strips of toast in it, one by one, before eating them—and looking benignantly on me from inside her nightcap.

"Well, Trot," she began, "what do you think of the proctor plan? Or have you not begun to think about it yet?"

"I have thought a good deal about it, my dear aunt, and I have talked a good deal about it with Steerforth. I like it very much indeed. I like it exceedingly."

"Come," said my aunt; "that's cheering."

"I have only one difficulty, aunt."

"Say what it is, Trot," she returned.

"Why, I want to ask, aunt, as this seems, from what I understand, to be a limited profession, whether my entrance into it would not be very expensive?"

"It will cost," returned my aunt, "to article you, just a thousand pounds."

"Now, my dear aunt," said I, drawing my chair nearer, "I am uneasy in my mind about that. It's a large sum of money. You have expended a great deal on my education, and have always been the soul of generosity. Surely there are some ways in which I might begin life with hardly any outlay, and yet begin with a good hope of getting on by resolution and exertion."

My aunt finished eating the piece of toast on which she was then engaged, looking me full in the face all the while; and then, setting her glass on the chimney-piece, and folding her hands upon her folded skirts, replied as follows:

"Trot, my child, if I have any object in life, it is to provide for your being a good, a sensible, and a happy man. I have no other claim upon my means; at least"—here to my surprise she hesitated, and was confused—"no, I have *no* other claim upon my means, and you are my adopted child. Only be a loving child to me in my age, and bear with my whims and fancies, and you will do more for an old woman whose prime of life was not so happy or conciliating as it might have been, than ever that old woman did for you."

It was the first time I had heard my aunt refer to her past history. There was a magnanimity in her quiet way of doing so, and of dismissing it, which would have exalted her in my respect and affection, if anything could.

"All is agreed and understood between us now, Trot," said my aunt, "and we need talk of this no more. Give me a kiss, and we'll go to the Commons after breakfast tomorrow."

At about mid-day we set out for the office of Messrs. Spenlow and Jorkins, in Doctors' Commons. My aunt, who had this other general opinion in reference to London, that every man she saw was a pickpocket, gave me her purse to carry for her, which had ten guineas in it and some silver.

We made a pause at the toy-shop in Fleet Street, to see the giants of St. Dunstan's strike upon the bells—we had timed our going so as to catch them at it, at twelve o'clock—and then went on toward Ludgate Hill and St. Paul's Churchyard. We were crossing to the former place, when I found that my aunt greatly accelerated her speed, and looked frightened. I observed, at the same time, that a lowering, ill-dressed man who had stopped and stared at us in passing, a little before, was coming so close after us as to brush against her.

"Trot! my dear Trot!" cried my aunt, in a terrified whisper, and pressing my arm, "I don't know what I am to do."

"Don't be alarmed," said I. "There's nothing to be afraid of. Step into a shop, and I'll soon get rid of this fellow."

"No, no, child!" she returned. "Don't speak to him for the world. I entreat, I order you!"

"Good Heavens, aunt!" said I, "he is nothing but a sturdy beggar."

"You don't know what he is!" replied my aunt. "You don't know who he is! You don't know what you say!"

We had stopped in an empty doorway, while this was passing, and he had stopped too.

"Don't look at him!" said my aunt, as I turned my head indignantly, "but get me a coach, my dear, and wait for me in St. Paul's Churchyard."

"Wait for you?" I repeated.

"Yes," rejoined my aunt. "I must go alone. I must go with him."

"With him, aunt? This man?"

"I am in my senses," she replied, "and I tell you I *must*. Get me a coach!"

However much astonished I might be, I was sensible that I had no right to refuse compliance with such a peremptory command. I hurried away a few paces, and called a hackney-chariot which was passing empty. Almost before I could let down the steps, my aunt sprang in, I don't know how, and the man followed. She waved her hand to me to go away, so earnestly, that, all confounded as I was, I turned from them at once. In doing so, I heard her say to the coachman, "Drive anywhere! Drive straight on!" and presently the chariot passed me, going up the hill.

What Mr. Dick had told me, and what I had supposed to be a delusion of his, now came into my mind. I could not doubt that this person was the person of whom he had made such mysterious mention, though what the nature of his hold upon my aunt could possibly be I was quite unable to imagine. After half an hour's cooling in the churchyard, I saw the chariot coming back. The driver stopped beside me, and my aunt was sitting in it alone.

She had not yet sufficiently recovered from her agitation to be quite prepared for the visit we had to make. She desired me to get into the chariot, and to tell the coachman to drive slowly up and down a little while. She said no more, except, "My dear child, never ask me what it was, and don't refer to it," until she had perfectly regained her composure, when she told me she was quite herself now, and we might get out. On her giving me her purse to pay the driver, I found that all the guineas were gone.

Doctors' Commons was approached by a little low archway. Before we had taken many paces down the street beyond it, the noise of the city seemed to melt, as if by magic, into a softened distance. A few dull courts and narrow ways brought us to the sky-lighted offices of Spenlow and Jorkins; in the vestibule of which temple, accessible to pilgrims without the ceremony of knocking, three or four clerks were at work as copyists. One of these, a little dry man, sitting by himself, who wore a stiff brown wig that looked as if it were made of gingerbread, rose to receive my aunt, and show us into Mr. Spenlow's room.

"Mr. Spenlow's in Court, ma'am," said the dry man, "but it's close by, and I'll send for him directly."

As we were left to look about us while Mr. Spenlow was fetched, I availed myself of the opportunity. The furniture of the room was old-fashioned and dusty, and the green baize on the top of the writing-table had lost all its color, and was as withered and pale as an old pauper. There were a great many bundles of papers on it. Besides these, there were sundry immense manuscript Books of Evidence tied together in massive sets. I was casting my eyes over these and many similar objects, when hasty footsteps were heard in the room outside, and Mr. Spenlow, in a black gown trimmed with white fur, came hurrying in, taking off his hat as he came.

He was a little, light-haired gentleman, with undeniable boots, and the stiffest of white cravats and shirt collars. He was buttoned up mighty trim and tight, and must have taken a great deal of pains with his whiskers, which were accurately curled. His gold watch-chain was so massive, that a fancy came across me that he ought to have a sinewy golden arm, to draw it out with, like those which are put up over the goldbeaters' shops. He was got up with such care, and was so stiff, that he could hardly bend himself, being obliged, when he glanced at some papers on his desk, after sitting down in his chair, to move his whole body, from the bottom of his spine, like Punch.

I had previously been presented by my aunt, and had been courteously received. He now said,

"And so, Mr. Copperfield, you think of entering into our profession? I casually mentioned to Miss Trotwood, when I had the pleasure of an interview with her the other day"—with another inclination of his body—Punch again—"that there was a vacancy here. Miss Trotwood was good enough to mention that she had a nephew who was her peculiar care, and for whom she was seeking to provide genteelly in life. That nephew, I believe, I have now the pleasure of"—Punch again.

I bowed my acknowledgments, and said my aunt had mentioned to me that there was that opening, and that I believed I should like it very much; that although it was little else than a matter of form, I presumed I should have an opportunity of trying how I liked it before I bound myself to it irrevocably.

"Oh, surely! surely!" said Mr. Spenlow. "We always, in this house, propose a month—an initiatory month. I should be happy, myself, to propose two months—three—an indefinite period, in fact —but I have a partner. Mr. Jorkins."

"And the premium, sir," I returned, "is a thousand pounds."

"And the premium, stamp included, is a thousand pounds," said Mr. Spenlow. "As I have mentioned to Miss Trotwood, I am actu-ated by no mercenary considerations—few men are less so, I be-lieve—but Mr. Jorkins has his opinions on these subjects, and I am bound to respect Mr. Jorkins's opinions. Mr. Jorkins thinks a thousand pounds too little, in short."

"I suppose, sir," said I, still desiring to spare my aunt, "that it is not the custom here, if an article clerk were particularly useful, and made himself a perfect master of his profession"—I could not help blushing, this looked so like praising myself—"I suppose it is not the custom, in the later years of his time, to allow him any——"

Mr. Spenlow, by a great effort, just lifted his head far enough out of his cravat to shake it, and answered, anticipating the word "salary":

"No. I will not say what consideration I might give to that point myself, Mr. Copperfield, if I were unfettered. Mr. Jorkins is immovable."

I was quite dismayed by the idea of this terrible Jorkins. But I found out afterwards that he was a mild man of a heavy temperament, whose place in the business was to keep himself in the background, and be constantly exhibited by name as the most obdurate and ruthless of men. If a clerk wanted his salary raised, Mr. Jorkins wouldn't listen to such a proposition. If a client were slow to settle his bill of costs, Mr. Jorkins was resolved to have it paid; and however painful these things might be (and always were) to the feelings of Mr. Spenlow, Mr. Jorkins would have his bond. The heart and hand of the good angel Spenlow would have been always open, but for the restraining demon Jorkins. As I have grown older, I think I have had experience of some other houses doing business on the principle of Spenlow and Jorkins!

It was settled that I should begin my month's probation as soon as I pleased, and that my aunt need neither remain in town nor return at its expiration. As I knew she was anxious to get home, I urged her not to be uncomfortable on my account, but to leave me to take care of myself.

"I have not been here a week tomorrow without considering that too, my dear," she returned.

With this brief introduction, she produced from her pocket an advertisement, carefully cut out of a newspaper, setting forth that in Buckingham Street in the Adelphi there was to be let furnished, with a view of the river, a singularly desirable and compact set of chambers, forming a genteel residence for a young gentleman. Terms moderate, and could be taken for a month only, if required.

"Why, this is the very thing, aunt!" said I, flushed with the possible dignity of living in chambers.

"Then come," replied my aunt. "We'll go and look at 'em."

Away we went. The advertisement directed us to apply to Mrs. Crupp on the premises, and we rung the area bell, which we supposed to communicate with Mrs. Crupp. It was not until we had rung three or four times that we could prevail on Mrs. Crupp to communicate with us; but at last she appeared, being a stout lady with a flounce of flannel petticoat below a nankeen gown.

"Let us see these chambers of yours, if you please, ma'am," said my aunt.

"For this gentleman?" said Mrs. Crupp, feeling in her pocket for her keys.

"Yes, for my nephew," said my aunt.

"And a sweet set they is for sich!" said Mrs. Crupp.

So we went upstairs.

They were on the top of the house—a great point with my aunt, being near the fire-escape—and consisted of a little half-blind entry where you could see hardly anything, a little stone-blind pantry where you could see nothing at all, a sitting-room, and a bedroom. The furniture was rather faded, but quite good enough for me; and, sure enough, the river was outside the windows.

As I was delighted with the place, my aunt and Mrs. Crupp withdrew into the pantry to discuss the terms, while I remained on the sitting-room sofa, hardly daring to think it possible that I could be destined to live in such a noble residence. After a single combat of some duration they returned.

"Is it the last occupant's furniture?" inquired my aunt.

"Yes, it is, ma'am," said Mrs. Crupp.

"What's become of him?" asked my aunt.

Mrs. Crupp was taken with a troublesome cough, in the midst of which she articulated with much difficulty. "He was took ill here, ma'am, and—ugh! ugh! ugh! dear me!—and he died!"

"Hey! What did he die of?" asked my aunt.

"Well, ma'am, he died of drink," said Mrs. Crupp, in confidence —"and smoke."

"Smoke? You don't mean chimneys?" said my aunt.

"No, ma'am," returned Mrs. Crupp—"cigars and pipes."

"*That's* not catching, Trot, at any rate," remarked my aunt.

"No, indeed," said I.

In short, my aunt, seeing how enraptured I was with the premises, took them for a month, with leave to remain for twelve months when that time was out. Mrs. Crupp was to find linen, and to cook; every other necessary was already provided; and Mrs. Crupp expressly intimated that she should always yearn toward me as a son. I was to take possession the day after tomorrow, and Mrs. Crupp said, thank Heaven she had now found summun she could care for!

I T WAS a wonderfully fine thing to have that lofty castle to myself, and to feel, when I shut my outer door, like Robinson Crusoe, when he had got into his fortification, and pulled his ladder up after him. It was a wonderfully fine thing to walk about town with the key of my house in my pocket. It was a wonderfully fine thing to ring Mrs. Crupp up, gasping, from the depths of the earth, when I wanted her—and when she was disposed to come. All this, I say, was wonderfully fine; but I must say, too, that there were times when it was very dreary.

I was taking my coffee and roll in the morning, before going to the Commons—and I may observe in this place that it is surprising how much coffee Mrs. Crupp used, and how weak it was, considering—when Steerforth himself walked in, to my unbounded joy.

"My dear Steerforth," cried I, "I began to think I should never see you again!"

I showed him over the establishment, not omitting the pantry, with no little pride, and he commended it highly. "I tell you what, old boy," he added, "I shall make quite a town house of this place, unless you give me notice to quit."

This was a delightful hearing. I told him if he waited for that, he would have to wait till doomsday.

"You'll come back to dinner?" said I.

"I can't, upon my life. There's nothing I should like better, but I *must* remain with two fellows. We are all three off together tomorrow morning."

"Then bring them here to dinner," I returned. "Do you think they would come?"

"Oh! they would come fast enough," said Steerforth; "but we should inconvenience you. You had better come and dine with us somewhere."

I would not by any means consent to this, for it occurred to me that I really ought to have a little house-warming, and that there never could be a better opportunity. I had a new pride in my rooms after his approval of them, and burned with a desire to develop their utmost resources. I therefore made him promise positively in the names of his two friends, and we appointed six o'clock as the dinner-hour.

These preparations happily completed, I bought a little dessert in Covent Garden Market, and gave a rather extensive order at a retail wine-merchant's in that vicinity. When I came home in the afternoon, and saw the bottles drawn up in a square on the pantry floor, they looked so numerous (though there were two missing, which made Mrs. Crupp very uncomfortable), that I was absolutely frightened at them.

One of Steerforth's friends was named Grainger, and the other Markham. They were both very gay and lively fellows: Grainger, something older than Steerforth; Markham, youthful-looking, and I should say not more than twenty. I observed that the latter always spoke of himself indefinitely as "a man," and seldom or never in the first person singular.

"A man might get on very well here, Mr. Copperfield," said Markham—meaning himself.

"It's not a bad situation," said I, "and the rooms are really commodious."

"I hope you have both brought appetites with you?" said Steerforth.

"Upon my honor," returned Markham, "town seems to sharpen a man's appetite. A man is hungry all day long. A man is perpetually eating."

Being a little embarrassed at first, and feeling much too young to preside, I made Steerforth take the head of the table when dinner was announced, and seated myself opposite to him. Everything was

161

very good; we did not spare the wine; and he exerted himself so brilliantly to make the thing pass off well, that there was no pause in our festivity.

I began by being singularly cheerful and light-hearted. All sorts of half-forgotten things to talk about came rushing into my mind, and made me hold forth in a most unwonted manner. I laughed heartily at my own jokes and everybody else's; called Steerforth to order for not passing the wine; made several engagements to go to Oxford; announced that I meant to have a dinner-party exactly like that once a week until further notice; and madly took so much snuff out of Grainger's box, that I was obliged to go into the pantry and have a private fit of sneezing ten minutes long.

I went on, by passing the wine faster and faster yet, and continually starting up with a corkscrew to open more wine, long before any was needed. I proposed Steerforth's health. I broke my glass in going round the table to shake hands with him, and I said (in two words), "Steerforth, you'retheguidingstarofmyexistence."

I went on, by finding suddenly that somebody was in the middle of a song. Markham was the singer, and he sang, "When the heart of a man is depressed with care." He said, when he had sung it, he would give us "Woman!" I took objection to that, and I couldn't allow it. I said it was not a respectful way of proposing the toast, and I would never permit that toast to be drunk in my house otherwise than as "The Ladies!" I was very high with him, mainly, I think, because I saw Steerforth and Grainger laughing at me—or at him—or at both of us. He said a man was not to be dictated to. I said a man *was*. He said a man was not to be insulted, then. I said he was right there—never under my roof, where the Lares were sacred, and the laws of hospitality paramount. He said it was no derogation from a man's dignity to confess that I was a devilish good fellow. I instantly proposed his health.

Somebody was smoking. We were all smoking. *I* was smoking, and trying to suppress a rising tendency to shudder.

Somebody was leaning out of my bedroom window, refreshing his forehead against the cool stone of the parapet, and feeling the air upon his face. It was myself. I was addressing myself as "Copperfield," and saying, "Why did you try to smoke? You might have known you couldn't do it." Now somebody was unsteadily contemplating his features in the looking-glass. That was I too. I was very pale in the looking-glass; my eyes had a vacant appearance; and my hair—only my hair, nothing else—looked drunk.

Somebody said to me, "Let us go to the theater, Copperfield!" The theater? To be sure. The very thing. Come along!

Owing to some confusion in the dark, the door was gone. I was feeling for it in the window-curtains, when Steerforth, laughing, took me by the arm and led me out. We went downstairs, one behind another. Near the bottom somebody fell, and rolled down. Somebody else said it was Copperfield. I was angry at that false report, until, finding myself on my back in the passage, I began to think there might be some foundation for it.

Then I was being ushered into one of the boxes, and found myself saying something as I sat down, and people about me crying "Silence!" to somebody, and ladies casting indignant glances at me, and—what! yes!—Agnes sitting on the seat before me, in the same box, with a lady and gentleman beside her whom I didn't know.

"Agnes!" I said thickly, "Lorblessmer! Agnes!"

"Hush, pray!" she answered, I could not conceive why; "you disturb the company. Look at the stage!"

I tried, on her injunction, to fix it, and to hear something of what was going on there, but quite in vain. I looked at her again by-and-by, and saw her shrink into her corner, and put her gloved hand to her forehead.

"Agnes!" said I, "I'mafraidyou'renorwell."

"Yes, yes. Do not mind me, Trotwood," she returned. "Listen! Are you going away soon?"

"Amigoarawaysoo?" I repeated.

"Yes."

I had a stupid intention of replying that I was going to wait to hand her downstairs. I suppose I expressed it somehow; for after she had looked at me attentively for a little while, she appeared to understand, and replied in a low tone,

"I know you will do as I ask you, if I tell you I am very earnest in it. Go away now, Trotwood, for my sake, and ask your friends to take you home."

She had so far improved me, for the time, that, though I was angry with her, I felt ashamed; and with a short "Goori!" (which I intended for "Good-night!") got up and went away. They followed, and I stepped at once out of the box-door into my bedroom, where only Steerforth was with me, helping me to undress, and where I was by turns telling him that Agnes was my sister, and adjuring him to bring the corkscrew that I might open another bottle of wine.

CHAPTER 25 ❦ GOOD AND BAD
ANGELS ◆ ◆ ◆

I WAS going out at my door, after a deplorable day of headache, sickness, and repentance, when I saw a ticket-porter coming upstairs with a letter in his hand. He was taking his time about his errand then; but when he saw me on the top of the staircase looking at him over the banisters, he swung into a trot, and came up panting, as if he had run himself into a state of exhaustion.

"T. Copperfield, Esquire," said the ticket-porter, touching his hat with his little cane.

I could scarcely lay claim to the name, I was so disturbed by the conviction that the letter came from Agnes. However, I told him I was T. Copperfield, Esquire, and he believed it, and gave me the letter, which he said required an answer. I shut him out on the landing and went into my chambers again.

It was a very kind note, containing no reference to my condition at the theater. All it said was, "My dear Trotwood,—I am staying at the house of papa's agent, Mr. Waterbrook, in Ely Place, Holborn. Will you come and see me today, at any time you like to appoint? —Ever yours affectionately, AGNES."

It took me such a long time to write an answer at all to my satisfaction, that I don't know what the ticket-porter can have thought, unless he thought I was learning to write. I must have written half a dozen answers at least. I began one, "How can I ever hope, my dear Agnes, to efface from your remembrance the disgusting impression"—there I didn't like it, and then I tore it up. I began another, "Shakespeare has observed, my dear Agnes, how strange it is that a man should put an enemy into his mouth"—that reminded me of Markham, and it got no further. I even tried poetry. I began one note in a six-syllable line, "Oh, do not remember"—but that associated itself with the fifth of November, and became an absurdity. After many attempts, I wrote, "My dear Agnes, Your letter is like you, and what could I say of it that would be higher praise than that? I will come at four o'clock.—Affectionately and sorrowfully, T. C." With this missive, which I was in twenty minds at once about recalling as soon as it was out of my hands, the ticket-porter at last departed.

Although I left the office at half-past three, and was prowling about the place of appointment within a few minutes afterwards, the appointed time was exceeded by a full quarter of an hour, according to the clock of St. Andrew's, Holborn, before I could muster up sufficient desperation to pull the private bell-handle let into the left-hand doorpost of Mr. Waterbrook's house. I was shown into a pretty but rather close drawing-room, and there sat Agnes, netting a purse.

She looked so quiet and good, and reminded me so strongly of my airy, fresh schooldays at Canterbury, and the sodden, smoky, stupid wretch I had been the other night, that, nobody being by, I yielded to my self-reproach and shame, and—in short, made a fool of myself. I cannot deny that I shed tears. To this hour I am undecided whether it was, upon the whole, the wisest thing I could have done, or the most ridiculous.

"If it had been anyone but you, Agnes," said I, turning away my head, "I should not have minded it half so much. But that it should have been you who saw me! I almost wish I had been dead first."

She put her hand—its touch was like no other hand—upon my arm for a moment; and I felt so befriended and comforted, that I could not help moving it to my lips and gratefully kissing it.

"Sit down," said Agnes cheerfully. "Don't be unhappy, Trotwood. If you cannot confidently trust me, whom will you trust?"

"Ah, Agnes," I returned, "you are my good Angel!"

She smiled rather sadly, I thought, and shook her head.

"Yes, Agnes, my good Angel—always my good Angel!"

"If I were indeed, Trotwood," she returned, "there is one thing that I should set my heart on very much."

I looked at her inquiringly, but already with a foreknowledge of her meaning.

"On warning you," said Agnes, with a steady glance, "against your bad Angel."

"My dear Agnes," I began, "if you mean Steerforth——"

"I do, Trotwood," she returned.

"Then, Agnes, you wrong him very much. He my bad Angel, or anyone's! He anything but a guide, a support, and a friend to me! My dear Agnes! Now is it not unjust, and unlike you, to judge him from what you saw of me the other night?"

"I do not judge him from what I saw of you the other night," she quietly replied. "I judge him partly from your account of him, Trotwood, and your character, and the influence he has over you."

There was always something in her modest voice that seemed to touch a chord within me answering to that sound alone. It was always earnest; but when it was very earnest, as it was now, there was a thrill in it that quite subdued me. I sat looking at her as she cast her eyes down on her work.

"I am not so unreasonable as to expect," said Agnes, resuming her usual tone, after a little while, "that you will, or that you can, at once, change any sentiment that has become a conviction to you; I only ask you, Trotwood, to think of what I have said. Do you forgive me for all this?"

"I will forgive you, Agnes," I replied, "when you come to do Steerforth justice, and to like him as well as I do."

"Not until then?" said Agnes.

I saw a passing shadow on her face; but she returned my smile, and we were again as unreserved in our mutual confidence as of old.

"And when, Agnes," said I, "will you forgive me the other night?"

"When I recall it," said Agnes. She dismissed the subject so; calmly changing the conversation, she asked me if I had seen Uriah Heep.

"Uriah Heep?" said I. "No. Is he in London?"

"He comes to the office downstairs every day," returned Agnes. "He was in London a week before me. I am afraid on disagreeable business, Trotwood."

"On some business that makes you uneasy, Agnes, I see," said I. "What can that be?"

Agnes laid aside her work, and replied, folding her hands upon one another, and looking pensively at me out of those beautiful soft eyes of hers,

"I believe he is going to enter into partnership with papa."

"What? Uriah? That mean, fawning fellow worm himself into such promotion!" I cried indignantly. "Have you made no remonstrance about it, Agnes? You must not allow your father to take such a mad step."

Still looking at me, Agnes shook her head while I was speaking, with a faint smile at my warmth, and then replied,

"You remember our last conversation about papa? It was not long after that—not more than two or three days—when he gave me the first intimation of what I tell you. It was sad to see him struggling between his desire to represent it to me as a matter of choice on his part, and his inability to conceal that it was forced upon him. I felt very sorry."

"Forced upon him, Agnes! Who forces it upon him?"

"Uriah," she replied, after a moment's hesitation, "has made himself indispensable to papa. He is subtle and watchful. He has mastered papa's weaknesses, fostered them, and taken advantage of them, until—to say all that I mean in a word, Trotwood—until papa is afraid of him."

There was more that she might have said, more that she knew, or that she suspected, I clearly saw. I could not give her pain by asking what it was, for I knew that she withheld it from me to spare her father. It had long been going on to this, I was sensible; yes, I could not but feel, on the least reflection, that it had been going on to this for a long time. I remained silent.

"His ascendancy over papa," said Agnes, "is very great. He professes humility and gratitude—with truth, perhaps; I hope so—but his position is really one of power, and I fear he makes a hard use of his power."

I said he was a hound, which, at the moment, was a great satisfaction to me.

"We are not likely to remain alone much longer," said Agnes; "and while I have an opportunity, let me earnestly entreat you, Trotwood, to be friendly to Uriah. Don't repel him. Don't resent (as I think you have a general disposition to do) what may be uncongenial to you in him. He may not deserve it, for we know no certain ill of him. In any case, think first of papa and me!"

Agnes had no time to say more, for the room-door opened, and Mrs. Waterbrook, who was a large lady—or who wore a large dress; I don't exactly know which, for I don't know which was dress and which was lady—came sailing in. I had a dim recollection of having seen her at the theater, as if I had seen her in a pale magic-lantern; but she appeared to remember me perfectly, and still to suspect me of being in a state of intoxication.

Finding by degrees, however, that I was sober, and (I hope) that I was a modest young gentleman, Mrs. Waterbrook softened toward me considerably, and inquired, firstly, if I went much into the parks, and secondly, if I went much into society. On my replying to both these questions in the negative, it occurred to me that I fell again in her good opinion; but she concealed the fact gracefully, and invited me to dinner next day. I accepted the invitation, and took my leave.

I went to dinner next day, and, on the street-door being opened, plunged into a vapor-bath of haunch of mutton. I found Mr. Waterbrook to be a middle-aged gentleman, with a short throat and a good deal of shirt collar, who only wanted a black nose to be the portrait of a pug-dog. He presented me, with much ceremony, to a very awful lady in a black velvet dress and a great black velvet hat, whom I remember as looking like a near relation of Hamlet's—say his aunt.

Mrs. Henry Spiker was this lady's name; and her husband was there too—so cold a man that his head, instead of being grey, seemed to be sprinkled with hoar-frost. Immense deference was shown to the Henry Spikers, male and female; which Agnes told me was on account of Mr. Henry Spiker being solicitor to something or to somebody, I forget what or which, remotely connected with the Treasury.

I found Uriah Heep among the company, in a suit of black, and in deep humility. He told me, when I shook hands with him, that he was proud to be noticed by me, and that he really felt obliged to me for my condescension. I could have wished he had been less obliged to me, for he hovered about me in his gratitude all the rest of the evening, and whenever I said a word to Agnes, was sure, with his shadowless eyes and cadaverous face, to be looking gauntly down upon us from behind.

There were other guests—all iced for the occasion, as it struck me, like the wine. But there was one who attracted my attention before he came in, on account of my hearing him announced as

Mr. Traddles. My mind flew back to Salem House; and could it be Tommy, I thought, who used to draw the skeletons?

I looked for Mr. Traddles with unusual interest. He was a sober, steady-looking young man of retiring manners, with a comic head of hair, and eyes that were rather wide open; and he got into an obscure corner so soon, that I had some difficulty in making him out. At length I had a good view of him, and either my vision deceived me, or it was the old unfortunate Tommy.

I made my way to Mr. Waterbrook, and said that I believed I had the pleasure of seeing an old schoolfellow there.

"Indeed!" said Mr. Waterbrook, surprised. "You are too young to have been at school with Mr. Henry Spiker."

"Oh, I don't mean him," I returned. "I mean the gentleman named Traddles."

"Oh! Ay, ay! Indeed!" said my host, with much-diminished interest. "Possibly."

I inquired what Mr. Traddles was by profession.

"Traddles," returned Mr. Waterbrook, "is a young man reading for the bar. Yes; he is quite a good fellow—nobody's enemy but his own."

"Is he his own enemy?" said I, sorry to hear this.

"Well," returned Mr. Waterbrook, pursing up his mouth, and playing with his watch-chain, in a comfortable, prosperous sort of way. "I should say he was one of those men who stand in their own light. Yes, I should say he would never, for example, be worth five hundred pound. Traddles was recommended to me by a professional friend. Oh, yes. Yes."

When dinner was announced, Mr. Waterbrook went down with Hamlet's aunt. Mr. Henry Spiker took Mrs. Waterbrook; Agnes, whom I should have liked to take myself, was given to a simpering fellow with weak legs. Uriah, Traddles, and I, as the junior part of the company, went down last, how we could. The dinner was very long, and the conversation was about the Aristocracy—and Blood. Mrs. Waterbrook repeatedly told us that if she had a weakness, it was Blood. We might have been a party of ogres, the conversation assumed such a sanguine complexion.

"I confess I am of Mrs. Waterbrook's opinion," said Mr. Waterbrook, with his wine-glass at his eye. "Other things are all very well in their way, but give me Blood!"

"Oh! there is nothing," observed Hamlet's aunt, "so satisfactory to one! There is nothing that is so much one's *beau idéal* of—of all that sort of thing, speaking generally. There are some low minds (not many, I am happy to believe, but there are *some*) that would prefer to do what *I* should call bow down before idols. Positively idols! Before services, intellect, and so on. But these are intangible points. Blood is not so. We see Blood in a nose, and we know it. We meet with it in a chin, and we say, 'There it is! That's Blood!' It is an actual matter of fact. We point it out. It admits of no doubt."

The simpering fellow with the weak legs, who had taken Agnes down, stated the question more decisively yet, I thought.

"Oh, you know, deuce take it," said this gentleman, looking round the board with an imbecile smile, "we can't forego Blood, you know. We must have Blood, you know. Some young fellows, you know, may be a little behind their station, perhaps, in point of education and behavior, and may go a little wrong, you know, and get themselves and other people into a variety of fixes—and all that —but deuce take it, it's delightful to reflect that they've got Blood in 'em! Myself, I'd rather at any time be knocked down by a man who had got Blood in him, than I'd be picked up by a man who hadn't!"

This sentiment, as compressing the general question into a nut-shell, gave the utmost satisfaction, and brought the gentleman into great notice until the ladies retired.

I was very glad indeed to get upstairs to Agnes, and to talk with her in a corner, and to introduce Traddles to her, who was shy, but agreeable, and the same good-natured creature still. As he was obliged to leave early, on account of going away next morning for a month, I had not nearly so much conversation with him as I could have wished; but we exchanged addresses, and promised ourselves the pleasure of another meeting when he should come back to town.

Uriah, who had never ceased to hover near us, was close behind me when I went downstairs. He was close beside me when I walked away from the house, slowly fitting his long skeleton fingers into the still longer fingers of a great Guy Fawkes pair of gloves.

It was in no disposition for Uriah's company, but in remembrance of the entreaty Agnes had made to me, that I asked him if he would come home to my rooms and have some coffee.

"Oh, really, Master Copperfield," he rejoined—"I beg your pardon, Mister Copperfield, but the other comes so natural—I don't like that you should put a constraint upon yourself to ask an umble person like me to your ouse."

"There is no constraint in the case," said I. "Will you come?"

"I should like to, very much," replied Uriah, with a writhe.

"Well, then, come along!" said I.

I could not help being rather short with him, but he appeared not to mind it. We went the nearest way, without conversing much upon the road; and he was so humble in respect of those scarecrow gloves, that he was still putting them on, and seemed to have made no advance in that labor, when we got to my place.

I led him up the dark stairs, to prevent his knocking his head against anything, and really his damp cold hand felt so like a frog in mine, that I was tempted to drop it and run away. Agnes and hospitality prevailed, however, and I conducted him to my fireside. When I lighted my candles, he fell into meek transports with the room that was revealed to him; and when I heated the coffee he professed so much emotion that I could joyfully have scalded him.

"Oh, really, Master Copperfield—I mean Mister Copperfield," said Uriah—"to see you waiting upon me is what I never could have expected! But, one way and another, so many things happen to me which I never could have expected, I am sure, in my umble station, that it seems to rain blessings on my ed. You have heard something, I des-say, of a change in my expectations, Master Copperfield—I should say, Mister Copperfield?"

As he sat on my sofa, with his long knees drawn up under his coffee-cup, his hat and gloves upon the ground close to him, his spoon going softly round and round, his shadowless red eyes, which looked as if they had scorched their lashes off, turned toward me without looking at me, the disagreeable dints in his nostrils coming and going with his breath, and a snaky undulation pervading his frame from his chin to his boots, I decided in my own mind that I disliked him intensely. It made me very uncomfortable to have him for a guest, for I was young then, and unused to disguise what I so strongly felt.

"You have heard something, I des-say, of a change in my expectations, Master Copperfield—I should say, Mister Copperfield?" observed Uriah.

"Yes," said I, "something."

"Ah! I thought Miss Agnes would know of it!" he quietly returned. "I'm glad to find Miss Agnes knows of it. Oh, thank you, Master—Mister Copperfield!"

I could have thrown my boot-jack at him (it lay ready on the rug), for having entrapped me into the disclosure of anything concerning Agnes, however immaterial. But I only drank my coffee.

"What a prophet you have shown yourself, Mister Copperfield!" pursued Uriah. "Dear me, what a prophet you have proved yourself to be! Don't you remember saying to me once that perhaps I should be a partner in Mr. Wickfield's business, and perhaps it might be Wickfield and Heep? *You* may not recollect it; but when a person is umble, Master Copperfield, a person treasures such things up."

"I recollect talking about it," said I, "though I certainly did not think it very likely then."

"Oh! who *would* have thought it likely, Mister Copperfield!" returned Uriah enthusiastically. "I am sure I didn't myself. I recollect saying with my own lips that I was much too umble. So I considered myself really and truly."

He sat, with that carved grin on his face, looking at the fire, as I looked at him.

"But the umblest persons, Master Copperfield," he presently resumed, "may be the instruments of good. I am glad to think I have been the instrument of good to Mr. Wickfield, and that I may be more so. Oh, what a worthy man he is, Mister Copperfield, but how imprudent he has been!"

"I am sorry to hear it," said I. I could not help adding, rather pointedly, "on all accounts."

"Decidedly so, Mister Copperfield," replied Uriah; "on all accounts. Miss Agnes' above all! You don't remember your own eloquent expressions, Master Copperfield, but *I* remember how you said one day that everybody must admire her, and how I thanked you for it! You have forgot that, I have no doubt, Master Copperfield?"

"No," said I dryly.

"Oh, how glad I am you have not!" exclaimed Uriah. "To think that you should be the first to kindle the sparks of ambition in my umble breast, and that you've not forgot it! Oh!—Would you excuse me asking for a cup more coffee?"

Something in the emphasis he laid upon the kindling of those sparks, and something in the glance he directed at me as he said it, had made me start as if I had seen him illuminated by a blaze of light. Recalled by his request, preferred in quite another tone of voice, I did the honors; but I did them with an unsteadiness of hand, a sudden sense of being no match for him, and a perplexed suspicious anxiety as to what he might be going to say next.

He said nothing at all. He stirred his coffee round and round, he sipped it, he felt his chin softly with his grisly hand, he looked at the fire, he looked about the room, he gasped rather than smiled at me, he writhed and undulated about in his deferential servility, he stirred and sipped again, but he left the renewal of the conversation to me.

"So Mr. Wickfield," said I at last, "who is worth five hundred of you—or me"—for my life, I think, I could not have helped dividing that part of the sentence with an awkward jerk—"has been imprudent, has he, Mr. Heep?"

"Oh, very imprudent indeed, Master Copperfield," returned Uriah, sighing modestly. "Oh, very much so! But I wish you'd call me Uriah, if you please. It's like old times."

"Well, Uriah," said I, bolting it out with some difficulty.

"Thank you," he returned, with fervor. "Thank you, Master Copperfield. It's like the blowing of old breezes or the ringing of old bellses to hear *you* say Uriah. I beg your pardon. Was I making any observation?"

"About Mr. Wickfield," I suggested.

"Oh dear, yes, Master Copperfield," he proceeded, in a soft voice, "there's no doubt of it. There would have been loss, disgrace, I don't know what all. Mr. Wickfield knows it. I am the umble instrument of umbly serving him; and he puts me on an eminence I hardly could have hoped to reach. How thankful should I be!"

I recollect well how indignantly my heart beat, as I saw his crafty face, with the appropriately red light of the fire upon it, preparing for something else.

"Master Copperfield," he began—"but am I keeping you up?"

"You are not keeping me up. I generally go to bed late."

"Thank you, Master Copperfield! I have risen from my umble station since first you used to address me, it is true, but I am umble still. I hope I never shall be otherwise than umble. You will not think the worse of my umbleness if I make a little confidence to you, Master Copperfield? Will you?"

"Oh, no," said I, with an effort.

"Thank you!" He took out his pocket-handkerchief, and began wiping the palms of his hands. "Miss Agnes, Master Copperfield——"

"Well, Uriah?"

"Oh, how pleasant to be called Uriah spontaneously!" he cried, and gave himself a jerk, like a convulsive fish. "You thought her looking very beautiful tonight, Master Copperfield?"

"I thought her looking as she always does—superior, in all respects, to everyone around her," I returned.

"Oh, thank you! it's so true!" he cried. "Oh, thank you very much for that!"

"Not at all," I said loftily; "there is no reason why you should thank me."

"Why that, Master Copperfield," said Uriah, "is, in fact, the confidence that I am going to take the liberty of reposing. Umble as I am" (he wiped his hands harder, and looked at them and at the fire by turns), "umble as my mother is, and lowly as our poor but honest roof has ever been, the image of Miss Agnes (I don't mind trusting you with my secret, Master Copperfield, for I have always overflowed toward you since the first moment I had the pleasure of beholding you in a pony-shay) has been in my breast for years. Oh, Master Copperfield, with what a pure affection do I love the ground my Agnes walks on!"

I believe I had a delirious idea of seizing the red-hot poker out of the fire and running him through with it. It went from me with a shock, like a ball fired from a rifle; but the image of Agnes, outraged by so much as a thought of this red-headed animal's, remained in my mind (when I looked at him, sitting all awry, as if his mean soul gripped his body), and made me giddy.

A timely observation of the sense of power that there was in his face did more to bring back to my remembrance the entreaty of Agnes, in its full force, than any effort I could have made. I asked him, with a better appearance of composure than I could have thought possible a minute before, whether he had made his feelings known to Agnes.

"Oh, no, Master Copperfield!" he returned; "oh dear, no! Not to anyone but you. You see, I am only just emerging from my lowly station. I rest a good deal of hope on her observing how useful I am to her father (for I trust to be very useful to him indeed, Master Copperfield), and how I smooth the way for him, and keep him straight. She's so much attached to her father, Master Copperfield (oh, what a lovely thing it is in a daughter!), that I think she may come, on his account, to be kind to me."

I fathomed the depth of the rascal's whole scheme, and understood why he laid it bare.

"If you'll have the goodness to keep my secret, Master Copperfield," he pursued, "and not, in general, to go against me, I shall take it as a particular favor. You wouldn't wish to make unpleasantness. I know what a friendly heart you've got; but having only known me on my umble footing (on my umblest, I should say, for

174

I am very umble still), you might, unbeknown, go against me rather with my Agnes. I call her mine, you see, Master Copperfield. There's a song that says, 'I'd crowns resign to call her mine!' I hope to do it one of these days."

Dear Agnes! so much too loving and too good for anyone that I could think of, was it possible that she was reserved to be the wife of such a wretch as this?

"There's no hurry at present, you know, Master Copperfield," Uriah proceeded, in his slimy way, as I sat gazing at him, with this thought in my mind. "My Agnes is very young still; and mother and me will have to work our way upwards, and make a good many new arrangements, before it would be quite convenient. So I shall have time gradually to make her familiar with my hopes, as opportunities offer. Oh, I'm so much obliged to you for this confidence! Oh, it's such a relief, you can't think, to know that you understand our situation, and are certain (as you wouldn't wish to make unpleasantness in the family) not to go against me!"

He took the hand which I dared not withhold, and having given it a damp squeeze, referred to his pale-faced watch.

"Dear me!" he said, "it's past one. The moments slip away so, in the confidence of old times, Master Copperfield, that it's almost halfpast one!"

I saw him going downstairs, and in the morning I charged Mrs. Crupp with particular directions to leave the windows open, that my sitting-room might be aired and purged of his presence.

DAYS and weeks slipped away. I was articled to Spenlow and Jorkins. I had ninety pounds a year (exclusive of my house rent and sundry collateral matters) from my aunt. My rooms were engaged for twelve months certain; and though I still found them dreary of an evening, and the evenings long, I could settle down into a state of equable low spirits, and resign myself to coffee. At about this time, too, I made three discoveries: first, that Mrs. Crupp was a martyr to a curious disorder called "the spazzums," which was generally accompanied with inflammation of the nose, and required to be constantly treated with peppermint; secondly, that something peculiar in the temperature of my pantry made the brandy bottles burst; thirdly, that I was alone in the world, and much given to record that circumstance in fragments of English versification.

On the day when I was articled, Mr. Spenlow remarked that he should have been happy to have seen me at his house at Norwood, to celebrate our becoming connected, but for his domestic arrangements being in some disorder on account of the expected return of his daughter from finishing her education at Paris. But he intimated that, when she came home, he should hope to have the pleasure of entertaining me. I knew that he was a widower with one daughter, and expressed my acknowledgments.

Mr. Spenlow was as good as his word. In a week or two he referred to this engagement, and said that if I would do him the favor to come down next Saturday, and stay till Monday, he would be extremely happy. Of course, I said I *would* do him the favor; and he was to drive me down in his phaëton, and to bring me back.

When the day arrived, my very carpet-bag was an object of veneration to the stipendiary clerks, to whom the house at Norwood was a sacred mystery. One of them informed me that he had heard that Mr. Spenlow ate entirely off plate and china; and another hinted at champagne being constantly on draft, after the usual custom of table-beer. The old clerk with the wig, whose name was Mr. Tiffey, had been down on business several times in the course of his career, and had on each occasion penetrated to the breakfast-parlor. He described it as an apartment of the most sumptuous nature.

The phaëton was a very handsome affair. The horses arched their necks and lifted up their legs as if they knew they belonged to Doctors' Commons. There was a good deal of competition in the Commons on all points of display, and it turned out some very choice equipages then; though I always have considered, and always shall consider, that in my time the great article of competition there was starch, which I think was worn among the proctors to as great an extent as it is in the nature of man to bear.

We were very pleasant going down, and Mr. Spenlow gave me some hints in reference to my profession. He said it was the genteelest profession in the world, and must on no account be confounded with the profession of a solicitor, being quite another sort of thing, infinitely more exclusive, less mechanical, and more profitable. We took things much more easily in the Commons than they could be taken anywhere else, he observed; and that sets us, as a privileged class, apart.

There was a lovely garden to Mr. Spenlow's house; and though that was not the best time of the year for seeing a garden, it was so beautifully kept, that I was quite enchanted. There was a charming lawn, there were clusters of trees, and there were perspective walks that I could just distinguish in the dark, arched over with trellis-work, on which shrubs and flowers grew in the growing season.

We went into the house, which was cheerfully lighted up, and into a hall where there were all sorts of hats, caps, great-coats, plaids, gloves, whips, and walking-sticks. "Where is Miss Dora?" said Mr. Spenlow to the servant. "Dora!" I thought. "What a beautiful name!"

We turned into a room near at hand and I heard a voice say, "Mr. Copperfield, my daughter Dora, and my daughter Dora's confidential friend!" It was, no doubt, Mr. Spenlow's voice; but I didn't know it, and I didn't care whose it was. All was over in a moment. I had fulfilled my destiny. I was a captive and a slave. I loved Dora Spenlow to distraction!

She was more than human to me. She was a Fairy, a Sylph, I don't know what she was—anything that no one ever saw, and everything that everybody ever wanted. I was swallowed up in an abyss of love in an instant. There was no pausing on the brink—no looking down, or looking back; I was gone, headlong, before I had sense to say a word to her.

"*I*," observed a well-remembered voice, when I had bowed and murmured something, "have seen Mr. Copperfield before."

The speaker was not Dora. No; the confidential friend, Miss Murdstone!

I don't think I was much astonished. To the best of my judgment, no capacity of astonishment was left in me. There was nothing worth mentioning in the material world, but Dora Spenlow, to be astonished about. I said, "How do you do, Miss Murdstone? I hope you are well." She answered, "Very well." I said, "How is Mr. Murdstone?" She replied, "My brother is robust, I am obliged to you." Mr. Spenlow, who, I suppose, had been surprised to see us recognize each other, then put in his word.

"I am glad to find," he said, "Copperfield, that you and Miss Murdstone are already acquainted."

"Mr. Copperfield and myself," said Miss Murdstone, with severe composure, "are connections. We were once slightly acquainted. It was in his childish days. Circumstances have separated us since. I should not have known him."

I replied that I should have known her anywhere.

"Miss Murdstone has had the goodness," said Mr. Spenlow to me, "to accept the office—if I may so describe it—of my daughter Dora's confidential friend. My daughter Dora having, unhappily, no mother, Miss Murdstone is obliging enough to become her companion and protector."

A bell rang, which Mr. Spenlow said was the first dinner-bell, and so carried me off to dress. The idea of dressing one's self, or doing anything in the way of action, in that state of love, was a little too ridiculous. I could only sit down before my fire, biting the key of my carpet-bag, and think of the captivating, girlish, bright-eyed, lovely Dora. What a form she had, what a face she had, what a graceful, variable, enchanting manner! I made a mere scramble of my dressing, instead of the careful operation I could have wished under the circumstances, and went downstairs.

I don't remember who was there, except Dora. I have not the least idea what we had for dinner, besides Dora. My impression is, that I dined off Dora entirely, and sent away half a dozen plates untouched. I sat next to her. I talked to her. She had the most delightful little voice, the gayest little laugh, the pleasantest and most fascinating little ways, that ever led a lost youth into hopeless slavery. She was rather diminutive altogether. So much the more precious, I thought.

When she went out of the room with Miss Murdstone (no other ladies were of the party), I fell into a reverie, only disturbed by the cruel apprehension that Miss Murdstone would disparage me to her. But when we went into the drawing-room I was relieved of them in an unexpected manner.

"David Copperfield," said Miss Murdstone, beckoning me aside into a window. "A word."

I confronted Miss Murdstone alone.

"David Copperfield," said Miss Murdstone, "I need not enlarge upon family circumstances. They are not a tempting subject."

"Far from it, ma'am," I returned.

Miss Murdstone shut her eyes, and inclined her head; then, slowly opening her eyes, resumed,

"David Copperfield, I shall not attempt to disguise the fact that I formed an unfavorable opinion of you in your childhood. It may have been a mistaken one, or you may have ceased to justify it. That is not in question between us now. I belong to a family remarkable, I believe, for some firmness, and I am not the creature of circumstance or change. I may have my opinion of you. You may have your opinion of me."

I inclined my head in my turn.

"But it is not necessary," said Miss Murdstone, "that these opinions should come into collision here. As the chances of life have brought us together again, and may bring us together on other occasions, I would say, let us meet here as distant acquaintances. It is quite unnecessary that either of us should make the other the subject of remark. Do you approve of this?"

"Miss Murdstone," I returned, "I think you and Mr. Murdstone used me very cruelly, and treated my mother with great unkindness. I shall always think so, as long as I live. But I quite agree in what you propose."

Miss Murdstone shut her eyes again and bent her head. Then, just touching the back of my hand with the tips of her cold, stiff fingers, she walked away.

All I know of the rest of the evening is, that I heard the empress of my heart sing enchanted ballads in the French language, generally to the effect that, whatever was the matter, we ought always to dance, Ta ra la, Ta ra la! accompanying herself on a glorified instrument resembling a guitar; that I was lost in blissful delirium; that I retired to bed in a most maudlin state of mind, and got up in a crisis of feeble infatuation.

It was a fine morning, and early, and I thought I would go and take a stroll down one of those wire-arched walks, and indulge my passion by dwelling on her image. On my way through the hall, I encountered her little dog, who was called Jip—short for Gipsy. I approached him tenderly, for I loved even him; but he showed his whole set of teeth, got under a chair expressly to snarl, and wouldn't hear of the least familiarity.

I had not been walking long, when I turned a corner, and met her. I tingle again from head to foot as my recollection turns that corner, and my pen shakes in my hand.

"You—are—out early, Miss Spenlow," said I.

"It's so stupid at home," she replied, "and Miss Murdstone is so absurd! She talks such nonsense about its being necessary for the day to be aired before I come out. Aired!" (She laughed, here, in the most melodious manner.) "On a Sunday morning, when I don't practice, I must do something. So I told papa last night I *must* come out. Besides, it's the brightest time of the whole day. Don't you think so?"

I hazarded a bold flight, and said (not without stammering) that it was very bright to me then, though it had been very dark to me a minute before.

"Do you mean a compliment?" said Dora, "or that the weather has really changed?"

I stammered worse than before, in replying that I meant no compliment, but the plain truth, though I was not aware of any change having taken place in the weather. It was in the state of my own feelings, I added bashfully, to clench the explanation.

I never saw such curls—how could I, for there never were such curls!—as those she shook out to hide her blushes. As to the straw hat and blue ribbons which was on the top of the curls, if I could only have hung it up in my room in Buckingham Street, what a priceless possession it would have been!

The little dog came running along the walk to our relief. He was mortally jealous of me, and persisted in barking at me. She took him up in her arms—oh my goodness!—and caressed him; but he insisted upon barking still. He wouldn't let me touch him, when I tried.

"You are not very intimate with Miss Murdstone, are you?" said Dora.—"My pet."

(The two last words were to the dog. Oh, if they had only been to me!)

"No," I replied. "Not at all so."

"She is a tiresome creature," said Dora, pouting. "I can't think what papa can have been about when he chose such a vexatious thing to be my companion. Who wants a protector? I am sure *I* don't want a protector. Jip can protect me a great deal better than Miss Murdstone—can't you, Jip dear?"

He only winked lazily when she kissed his ball of a head.

"Papa calls her my confidential friend, but I am sure she is no such thing—is she, Jip? We are not going to confide in such cross people, Jip and I. We mean to bestow our confidence where we like, and to find out our own friends, instead of having them found out for us—don't we, Jip?"

Jip made a comfortable noise, in answer, a little like a teakettle when it sings. As for me, every word was a new heap of fetters riveted above the last.

We had a quiet day. No company, a walk, a family dinner of four, and an evening of looking over books and pictures; Miss Murdstone with a homily before her, and her eye upon us, keeping guard vigilantly. Ah! little did Mr. Spenlow imagine, when he sat opposite to me after dinner that day, with his pocket-handkerchief over his head, how fervently I was embracing him, in my fancy, as his son-in-law!

Within the first week of my passion, I bought four sumptuous waistcoats (not for myself—*I* had no pride in them—for Dora), and took to wearing straw-colored kid gloves in the streets, and laid the

181

foundations of all the corns I have ever had. If the boots I wore at that period could only be produced and compared with the natural size of my feet, they would show what the state of my heart was.

And yet, wretched cripple as I made myself by this act of homage to Dora, I walked miles upon miles daily in the hope of seeing her. Not only was I soon as well known on the Norwood Road as the postmen on that beat, but I pervaded London likewise. I walked about the streets where the best shops for ladies were; I haunted the Bazaar like an unquiet spirit; I fagged through the Park again and again, long after I was quite knocked up. Sometimes, at long intervals and on rare occasions, I saw her. Perhaps I saw her glove waved in a carriage window; perhaps I met her, walked with her and Miss Murdstone a little way, and spoke to her. In the latter case I was always very miserable afterwards to think that I had said nothing to the purpose, or that she had no idea of the extent of my devotion, or that she cared nothing about me. I was always looking out, as may be supposed, for another invitation to Mr. Spenlow's house. I was always being disappointed, for I got none.

Mrs. Crupp must have been a woman of penetration; for when this attachment was but a few weeks old, she found it out. She came up to me one evening, when I was very low, to ask (she being then afflicted with the disorder I have mentioned) if I could oblige her with a little tincture of cardamums mixed with rhubarb, and flavored with seven drops of the essence of cloves, which was the best remedy for her complaint; or, if I had not such a thing by me, with a little brandy, which was the next best. I gave Mrs. Crupp a glass of the second, which (that I might have no suspicion of its being devoted to any improper use) she began to take in my presence.

"Cheer up, sir," said Mrs. Crupp. "I can't bear to see you so, sir. If She don't smile upon you, there's a many as will. You're a young gentleman to *be* smiled on, Mr. Copperfull, and you must learn your walue, sir."

"What makes you suppose there is any young lady in the case, Mrs. Crupp?" said I.

"Mr. Copperfull," said Mrs. Crupp, with a great deal of feeling, "I'm a mother myself. I ask your pardon, sir, if I intrude. But my advice to you is, to cheer up, sir, to keep a good heart, and to know your own walue."

With these words, Mrs. Crupp, affecting to be very careful of the brandy—which was all gone—thanked me with a majestic curtsy, and retired.

IT MAY have been in consequence of Mrs. Crupp's advice, and, perhaps, for no better reason than because there was a certain similarity in the sound of the word skittles and Traddles, that it came into my head, next day, to go and look after Traddles. He lived in a little street near the Veterinary College at Camden Town, which was principally tenanted, as one of our clerks who lived in that direction informed me, by gentlemen students, who bought live donkeys, and made experiments on them in their apartments.

I found that the street was not as desirable a one as I could have wished it to be, for the sake of Traddles. The inhabitants appeared to have a propensity to throw any little trifles they were not in want of into the road, which not only made it rank and sloppy, but untidy too, on account of the cabbage-leaves. The refuse was not wholly vegetable either, for I myself saw a shoe, a doubled-up saucepan, a black bonnet, and an umbrella, in various stages of decomposition, as I was looking out for the number I wanted.

The general air of the place reminded me forcibly of the days when I lived with Mr. and Mrs. Micawber. An indescribable character of faded gentility that attached to the house I sought, and made it unlike all the other houses in the street—though they were all built on one monotonous pattern—reminded me still more of Mr. and Mrs. Micawber. Happening to arrive at the door as it was opened to the afternoon milkman, I was reminded of Mr. and Mrs. Micawber more forcibly yet.

"Now," said the milkman to a very youthful servant-girl, "has that there little bill of mine been heerd on?"

"Oh, master says he'll attend to it immediate," was the reply.

"Because," said the milkman, going on as if he had received no answer, and speaking, as I judged from his tone, rather for the edification of somebody within the house than of the youthful servant—an impression which was strengthened by his manner of glaring down the passage—"because that there little bill has been running so long, that I begin to believe it's run away altogether, and never won't be heerd of. Now, I'm not a-going to stand it, you know!" said the milkman, still throwing his voice into the house, and glaring down the passage.

The voice of the youthful servant became faint, but she seemed to me, from the action of her lips, again to murmur that it would be attended to immediate.

"I tell you what," said the milkman, looking hard at her for the first time, and taking her by the chin, "are you fond of milk?"

"Yes, I likes it," she replied.

"Good," said the milkman. "Then you won't have none to-morrow. D'ye hear? Not a fragment of milk you won't have to-morrow."

I thought she seemed, upon the whole, relieved by the prospect of having any today. The milkman, after shaking his head at her darkly, released her chin, and with anything rather than good-will opened his can, and deposited the usual quantity in the family jug. This done, he went away muttering, and uttered the cry of his trade next door in a vindictive shriek.

When I got to the top of the stairs—the house was only a story high above the ground floor—Traddles was on the landing to meet me. He was delighted to see me, and gave me welcome, with great heartiness, to his little room. It was in the front of the house, and extremely neat, though sparely furnished. It was his only room, I saw; for there was a sofa-bedstead in it, and his blacking-brushes and blacking were among his books—on the top shelf, behind a dictionary. His table was covered with papers, and he was hard at work in an old coat. In a corner of the room was something neatly covered up with a large white cloth. I could not make out what.

"Traddles," said I, shaking hands with him again, after I had sat down, "I am delighted to see you."

"I am delighted to see *you*, Copperfield," he returned. "I am very glad indeed to see you. It was because I was thoroughly glad to see you when we met in Ely Place, and was sure you were thoroughly glad to see me, that I gave you this address instead of my address at chambers."

"Oh! you have chambers?" said I.

"Why, I have the fourth of a room and a passage, and the fourth of a clerk," returned Traddles. "Three others and myself unite to have a set of chambers—to look business-like—and we quarter the clerk too. Half a crown a week he costs me."

His old simple character and good temper, and something of his old unlucky fortune also, I thought, smiled at me in the smile with which he made this explanation.

"It's not because I have the least pride, Copperfield, you understand," said Traddles, "that I don't usually give my address here. It's only on account of those who come to me, who might not like to come here. For myself, I am fighting my way on in the world against difficulties, and it would be ridiculous if I made a pretense of doing anything else."

"You are reading for the bar, Mr. Waterbrook informed me?" said I.

"Why, yes," said Traddles, rubbing his hands slowly over one another, "I am reading for the bar. The fact is, I have just begun to keep my terms, after rather a long delay. It's some time since I was articled, but the payment of that hundred pounds was a great pull. A great pull!" said Traddles, with a wince, as if he had had a tooth out.

"You were brought up by an uncle?" said I.

"Yes. He was a retired—what do you call it?—draper—cloth-merchant—and had made me his heir. But he didn't like me when I grew up."

"Did you get nothing, Traddles, after all?"

"Oh dear, yes!" said Traddles. "I got fifty pounds. I had never been brought up to any profession, and at first I was at a loss what to do for myself. However, I began to copy law writings. That didn't answer very well; and then I began to state cases for them, and make abstracts, and do that sort of work. Well, that put it in my head to enter myself as a law student; and that ran away with all that was left of the fifty pounds. I was fortunate enough, too, to become

185

acquainted with a person in the publishing way, who was getting up an Encyclopædia, and he set me to work; and, indeed" (glancing at his table), "I am at work for him at this minute. I am not a bad compiler, Copperfield," said Traddles, preserving the same air of cheerful confidence in all he said, "but I have no invention at all, not a particle. I suppose there never was a young man with less originality than I have."

As Traddles seemed to expect that I should assent to this as a matter of course, I nodded; and he went on, with the same sprightly patience—I can find no better expression—as before.

"So, by little and little, and not living high, I managed to scrape up the hundred pounds at last," said Traddles; "and thank Heaven that's paid—though it was—though it certainly was," said Traddles, wincing again as if he had had another tooth out, "a pull. Now, Copperfield, it's so pleasant to see you, that I shan't conceal anything. Therefore you must know that I am engaged."

Engaged! O Dora!

"She is a curate's daughter," said Traddles; "one of ten, down in Devonshire. A little older than me, but the dearest girl! I told you I was going out of town? I have been down there. I walked there, and I walked back, and I had the most delightful time! I dare say ours is likely to be a rather long engagement, but our motto is, 'Wait and hope!' We always say that. 'Wait and hope,' we always say. And she would wait, Copperfield, till she was sixty—any age you can mention—for me!"

Traddles rose from his chair, and, with a triumphant smile, put his hand upon the white cloth I had observed.

"However," he said, "it's not that we haven't made a beginning towards housekeeping. No, no; we have begun. We must get on by degrees, but we have begun. Here," drawing the cloth off with great pride and care, "are two pieces of furniture to commence with. This flower-pot and stand she bought herself. You put that in a parlor window," said Traddles, falling a little back from it to survey it with the greater admiration, "with a plant in it, and—and there you are! This little round table with the marble top (it's two feet ten in circumference), *I* bought. You want to lay a book down, you know, or somebody comes to see you and wants a place to stand a cup of tea upon, and—and there you are again!" said Traddles. "It's an admirable piece of workmanship—firm as a rock!"

I praised them both highly, and Traddles replaced the covering as carefully as he had removed it.

186

"In the meantime," said Traddles, coming back to his chair—
"and this is the end of my prosing about myself—I get on as well as
I can. I don't make much, but I don't spend much. In general, I
board with the people downstairs, who are very agreeable people
indeed. Both Mr. and Mrs. Micawber have seen a good deal of life,
and are excellent company."

"My dear Traddles!" I quickly exclaimed, "what are you talking
about?"

Traddles looked at me, as if he wondered what *I* was talking
about.

"Mr. and Mrs. Micawber!" I repeated. "Why, I am intimately
acquainted with them!"

An opportune double knock at the door, which I knew well from
old experience in Windsor Terrace, resolved any doubt in my mind
as to their being my old friends. I begged Traddles to ask his landlord to walk up. Traddles accordingly did so, over the banister; and
Mr. Micawber, not a bit changed—his tights, his stick, his shirt
collar, and his eye-glass, all the same as ever—came into the room
with a genteel and youthful air.

"I beg your pardon, Mr. Traddles," said Mr. Micawber, with the
old roll in his voice, as he checked himself in humming a soft tune.
"I was not aware that there was any individual, alien to this tene-
ment, in your sanctum."

Mr. Micawber slightly bowed to me, and pulled up his shirt
collar.

"How do you do, Mr. Micawber?" said I.

"Sir," said Mr. Micawber, "you are exceedingly obliging. I am
in statu quo."

"And Mrs. Micawber?" I pursued.

"Sir," said Mr. Micawber, "she is also, thank God, *in statu quo.*"

"And the children, Mr. Micawber?"

"Sir," said Mr. Micawber, "I rejoice to reply that they are likewise in the enjoyment of salubrity."

All this time, Mr. Micawber had not known me in the least,
though he had stood face to face with me. But now, seeing me smile,
he examined my features with more attention, fell back, cried, "Is it
possible? Have I the pleasure of again beholding Copperfield?" and
shook me by both hands with the utmost fervor.

"Good Heaven, Mr. Traddles!" said Mr. Micawber, "to think
that I should find you acquainted with the friend of my youth, the
companion of earlier days!—My dear!" calling over the banisters to

Mrs. Micawber, while Traddles looked (with reason) not a little amazed at this description of me, "here is a gentleman in Mr. Traddles's apartment, whom he wishes to have the pleasure of presenting to you, my love!"

Mr. Micawber immediately reappeared, and shook hands with me again.

"You find us, Copperfield," said Mr. Micawber, with one eye on Traddles, "at present established on what may be designated as a small and unassuming scale; but you are aware that I have, in the course of my career, surmounted difficulties and conquered obstacles. You are no stranger to the fact that there have been periods of my life when it has been requisite that I should pause, until certain expected events should turn up; when it has been necessary that I should fall back, before making what I trust I shall not be accused of presumption in terming—a spring. The present is one of those momentous stages in the life of man. You find me fallen back, *for* a spring; and I have every reason to believe that a vigorous leap will shortly be the result."

I was expressing my satisfaction, when Mrs. Micawber came in— a little more slatternly than she used to be, or so she seemed now, to my unaccustomed eyes, but still with some preparation of herself for company, and with a pair of brown gloves on.

"My dear," said Mr. Micawber, leading her toward me, "here is a gentleman of the name of Copperfield, who wishes to renew his acquaintance with you."

It would have been better, as it turned out, to have led gently up to his announcement; for Mrs. Micawber, being in a delicate state of health, was overcome by it, and was taken so unwell, that Mr. Micawber was obliged, in great trepidation, to run down to the water-butt and draw a basinful to lave her brow with. She presently revived, however, and was really pleased to see me.

Mr. Micawber was very anxious that I should stay to dinner. I should not have been averse to do so, but that I imagined I detected trouble, and calculation relative to the extent of the cold meat, in Mrs. Micawber's eye. I therefore pleaded another engagement; and observing that Mrs. Micawber's spirits were immediately lightened, I resisted all persuasion to forego it.

But I told Traddles, and Mr. and Mrs. Micawber, that before I could think of leaving, they must appoint a day when they would come and dine with me. An appointment was made for the purpose that suited us all, and then I took my leave.

CHAPTER 28  MR. MICAWBER'S
GAUNTLET • • •

U NTIL the day arrived on which I was to entertain my newly
found old friends, I lived principally on Dora and coffee.
In my love-lorn condition my appetite languished; and I was
glad of it, for I felt as though it would have been an act of perfidy
toward Dora to have a natural relish for my dinner.

On the occasion of this domestic little party, I merely provided
a pair of soles, a small leg of mutton, and a pigeon-pie. Mrs. Crupp
broke out into rebellion on my first bashful hint in reference to the
cooking of the fish and joint, and said, with a dignified sense of
injury, "No! No, sir! You will not ask me sich a thing, for you are
better acquainted with me than to suppose me capable of doing
what I cannot do with ampial satisfaction to my own feelings!" But,
in the end, a compromise was effected, and Mrs. Crupp consented to
achieve this feat, on condition that I dined from home for a fortnight afterwards.

And here I may remark, that what I underwent from Mrs. Crupp,
in consequence of the tyranny she established over me, was dreadful. I never was so much afraid of anyone. We made a compromise
of everything. If I hesitated, she was taken with that wonderful
disorder which was always lying in ambush in her system, ready, at

the shortest notice, to prey upon her vitals. I would have done anything in an honorable way rather than give Mrs. Crupp offense.

At the appointed time my three visitors arrived together—Mr. Micawber with more shirt collar than usual, and a new ribbon to his eye-glass; Mrs. Micawber with her cap in a whity-brown paper parcel; Traddles carrying the parcel, and supporting Mrs. Micawber on his arm. They were all delighted with my residence.

"My dear Copperfield," said Mr. Micawber, "this is luxurious. This is a way of life which reminds me of the period when I was myself in a state of celibacy, and Mrs. Micawber had not yet been solicited to plight her faith at the Hymeneal altar."

"He means, solicited by him, Mr. Copperfield," said Mrs. Micawber archly. "He cannot answer for others."

"My dear," returned Mr. Micawber, with sudden seriousness, "I have no desire to answer for others. I am too well aware that when, in the inscrutable decrees of Fate, you were reserved for me, it is possible you may have been reserved for one destined, after a protracted struggle, at length to fall a victim to pecuniary involvements of a complicated nature. I understand your allusion, my love. I regret it, but I can bear it."

"Micawber!" exclaimed Mrs. Micawber, in tears, "have I deserved this?—I, who never have deserted you; who never *will* desert you, Micawber!"

Mr. Micawber then embraced Mrs. Micawber, and pressed my hand. To divert his thoughts, I informed Mr. Micawber that I relied upon him for a bowl of punch, and led him to the lemons. His recent despondency, not to say despair, was gone in a moment. I never saw a man so thoroughly enjoy himself amid the fragrance of lemon-peel and sugar, the odor of burning rum, and the steam of boiling water, as Mr. Micawber did that afternoon. As to Mrs. Micawber, the lark was never gayer than that excellent woman.

I suppose—I never ventured to inquire, but I suppose—that Mrs. Crupp, after frying the soles, was taken ill. Because we broke down at that point. The leg of mutton came up very red within, and very pale without; besides having a foreign substance of a gritty nature sprinkled over it, as if it had had a fall into the ashes of that remarkable kitchen fireplace. The pigeon-pie was not bad, but it was a delusive pie; the crust being like a disappointing head, phrenologically speaking—full of lumps and bumps, with nothing particular underneath. In short, the banquet was such a failure that I should have been quite unhappy if I had not been relieved by the great good-humor of my company, and by a bright suggestion from Mr. Micawber.

"My dear friend Copperfield," said Mr. Micawber, "accidents will occur in the best-regulated families; and in families not regulated by that pervading influence which sanctifies while it enhances the—a—I would say, in short, by the influence of Woman, in the lofty character of Wife, they may be expected with confidence, and must be borne with philosophy. If you will allow me to take the liberty of remarking that there are few comestibles better, in their way, than a devil, and that I believe, with a little division of labor, we could accomplish a good one, I would put it to you that this little misfortune may be easily repaired."

There was a gridiron in the pantry, on which my morning rasher of bacon was cooked. We had it in, in a twinkling, and immediately applied ourselves to carrying Mr. Micawber's idea into effect. The division of labor to which he had referred was this: Traddles cut the mutton into slices; Mr. Micawber (who could do anything of this sort to perfection) covered them with pepper, mustard, salt, and cayenne; I put them on the gridiron, turned them with a fork, and took them off, under Mr. Micawber's direction; and Mrs. Micawber heated, and continually stirred, some mushroom ketchup in a little saucepan.

When we had slices enough done to begin upon, we fell to, with our sleeves still tucked up at the wrists, more slices sputtering and blazing on the fire, and our attention divided between the mutton on our plates and the mutton then preparing.

What with the novelty of this cookery, the excellence of it, the bustle of it, the frequent starting up to look after it, the frequent sitting down to dispose of it as the crisp slices came off the gridiron hot and hot, the being so busy, so flushed with the fire, so amused, and in the midst of such a tempting noise and savor, we reduced the leg of mutton to the bone. My own appetite came back miraculously. I am ashamed to record it, but I really believe I forgot Dora for a little while. I am satisfied that Mr. and Mrs. Micawber could not have enjoyed the feast more, if they had sold a bed to provide it. Traddles laughed as heartily, almost the whole time, as he ate and worked. Indeed we all did, all at once; and I dare say there never was a greater success.

We were at the height of our enjoyment, and were all busily engaged, in our several departments, endeavoring to bring the last batch of slices to a state of perfection that should crown the feast, when I was aware of a strange presence in the room, and my eyes encountered those of the staid Littimer, standing hat in hand before me.

"What's the matter?" I involuntarily asked.

"I beg your pardon, sir. I was directed to come in. Is my master not here, sir?"

"No."

"Have you not seen him, sir?"

"No; don't you come from him?"

"Not immediately so, sir."

"Did he tell you you would find him here?"

"Not exactly so, sir; but I should think he might be here tomorrow, as he has not been here today."

"Is he coming up from Oxford?"

"I beg, sir," he returned respectfully, "that you will be seated, and allow me to do this." With which he took the fork from my unresisting hand, and bent over the gridiron, as if his whole attention were concentrated on it.

We should not have been much discomposed, I dare say, by the appearance of Steerforth himself; but we became in a moment the meekest of the meek before his respectable serving-man. Mr. Micawber, humming a tune to show that he was quite at ease, subsided into his chair, with the handle of a hastily concealed fork sticking out of the bosom of his coat, as if he had stabbed himself. Mrs. Micawber put on her brown gloves, and assumed a genteel languor. Traddles ran his greasy hands through his hair, and stood it bolt upright, and stared in confusion on the table-cloth. As for me, I was a mere infant at the head of my own table, and hardly ventured to glance at the respectable phenomenon who had come from Heaven knows where to put my establishment to rights.

Meanwhile he took the mutton off the gridiron, and gravely handed it round. We all took some, but our appreciation of it was gone, and we merely made a show of eating it. As we severally pushed away our plates, he noiselessly removed them, and set on the cheese. He took that off, too, when it was done with, cleared the table, piled everything on the dumb-waiter, gave us our wine-glasses, and, of his own accord, wheeled the dumb-waiter into the pantry. All this was done in a perfect manner, and he never raised his eyes from what he was about.

"Can I do anything more, sir?"

I thanked him, and said, No; but would he take no dinner himself?

"None; I am obliged to you, sir."

He was moving softly to the door, when, in a forlorn hope of saying something naturally—which I never could, to this man—I said,

"Oh, Littimer!"

"Sir."

"Did you remain long at Yarmouth, that time?"

"Not particularly so, sir."

"You saw the boat completed?"

"Yes, sir. I remained behind on purpose to see the boat completed."

"I know." He raised his eyes to mine respectfully. "Mr. Steerforth has not seen it yet, I suppose?"

"I really can't say, sir. I think—but I really can't say, sir. I wish you good-night, sir."

He comprehended everybody present in the respectful bow with which he followed these words, and disappeared. My visitors seemed to breathe more freely when he was gone.

"But punch, my dear Copperfield," said Mr. Micawber, tasting it, "like time and tide, waits for no man. Ah! it is at the present moment in high flavor. My love, will you give me your opinion?"

Mrs. Micawber pronounced it excellent.

"Then I will drink," said Mr. Micawber, "if my friend Copperfield will permit me to take that social liberty, to the days when my friend Copperfield and myself were younger, and fought our way in the world side by side. I may say, of myself and Copperfield, in words we have sung together before now, that—

'We twa hae run about the braes,
And pu'd the gowans fine,'

—in a figurative point of view—on several occasions. I am not exactly aware," said Mr. Micawber, with the old roll in his voice, and the old indescribable air of saying something genteel, "what gowans may be, but I have no doubt that Copperfield and myself would frequently have taken a pull at them, if it had been feasible."

Mr. Micawber, at the then present moment, took a pull at his punch. So we all did—Traddles evidently lost in wondering at what distant time Mr. Micawber and I could have been comrades in the battle of the world.

"Ahem!" said Mr. Micawber, clearing his throat, and warming with the punch and with the fire. "My dear, another glass?"

Mrs. Micawber said it must be very little; but we couldn't allow that, so it was a glassful.

"As we are quite confidential here, Mr. Copperfield," said Mrs. Micawber, sipping her punch, "Mr. Traddles being a part of our domesticity, I should much like to have your opinion on Mr. Micawber's prospects."

Mr. Micawber, leaning back in his chair with his hands in his pockets, eyes us aside, and nodded his head, as much as to say that the case was very clearly put. Mrs. Micawber went on to say, still with the same air of putting a case lucidly,

"What is the conclusion, my dear Mr. Copperfield, to which I am irresistibly brought? Am I wrong in saying it is clear that we must live?"

I answered, "Not at all!" and Traddles answered, "Not at all!" and I found myself afterwards sagely adding, alone, that a person must either live or die.

"Just so," returned Mrs. Micawber. "It is precisely that. And the fact is, my dear Mr. Copperfield, that we can *not* live without something widely different from existing circumstances shortly turning up. Now I am convinced myself, and this I have pointed out to Mr. Micawber several times of late, that things cannot be expected to turn up of themselves. We must, in a measure, assist to turn them up. I may be wrong, but I have formed that opinion."

Both Traddles and I applauded it highly.

"Very well," said Mrs. Micawber. "Then what do I recommend? Here is Mr. Micawber with a variety of qualifications—with great talent——"

"Really, my love," said Mr. Micawber.

"Pray, my dear, allow me to conclude. Here is Mr. Micawber, with a variety of qualifications, with great talent—*I* should say with genius, but that may be the partiality of a wife."

Traddles and I both murmured, "No."

"And here is Mr. Micawber without any suitable position or employment. Where does that responsibility rest? Clearly on society. Then I would make a fact so disgraceful known, and boldly challenge society to set it right. It appears to me, my dear Mr. Copperfield," said Mrs. Micawber forcibly, "that what Mr. Micawber has to do, is to throw down the gauntlet to society, and say, in effect, 'Show me who will take that up. Let the party immediately step forward.'"

I ventured to ask Mrs. Micawber how this was to be done.

"By advertising," said Mrs. Micawber, "in all the papers. It appears to me that what Mr. Micawber has to do, in justice to himself, in justice to his family, and I will even go so far as to say in justice to society, by which he has been hitherto overlooked, is to advertise in all the papers; to describe himself plainly as so-and-so, with such and such qualifications, and to put it thus: '*Now* employ me, on remunerative terms, and address, post-paid, to *W. M.*, Post Office, Camden Town.'"

"This idea of Mrs. Micawber's, my dear Copperfield," said Mr. Micawber, making his shirt collar meet in front of his chin, and glancing at me sideways, "is, in fact, the leap to which I alluded when I last had the pleasure of seeing you."

"Advertising is rather expensive," I remarked dubiously.

"Exactly so," said Mrs. Micawber, preserving the same logical air. "Quite true, my dear Mr. Copperfield. I have made the identical observation to Mr. Micawber. It is for that reason especially that I think Mr. Micawber ought (as I have already said, in justice to himself, in justice to his family, and in justice to society) to raise a certain sum of money—on a bill."

Mr. Micawber, leaning back in his chair, tried with his eye-glass, and cast his eyes up at the ceiling; but I thought him observant of Traddles, too, who was looking at the fire.

"If no member of my family," said Mrs. Micawber, "is possessed of sufficient natural feeling to negotiate that bill—I believe there is a better business term to express what I mean——"

Mr. Micawber, with his eyes still cast up at the ceiling, suggested "Discount."

"To discount that bill," said Mrs. Micawber, "then my opinion is, that Mr. Micawber should go into the City, should take that bill into the Money Market, and should dispose of it for what he can get."

I felt, but I am sure I don't know why, that this was self-denying and devoted in Mrs. Micawber, and I uttered a murmur to that effect. Traddles, who took his tone from me, did likewise, still looking at the fire.

"I will not," said Mrs. Micawber, finishing her punch, and gathering her scarf about her shoulders, preparatory to her withdrawal to my bedroom—"I will not protract these remarks on the subject of Mr. Micawber's pecuniary affairs. At your fireside, by dear Mr. Copperfield, and in the presence of Mr. Traddles, who, though not so old a friend, is quite one of ourselves, I could not refrain from making you acquainted with the course *I* advise Mr. Micawber to take."

With these words, and resisting our entreaties that she would grace the remaining circulation of the punch with her presence, Mrs. Micawber retired to my bedroom.

After tea, we discussed a variety of topics before the fire, and Mrs. Micawber was good enough to sing us (in a small, thin, flat voice, which I remembered to have considered, when I first knew her, the very table-beer of acoustics) the favorite ballads of "The Dashing White Serjeant," and "Little Tafflin." It was between ten and eleven o'clock when Mrs. Micawber rose to replace her cap in the whity-brown paper parcel, and to put on her bonnet. Mr. Micawber took the opportunity to slip a letter into my hand, with a whispered request that I would read it at my leisure. I also took the opportunity, when Mr. Micawber was going first, leading Mrs. Micawber, and Traddles was following with the cap, to detain Traddles for a moment on the top of the stairs.

"Traddles," said I, "Mr. Micawber don't mean any harm, poor fellow; but if I were you, I wouldn't lend him anything."

"My dear Copperfield," returned Traddles, smiling, "I haven't got anything to lend."

"You have got a name, you know," said I.

"Oh! you call *that* something to lend?" returned Traddles, with a thoughtful look.

"Certainly."

"Oh!" said Traddles. "Yes, to be sure! I am very much obliged to you, Copperfield; but—I am afraid I have lent him that already."

"For the bill that is to be a certain investment?" I inquired.

"No," said Traddles; "not for that one. This is the first I have heard of that one. I have been thinking that he will most likely propose that one, on the way home. Mine's another."

"I hope there will be nothing wrong about it," said I.

"I hope not," said Traddles. "I should think not, though, because he told me, only the other day, that it was provided for. That was Mr. Micawber's expression—'provided for.'"

Mr. Micawber looking up at this juncture to where we were standing, I had only time to repeat my caution. Traddles thanked me, and descended. But I was much afraid, when I observed the good-natured manner in which he went down with the cap in his hand, and gave Mrs. Micawber his arm, that he would be carried into the Money Market neck and heels.

I returned to my fireside, and was musing, half gravely and half laughing, on the character of Mr. Micawber and the old relations between us, when I heard a quick step ascending the stairs. I knew it, and felt my heart beat high, and the blood rush to my face, for it was Steerforth's.

"Why, Daisy, old boy, dumb-foundered!" laughed Steerforth, shaking my hand heartily, and throwing it gaily away. "Have I detected you in another feast, you Sybarite? These Doctors' Commons fellows are the gayest men in town, I believe, and beat us sober Oxford people all to nothing!" His bright glance went merrily round the room, as he took the seat on the sofa opposite to me which Mrs. Micawber had recently vacated, and stirred the fire into a blaze.

"I was so surprised at first," said I, giving him welcome with all the cordiality I felt, "that I had hardly breath to greet you with, Steerforth."

"Well, the sight of me *is* good for sore eyes, as the Scotch say," replied Steerforth, "and so is the sight of you, Daisy, in full bloom. How are you, my bacchanal?"

"I am very well," said I; "and not at all bacchanalian tonight, though I confess to another party of three."

"All of whom I met in the street, talking loud in your praise," returned Steerforth. "Who's our friend in the tights?"

I gave him the best idea I could, in a few words, of Mr. Micawber. He laughed heartily at my feeble portrait of that gentleman, and said he was a man to know, and he must know him. Dismissing the subject, he inquired if I could give him anything to eat? During most of this short dialogue, when he had not been speaking in a wild vivacious manner, he had sat idly beating on the lump of coal with the poker. I observed that he did the same thing while I was getting out the remains of the pigeon-pie, and so forth.

"Why, Daisy, here's a supper for a king!" he exclaimed, starting out of his silence with a burst, and taking his seat at the table. "I shall do it justice, for I have come from Yarmouth."

"I thought you came from Oxford," I returned.

"Not I," said Steerforth. "I have been seafaring—better employed."

"Littimer was here today, to inquire for you," I remarked.

"Littimer is a greater fool than I thought him, to have been inquiring for me at all," said Steerforth, jovially pouring out a glass of wine, and drinking to me. "As to understanding him, you are a cleverer fellow than most of us, Daisy, if you can do that."

197

"That's true, indeed," said I, moving my chair to the table. "So you have been at Yarmouth, Steerforth?" interested to know all about it. "Have you been there long?"

"No," he returned. "An escapade of a week or so."

"And how are they all? Of course, little Em'ly is not married yet?"

"Not yet. Going to be, I believe—in so many weeks, or months, or something or other. I have not seen much of 'em. By-the-by"—he laid down his knife and fork, which he had been using with great diligence, and began feeling in his pockets—"I have a letter for you."

"From whom?"

"Why, from your old nurse," he returned, taking some papers out of his breast-pocket. " 'J. Steerforth, Esquire, debtor to The Willing Mind;' that's not it. Patience, and we'll find it presently. Old what's-his-name's in a bad way, and it's about that, I believe."

"Barkis, do you mean?"

"Yes!" still feeling in his pockets, and looking over their contents; "it's all over with poor Barkis, I am afraid.—Put your hand into the breast-pocket of my greatcoat on the chair yonder, and I think you'll find the letter. Is it there?"

"Here it is!" said I.

"That's right!"

It was from Peggotty—something less legible than usual, and brief. It informed me of her husband's hopeless state, and hinted at his being "a little nearer" than heretofore, and consequently more difficult to manage for his own comfort. It said nothing of her weariness and watching, and praised him highly.

"I tell you what, Steerforth," said I, "if your high spirits will listen to me——"

"They are potent spirits, and will do whatever you like," he answered, moving from the table to the fireside again.

"Then I tell you what, Steerforth. I think I will go down and see my old nurse. It is not that I can do her any good, or render her any real service; but she is so attached to me, that my visit will have as much effect on her as if I could do both. She will take it so kindly, that it will be a comfort and support to her."

His face was thoughtful, and he sat considering a little before he answered, in a low voice, "Well, go! You can do no harm."

"You have just come back," said I, "and it would be in vain to ask you to go with me?"

"Quite," he returned. "I am for Highgate tonight. I have not seen my mother this long time, and it lies upon my conscience, for it's something to be loved as she loves her prodigal son.—Bah! Nonsense!—You mean to go tomorrow, I suppose?" he said, holding me out at arm's-length, with a hand on each of my shoulders.

"Yes, I think so."

"Well, then, don't go till next day. I wanted you to come and stay a few days with us. Here I am, on purpose to bid you, and you fly off to Yarmouth!"

"You are a nice fellow to talk of flying off, Steerforth, who are always running wild on some unknown expedition or other!"

He looked at me for a moment without speaking, and then rejoined, still holding me as before, and giving me a shake,

"Come! say the next day, and pass as much of tomorrow as you can with us! Who knows when we may meet again, else? Come! say the next day! I want you to stand between Rosa Dartle and me, and keep us asunder."

"Would you love each other too much without me?"

"Yes, or hate," laughed Steerforth; "no matter which. Come! say the next day!"

I said the next day; and he put on his greatcoat and lighted his cigar, and set off to walk home.

I was undressing in my own room when Mr. Micawber's letter tumbled on the floor. Thus reminded of it, I broke the seal, and read as follows. It was dated an hour and a half before dinner.

"Sir—for I dare not say my dear Copperfield,

"It is expedient that I should inform you that the undersigned is Crushed. Some flickering efforts to spare you the premature knowledge of his calamitous position, you may observe in him this day; but hope has sunk beneath the horizon, and the undersigned is Crushed.

"The present communication is penned within the personal range (I cannot call it the society) of an individual, in a state closely bordering on intoxication, employed by a broker. That individual is in legal possession of the premises, under a distress for rent. His inventory includes, not only the chattels and effects of every description belonging to the undersigned, as yearly tenant of this habitation, but also those appertaining to Mr. Thomas Traddles, lodger, a member of the Honourable Society of the Inner Temple.

"If any drop of gloom were wanting in the overflowing cup, which is now 'commended' (in the language of an immortal Writer) to the lips of the undersigned, it would be found in the fact that a friendly acceptance granted to the undersigned, by the before-mentioned Mr. Thomas Traddles, for the sum of £23, 4s. 9½d., is overdue, and is NOT provided for. Also, in the fact, that the living responsibilities clinging to the undersigned will, in the course of nature, be increased by the sum of one more helpless victim, whose miserable appearance may be looked for—in round numbers—at the expiration of a period not exceeding six lunar months from the present date.

"After premising thus much, it would be a work of supererogation to add that dust and ashes are for ever scattered

"On

"The

"Head

"Of

"WILKINS MICAWBER."

Poor Traddles! I knew enough of Mr. Micawber by this time to foresee that *he* might be expected to recover the blow; but my night's rest was sorely distressed by thoughts of Traddles, and of the curate's daughter, who was one of ten, down in Devonshire, and who was such a dear girl, and who would wait for Traddles (ominous praise!) until she was sixty, or any age that could be mentioned.

The party at Mr. Peggotty's house

CHAPTER 29 ❧ I VISIT STEERFORTH AT HIS HOME AGAIN ◆ ◆ ◆

Mrs. STEERFORTH was pleased to see me, and so was Rosa Dartle. I was agreeably surprised to find that Littimer was not there, and that we were attended by a modest little parlor-maid, with blue ribbons in her cap. But what I particularly observed, before I had been half an hour in the house, was the close and attentive watch Miss Dartle kept upon me. So surely as I looked toward her did I see that eager visage, with its gaunt black eyes and searching brow, intent on mine; or passing suddenly from mine to Steerforth's; or comprehending both of us at once.

All day she seemed to pervade the whole house. If I talked to Steerforth in his room, I heard her dress rustle in the little gallery outside. When he and I engaged in some of our old exercises on the lawn behind the house, I saw her face pass from window to window, like a wandering light, until it fixed itself in one, and watched us. When we all four went out walking in the afternoon, she closed her thin hand on my arm like a spring, to keep me back, while Steerforth and his mother went on out of hearing and then spoke to me.

"You have been a long time," she said, "without coming here. Is your profession really so engaging and interesting as to absorb your whole attention? I ask, because I always want to be informed when I am ignorant. Is it really, though?"

I replied that I liked it well enough, but that I certainly could not claim so much for it.

"Oh! I am glad to know that, because I always like to be put right when I am wrong," said Rosa Dartle. "You mean it is a little dry, perhaps?"

"Well," I replied; "perhaps it *was* a little dry."

"Oh! and that's a reason why you want relief and change—excitement, and all that?" said she. "Ah, very true! But isn't it a little—eh? —for him; I don't mean you?"

A quick glance of her eye toward the spot where Steerforth was walking, with his mother leaning on his arm, showed me whom she meant; but beyond that I was quite lost. And I looked so, I have no doubt.

"Don't it—I don't say that it *does;* mind I want to know—don't it rather engross him? Don't it make him, perhaps, a little more remiss than usual in his visits to his blindly-doting—eh?" With another quick glance at them, and such a glance at me as seemed to look into my innermost thoughts.

"Miss Dartle," I returned, "pray do not think——"

"I don't!" she said. "Oh, dear me, don't suppose that I think anything! I am not suspicious. I only ask a question. I don't state any opinion. I want to found an opinion on what you tell me. Then, it's not so? Well, I am very glad to know it!"

"It certainly is not the fact," said I, perplexed, "that I am accountable for Steerforth's having been away from home longer than usual—if he has been; which I really don't know at this moment, unless I understand it from you. I have not seen him this long while, until last night."

"No?"

"Indeed, Miss Dartle, no!"

As she looked full at me, I saw her face grow sharper and paler, and the marks of the old wound lengthen out until it cut through the disfigured lip, and deep into the nether lip, and slanted down the face. There was something positively awful to me in this, and in the brightness of her eyes, as she said, looking fixedly at me,

"What is he doing?"

I repeated the words, more to myself than her, being so amazed.

"What is he doing?" she said, with an eagerness that seemed enough to consume her like a fire. "In what is that man assisting him, who never looks at me without an inscrutable falsehood in his eyes? If you are honorable and faithful, I don't ask you to betray your friend. I ask you only to tell me, is it anger, is it hatred, is it pride, is it restlessness, is it some wild fancy, is it love, *what is it*, that is leading him?"

"Miss Dartle," I returned, "how shall I tell you, so that you will believe me, that I know of nothing in Steerforth different from what there was when I first came here? I can think of nothing. I firmly believe there is nothing. I hardly understand even what you mean."

As she still stood looking fixedly at me, a twitching or throbbing, from which I could not dissociate the idea of pain, came into that cruel mark, and lifted up the corner of her lip as if with scorn, or with a pity that despised its object. She put her hand upon it hurriedly—a hand so thin and delicate, that when I had seen her hold it up before the fire to shade her face, I had compared it in my thoughts to fine porcelain—and saying, in a quick, fierce, passionate way, "I swear you to secrecy about this!" said not a word more.

During the whole of this day, but especially from this period of it, Steerforth exerted himself with his utmost skill to charm this singular creature into a pleasant and pleased companion. That he should succeed was no matter of surprise to me. I saw her features and her manner slowly change; I saw her look at him with growing admiration; I saw her try, more and more faintly, but always angrily, as if she condemned a weakness in herself, to resist the captivating power that he possessed; and finally, I saw her sharp glance soften, and her smile become quite gentle.

"My dear Rosa, be kind for once, and sing us an Irish song," said Steerforth. "Here is Daisy, too—loves music from his soul. Sing us an Irish song, Rosa; and let me sit and listen as I used to do."

He did not touch her, or the chair from which she had risen, but sat himself near the harp. She stood beside it for some little while, in a curious way, going through the motion of playing it with her right hand, but not sounding it. At length she sat down, and drew it to her with one sudden action, and played and sang.

I don't know what it was, in her touch or voice, that made that song the most unearthly I have ever heard in my life, or can imagine. There was something fearful in the reality of it. It was as if it had never been written, or set to music, but sprung out of the passion within her, which found imperfect utterance in the low sounds of her voice, and crouched again when all was still. I was dumb when she leaned beside the harp again, playing it, but not sounding it, with her right hand.

A minute more, and this had roused me from my trance: Steerforth had left his seat, and gone to her, and had put his arm laughingly about her, and had said, "Come, Rosa, for the future we will love each other very much!" And she had struck him, and had thrown him off with the fury of a wild cat, and had burst out of the room.

"What is the matter with Rosa?" said Mrs. Steerforth, coming in.

"She has been an angel, mother," returned Steerforth, "for a little while; and has run into the opposite extreme, since, by way of compensation."

"You should be careful not to irritate her, James. Her temper has been soured, remember, and ought not to be tried."

Rosa did not come back, and no other mention was made of her, until I went with Steerforth into his room to say good-night. Then he laughed about her, and asked me if I had ever seen such a fierce little piece of incomprehensibility.

I expressed as much of my astonishment as was then capable of expression, and asked if he could guess what it was that she had taken so much amiss so suddenly.

"Oh, Heaven knows," said Steerforth. "She is an edge-tool, and requires great care in dealing with. She is always dangerous. Good-night!"

"Good-night," said I, "my dear Steerforth! I shall be gone before you wake in the morning. Good-night!"

He was unwilling to let me go, and stood, holding me out, with a hand on each of my shoulders, as he had done in my own room.

"Daisy," he said with a smile—"for though that's not the name your godfathers and godmothers gave you, it's the name I like best to call you by—and I wish, I wish, I wish you could give it to me!"

"Why, so I can, if I choose," said I.

"Daisy, if anything should ever separate us, you must think of me at my best, old boy. Come! let us make that bargain. Think of me at my best, if circumstances should ever part us."

"You have no best to me, Steerforth," said I, "and no worst. You are always equally loved, and cherished in my heart."

He said, "God bless you, Daisy, and good-night!" We shook hands, and we parted.

I GOT down to Yarmouth in the evening, and went to the inn. It was ten o'clock when I went out. Many of the shops were shut, and the town was dull. When I came to Omer and Joram's, I found the shutters up, but the shop door standing open. As I could obtain a perspective view of Mr. Omer inside, smoking his pipe by the parlor door, I entered, and asked him how he was.

"Why, bless my life and soul!" said Mr. Omer, "how do you find yourself? Take a seat. Smoke not disagreeable, I hope?"

"By no means," said I. "I like it—in somebody else's pipe."

Mr. Omer had made room for me, and placed a chair.

"I am sorry to have heard bad news of Mr. Barkis," said I.

Mr. Omer looked at me with a steady countenance, and shook his head.

"Do you know how he is tonight?" I asked.

"The very question I should have put to you, sir," returned Mr. Omer, "but on account of delicacy. It's one of the drawbacks of our line of business. When a party's ill, we *can't* ask how the party is."

The difficulty had not occurred to me, though on its being mentioned, I recognized it.

205

Mr. Omer, with a very complacent and amiable face, took several puffs in silence; and then said,

"Accordingly we're obleeged, in ascertaining how Barkis goes on, to limit ourselves to Em'ly. She knows what our real objects are. Minnie and Joram have just stepped down to the house, in fact (she's there, after hours, helping her aunt a bit), to ask her how he is to-night; and if you was to please to wait till they come back, they'd give you full partic'lers."

She and her husband came in immediately afterwards. Their report was, that Mr. Barkis was "as bad as bad could be." Hearing this, and learning that Mr. Peggotty was there, I determined to go to the house at once.

I shook hands with Mr. Peggotty, and passed into the kitchen, while he softly closed the door. Little Emily was sitting by the fire, with her hands before her face. Ham was standing near her.

Peggotty took me in her arms, and blessed and thanked me over and over again for being such a comfort to her (that was what she said) in her distress. She then entreated me to come upstairs, sobbing that Mr. Barkis had always liked me and admired me; and that she believed, in case of his coming to himself again, he would brighten up at sight of me, if he could brighten up at any earthly thing.

The probability of his ever doing so appeared to me, when I saw him, to be very small. He was lying with his head and shoulders out of bed, in an uncomfortable attitude, half resting on the box which had cost him so much pain and trouble. I learned that, when he was past creeping out of bed to open it, and past assuring himself of its safety by means of the divining rod I had seen him use, he had required to have it placed on the chair at the bedside, where he had ever since embraced it, night and day. His arm lay on it now. Time and the world were slipping from beneath him, but the box was there; and the last words he had uttered were (in an explanatory tone), "Old clothes!"

"Barkis, my dear!" said Peggotty, almost cheerfully, bending over him, while her brother and I stood at the bed's foot, "here's my dear boy—my dear boy, Master Davy, who brought us together, Barkis! That you sent messages by, you know! Won't you speak to Master Davy?"

He was as mute and senseless as the box, from which his form derived the only expression it had.

"He's a-going out with the tide," said Mr. Peggotty to me, behind his hand.

My eyes were dim, and so were Mr. Peggotty's; but I repeated in a whisper, "With the tide?"

"People can't die, along the coast," said Mr. Peggotty, "except when the tide's pretty nigh out. They can't be born, unless it's pretty nigh in—not properly born, till flood. He's a-going out with the tide. It's ebb at half-arter three, slack water half an hour. If he lives till it turns, he'll hold his own till past the flood, and go out with the next tide."

We remained there, watching him, a long time—hours. What mysterious influence my presence had upon him in that state of his senses, I shall not pretend to say; but when he at last began to wander feebly, it is certain he was muttering about driving me to school.

"He's coming to himself," said Peggotty.

Mr. Peggotty touched me, and whispered with much awe and reverence, "They are both a-going out fast."

"Barkis, my dear!" said Peggotty.

"C. P. Barkis," he cried faintly. "No better woman anywhere!"

"Look! Here's Master Davy!" said Peggotty. For he now opened his eyes.

I was on the point of asking him if he knew me, when he tried to stretch out his arm, and said to me distinctly, with a pleasant smile,

"Barkis is willin'!"

And, it being low water, he went out with the tide.

IT was not difficult for me, on Peggotty's solicitation, to resolve to stay where I was until after the remains of the poor carrier should have made their last journey to Blunderstone. She had long ago bought, out of her own savings, a little piece of ground in our old churchyard near the grave "of her sweet girl," as she always called my mother; and there they were to rest.

I may claim the merit of having originated the suggestion that the will should be looked for in the box. After some search, it was found in the box, at the bottom of a horse's nose-bag; wherein (besides hay) there was discovered an old gold watch, with chain and seals, which Mr. Barkis had worn on his wedding-day, and which had never been seen before or since; a silver tobacco-stopper, in the form of a leg; an imitation lemon, full of minute cups and saucers, which I have some idea Mr. Barkis must have purchased to present to me when I was a child, and afterwards found himself unable to part with; eighty-seven guineas and a half, in guineas and half-guineas; two hundred and ten pounds, in perfectly clean bank-notes; certain receipts for Bank of England stock; an old horseshoe, a bad shilling, a piece of camphor, and an oyster-shell.

His property in money amounted to nearly three thousand pounds. Of this he bequeathed the interest of one thousand to Mr. Peggotty for his life; on his decease, the principal to be equally divided between Peggotty, little Emily, and me, or the survivor or survivors of us, share and share alike. All the rest he died possessed of he bequeathed to Peggotty, whom he left residuary legatee and sole executrix of that his last will and testament.

I felt myself quite a proctor when I read this document aloud with all possible ceremony, and set forth its provisions any number of times to those whom they concerned. I examined the will with the deepest attention, pronounced it perfectly formal in all respects, made a pencil-mark or so in the margin, and thought it rather extraordinary that I knew so much.

In this abstruse pursuit, in making an account for Peggotty of all the property, and in being her adviser on every point, I passed the week before the funeral. My old nurse was to go to London with me next day, on the business of the will. We were all to meet in the old boathouse that night.

Rain was falling heavily by that time, and it was a wild night; but there was a moon behind the clouds, and it was not dark. I was soon within sight of Mr. Peggotty's house, and of the light within it shining through the window. A little floundering across the sand, which was heavy, brought me to the door, and I went in.

"You're first of the lot, Mas'r Davy," said Mr. Peggotty, with a happy face. "Sit ye down, sir. It ain't o' no use saying welcome to you, but you're welcome, kind and hearty."

"Thank you, Mr. Peggotty; I am sure of that.—Well, Peggotty," said I, giving her a kiss, "and how are you, old woman?"

"Ha, ha!" laughed Mr. Peggotty, sitting down beside us, and rubbing his hands in his sense of relief from recent trouble, and in the genuine heartiness of his nature; "there's not a woman in the wureld, sir (as I tell her), that need to feel more easy in her mind than her. She done her dooty by the departed, and the departed know'd it."

Mrs. Gummidge groaned.

"Cheer up, my pretty mawther!" said Mr. Peggotty; "don't be down! Cheer up, for your own self, on'y a little bit, and see if a good deal more doen't come nat'ral!"

"Not to me, Dan'l," returned Mrs. Gummidge: "nothink's nat'ral to me but to be lone and lorn."

"No, no," said Mr. Peggotty, soothing her sorrows. He glanced at the Dutch clock, rose, snuffed the candle, and put it in the window.

"Theer!" said Mr. Peggotty cheerily; "theer we are, Missis Gummidge!" (Mrs. Gummidge slightly groaned)—"lighted up, accordin' to custom!—You're a-wonderin' what that's fur, sir! Well, it's fur our little Em'ly. You see, the path ain't overlight or cheerful arter dark; and when I'm here at the hour she's a-comin' home, I puts the light in the winder. That, you see," said Mr. Peggotty, bending over me with great glee, "meets two objects: she says, says Em'ly, 'Theer's home!' she says; and likewise, says Em'ly, 'My uncle's theer!'—fur if I ain't theer, I never have no light showed."

"You're a baby!" said Peggotty, very fond of him for it, if she thought so.

"Well," returned Mr. Peggotty, standing with his legs pretty wide apart, and rubbing his hands up and down them in his comfortable satisfaction, as he looked alternately at us and at the fire, "I doen't know but I am—not, you see, to look at."

"Not azackly," observed Peggotty.

"Why, this here candle, now!" said Mr. Peggotty, gleefully holding out his hand toward it, "*I* know very well that arter she's married and gone, I shall put that candle theer, just that same as now, pretending I'm expecting of her, like I'm a-doing now. *There's* a babby for you, in the form of a sea porkypine! Right for all that," said Mr. Peggotty, smiting his hands together—"fur here she is!"

It was only Ham. The night should have turned more wet since I came in, for he had a large sou'wester hat on, slouched over his face.

"Wheer's Em'ly?" said Mr. Peggotty.

Ham, who had not moved, said, "Mas'r Davy, will you come out a minute, and see what Em'ly and me has got to show you?"

We went out. As I passed him at the door, I saw, to my astonishment and fright, that he was deadly pale. He pushed me hastily into the open air, and closed the door upon us—only upon us two.

"Ham! what's the matter?"

"Mas'r Davy!——" Oh, for his broken heart, how dreadfully he wept!

I was paralyzed by the sight of such grief. I don't know what I thought, or what I dreaded. I could only look at him.

"Ham! poor, good fellow! for Heaven's sake, tell me what's the matter!"

"My love, Mas'r Davy—the pride and hope of my 'art—her that I'd have died for, and would die for now—she's gone!"

"Gone!"

"Em'ly's run away! Oh, Mas'r Davy, think *how* she's run away, when I pray my good and gracious God to kill her (her that is so dear above all things!) sooner than let her come to ruin and disgrace!"

I saw the door move, and instinctively tried to hold the latch on the outside, to gain a moment's time. It was too late. I remember a great wail and cry, and we all standing in the room—I with a paper in my hand, which Ham had given me; Mr. Peggotty, with his vest torn open, his hair wild, his face and lips quite white, and blood trickling down his bosom (it had sprung from his mouth, I think), looking fixedly at me.

"Read it, sir," he said, in a low, shivering voice. "Slow, please. I don't know as I can understand."

In the midst of the silence of death I read thus, from a blotted letter:

" 'When you, who love me so much better than I ever have deserved, even when my mind was innocent, see this, I shall be far away.' "

" 'I shall be fur away,' " he repeated slowly. "Stop! Em'ly fur away. Well?"

" 'When I leave my dear home—oh, my dear home!—in the morning' "—

the letter bore date on the previous night—

" 'it will be never to come back, unless he brings me back a lady. This will be found at night, many hours after, instead of me. Oh, if you knew how my heart is torn! If even you, that I have wronged so much, that never can forgive me, could only know what I suffer! I am too wicked to write about myself. Oh, take comfort in thinking that I am so bad. Oh, don't remember how affectionate and kind you have all been to me—don't remember we were ever to be married—but try to think as if I died when I was little, and was buried somewhere. Tell uncle that I never loved him half so dear as now. Be his comfort. Love some good girl, that will be what I was once to uncle, and be true to you, and worthy of you, and know no shame but me. God bless all! My parting love to uncle, my last tears, and my last thanks, for uncle!' "

That was all.

He stood, long after I had ceased to read, still looking at me. Slowly, at last he moved his eyes from my face, as if he were waking from a vision, and cast them round the room. Then he said, in a low voice,

"Who's the man? I want to know his name."

Ham glanced at me, and suddenly I felt a shock that struck me back.

"There's a man suspected," said Mr. Peggotty—"who is it?"

"Mas'r Davy!" implored Ham, "go out a bit, and let me tell him what I must. You doen't ought to hear it, sir."

I felt the shock again. I sank down in a chair, and tried to utter some reply; but my tongue was fettered, and my sight was weak.

"I want to know his name!" I heard said, once more.

"For some time past," Ham faltered, "there's been a servant about here, at odd times. There's been a gen'lm'n too. Both of 'em belonged to one another."

Mr. Peggotty stood fixed as before, but now looking at him.

I felt Peggotty's arm round my neck, but I could not have moved if the house had been about to fall upon me.

"A strange chay and hosses was outside town, this morning, on the Norwich road, a'most afore the day broke," Ham went on. "The servant went to it, and come from it, and went to it again. When he went to it again, Em'ly was nigh him. The t'other was inside. He's the man."

"For the Lord's love," said Mr. Peggotty, falling back, and putting out his hand, as if to keep off what he dreaded, "doen't tell me his name's Steerforth!"

"Mas'r Davy," exclaimed Ham, in a broken voice, "it ain't no fault of yourn—and I am far from laying of it to you—but his name is Steerforth, and he's a damned villain!"

Mr. Peggotty uttered no cry, and shed no tear, and moved no more, until he seemed to wake again, all at once, and pulled down his rough coat from its peg in a corner.

"Bear a hand with this! I'm struck of a heap, and can't do it," he said impatiently. "Bear a hand and help me. Well!" when somebody had done so. "Now give me that theer hat!"

Ham asked him whither he was going.

"I'm a-going to seek my niece. I'm a-going to seek my Em'ly. I am a-going, first, to stave in that theer boat, and sink it where I would have drowned *him*, as I'm a livin' soul, if I had had one thought of what was in him," he said wildly, holding out his clenched right hand—"I'd have drowned him, and thought it right!—I'm a-going to seek my niece!"

"Where?" cried Ham, interposing himself before the door.

"Anywhere! I'm a-going to seek my niece through the wureld.

I'm a-going to find my poor niece in her shame, and bring her back. No one stop me! I tell you I'm a-going to seek my niece!"

"No, no!" cried Mrs. Gummidge, coming between them, in a fit of crying. "No, no, Dan'l, not as you are now. Seek her in a little while, my lone lorn Dan'l, and that'll be but right! but not as you are now. Sit ye down, and give me your forgiveness for having ever been a worrit to you, Dan'l—what have my contrairies ever been to this!—and let us speak a word about them times when she was first an orphan, and when Ham was too, and when I was a poor widder woman, and you took me in. It'll soften your poor heart, Dan'l," laying her head upon his shoulder, "and you'll bear your sorrow better; for you know the promise, Dan'l, 'As you have done it unto one of the least of these, you have done it unto me.'"

He was quite passive now; and when I heard him crying, the impulse that had been upon me to go down upon my knees, and ask their pardon for the desolation I had caused, and curse Steerforth, yielded to a better feeling. My overcharged heart found the same relief, and I cried too.

CHAPTER 32 ⚓ THE BEGINNING OF A LONG JOURNEY ◆ ◆ ◆

THE news of what had happened soon spread through the town, insomuch that as I passed along the streets next morning I overheard the people speaking of it at their doors. Many were hard upon her, some few were hard upon him, but toward her second father and her lover there was but one sentiment. Among all kinds of people a respect for them in their distress prevailed, which was full of gentleness and delicacy. The seafaring men kept apart, when those two were seen early, walking with slow steps on the beach, and stood in knots, talking compassionately among themselves.

It was on the beach, close down by the sea, that I found them. It would have been easy to perceive that they had not slept all last night. They looked worn, and I thought Mr. Peggotty's head was bowed more in one night than in all the years I had known him. But they were both as grave and steady as the sea itself.

"We have had a mort of talk, sir," said Mr. Peggotty to me, when we had all three walked a little while in silence, "of what we ought and doen't ought to do. But we see our course now."

I happened to glance at Ham, then looking out to sea upon the distant light, and a frightful thought came into my mind—not that his face was angry, for it was not; I recall nothing but an expression of stern determination in it—that if ever he encountered Steerforth, he would kill him.

"My dooty here, sir," said Mr. Peggotty, "is done. I'm a-going to seek my—" he stopped, and went on in a firmer voice—"I'm a-going to seek her. That's my dooty evermore."

He shook his head when I asked him where he would seek her, and inquired if I were going to London tomorrow? I told him I had not gone today, fearing to lose the chance of being of any service to him; but that I was ready to go when he would.

"I'll go along with you, sir," he rejoined, "if you're agreeable, tomorrow."

We walked again, for a while, in silence.

"Ham," he presently resumed, "he'll hold to his present work, and go and live along with my sister. The old boat yonder——"

"Will you desert the old boat, Mr. Peggotty?" I gently interposed.

"My wishes is, sir, as it shall look, day and night, winter and summer, as it has always looked since she fust know'd it. If ever she should come a-wandering back, I wouldn't have the old place seem to cast her off, you understand, but seem to tempt her to draw nigher to 't."

I could not speak to him in reply, though I tried.

"Every night," said Mr. Peggotty, "as reg'lar as the night comes, the candle must be stood in its old pane of glass, that if ever she should see it, it may seem to say, 'Come back, my child, come back!' If ever there's a knock, Ham (partic'ler a soft knock), arter dark, at your aunt's door, doen't you go nigh it. Let it be her—not you—that sees my fallen child!"

In the morning I was joined by Mr. Peggotty and by my old nurse, and went at an early hour to the coach-office, where Mrs. Gummidge and Ham were waiting to take leave of us.

"Mas'r Davy," Ham whispered, drawing me aside, while Mr. Peggotty was stowing his bag among the luggage, "his life is quite broke up. He doen't know wheer he's going; he doen't know what's afore him; he's bound upon a voyage that'll last, on and off, all the rest of his days, take my wured for't, unless he finds what's he's a-seeking of. I am sure you'll be a friend to him, Mas'r Davy?"

"Trust me, I will indeed," said I, shaking hands with Ham earnestly.

When we got to our journey's end, our first pursuit was to look about for a little lodging for Peggotty, where her brother could have a bed. We were so fortunate as to find one, of a very clean

and cheap description, over a chandler's shop, only two streets removed from me. When we had engaged this domicile, I bought
some cold meat at an eating-house, and took my fellow-travelers
home to tea—a proceeding, I regret to state, which did not meet
with Mrs. Crupp's approval, but quite the contrary. I ought to observe, however, in explanation of that lady's state of mind, that she
was much offended by Peggotty's tucking up her widow's gown
before she had been ten minutes in the place and setting to work
to dust my bedroom. This Mrs. Crupp regarded in the light of a
liberty; and a liberty, she said, was a thing she never allowed.

Mr. Peggotty purposed first seeing Mrs. Steerforth. As I felt
bound to assist him in this, and also to mediate between them, with
the view of sparing the mother's feelings as much as possible, I wrote
to her that night. I told her as mildly as I could what his wrong was,
and what my own share in his injury. I said he was a man in very
common life, but of a most gentle and upright character; and that
I ventured to express a hope that she would not refuse to see him in
his heavy trouble. I mentioned two o'clock in the afternoon as the
hour of our coming, and I sent the letter myself by the first coach
in the morning.

At the appointed time we stood at the door. No Littimer appeared.
The pleasanter face which had replaced his on the occasion of my
last visit answered to our summons, and went before us to the
drawing-room. Mrs. Steerforth was sitting there. Rosa Dartle glided,
as we went in, from another part of the room, and stood behind
her chair.

I saw, directly, in his mother's face, that she knew from himself
what he had done. She sat upright in her arm-chair, with a stately,
immovable, passionless air, that it seemed as if nothing could disturb.
She looked very steadfastly at Mr. Peggotty when he stood before
her, and he looked quite as steadfastly at her. Rosa Dartle's keen
glance comprehended all of us. For some moments not a word was
spoken. She motioned to Mr. Peggotty to be seated. He said, in a
low voice, "I shouldn't feel it nat'ral, ma'am, to sit down in this
house. I'd sooner stand." And this was succeeded by another silence,
which she broke thus,

"I know, with deep regret, what has brought you here. What
do you want of me? What do you ask me to do?"

He put his hat under his arm, and feeling in his breast for Emily's
letter, took it out, unfolded it, and gave it to her.

"Please to read that, ma'am. That's my niece's hand!"

She read it, in the same stately and impassive way—untouched by its contents, as far as I could see—and returned it to him.

"'Unless he brings me back a lady,'" said Mr. Peggotty, tracing out that part with his finger. "I come to know, ma'am, whether he will keep his wured?"

"No," she returned.

"Why not?" said Mr. Peggotty.

"It is impossible. He would disgrace himself. You cannot fail to know that she is far below him."

"Raise her up!" said Mr. Peggotty.

"She is uneducated and ignorant."

"Maybe she's not, maybe she is," said Mr. Peggotty. "*I* think not, ma'am; but I'm no judge of them things. Teach her better!"

"Since you oblige me to speak more plainly, which I am very unwilling to do, her humble connections would render such a thing impossible, if nothing else did."

"Hark to this, ma'am," he returned, slowly and quietly. "You know what it is to love your child. So do I. If she was a hundred times my child, I couldn't love her more. You doen't know what it is to lose your child. I do. All the heaps of riches in the wureld would be nowt to me (if they was mine) to buy her back! But save her from this disgrace, and she shall never be disgraced by us. Not one of us that she's growed up among, not one of us that's lived along with her, and had her for their all in all, these many year, will ever look upon her pritty face again. We'll be content to let her be; we'll be content to think of her, far off, as if she was underneath another sun and sky; we'll be content to trust her to her husband— to her little children, p'raps—and bide the time when all of us shall be alike in quality afore our God!"

The rugged eloquence with which he spoke was not devoid of all effect. She still preserved her proud manner, but there was a touch of softness in her voice as she answered,

"I justify nothing. I make no counter-accusations. But I am sorry to repeat, it is impossible. Such a marriage would irretrievably blight my son's career and ruin his prospects. Nothing is more certain than that it never can take place, and never will. If there is any other compensation—"

"I am looking at the likeness of the face," interrupted Mr. Peggotty, with a steady but a kindling eye, "that has looked at me, in my home, at my fireside, in my boat—wheer not?—smiling and friendly, when it was so treacherous that I go half wild when I think of it. If the likeness of that face don't turn to burning fire at the thought of offering money to me for my child's blight and ruin, it's as bad. I doen't know, being a lady's, but what it's worse."

She changed now, in a moment. An angry flush overspread her features, and she said, in an intolerant manner, grasping the arm-chair tightly with her hands,

"What compensation can you make to *me* for opening such a pit between me and my son? What is your love to mine? What is your separation to ours?"

Miss Dartle softly touched her, and bent down her head to whisper, but she would not hear a word.

"No, Rosa, not a word! Let the man listen to what I say! My son, who has been the object of my life, to whom its every thought has been devoted, whom I have gratified from a child in every wish, from whom I have had no separate existence since his birth—to take up in a moment with a miserable girl, and avoid me! To repay my confidence with systematic deception, for her sake, and quit me for her! To set this wretched fancy against his mother's claims upon his duty, love, respect, gratitude—claims that every day and hour of his life should have strengthened into ties that nothing could be proof against! Is this no injury?"

Again Rosa Dartle tried to soothe her; again ineffectually.

"I say, Rosa, not a word! If he can stake his all upon the lightest object, I can stake my all upon a greater purpose. Let him go where he will, with the means that my love has secured to him! Does he think to reduce me by long absence? He knows his mother very little if he does. Let him put away his whim now, and he is welcome back. Let him not put her away now, and he never shall come near me, living or dying, while I can raise my hand to make a sign against it, unless, being rid of her forever, he comes humbly to me and begs for my forgiveness. This is my right. This is the acknowledgment I *will have*. This is the separation that there is between us! And is this," she added, looking at her visitor with the proud intolerant air with which she had begun, "no injury?"

While I heard and saw the mother as she said these words, I seemed to hear and see the son defying them. All that I had ever seen in him of an unyielding, wilful spirit, I saw in her. She rose with an air of dignity to leave the room, when Mr. Peggotty signified that it was needless. With this we departed, leaving her standing by her elbow-chair, a picture of a noble presence and a handsome face.

We had, on our way out, to cross a paved hall, with glass sides and roof, over which a vine was trained. Its leaves and shoots were green then, and the day being sunny a pair of glass doors leading to the garden were thrown open. Rosa Dartle, entering this way with a noiseless step, when we were close to them, addressed herself to me.

"You do well," she said, "indeed, to bring this fellow here!"

Such a concentration of rage and scorn as darkened her face, and flashed in her jet-black eyes, I could not have thought compressible even into that face. The scar made by the hammer was, as usual in this excited state of her features, strongly marked. When the throbbing I had seen before came into it as I looked at her, she absolutely lifted up her hand and struck it.

"This is a fellow," she said, "to champion and bring here, is he not? You are a true man!"

"Miss Dartle," I returned, "you are surely not so unjust as to condemn *me!*"

"Why do you bring division between these two mad creatures?" she returned. "Don't you know that they are both mad with their own self-will and pride?"

"Is it my doing?" I returned.

"Is it your doing?" she retorted. "Why do you bring this man here?"

"He is a deeply injured man, Miss Dartle," I replied. "You may not know it."

"I know that James Steerforth," she said, with her hand on her bosom, as if to prevent the storm that was raging there from being loud, "has a false, corrupt heart, and is a traitor. But what need I know or care about this fellow, and his common niece?"

"Miss Dartle," I returned, "you deepen the injury. It is sufficient already. I will only say, at parting, that you do him a great wrong."

"I do him no wrong," she returned. "They are a depraved, worthless set. I would have her whipped!"

Mr. Peggotty passed on, without a word, and went out at the door.

"Oh, shame, Miss Dartle! shame!" I said indignantly. "How can you bear to trample on his undeserved affliction!"

"I would trample on them all," she answered. "I would have his house pulled down. I would have her branded on the face, dressed in rags, and cast out in the streets to starve. If I had the power to sit in judgment on her, I would see it done. See it done? I would do it! I detest her. If I ever could reproach her with her infamous condition, I would go anywhere to do so. If I could hunt her to her grave, I would. If there was any word of comfort that would be a solace to her in her dying hour, and only I possessed it, I wouldn't part with it for life itself."

The mere vehemence of her words can convey, I am sensible, but a weak impression of the passion by which she was possessed, and which made itself articulate in her whole figure, though her voice, instead of being raised, was lower than usual. I have seen passion in many forms, but I have never seen it in such a form as that.

When I joined Mr. Peggotty, he was walking slowly and thought-fully down the hill. He told me, as soon as I came up with him, that having now discharged his mind of what he had purposed doing in London, he meant "to set out on his travels" that night. I asked him where he meant to go. He only answered, "I'm a-going, sir, to seek my niece."

He accepted, from his sister's stock of ready money, a small sum on account of his legacy; barely enough, I should have thought, to keep him for a month. He promised to communicate with me when anything befell him; and he slung his bag about him, took his hat and stick, and bade us both "Good-bye!"

All this time I had gone on loving Dora harder than ever. Her idea was my refuge in disappointment and distress, and made some amends to me even for the loss of my friend. If I may so express it, I was steeped in Dora. I was not merely over head and ears in love with her, but I was saturated through and through.

Peggotty was strongly interested, but I could not get her into my view of the case at all. She was audaciously prejudiced in my favor, and quite unable to understand why I should have any misgivings, or be low-spirited about it. "The young lady might think herself well off," she observed, "to have such a beau. And as to her pa," she said, "what *did* the gentleman expect, for gracious sake!"

I observed, however, that Mr. Spenlow's proctorial gown and stiff cravat took Peggotty down a little, and inspired her with a greater reverence for the man who was gradually becoming more and more etherealized in my eyes every day. Peggotty's business, which was what we used to call "common-form business" in the Commons (and very light and lucrative the common-form business was), being settled, I took her down to the office one morning to pay her bill. Mr. Spenlow, settling his chin in his cravat and rubbing it softly, went over the items with a deprecatory air—as if it were all Jorkins' doing.

"Yes," he said; "that's right—quite right. I should have been extremely happy, Copperfield, to have limited these charges to the actual expenditure out of pocket, but it is an irksome incident in my professional life that I am not at liberty to consult my own wishes. I have a partner—Mr. Jorkins."

As he said this with a gentle melancholy, which was the next thing to making no charge at all, I expressed my acknowledgments on Peggotty's behalf, and paid Tiffey in bank-notes. Peggotty then retired to her lodging, and Mr. Spenlow and I went into court, where we had a divorce suit coming on, under an ingenious little statute (repealed now, I believe, but in virtue of which I have seen several marriages annulled), of which the merits were these. The husband, whose name was Thomas Benjamin, had taken out his marriage licence as Thomas only, suppressing the Benjamin in case he should not find himself as comfortable as he expected. *Not* finding himself as comfortable as he expected, or being a little fatigued with his wife, poor fellow, he now came forward, by a friend, after being married a year or two, and declared that his name was Thomas Benjamin, and therefore he was not married at all. Which the court confirmed, to his great satisfaction.

I must say that I had my doubts about the strict justice of this, but Mr. Spenlow argued the matter with me. He said, Look at the world; there was good and evil in that. Look at the ecclesiastical law; there was good and evil in *that*. It was all part of a system. Very good. There you were!

Mr. Spenlow and I falling into this conversation, prolonged it and our saunter to and fro, until we diverged into general topics. And so it came about, in the end, that Mr. Spenlow told me this day week was Dora's birthday, and he would be glad if I would come down and join a little picnic on the occasion. I went out of my senses immediately; became a mere driveler next day, on receipt of a little lace-edged sheet of note-paper, "Favored by papa—to remind"; and passed the intervening period in a state of dotage.

I think I committed every possible absurdity in the way of preparation for this blessed event. I turn hot when I remember the cravat I bought. My boots might be placed in any collection of instruments of torture. I provided, and sent down by the Norwood coach the night before, a delicate little hamper, amounting in itself, I thought, almost to a declaration: there were crackers in it, with the tenderest mottoes that could be got for money. At six in the morning I was in Covent Garden Market, buying a bouquet for

Dora; at ten I was on horseback (I hired a gallant grey for the occasion), with the bouquet in my hat, to keep it fresh, trotting down to Norwood.

I suppose that when I saw Dora in the garden, and pretended not to see her, and rode past the house pretending to be anxiously looking for it, I committed two small fooleries which other young gentlemen in my circumstance might have committed, because they came so very natural to me. But, oh! when I *did* find the house, and *did* dismount at the garden gate, and drag those stony-hearted boots across the lawn to Dora sitting on a garden seat under a lilac tree, what a spectacle she was upon that beautiful morning, among the butterflies, in a white chip-bonnet and a dress of celestial blue!

There was a young lady with her—comparatively stricken in years—almost twenty, I should say. Her name was Miss Mills, and Dora called her Julia. She was the bosom friend of Dora. Happy Miss Mills!

Jip was there, and Jip *would* bark at me again. When I presented my bouquet, he gnashed his teeth with jealousy. Well he might! If he had the least idea how I adored his mistress, well he might!

"Oh, thank you, Mr. Copperfield! What dear flowers!" said Dora.

I had had an intention of saying (and had been studying the best form of words for three miles) that I thought them beautiful before I saw them so near *her*. But I couldn't manage it; she was too bewildering. To see her lay the flowers against her little dimpled chin was to lose all presence of mind and power of language in a feeble ecstasy. I wonder I didn't say, "Kill me, if you have a heart, Miss Mills. Let me die here!"

I learnt that Miss Mills had had her trials in the course of a chequered existence; Miss Mills having been unhappy in a misplaced affection, and being understood to have retired from the world on her awful stock of experience, but still to take a calm interest in the unblighted hopes and loves of youth.

But now Mr. Spenlow came out of the house, and we all walked from the lawn toward the carriage, which was getting ready.

I don't know how long we were going, and to this hour I know as little where we went. It was a green spot, on a hill, carpeted with soft turf. There were shady trees, and heather, and, as far as the eye could see, a rich landscape.

It was a trying thing to find people here, waiting for us; and my jealousy, even of the ladies, knew no bounds. But all of my own sex—especially one impostor, three or four years my elder, with

223

a red whisker, on which he established an amount of presumption not to be endured—were my mortal foes.

We all unpacked our baskets, and employed ourselves in getting dinner ready. Red Whisker pretended he could make a salad (which I don't believe), and obtruded himself on public notice. Some of the young ladies washed the lettuces for him, and sliced them under his directions. Dora was among these. By-and-by I saw him, with the majority of a lobster on his plate, eating his dinner at the feet of Dora!

I have but an indistinct idea of what happened for some time after this baleful object presented itself to my view. I was very merry, I know; but it was hollow merriment. I attached myself to a young creature in pink, with little eyes, and flirted with her desperately. She received my attentions with favor; but whether on my account solely, or because she had any designs on Red Whisker, I can't say. I caught Dora's eye as I bowed to her, and I thought it looked appealing; but it looked at me over the head of Red Whisker, and I was adamant.

There was a general breaking up of the party while the remnants of the dinner were being put away; and I strolled off by myself among the trees, in a raging and remorseful state. I was debating whether I should pretend that I was not well, and fly—I don't know where—upon my gallant grey, when Dora and Miss Mills met me.

"Mr. Copperfield," said Miss Mills, "you are dull."

I begged her pardon. Not at all.

"And, Dora," said Miss Mills, "*you* are dull."

Oh, dear, no! not in the least.

"Mr. Copperfield and Dora," said Miss Mills, with an almost venerable air, "enough of this. Do not allow a trivial misunderstanding to wither the blossoms of spring, which, once put forth and blighted, cannot be renewed. I speak," said Miss Mills, "from experience of the past—the remote, irrevocable past. The gushing fountains which sparkle in the sun must not be stopped in mere caprice; the oasis in the desert of Sahara must not be plucked up idly."

I hardly knew what I did, I was burning all over to that extraordinary extent; but I took Dora's little hand and kissed it—and she let me! I kissed Miss Mills's hand; and we all seemed, to my thinking, to go straight up to the seventh heaven.

We did not come down again; we stayed up there all the evening. At first we strayed to and fro among the trees, I with Dora's shy arm drawn through mine; but, much too soon, we heard the others laughing and talking, and calling, "Where's Dora?" So we went back, and they wanted Dora to sing. Red Whisker would have got the guitar-case out of the carriage; but Dora told him nobody knew where it was but I. So Red Whisker was done for in a moment; and *I* got it, and *I* unlocked it, and *I* took the guitar out, and *I* sat by her, and *I* held her handkerchief and gloves, and *I* drank in every note of her dear voice, and she sang to *me* who loved her; and all the others might applaud as much as they liked, but they had nothing to do with it!

I was happier than ever when the party broke up, and the other people, defeated Red Whisker and all, went their several ways, and we went ours through the still evening and the dying light, with sweet scents rising up around us. I rode by the side and talked to Dora. She admired my horse, and patted him (oh, what a dear little hand it looked upon a horse!); and her shawl would not keep right, and now and then I drew it round her with my arm; and I even fancied that Jip began to see how it was, and to understand that he must make up his mind to be friends with me.

"Mr. Copperfield," said Miss Mills, "come to this side of the carriage a moment—if you can spare a moment. I want to speak to you." Behold me, on my gallant grey, bending at the side of Miss Mills, with my hand upon the carriage door!

"Dora is coming to stay with me. She is coming home with me the day after tomorrow. If you would like to call, I am sure papa would be happy to see you."

Then Miss Mills benignantly dismissed me, saying, "Go back to Dora!" and I went; and Dora leaned out of the carriage to talk to me, and we talked all the rest of the way.

When I awoke next morning, I was resolute to declare my passion to Dora, and know my fate. I passed three days in a luxury of wretchedness, torturing myself by putting every conceivable variety of discouraging construction on all that ever had taken place between Dora and me. At last, arrayed for the purpose at a vast expense, I went to Miss Mills's, fraught with a declaration.

Mr. Mills was not at home. I did not expect he would be. Nobody wanted *him*. Miss Mills was at home. Miss Mills would do.

I was shown into a room upstairs, where Miss Mills and Dora were. Jip was there. Miss Mills was copying music and Dora was painting flowers. What were my feelings when I recognized my own flowers—the identical Covent Garden Market purchase!

Miss Mills was very glad to see me, and very sorry her papa was not at home, though I thought we all bore that with fortitude. Miss Mills was conversational for a few minutes, and then, laying down her pen, got up, and left the room.

I began to think I would put it off till tomorrow.

"I hope your poor horse was not tired when he got home at night," said Dora, lifting up her beautiful eyes. "It was a long way for him."

I began to think I would do it today.

"It was a long way for *him*," said I, "for *he* had nothing to up-hold him on the journey."

"Wasn't he fed, poor thing?" asked Dora.

I began to think I would put it off till tomorrow.

"Ye—yes," I said, "he was well taken care of. I mean he had not the unutterable happiness that I had in being so near you."

Dora bent her head over her drawing, and said, after a little while —I had sat, in the interval, in a burning fever, and with my legs in a very rigid state—

"You didn't seem to be sensible of that happiness yourself, at one time of the day."

I saw now that I was in for it, and it must be done on the spot.

"You didn't care for that happiness in the least," said Dora, slightly raising her eyebrows, and shaking her head, "when you were sitting by Miss Kitt."

Kitt, I should observe, was the name of the creature in pink, with the little eyes.

"Though certainly I don't know why you should," said Dora, "or why you should call it a happiness at all. But of course you don't mean what you say. And I am sure no one doubts your being at liberty to do whatever you like.—Jip, you naughty boy, come here!"

I don't know how I did it. I did it in a moment. I intercepted Jip. I had Dora in my arms. I was full of eloquence. I never stopped for a word. I told her how I loved her. I told her I should die without her. I told her that I idolized and worshiped her. Jip barked madly all the time.

When Dora hung her head and cried, and trembled, my eloquence increased so much the more. If she would like me to die for her, she had but to say the word, and I was ready. Life without Dora's love was not a thing to have on any terms. I couldn't bear it, and I wouldn't. I had loved her every minute, day and night,

226

since I first saw her. I loved her at that minute to distraction. I should always love her, every minute, to distraction. Lovers had loved before, and lovers would love again; but no lover had ever loved, might, could, would, or should ever love, as I loved Dora. The more I raved, the more Jip barked. Each of us, in his own way, got more mad every moment.

Well, well! Dora and I were sitting on the sofa by-and-by, quiet enough, and Jip was lying in her lap, winking peacefully at me. It was off my mind. I was in a state of perfect rapture. Dora and I were engaged.

I suppose we had some notion that this was to end in marriage. We must have had some, because Dora stipulated that we were never to be married without her papa's consent. But, in our youthful ecstasy, I don't think that we really looked before us or behind us, or had any aspiration beyond the ignorant present. We were to keep our secret from Mr. Spenlow; but I am sure the idea never entered my head, then, that there was anything dishonorable in that.

What an idle time it was! What an unsubstantial, happy, foolish time it was!

When I measured Dora's finger for a ring that was to be made of forget-me-nots; and when the jeweler, to whom I took the measure, found me out, and laughed over his order book, and charged me anything he liked for the pretty little toy with its blue stones!

When we had those meetings in the garden of the square, and sat within the dingy summer-house, so happy, that I love the London sparrows to this hour, for nothing else!

When we had our first great quarrel (within a week of our betrothal), and when Dora sent me back the ring, enclosed in a despairing cocked-hat note, wherein she used the terrible expression that "our love had begun in folly, and ended in madness!"

When we cried, and made it up, and arranged a plan of correspondence through Miss Mills, always to comprehend at least one letter on each side every day!

What an idle time! What an unsubstantial, happy, foolish time! Of all the times of mine that Time has in his grip, there is none that in one retrospection I can smile at half so much, and think of half so tenderly.

CHAPTER 34 ❧ MY AUNT ASTONISHES ME · · ·

MRS. CRUPP had resigned everything appertaining to her office (the salary excepted), until Peggotty should cease to present herself. Mrs. Crupp, after holding divers conversations respecting Peggotty, in a very high-pitched voice, on the staircase—with some invisible Familiar, it would appear, for corporeally speaking she was quite alone at those times—addressed a letter to me, developing her views. Beginning it with that statement of universal application, which fitted every occurrence of her life—namely, that she was a mother herself—she went on to inform me that she had once seen very different days, but that at all periods of her existence she had had a constitutional objection to spies, intruders, and informers. She named no names, she said—let them the cap fitted wear it; but spies, intruders, and informers, especially in widders' weeds (this clause was underlined), she had ever accustomed herself to look down upon. If a gentleman was the victim of spies, intruders, and informers (but still naming no names), that was his own pleasure. He had a right to please himself; so let him do. All that she, Mrs. Crupp, stipulated for, was, that she should not be "brought in contract" with such persons. Therefore she begged to be excused from any further attendance on the top set, until things were as they formerly was, and as they could be wished to be; and further mentioned that her little book would be found upon the breakfast-table every Saturday morning, when she requested an immediate settlement of the same, with the benevolent view of saving trouble, "and an ill-conwenience," to all parties.

After this, Mrs. Crupp confined herself to making pitfalls on the stairs, principally with pitchers, and endeavoring to delude Peggotty into breaking her legs. I found it rather harassing to live in this state of siege, but was too much afraid of Mrs. Crupp to see any way out of it.

"My dear Copperfield," cried Traddles, appearing at my door in spite of all these obstacles, "how do you do?"

"My dear Traddles," said I, "I am delighted to see you at last. I have been so much engaged——"

"Yes, yes, I know," said Traddles—"of course. Yours lives in London, I think?"

"What did you say?"

"She—excuse me—Miss D., you know," said Traddles, coloring in his great delicacy, "lives in London, I believe?"

"Oh, yes. Near London."

"Mine, perhaps you recollect," said Traddles, with a serious look, "lives down in Devonshire—one of ten. Consequently, I am not so much engaged as you—in that sense."

"I wonder you can bear," I returned, "to see her so seldom."

"Hah!" said Traddles thoughtfully. "It does seem a wonder. I suppose it is, Copperfield, because there's no help for it. She is always forgetting herself, and taking care of the other nine."

"Is she the eldest?" I inquired.

"Oh dear, no," said Traddles. "The eldest is a Beauty."

He saw, I suppose, that I could not help smiling at the simplicity of this reply; and added, with a smile upon his own ingenuous face,

"Not, of course, but that my Sophy—pretty name, Copperfield, I always think."

"Very pretty!" said I.

"Not, of course, but that Sophy is beautiful too in my eyes, and would be one of the dearest girls that ever was, in anybody's eyes (I should think). But when I say the eldest is a Beauty, I mean she really is a"—he seemed to be describing clouds about himself with both hands—"Splendid, you know," said Traddles energetically.

"Indeed!" said I.

"Oh, I assure you," said Traddles, "something very uncommon, indeed! Then, you know, being formed for society and admiration, and not being able to enjoy much of it in consequence of their limited means, she naturally gets a little irritable and exacting sometimes. Sophy puts her in good humor!"

"Is Sophy the youngest?" I hazarded.

"Oh dear, no!" said Traddles, stroking his chin. "The two youngest are only nine and ten. Sophy educates 'em."

"The second daughter, perhaps?" I hazarded.

"No," said Traddles. "Sarah's the second. Sarah has something the matter with her spine, poor girl. The malady will wear out by-and-by, the doctors say; but in the meantime she has to lie down for a twelvemonth. Sophy nurses her. Sophy's the fourth."

"Is the mother living?" I inquired.

"Oh, yes," said Traddles, "she is alive. She is a very superior woman indeed; but the damp country is not adapted to her constitution, and—in fact, she has lost the use of her limbs."

"Dear me!" said I.

"Very sad, is it not?" returned Traddles. "But in a merely domestic view it is not so bad as it might be, because Sophy takes her place. She is quite as much a mother *to* her mother, as she is to the other nine."

I felt the greatest admiration for the virtues of this young lady; and to prevent Traddles from being imposed upon, to the detriment of their joint prospects in life, I inquired how Mr. Micawber was.

"He is quite well, Copperfield, thank you," said Traddles. "I am not living with him at present."

"No?"

"No. You see the truth is," said Traddles, in a whisper, "he has changed his name to Mortimer, in consequence of his temporary embarrassments; and he don't come out till after dark—and then in spectacles. There was an execution put into our house for rent. Mrs. Micawber was in such a dreadful state that I really couldn't resist giving my name to that second bill we spoke of here. You may imagine how delightful it was to my feelings, Copperfield, to see the matter settled with it, and Mrs. Micawber recover her spirits."

"Hum!" said I.

"Not that her happiness was of long duration," pursued Traddles, "for, unfortunately, within a week another execution came in. It broke up the establishment. I have been living in a furnished apartment since then, and the Mortimers have been very private indeed.

I hope you won't think it selfish, Copperfield, if I mention that the broker carried off my little round table with the marble top, and Sophy's flowerpot and stand?"

"What a hard thing!" I exclaimed indignantly.

"It was a——it was a pull," said Traddles, with his usual wince at that expression. "I don't mention it reproachfully, however, but with a motive. The fact is, Copperfield, I was unable to repurchase them at the time of their seizure: in the first place, because the broker, having an idea that I wanted them, ran the price up to an extravagant extent; and, in the second place, because I—hadn't any money. What has occurred to me, having now the money, is, that perhaps you wouldn't object to ask that good nurse of yours to come with me to the shop and make the best bargain for them, as if they were for herself, that she can!"

I told him that my old nurse would be delighted to assist him, and that we would all three take the field together, but on one condition. That condition was, that he should make a solemn resolution to grant no more loans of his name, or anything else, to Mr. Micawber.

"My dear Copperfield," said Traddles, "I have already done so, because I begin to feel that I have not only been inconsiderate, but that I have been positively unjust to Sophy. My word being passed to myself, there is no longer any apprehension; but I pledge it to you, too, with the greatest readiness. That first unlucky obligation I have paid. I have no doubt Mr. Micawber would have paid it if he could, but he could not. One thing I ought to mention, which I like very much in Mr. Micawber, Copperfield. It refers to the second obligation, which is not yet due. He don't tell me that it *is* provided for, but he says it *will be*. Now, I think there is something very fair and honest about that!"

I was unwilling to damp my good friend's confidence, and therefore assented. After a little further conversation, we went round to the chandler's shop, to enlist Peggotty. She bought the property on tolerably easy terms, and Traddles was transported with pleasure. He overwhelmed her with thanks, and went his way up Tottenham Court Road, with one of the most delighted expressions of countenance I ever saw.

We then turned back toward my chambers. What was my amazement to find, of all people upon earth, my aunt there, and Mr. Dick!—my aunt sitting on a quantity of luggage, with her two birds before her, and her cat on her knee, like a female Robinson

Crusoe, drinking tea; Mr. Dick leaning thoughtfully on a great kite, such as we had often been out together to fly, with more luggage piled about him!

"My dear aunt!" cried I. "Why, what an unexpected pleasure!"

We cordially embraced, and Mr. Dick and I cordially shook hands; and Mrs. Crupp, who was busy making tea, and could not be too attentive, cordially said she had knowed well as Mr. Copperfull would have his heart in his mouth, when he see his dear relations.

"Holloa!" said my aunt, to Peggotty, who quailed before her awful presence; "how are *you?*"

"You remember my aunt, Peggotty?" said I.

"For the love of goodness, child," exclaimed my aunt, "don't call the woman by that South Sea Island name! If she married and got rid of it, which was the best thing she could do, why don't you give her the benefit of the change? What's your name now—P?" said my aunt, as a compromise for the obnoxious appellation.

"Barkis, ma'am," said Peggotty, with a curtsy.

"Well, that's human," said my aunt. "It sounds less as if you wanted a missionary. How d'ye do, Barkis? I hope you're well?"

Encouraged by these gracious words, and by my aunt's extending her hand, Barkis came forward and took the hand, and curtsied her acknowledgments.

"We are older than we were, I see," said my aunt. "We have only met each other once before, you know. A nice business we made of it then!—Trot, my dear, another cup."

I handed it dutifully to my aunt, who was in her usual inflexible state of figure, and ventured a remonstrance with her on the subject of her sitting on a box.

"Let me draw the sofa here, or the easy-chair, aunt," said I. "Why should you be so uncomfortable?"

"Thank you, Trot," replied my aunt, "I prefer to sit upon my property." Here my aunt looked hard at Mrs. Crupp, and observed, "We needn't trouble you to wait, ma'am."

"Shall I put a little more tea in the pot afore I go, ma'am?" said Mrs. Crupp.

"No, I thank you, ma'am," replied my aunt.

"Would you let me fetch another pat of butter, ma'am?" said Mrs. Crupp. "Or would you be persuaded to try a new-laid hegg?

"Em'ly's run away! Oh, Mas'r Davy!" Ham

exclaimed.

or should I brile a rasher?—Ain't there nothing I could do for your dear aunt, Mr. Copperfull?"

"Nothing, ma'am," returned my aunt. "I shall do very well, I thank you."

I knew my aunt sufficiently well to know that she had something of importance on her mind, and that there was far more matter in this arrival than a stranger might have supposed. As I knew she would only speak in her own good time, I sat down near her, and spoke to the birds, and played with the cat, and was as easy as I could be.

"Trot," said my aunt at last, when she had finished her tea, and carefully smoothed down her dress, and wiped her lips—"you needn't go, Barkis!—Trot, have you got to be firm and self-reliant?"

"I hope so, aunt."

"What do you think?" inquired Miss Betsey.

"I think so, aunt."

"Then why, my love," said my aunt, looking earnestly at me, "why do you think I prefer to sit upon this property of mine to-night?"

I shook my head, unable to guess.

"Because," said my aunt, "it's all I have. Because I'm ruined, my dear!"

If the house, and every one of us, had tumbled out into the river together, I could hardly have received a greater shock.

"Dick knows it," said my aunt, laying her hand calmly on my shoulder. "I am ruined, my dear Trot! All I have in the world is in this room, except the cottage; and that I have left Janet to let.—Barkis, I want to get a bed for this gentleman tonight.—To save expense, perhaps you can make up something here for myself. Anything will do. It's only for tonight. We'll talk about this, more, to-morrow."

I was roused from my amazement, and concern for her—I am sure, for her—by her falling on my neck for a moment, and crying that she only grieved for me. In another moment she suppressed this emotion, and said with an aspect more triumphant than dejected,

"We must meet reverses boldly, and not suffer them to frighten us, my dear. We must learn to act the play out. We must live misfortune down, Trot!"

233

As soon as I could recover my presence of mind, I proposed to Mr. Dick to take possession of the bed which Mr. Peggotty had lately vacated. I tried to ascertain whether Mr. Dick had any understanding of the causes of this sudden and great change in my aunt's affairs. As I might have expected, he had none at all. The only account he could give of it was, that my aunt had said to him, the day before yesterday, "Now, Dick, are you really and truly the philosopher I take you for?" That then he had said, Yes, he hoped so. That then my aunt had said, "Dick, I am ruined." That then he had said, "Oh, indeed!" That then my aunt had praised him highly, which he was very glad of. And that then they had come to me, and had had bottled porter and sandwiches on the road.

My aunt was in a composed frame of mind, which was a lesson to all of us—to me, I am sure. She was extremely gracious to Peggotty, except when I inadvertently called her by that name; and, strange as I knew she felt in London, appeared quite at home.

"Trot," said she, when she saw me compounding her usual night draft. "I don't care for strange faces in general, but I rather like that

Barkis of yours, do you know!"

"It's better than a hundred pounds to hear you say so!" said I.

"It's a most extraordinary world," observed my aunt, rubbing her nose. "How that woman ever got into it with that name is unaccountable to me. It would be much more easy to be born a Jackson, or something of that sort, one would think."

"Perhaps she thinks so too; it's not her fault," said I.

"I suppose not," returned my aunt, rather grudging the admission; "but it's very aggravating. However, she's Barkis *now*. That's some comfort. Barkis is uncommonly fond of you, Trot."

"There is nothing she would leave undone to prove it," said I.

"Nothing, I believe," returned my aunt. "Here the poor fool has been begging and praying about handing over some of her money— because she has got too much of it! A simpleton!"

My aunt's tears of pleasure were positively trickling down into the warm ale.

"She's the most ridiculous creature that ever was born," said my aunt. "I knew, from the first moment when I saw her with that poor dear blessed baby of a mother of yours, that she was the most ridiculous of mortals. But there are good points in Barkis!"

Affecting to laugh, she got an opportunity of putting her hand to her eyes. Having availed herself of it, she resumed her toast and her discourse.

"O Trot, Trot! And so you fancy yourself in love, do you?"

"Fancy, aunt!" I exclaimed, as red as I could be. "I adore her with my whole soul!"

"Dora, indeed!" returned my aunt. "And you mean to say the little thing is very fascinating, I suppose?"

"My dear aunt," I replied, "no one can form the least idea what she is."

"Ah! And not silly?" said my aunt.

"Silly, aunt!"

I seriously believe it had never once entered my head for a single moment to consider whether she was or not. I resented the idea, of course; but I was in a manner struck by it, as a new one altogether.

"Not light-headed?" said my aunt.

"Light-headed, aunt!" I could only repeat this daring speculation with the same kind of feeling with which I had repeated the preceding question.

"Well, well," said my aunt, "I only ask. I don't depreciate her. Poor little couple! And so you think you were formed for one another, and are to go through a party-supper-table kind of life, like two pretty pieces of confectionery, do you, Trot?"

She asked me this so kindly, and with such a gentle air, half playful and half sorrowful, that I was quite touched.

"We are young and inexperienced, aunt, I know," I replied, "and I dare say we say and think a good deal that is rather foolish; but we love one another truly, I am sure. If I thought Dora could ever love anybody else, or cease to love me, or that I could ever love anybody else, or cease to love her, I don't know what I should do —go out of my mind, I think."

"Ah, Trot!" said my aunt, shaking her head and smiling gravely, "blind, blind, blind!"

This was not upon the whole very comforting to a rapturous lover; but I was mindful of her being fatigued. So I thanked her ardently for this mark of her affection, and for all her other kindnesses toward me; and after a tender good-night, she took her nightcap into my bedroom.

How miserable I was when I lay down. How I thought and thought about my being poor in Mr. Spenlow's eyes; about the chivalrous necessity of telling Dora what my worldly condition was, and releasing her from her engagement if she thought fit; about how I should contrive to live during the long term of my articles, when I was earning nothing; about doing something to assist my aunt, and seeing no way of doing anything; about coming down to have no money in my pocket, and to wear a shabby coat, and to be able to carry Dora no little presents, and to ride no gallant greys, and to show myself in no agreeable light! Sordid and selfish as I knew it was, and as I tortured myself by knowing that it was, to let my mind run on my own distress so much, I was so devoted to Dora that I could not help it. I knew that it was base in me not to think more of my aunt, and less of myself; but, so far, selfishness was inseparable from Dora, and I could not put Dora on one side for any mortal creature. How exceedingly miserable I was that night!

I arrived at the office so soon that I had half an hour's loitering about the Commons until Mr. Spenlow came in, crisp and curly.

"How are you, Copperfield?" said he. "Fine morning!"

"Beautiful morning, sir," said I. "Could I say a word to you before you go into court?"

"By all means," said he. "Come into my room."

I followed him into his room, and he began putting on his gown, and touching himself up before a little glass he had hanging inside a closet door.

"I am sorry to say," said I, "that I have some rather disheartening intelligence from my aunt."

"No!" said he. "Dear me! Not paralysis, I hope?"

"It has no reference to her health, sir," I replied. "She has met with some large losses—in fact, she has very little left indeed."

"You as-tound me, Copperfield!" cried Mr. Spenlow.

I shook my head. "Indeed, sir," said I, "her affairs are so changed, that I wished to ask you whether it would be possible—at a sacrifice on our part of some portion of the premium, of course"—(I put in this on the spur of the moment, warned by the blank expression of his face)—"to cancel my articles?"

What it cost me to make this proposal, nobody knows. It was like asking, as a favor, to be sentenced to transportation from Dora.

"To cancel your articles, Copperfield? Cancel?"

I explained, with tolerable firmness, that I really did not know where my means of subsistence were to come from, unless I could earn them for myself. I had no fear for the future, I said—and I laid great emphasis on that, as if to imply that I should still be decidedly eligible for a son-in-law one of these days—but, for the present, I was thrown upon my own resources.

"I am extremely sorry to hear this, Copperfield," said Mr. Spenlow—"extremely sorry. It is not usual to cancel articles for any such reason. It is not a professional course of proceeding. It is not a convenient precedent at all—far from it. At the same time——"

"You are very good, sir," I murmured, anticipating a concession.

"Not at all; don't mention it," said Mr. Spenlow. "At the same time, I was going to say, if it had been my lot to have my hands unfettered—if I had not a partner—Mr. Jorkins——"

My hopes were dashed in a moment, but I made another effort.

"Do you think, sir," said I, "if I were to mention it to Mr. Jorkins——"

Mr. Spenlow shook his head discouragingly. "Heaven forbid, Copperfield," he replied, "that I should do any man an injustice!—still less Mr. Jorkins. But I know my partner, Copperfield. Mr. Jorkins is *not* a man to respond to a proposition of this peculiar nature. Mr. Jorkins is very difficult to move from the beaten track. You know what he is!"

I am sure I knew nothing about him, except that he had originally been alone in the business, and now lived by himself in a house near

Montagu Square, which was fearfully in want of painting; that he came very late of a day, and went away very early; that he never appeared to be consulted about anything; and that he had a dingy little black-hole of his own upstairs, where no business was ever done, and where there was a yellow old cartridge-paper pad upon his desk, unsoiled by ink, and reported to be twenty years of age.

"Would you object to my mentioning it to him, sir?" I asked.

"By no means," said Mr. Spenlow. "But I have some experience of Mr. Jorkins, Copperfield. I wish it were otherwise, for I should be happy to meet your views in any respect. I cannot have the least objection to your mentioning it to Mr. Jorkins, Copperfield, if you think it worth while."

Availing myself of this permission, which was given with a warm shake of the hand, I sat thinking about Dora, and looking at the sunlight stealing from the chimney-pots down the wall of the opposite house, until Mr. Jorkins came. I then went up to Mr. Jorkins' room, and evidently astonished Mr. Jorkins very much by making my appearance there.

"Come in, Mr. Copperfield," said Mr. Jorkins; "come in."

I went in, and sat down, and stated my case to Mr. Jorkins pretty much as I had stated it to Mr. Spenlow. Mr. Jorkins was not by any means the awful creature one might have expected, but a large, mild, smooth-faced man of sixty, who took so much snuff that there was a tradition in the Commons that he lived principally on that stimulant, having little room in his system for any other article of diet.

"You have mentioned this to Mr. Spenlow, I suppose?" said Mr. Jorkins, when he had heard me, very restlessly, to an end.

I answered, "Yes," and told him that Mr. Spenlow had introduced his name.

"He said I should object?" asked Mr. Jorkins.

I was obliged to admit that Mr. Spenlow had considered it probable.

"I am sorry to say, Mr. Copperfield, I can't advance your object," said Mr. Jorkins nervously. "The fact is—but I have an appointment at the Bank, if you'll have the goodness to excuse me."

With that he rose in a great hurry, and was going out of the room, when I made bold to say that I feared, then, there was no way of arranging the matter.

"No!" said Mr. Jorkins, stopping at the door to shake his head. "Oh, no! I object, you know!"—which he said very rapidly, and went out. "You must be aware, Mr. Copperfield," he added, looking restlessly in at the door again, "if Mr. Spenlow objects——"

"Personally, he does not object, sir," said I.

"Oh! personally!" repeated Mr. Jorkins, in an impatient manner. "I assure you there's an objection, Mr. Copperfield. Hopeless! What you wish to be done can't be done. I—I really have got an appointment at the Bank." With that he fairly ran away, and, to the best of my knowledge, it was three days before he showed himself in the Commons again.

I left the office, and went homeward. I was trying to familiarize my mind with the worst, when a hackney-chariot coming after me, and stopping at my very feet, occasioned me to look up. A fair hand was stretched forth to me from the window, and the face I had never seen without a feeling of serenity and happiness was smiling on me.

"Agnes!" I joyfully exclaimed. "Oh, my dear Agnes, of all people in the world, what a pleasure to see you!"

Agnes had come to London to see my aunt. She was not alone, she said: her papa was with her—and Uriah Heep.

"And now they are partners," I said. "Confound him!"

"Yes," said Agnes. "They have some business here, and I took advantage of their coming to come too. You must not think my visit all friendly and disinterested, Trotwood, for—I am afraid I may be cruelly prejudiced—I do not like to let papa go away alone with him."

"Does he exercise the same influence over Mr. Wickfield still, Agnes?"

Agnes shook her head. "There is such a change at home," said she, "that you would scarcely know the dear old house. They live with us now."

"They?" said I.

"Mr. Heep and his mother. He sleeps in your old room," said Agnes, looking up into my face.

"I wish I had the ordering of his dreams," said I; "he wouldn't sleep there long."

We found my aunt alone, in a state of some excitement. A difference of opinion had arisen between herself and Mrs. Crupp on an abstract question (the propriety of chambers being inhabited by the gentler sex); and my aunt, utterly indifferent to spasms on the part of Mrs. Crupp, had cut the dispute short by informing that lady that she smelt of my brandy, and that she would trouble her to

239

walk out. Both of these expressions Mrs. Crupp considered actionable, and had expressed her intention of bringing before a "British Judy"—meaning, it was supposed, the bulwark of our national liberties.

We began to talk about my aunt's losses, and I told them what I had tried to do that morning.

"Which was injudicious, Trot," said my aunt, "but well meant. You are a generous boy—I suppose I must say 'young man' now—and I am proud of you, my dear. So far, so good. Now, Trot and Agnes, let us look the case of Betsey Trotwood in the face, and see how it stands."

I observed Agnes turn pale, as she looked very attentively at my aunt. My aunt, patting her cat, looked very attentively at Agnes.

"What's to be done? Here's the cottage, taking one time with another, will produce, say seventy pounds a year; I think we may safely put it down at that. Well! that's all we've got," said my aunt —with whom it was an idiosyncrasy, as it is with some horses, to stop very short when she appeared to be in a fair way of going on for a long while.

"Then," said my aunt, after a rest, "there's Dick. He's good for a hundred a year; but, of course, that must be expended on himself. I would sooner send him away, though I know I am the only person who appreciates him, than have him, and not spend his money on himself. How can Trot and I do best upon our means? What do you say, Agnes?"

"*I* say, aunt," I interposed, "that I must do something!"

"Go for a soldier, do you mean?" returned my aunt, alarmed; "or go to sea? I won't hear of it. You are to be a proctor. We're not going to have any knockings on the head in *this* family, if you please, sir."

"I've been thinking, Trotwood," said Agnes diffidently, "that if you had time——"

"I have a good deal of time, Agnes. I am always disengaged after four or five o'clock, and I have time early in the morning. In one way and another," said I, conscious of reddening a little as I thought of the hours and hours I had devoted to fagging about town, and to and fro upon the Norwood Road, "I have abundance of time."

"I know you would not mind," said Agnes, coming to me, and speaking in a low voice, so full of sweet and hopeful consideration that I hear it now, "the duties of a secretary."

"Mind, my dear Agnes!"

240

"Because," continued Agnes, "Doctor Strong has acted on his intention of retiring, and has come to live in London; and he asked papa, I know, if he could recommend him one. Don't you think he would rather have his favorite old pupil near him than anybody else?"

"Dear Agnes!" said I, "what should I do without you? You are always my good angel. I told you so. I never think of you in any other light."

Agnes answered, with her pleasant laugh, that one good angel (meaning Dora) was enough; and went on to remind me that the Doctor had been used to occupy himself in his study, early in the morning, and in the evening, and that probably my leisure would suit his requirements very well. I was scarcely more delighted with the prospect of earning my own bread than with the hope of earning it under my old master; in short, acting on the advice of Agnes, I sat down and wrote a letter to the Doctor, stating my object, and appointing to call on him next day at ten in the forenoon. This I addressed to Highgate—for in that place, so memorable to me, he lived—and went and posted, myself, without losing a minute.

Wherever Agnes was, some agreeable token of her noiseless presence seemed inseparable from the place. When I came back I found my aunt's birds hanging, just as they had hung so long in the parlor window of the cottage; and my easy-chair, imitating my aunt's much easier chair, in its position at the open window; and I was looking on, thinking how little even Peggotty seemed to do with a good deal of bustle, and how much Agnes did without any bustle at all.

We sat there, talking about our pleasant old Canterbury days, an hour or two. I pray Heaven that I never may forget the dear girl in her love and truth, at that time of my life. Oh, Agnes, sister of my boyhood, if I had known then, what I knew long afterwards!——

There was a beggar in the street when I went down, and as I turned my head toward the window, thinking of her calm, seraphic eyes, he made me start by muttering, as if he were an echo of the morning,

"Blind! blind! blind!"

I was not dispirited now. I was not afraid of the shabby coat, and had no yearnings after gallant greys. My whole manner of thinking of our late misfortune was changed. What I had to do was, to show my aunt that her past goodness to me had not been thrown away on an insensible, ungrateful object. What I had to do was, to turn the painful discipline of my younger days to account, by going to work with a resolute and steady heart. What I had to do was, to take my woodman's axe in my hand, and clear my own way through the forest of difficulty, by cutting down the trees until I came to Dora. And I went on at a mighty rate, as if it could be done by walking.

When I found myself on the familiar Highgate road, pursuing such a different errand from that old one of pleasure with which it was associated, it seemed as if a complete change had come on my whole life. But that did not discourage me. With the new life came new purpose, new intention. Great was the labor; priceless the reward. Dora was the reward, and Dora must be won.

I got into such a transport that I felt quite sorry my coat was not a little shabby already. In this state, I went into a cottage that I saw was to let, and examined it narrowly; for I felt it necessary to be practical. It would do for me and Dora admirably—with a little front garden for Jip to run about in, and bark at the tradespeople through the railings, and a capital room upstairs for my aunt. I came out again, hotter and faster than ever, and dashed up to Highgate, at such a rate that I was there an hour too early.

When I approached the Doctor's cottage—a pretty, old place—I saw him walking in the garden at the side, gaiters and all, as if he had never left off walking since the days of my pupilage. He looked at me thoughtfully, for a few moments, evidently without thinking about me at all; and then his benevolent face expressed extraordinary pleasure, and he took me by both hands.

"Why, my dear Copperfield," said the Doctor, "you are a man! How do you do? I am delighted to see you. My dear Copperfield, how very much you have improved! You are quite—yes—dear me!"

I hoped he was well, and Mrs. Strong too.

"Oh dear, yes!" said the Doctor; "Annie's quite well, and she'll be delighted to see you. You were always her favorite. She said so, last night, when I showed her your letter."

The Doctor, walking up and down with his hand on my shoulder, and his kind face turned encouragingly to mine, went on,

"Now, my dear Copperfield, in reference to this proposal of yours. It's very gratifying and agreeable to me, I am sure, but don't you think you could do better? You achieved distinction, you know, when you were with us. You are qualified for many good things."

I urged my request strongly, reminding the Doctor that I had already a profession.

"Well, well," returned the Doctor, "that's true. But, my good young friend, what's seventy pounds a year?"

"It doubles our income, Doctor Strong," said I.

"Dear me!" replied the Doctor. "To think of that! Not that I mean to say it's rigidly limited to seventy pounds a year, because I have always contemplated making any young friend I might thus employ a present too. Undoubtedly," said the Doctor, still walking me up and down with his hand on my shoulder, "I have always taken an annual present into account."

"My dear tutor," said I (now, really, without any nonsense), "to whom I owe more obligations already than I ever can acknowl-edge——"

"No, no," interposed the Doctor. "Pardon me!"

"If you will take such time as I have, and that is my mornings and evenings, and can think it worth seventy pounds a year, you will do me such a service as I cannot express."

"Then be it so," said the Doctor, clapping me on the shoulder, and still keeping his hand there, as we still walked up and down.

"And I shall be twenty times happier, sir," said I, with a little—I hope innocent—flattery, "if my employment is to be on the Dictionary."

The Doctor stopped, smilingly clapped me on the shoulder again, and exclaimed, with a triumph most delightful to behold, as if I had penetrated to the profoundest depths of mortal sagacity, "My dear young friend, you have hit it. It is the Dictionary!"

The Doctor was quite happy in the prospect of our going to work together on that wonderful performance, and we settled to begin next morning at seven o'clock. We were to work two hours every morning, and two or three hours every night, except on Saturdays, when I was to rest. On Sundays, of course, I was to rest also; and I considered these very easy terms.

Our plans being thus arranged to our mutual satisfaction, the Doctor took me into the house to present me to Mrs. Strong, whom we found in the Doctor's new study, dusting his books—a freedom which he never permitted anybody else to take with those sacred favorites.

They had postponed their breakfast on my account, and we sat down to table together. We had not been seated long, when I saw an approaching arrival in Mrs. Strong's face before I heard any sound of it. A gentleman on horseback came to the gate, and leading his horse into the little court, with the bridle over his arm, as if he were quite at home, tied him to a ring in the empty coach-house wall, and came into the breakfast-parlor, whip in hand.

"Mr. Jack!" said the Doctor. "Copperfield!"

Mr. Jack Maldon shook hands with me, but not very warmly, I believed, and with an air of languid patronage, at which I secretly took great umbrage. But his languor altogether was quite a wonderful sight—except when he addressed himself to his cousin Annie.

"Have you breakfasted this morning, Mr. Jack?" said the Doctor.

"I hardly ever take breakfast, sir," he replied, with his head thrown back in an easy-chair. "I find it bores me."

"Is there any news today?" inquired the Doctor.

"Nothing at all, sir," replied Mr. Maldon. "There's an account about the people being hungry and discontented down in the North; but they are always being hungry and discontented somewhere."

244

The Doctor looked grave, and said, as though he wished to change the subject, "Then there's no news at all; and no news, they say, is good news."

"There's a long statement in the papers, sir, about a murder," observed Mr. Maldon. "But somebody is always being murdered, and I didn't read it."

A display of indifference to all the actions and passions of mankind was not supposed to be such a distinguished quality at that time, I think, as I have observed it to be considered since. I have known it very fashionable indeed. I have seen it displayed with such success, that I have encountered some fine ladies and gentlemen who might as well have been born caterpillars. Perhaps it impressed me the more then, because it was new to me; but it certainly did not tend to exalt my opinion of, or to strengthen my confidence in, Mr. Jack Maldon.

"I came out to inquire whether Annie would like to go to the opera tonight," said Mr. Maldon, turning to her. "It's the last good night there will be this season, and there's a singer there whom she really ought to hear. She is perfectly exquisite. Besides which, she is so charmingly ugly," relapsing into languor.

The Doctor, ever pleased with what was likely to please his young wife, turned to her and said,

"You must go, Annie. You must go."

"I would rather not," she said to the Doctor. "I prefer to remain at home. I would much rather remain at home."

Without looking at her cousin, she then addressed me, and asked me about Agnes, and whether she should see her, and whether she was not likely to come that day; and was so much disturbed, that I wondered how even the Doctor, buttering his toast, could be blind to what was so obvious.

But he saw nothing. He told her, good-naturedly, that she was young, and ought to be amused and entertained, and must not allow herself to be made dull by a dull old fellow. Moreover, he said, he wanted to hear her sing all the new singer's songs to him; and how could she do that well unless she went? So the Doctor persisted in making the engagement for her, and Mr. Jack Maldon was to come back to dinner.

I was curious to find out next morning whether she had been. She had not, but had sent into London to put her cousin off; and had gone out in the afternoon to see Agnes, and had prevailed upon the Doctor to go with her; and they had walked home by the fields,

245

the Doctor told me, the evening being delightful. When I left, at nine o'clock, she was kneeling on the ground at the Doctor's feet, putting on his shoes and gaiters for him.

I was pretty busy now—up at five in the morning, and home at nine or ten at night. But I had infinite satisfaction in being so closely engaged, and never walked slowly on any account, and felt enthusiastically that the more I tired myself, the more I was doing to deserve Dora. I had not revealed myself in my altered character to Dora yet, because she was coming to see Miss Mills in a few days, and I deferred all I had to tell her until then; merely informing her in my letters (all our communications were secretly forwarded through Miss Mills) that I had much to tell her. In the meantime, I put myself on a short allowance of bear's-grease, wholly abandoned scented soap and lavender water, and sold off three waistcoats at a prodigious sacrifice, as being too luxurious for my stern career.

Not satisfied with all these proceedings, but burning with impatience to do something more, I went to see Traddles. I took Mr. Dick with me, because he had begun to fret and worry himself out of spirits and appetite, as having nothing useful to do. Seriously apprehending that his malady would increase, I made up my mind to try if Traddles could help us.

The first subject on which I had to consult Traddles was this: I had heard that many men distinguished in various pursuits had begun life by reporting the debates in Parliament. Traddles having mentioned newspapers to me, as one of his hopes, I had put the two things together, and told Traddles that I wished to know how I could qualify myself for this pursuit. Traddles now informed me that a perfect and entire command of the mystery of shorthand was about equal in difficulty to the mastery of six languages; and that it might perhaps be attained, by dint of perseverance, in the course of a few years. Traddles reasonably supposed that this would settle the business.

"I am very much obliged to you, my dear Traddles!" said I. "I'll begin tomorrow."

Traddles looked astonished, as he well might; but he had no notion as yet of my rapturous condition.

"I'll buy a book," said I, "with a good scheme of this art in it. I'll work at it at the Commons, where I haven't half enough to do. I'll take down the speeches in our court for practice—Traddles, my dear fellow, I'll master it!"

246

"Dear me," said Traddles, opening his eyes, "I had no idea you were such a determined character, Copperfield!"

I don't know how he should have had, for it was new enough to me. I passed that off, and brought Mr. Dick on the carpet.

"You see," said Mr. Dick wistfully, "if I could exert myself, Mr. Traddles—if I could beat a drum, or blow anything!"

Poor fellow! I have little doubt he would have preferred such an employment in his heart to all others. Traddles, who would not have smiled for the world, replied composedly,

"But you are a very good penman, sir.—You told me so, Copperfield?"

"Excellent!" said I. And indeed he was. He wrote with extraordinary neatness.

"Don't you think," said Traddles, "you could copy writings, sir, if I got them for you?"

Mr. Dick looked doubtfully at me. "Eh, Trotwood?"

I shook my head. Mr. Dick shook his, and sighed, "Tell him about the Memorial," said Mr. Dick.

I explained to Traddles that there was a difficulty in keeping King Charles the First out of Mr. Dick's manuscripts; Mr. Dick in the meanwhile looking very deferentially and seriously at Traddles, and sucking his thumb.

"But these writings, you know, that I speak of, are already drawn up and finished," said Traddles, after a little consideration. "Mr. Dick has nothing to do with them. Wouldn't that make a difference, Copperfield? At all events, wouldn't it be well to try?"

This gave us new hope. Traddles and I laying our heads together apart, while Mr. Dick anxiously watched us from his chair, we concocted a scheme, in virtue of which we got him to work next day, with triumphant success.

On a table by the window in Buckingham Street we set out the work Traddles procured for him—which was to make, I forget how many copies of a legal document about some right of way—and on another table we spread the last unfinished original of the great Memorial. Our instructions to Mr. Dick were that he should copy exactly what he had before him, without the least departure from the original; and that when he felt it necessary to make the slightest allusion to King Charles the First, he should fly to the Memorial. My aunt reported to us, afterwards, that at first he was like a man playing the kettle-drums, and constantly divided his attentions between the two; but that, finding this confuse and fatigue him, and having his copy there, plainly before his eyes, he soon sat at it in an orderly, business-like manner, and postponed the Memorial to a more convenient time. In a word, although we took great care that he should have no more to do than was good for him, he earned by the following Saturday night ten shillings and ninepence; and never, while I live, shall I forget his going about to all the shops in the neighborhood to change this treasure into sixpences, or his bringing them to my aunt arranged in the form of a heart upon a waiter, with tears of joy and pride in his eyes.

"No starving now, Trotwood," said Mr. Dick, shaking hands with me in a corner. "I'll provide for her, sir!" and he flourished his ten fingers in the air, as if they were ten banks.

I hardly know which was the better pleased, Traddles or I. "It really," said Traddles suddenly, taking a letter out of his pocket, and giving it to me, "put Mr. Micawber quite out of my head!"

The letter (Mr. Micawber never missed any possible opportunity of writing a letter) was addressed to me, "By the kindness of T. Traddles, Esquire, of the Inner Temple." It ran thus:

"My Dear Copperfield,

"You may possibly not be unprepared to receive the intimation that something has turned up. I may have mentioned to you on a former occasion that I was in expectation of such an event.

"I am about to establish myself in one of the provincial towns of our favored island (where the society may be described as a happy admixture of the agricultural and the clerical), in immediate connection with one of the learned professions. Mrs. Micawber and our offspring will accompany me. Our ashes, at a future period, will probably be found commingled in the cemetery attached to a venerable pile, for which the spot to which I refer has acquired a reputation, shall I say from China to Peru?

"In bidding adieu to the modern Babylon, where we have undergone many vicissitudes, I trust not ignobly, Mrs. Micawber and myself cannot disguise from our minds that we part, it may be for years and it may be forever, with an individual linked by strong associations to the altar of our domestic life. If, on the eve of such a departure, you will accompany our mutual friend, Mr. Thomas Traddles, to our present abode, and there reciprocate the wishes natural to the occasion, you will confer a Boon

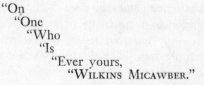

"On
"One
"Who
"Is
"Ever yours,
"Wilkins Micawber."

Learning from Traddles that the invitation referred to the evening then wearing away, I expressed my readiness to do honor to it; and we went off together to the lodging which Mr. Micawber occupied as Mr. Mortimer.

The resources of this lodging were so limited, that we found the twins, now some eight or nine years old, reposing in a turn-up bedstead in the family sitting-room, where Mr. Micawber had prepared, in a washhand-stand jug, what he called a "brew" of the agreeable beverage for which he was famous. I had the pleasure, on this occasion, of renewing the acquaintance of Master Micawber, whom I found a promising boy of about twelve or thirteen, very subject to that restlessness of limb which is not an infrequent phenomenon in youths of his age. I also became once more known to his sister, Miss Micawber, in whom, as Mr. Micawber told us, "her mother renewed her youth, like the Phœnix."

"My dear Copperfield," said Mr. Micawber, "yourself and Mr. Traddles find us on the brink of migration, and will excuse any little discomforts incidental to that position."

Glancing round as I made a suitable reply, I observed that the family effects were already packed, and that the amount of luggage was by no means overwhelming. I congratulated Mrs. Micawber on the approaching change.

"My dear Mr. Copperfield," said Mrs. Micawber, "of your friendly interest in all our affairs, I am well assured. My family may consider it banishment, if they please; but I am a wife and mother, and I never will desert Mr. Micawber."

Traddles, appealed to by Mrs. Micawber's eye, feelingly acquiesced.

"That," said Mrs. Micawber, "that, at least, is my view, my dear Mr. Copperfield and Mr. Traddles, of the obligation which I took upon myself when I repeated the irrevocable words, 'I, Emma, take thee, Wilkins.' I read the service over with a flat-candle on the previous night, and the conclusion I derived from it was, that I never could desert Mr. Micawber. And," said Mrs. Micawber, "though it is possible I may be mistaken in my view of the ceremony, I never will!"

"My dear," said Mr. Micawber, a little impatiently, "I am not conscious that you are expected to do anything of the sort."

"It may be a sacrifice," said Mrs. Micawber, "to immure one's self in a cathedral town; but surely, Mr. Copperfield, if it is a sacrifice in me, it is much more a sacrifice in a man of Mr. Micawber's abilities."

"Oh! you are going to a cathedral town?" said I.

Mr. Micawber, who had been helping us all out of the washhand-stand jug, replied,

"To Canterbury. In fact, my dear Copperfield, I have entered into arrangements, by virtue of which I stand pledged and contracted to our friend Heep, to assist and serve him in the capacity of —and to be—his confidential clerk."

I stared at Mr. Micawber, who greatly enjoyed my surprise.

"I am bound to state to you," he said, with an official air, "that the business habits, and the prudent suggestions of Mrs. Micawber, have in a great measure conducted to this result. The gauntlet, to which Mrs. Micawber referred upon a former occasion, being thrown down in the form of an advertisement, was taken up by my friend Heep, and led to a mutual recognition. Of my friend Heep," said Mr. Micawber, "who is a man of remarkable shrewdness, I desire to speak with all possible respect. My friend Heep has not fixed the positive remuneration at too high a figure, but he has made a great deal, in the way of extrication from the pressure of pecuniary difficulties, contingent on the value of my services; and on the value of those services, I pin my faith. Such address and intelligence as I chance to possess," said Mr. Micawber, boastfully disparaging himself, with the old genteel air, "will be devoted to my friend Heep's service. I have already some acquaintance with the law—as a defendant on civil process—and I shall immediately apply myself to the commentaries of one of the most eminent and remarkable of our English jurists. I believe it is unnecessary to add that I allude to Mr. Justice Blackstone."

"What I particularly request Mr. Micawber to be careful of, is," said Mrs. Micawber, "that he does not, my dear Mr. Copperfield, in applying himself to this subordinate branch of the law, place it out of his power to rise, ultimately, to the top of the tree. Now, for example, Mr. Traddles," said Mrs. Micawber, assuming a profound air, "a Judge, or even say a Chancellor."

Mr. Micawber coughed, and drank his punch with an air of exceeding satisfaction—glancing at Traddles, as if he desired to have his opinion.

"Why, the plain state of the case, Mrs. Micawber," said Traddles, mildly breaking the truth to her—"I mean the real prosaic fact, you know——"

"Just so," said Mrs. Micawber. "My dear Mr. Traddles, I wish to be as prosaic and literal as possible on a subject of so much importance."

"Is," said Traddles, "that this branch of the law, even if Mr. Micawber were a regular solicitor——"

"Exactly so," returned Mrs. Micawber. ("Wilkins, you are squinting, and will not be able to get your eyes back.")

"Has nothing," pursued Traddles, "to do with that. Only a barrister is eligible for such preferments; and Mr. Micawber could not be a barrister, without being entered at an inn of court as a student, for five years."

"Do I follow you?" said Mrs. Micawber, with her most affable air of business. "Do I understand, my dear Mr. Traddles, that, at the expiration of that period, Mr. Micawber would be eligible as a Judge or Chancellor?"

"He would be *eligible*," returned Traddles, with a strong emphasis on that word.

"Thank you," said Mrs. Micawber. "That is quite sufficient. If such is the case, and Mr. Micawber forfeits no privilege by entering on these duties, my anxiety is set at rest. I speak," said Mrs. Micawber, "as a female, necessarily; but I have always been of the opinion that Mr. Micawber possesses what I have heard my papa call, when I lived at home, the judicial mind."

I quite believe that Mr. Micawber saw himself, in his judicial mind's eye, on the woolsack. He passed his hand complacently over his bald head, and said with ostentatious resignation,

"My dear, we will not anticipate the decrees of fortune. If I am reserved to wear a wig, I am at least prepared, externally," in allusion to his baldness, "for that distinction. I do not," said Mr. Micawber, "regret my hair, and I may have been deprived of it for a specific purpose."

We fell into some general conversation; and as I was too full of my desperate intentions to keep my altered circumstances to myself, I made them known to Mr. and Mrs. Micawber. I cannot express how extremely delighted they both were by the idea of my aunt's being in difficulties, and how comfortable and friendly it made them.

When we were nearly come to the last round of the punch, Mr. Micawber said with much solemnity,

"One thing more I have to do, before this separation is complete, and that is to perform an act of justice. My friend Mr. Thomas

Traddles has, on two several occasions, 'put his name,' if I may use a common expression, to bills of exchange for my accommodation. On the first occasion Mr. Thomas Traddles was left—let me say, in short, in the lurch. The fulfilment of the second has not yet arrived.

"To leave this metropolis," said Mr. Micawber, "and my friend Mr. Thomas Traddles, without acquitting myself of the pecuniary part of this obligation, would weigh upon my mind to an insupportable extent. I have, therefore, prepared for my friend Mr. Thomas Traddles, and I now hold in my hand, a document which accomplishes the desired object. I beg to hand to my friend Mr. Thomas Traddles my I. O. U. for forty-one, ten, eleven and a half; and I am happy to recover my moral dignity, and to know that I can once more walk erect before my fellow-man!"

With this introduction (which greatly affected him), Mr. Micawber placed his I. O. U. in the hands of Traddles, and said he wished him well in every relation of life. I am persuaded, not only that this was quite the same to Mr. Micawber as paying the money, but that Traddles himself hardly knew the difference until he had had time to think about it.

Mr. Micawber walked so erect before his fellow-man, on the strength of this virtuous action, that his chest looked half as broad again when he lighted us downstairs. We parted with great heartiness on both sides; and when I had seen Traddles to his own door, and was going home alone, I thought, among the other odd and contradictory things I mused upon, that, slippery as Mr. Micawber was, I was probably indebted to some compassionate recollection he retained of me as his boy-lodger, for never having been asked by him for money. I certainly should not have had the moral courage to refuse it; and I have no doubt he knew that (to his credit be it written) quite as well as I did.

CHAPTER 37 ⅋ A LITTLE COLD WATER • • •

M<small>Y NEW</small> life had lasted for more than a week, and I was stronger than ever in those tremendous practical resolutions that I felt the crisis required. As yet, little Dora was quite unconscious of my desperate firmness, otherwise than as my letters darkly shadowed it forth. But another Saturday came, and on that Saturday evening she was to be at Miss Mills's; and when Mr. Mills had gone to his whist-club (telegraphed to me in the street by a bird-cage in the drawing-room middle window), I was to go there to tea.

Dora came to the drawing-room door to meet me; and Jip came scrambling out, tumbling over his own growls, under the impression that I was a bandit; and we all three went in, as happy and loving as could be. I soon carried desolation into the bosom of our joys— not that I meant to do it, but that I was so full of the subject—by asking Dora, without the smallest preparation, if she could love a beggar?

My pretty, little, startled Dora! Her only association with the word was a yellow face and a nightcap, or a pair of crutches, or a wooden leg, or a dog with a decanter-stand in his mouth, or something of that kind; and she stared at me with the most delightful wonder.

"How can you ask me anything so foolish?" pouted Dora. "Love a beggar!"

"Dora, my own dearest!" said I, "*I* am a beggar."

"How can you be such a silly thing," replied Dora, slapping my hand, "as to sit there telling such stories? I'll make Jip bite you!"

Her childish way was the most delicious way in the world to me; but it was necessary to be explicit, and I solemnly repeated,

"Dora, my own life, I am your ruined David!"

"I declare I'll make Jip bite you!" said Dora, shaking her curls, "if you are so ridiculous."

But I looked so serious that Dora left off shaking her curls, and laid her trembling little hand upon my shoulder, and first looked scared and anxious, then began to cry. That was dreadful. I fell upon my knees before the sofa, caressing her, and imploring her not to rend my heart; but, for some time, poor little Dora did nothing but exclaim, "Oh dear! oh dear! And oh, she was so frightened! And where was Julia Mills? And oh, take her to Julia Mills, and go away, please!" until I was almost beside myself.

At last, after an agony of supplication and protestation, I got Dora to look at me, with a horrified expression of face, which I gradually soothed until it was only loving, and her soft, pretty cheek was lying against mine. Then I told her, with my arms clasped round her, how I loved her so dearly, and so dearly; how I felt it right to offer to release her from her engagement, because now I was poor; how I never could bear it, or recover it, if I lost her; how I had no fears of poverty, if she had none, my arm being nerved and my heart inspired by her; how I was already working with a courage such as none but lovers knew; how I had begun to be practical, and to look into the future; how a crust well-earned was sweeter far than a feast inherited; and much more to the same purpose, which I delivered in a burst of passionate eloquence quite surprising to myself, though I had been thinking about it, day and night, ever since my aunt had astonished me.

"Is your heart mine still, dear Dora?" said I rapturously, for I knew by her clinging to me that it was.

"Oh, yes!" cried Dora; "oh, yes, it's all yours. Oh, don't be dreadful!"

I dreadful! To Dora!

"Don't talk about being poor and working hard!" said Dora, nestling closer to me. "Oh, don't, don't!"

"My dearest love," said I, "the crust well-earned——"

"Oh, yes; but I don't want to hear any more about crusts!" said Dora. "And Jip must have a mutton-chop every day at twelve, or he'll die!"

I was charmed with her childish, winning way. I fondly explained to Dora that Jip should have his mutton-chop with his accustomed regularity. I drew a picture of our frugal home, made independent by my labor—sketching in the little house I had seen at Highgate, and my aunt in her room upstairs.

"I am not dreadful now, Dora?" said I tenderly.

"Oh, no, no!" cried Dora. "But I hope your aunt will keep in her own room a good deal. And I hope she's not a scolding old thing!"

If it were possible for me to love Dora more than ever, I am sure I did. But I became grave, and said,

"My own, may I mention something?"

"Oh, please don't be practical," said Dora coaxingly, "because it frightens me so!"

"Sweetheart," I returned, "there is nothing to alarm you in all this. I want you to think of it quite differently. I want to make it nerve you and inspire you, Dora."

"Oh, but that's so shocking!" cried Dora.

"My love, no. Perseverance and strength of character will enable us to bear much worse things."

"But I haven't got any strength at all," said Dora, shaking her curls.—"Have I, Jip?—Oh, do kiss Jip, and be agreeable!"

It was impossible to resist kissing Jip when she held him up to me for that purpose, putting her own bright, rosy little mouth into kissing form as she directed the operation, which she insisted should be performed symmetrically on the center of his nose. I did as she bade me—rewarding myself afterwards for my obedience—and she charmed me out of my graver character for I don't know how long.

"But, Dora, my beloved!" said I, at last resuming it; "I was going to mention something."

The Judge of the Prerogative Court might have fallen in love with her, to see her fold her little hands and hold them up, begging and praying me not to be dreadful any more.

"Indeed I am not going to be, my darling!" I assured her. "But, Dora, my love, if you will sometimes think—not despondingly, you know; far from that!—but if you will sometimes think—just to encourage yourself—that you are engaged to a poor man——"

"Don't, don't! Pray don't!" cried Dora. "It's so very dreadful!"

"My soul, not at all!" said I cheerfully. "If you will sometimes

255

think of that, and look about now and then at your papa's house-keeping, and endeavor to acquire a little habit—of accounts, for instance——"

Poor little Dora received this suggestion with something that was half a sob and half a scream.

"—it would be so useful to us afterwards," I went on. "And if you would promise me to read a little—a little Cookery Book that I would send you, it would be so excellent for both of us. For our path in life, my Dora," said I, warming with the subject, "is stony and rugged now, and it rests with us to smooth it. We must fight our way onward. We must be brave. There are obstacles to be met, and we must meet and crush them!"

I was going on at a great rate, with a clenched hand and a most enthusiastic countenance; but it was quite unnecessary to proceed. I had said enough. I had done it again. Oh, she was so frightened! Oh, where was Julia Mills? Oh, take her to Julia Mills, and go away, please! So that, in short, I was quite distracted, and raved about the drawing-room.

At first Miss Mills thought it was a quarrel, and that we were verging on the Desert of Sahara. But she soon found out how matters stood; for my dear affectionate little Dora, embracing her, began exclaiming that I was "a poor laborer"; and then cried for me, and embraced me, and asked me would I let her give me all her money to keep; and then fell on Miss Mills's neck, sobbing as if her tender heart were broken.

Miss Mills must have been born to be a blessing to us. She ascertained from me in a few words what it was all about, com-forted Dora, and gradually convinced her that I was not a laborer. When we were quite composed, and Dora had gone upstairs to put some rose-water to her eyes, Miss Mills rang for tea.

After tea we had the guitar, and Dora sang those same dear old French songs about the impossibility of ever on any account leaving off dancing, La ra la, La ra la, until I felt a much greater monster than before.

We had only one check to our pleasure, and that happened a little while before I took my leave, when, Miss Mills chancing to make some allusion to tomorrow morning, I unluckily let out that, being obliged to exert myself now, I got up at five o'clock. Whether Dora had any idea that I was a private watchman, I am unable to say; but it made a great impression on her, and she neither played nor sang any more.

256

It was still on her mind when I bade her adieu, and she said to me, in her pretty, coaxing way—as if I were a doll, I used to think,

"Now don't get up at five o'clock, you naughty boy. It's so non-sensical!"

"My love," said I, "I have work to do."

"But don't do it!" returned Dora. "Why should you?"

It was impossible to say to that sweet little surprised face, other-wise than lightly and playfully, that we must work to live.

"Oh, how ridiculous!" cried Dora.

"How shall we live without, Dora?" said I.

"How? Any how!" said Dora.

She seemed to think she had quite settled the question, and gave me such a triumphant little kiss, direct from her innocent heart, that I would hardly have put her out of conceit with her answer for a fortune.

Well, I loved her, and I went on loving her, most absorbingly, entirely, and completely. But going on, too, working pretty hard, and busily keeping red-hot all the irons I now had in the fire, I would sit sometimes of a night, opposite my aunt, thinking how I had frightened Dora that time, and how I could best make my way with a guitar-case through the forest of difficulty, until I used to fancy that my head was turning quite grey.

CHAPTER 38  A DISSOLUTION OF
PARTNERSHIP ✦ ✦ ✦

I DID not allow my resolution with respect to the parliamentary
debates to cool. I bought an approved scheme of the noble art
and mystery of stenography (which cost me ten and sixpence),
and night after night, almost every night, for a long time, we had
a sort of private Parliament in Buckingham Street, after I came
home from the Doctor's.

Often and often we pursued these debates until the clock pointed
to midnight, and the candles were burning down. I was always
punctual at the office, at the Doctor's too; and I really did work, as
the common expression is, like a cart-horse.

One day, when I went to the Commons as usual, I found Mr.
Spenlow in the doorway looking extremely grave, and talking to
himself. Instead of returning my "Good-morning" with his usual
affability, he looked at me in a distant, ceremonious manner, and
coldly requested me to accompany him to a certain coffee-house.
I followed him and found Miss Murdstone there, supported by a
background of sideboard. Miss Murdstone gave me her chilly finger-
nails, and sat severely rigid. Mr. Spenlow shut the door, motioned
me to a chair, and stood on the hearthrug in front of the fireplace.

258

"Have the goodness to show Mr. Copperfield," said Mr. Spenlow, "what you have in your reticule, Miss Murdstone."

I believe it was the old identical steel-clasped reticule of my childhood, that shut up like a bite. Compressing her lips, in sympathy with the snap, Miss Murdstone opened it—opening her mouth a little at the same time—and produced my last letter to Dora, teeming with expressions of devoted affection.

"I believe that is your writing, Mr. Copperfield?" said Mr. Spenlow.

I was very hot, and the voice I heard was very unlike mine, when I said, "It is, sir!"

"If I am not mistaken," said Mr. Spenlow, as Miss Murdstone brought a parcel of letters out of her reticule, tied round with the dearest bit of blue ribbon, "those are also from your pen, Mr. Copperfield?"

I took them from her with a most desolate sensation, and glancing at such phrases at the top as "My ever dearest and own Dora," "My best beloved angel," "My blessed one forever," and the like, blushed deeply, and inclined my head.

"No, thank you!" said Mr. Spenlow coldly, as I mechanically offered them back to him. "I will not deprive you of them.—Miss Murdstone, be so good as to proceed!"

That gentle creature, after a moment's thoughtful survey of the carpet, delivered herself with much dry unction as follows:

"I must confess to having entertained my suspicions of Miss Spenlow, in reference to David Copperfield, for some time. I observed Miss Spenlow and David Copperfield when they first met, and the impression made upon me then was not agreeable. The depravity of the human heart is such——"

"You will oblige me, ma'am," interrupted Mr. Spenlow, "by confining yourself to facts."

Miss Murdstone cast down her eyes, shook her head as if protesting against this unseemly interruption, and with frowning dignity resumed,

"I have already said, sir, that I have had my suspicions of Miss Spenlow, in reference to David Copperfield, for some time. I have frequently endeavored to find decisive corroboration of those suspicions, but without effect. I have therefore forborne to mention them to Miss Spenlow's father"—looking severely at him—"knowing how little disposition there usually is in such cases to acknowledge the conscientious discharge of duty."

Mr. Spenlow seemed quite cowed by the gentlemanly sternness of Miss Murdstone's manner, and deprecated her severity with a conciliatory little wave of his hand.

"Last evening after tea," pursued Miss Murdstone, "I observed the little dog starting, rolling, and growling about the drawing-room, worrying something. I said to Miss Spenlow, 'Dora, what is that the dog has in his mouth? It's paper.' Miss Spenlow immediately put her hand to her frock, gave a sudden cry, and ran to the dog. I interposed, and said, 'Dora my love, you must permit me.'"

Oh, Jip, miserable spaniel, this wretchedness, then, was your work!

"Miss Spenlow endeavored," said Miss Murdstone, "to bribe me with kisses, work-boxes, and small articles of jewelry—that, of course, I pass over. The little dog still kept the letter in his mouth; and on my endeavoring to take it from him, at the imminent risk of being bitten, he kept it between his teeth so pertinaciously as to suffer himself to be held suspended in the air by means of the document. At length I obtained possession of it. After perusing it, I taxed Miss Spenlow with having many such letters in her possession, and ultimately obtained from her the packet which is now in David Copperfield's hand."

Here she ceased, and snapping her reticule again, and shutting her mouth, looked as if she might be broken, but could never be bent.

"You have heard Miss Murdstone," said Mr. Spenlow, turning to me. "I beg to ask, Mr. Copperfield, if you have anything to say in reply?"

The picture I had before me of the beautiful little treasure of my heart sobbing and crying all night—of her being alone, frightened, and wretched, then—of her having so piteously begged and prayed that stony-hearted woman to forgive her—of her having vainly offered her those kisses, work-boxes, and trinkets—of her being in such grievous distress, and all for me—very much impaired the little dignity I had been able to muster.

"There is nothing I can say, sir," I returned, "except that all the blame is mine. Dora——"

"Miss Spenlow, if you please," said her father majestically.

"—was induced and persuaded by me," I went on, swallowing that colder designation, "to consent to this concealment, and I bitterly regret it."

"You are very much to blame, sir," said Mr. Spenlow, walking to and fro upon the hearthrug, and emphasizing what he said with his whole body instead of his head, on account of the stiffness of his cravat and spine. "You have done a stealthy and unbecoming action, Mr. Copperfield."

"I feel it, sir, I assure you," I returned. "But I never thought so before. I love Miss Spenlow to that extent——"

"Pooh! nonsense!" said Mr. Spenlow, reddening. "Pray don't tell me to my face that you love my daughter, Mr. Copperfield."

"Could I defend my conduct if I did not, sir?" I returned, with all humility.

"Can you defend your conduct if you do, sir?" said Mr. Spenlow, stopping short upon the hearthrug. "Have you considered your years, and my daughter's years, Mr. Copperfield? Have you considered my daughter's station in life, the projects I may contemplate for her advancement, the testamentary intentions I may have with reference to her? Have you considered anything, Mr. Copperfield?"

"Very little, sir, I am afraid," I answered, speaking to him as respectfully and sorrowfully as I felt; "but pray believe me, I have considered my own worldly position. When I explained it to you, we were already engaged——"

"I BEG," said Mr. Spenlow, more like Punch than I had ever seen him, as he energetically struck one hand upon the other—"that you will NOT talk to me of engagements, Mr. Copperfield."

The otherwise immovable Miss Murdstone laughed contemptuously in one short syllable.

"When I explained my altered position to you, sir," I began again, substituting a new form of expression for what was so unpalatable to him, "this concealment, into which I am so unhappy as to have led Miss Spenlow, had begun. Since I have been in that altered position, I have strained every nerve. I have exerted every energy, to improve it. I am sure I shall improve it in time. Will you grant me time—any length of time? We are both so young, sir——"

"You are right," interrupted Mr. Spenlow, nodding his head a great many times, and frowning very much—"you are both very young. It's all nonsense. Let there be an end of the nonsense. Take away those letters and throw them in the fire. Give me Miss Spenlow's letters to throw in the fire; and although our future intercourse must, you are aware, be restricted to the Commons here, we will agree to make no further mention of the past. Come, Mr. Copperfield, you don't want sense, and this is the sensible course."

No. I couldn't think of agreeing to it. I was very sorry, but there was a higher consideration than sense. Love was above all earthly considerations, and I loved Dora to idolatry, and Dora loved me.

"Very well, Mr. Copperfield," said Mr. Spenlow, "I must try my influence with my daughter."

A silence succeeding, I was undecided whether to go or stay. At length I was moving quietly toward the door, with the intention of saying that perhaps I should consult his feelings best by withdrawing, when he said, with his hands in his coat pockets, into which it was as much as he could do to get them,

"You may make it necessary, if you are foolish or obstinate, Mr. Copperfield, for me to send my daughter abroad again, for a term; but I have a better opinion of you. I hope you will be wiser than that, in a few days. As to Miss Murdstone, I respect that lady's vigilance, and feel obliged to her; but she has strict charge to avoid the subject. All I desire, Mr. Copperfield, is that it should be forgotten. All you have got to do, Mr. Copperfield, is to forget it."

All! In the note I wrote to Miss Mills I bitterly quoted this sentiment. All I had to do, I said, with gloomy sarcasm, was to forget Dora. That was all, and what was that? I informed her that my reason was tottering on its throne. I signed myself hers distractedly; and I couldn't help feeling, while I read this composition over, before sending it by a porter, that it was something in the style of Mr. Micawber.

I confided all to my aunt when I got home, and in spite of all she could say to me, went to bed despairing. I got up despairing, and went out despairing. It was Saturday morning, and I went straight to the Commons.

I was surprised, when I came within sight of our office door, to see the ticket-porters standing outside talking together, and some half-dozen stragglers gazing at the windows, which were shut up. I quickened my pace, and, passing among them, wondering at their looks, went hurriedly in.

The clerks were there, but nobody was doing anything. Old Tiffey, for the first time in his life, I should think, was sitting on somebody else's stool, and had not hung up his hat.

"This is a dreadful calamity, Mr. Copperfield," said he, as I entered.

"What is?" I exclaimed. "What's the matter?"

"Don't you know?" cried Tiffey, and all the rest of them, coming round me.

"No!" said I, looking from face to face.

"Mr. Spenlow," said Tiffey.

"What about him?"

"Dead!"

I thought it was the office reeling, and not I, as one of the clerks caught hold of me. They sat me down in a chair, untied my neck-cloth, and brought me some water. I have no idea whether this took any time.

"Dead?" said I.

"He dined in town yesterday, and drove down in the phaëton by himself," said Tiffey, "having sent his own groom home by the coach, as he sometimes did, you know——"

"Well?"

"The phaëton went home without him. The house was roused up directly, and three of them went out along the road. They found him a mile off."

"More than a mile off, Mr. Tiffey," interposed a junior.

"Was it? I believe you are right," said Tiffey—"*more* than a mile off—not far from the church—lying partly on the roadside, and partly on the path, upon his face. Whether he fell out in a fit, or got out, feeling ill before the fit came on—or even whether he was quite dead then, though there is no doubt he was quite insensible—no one appears to know. If he breathed, certainly he never spoke. Medical assistance was got as soon as possible, but it was quite useless."

I went down to Norwood that night; and finding from one of the servants, when I made my inquiries at the door, that Miss Mills was there, got my aunt to direct a letter to her, which I wrote. I deplored the untimely death of Mr. Spenlow most sincerely, and shed tears in doing so. I entreated her to tell Dora, if Dora were in a state to hear it, that he had spoken to me with the utmost kindness and considera-tion, and had coupled nothing but tenderness, not a single or re-proachful word, with her name.

My aunt received a few lines next day in reply—addressed, out-side, to her; within, to me. Dora was overcome by grief, and when her friend had asked her should she send her love to me, had only cried, as she was always crying, "Oh, dear papa! oh, poor papa!" But she had not said No, and that I made the most of.

Mr. Jorkins, who had been at Norwood since the occurrence, came to the office a few days afterwards. He and Tiffey were closeted together for some few moments, and then Tiffey looked out at the door and beckoned me in.

"Oh!" said Mr. Jorkins, "Mr. Tiffey and myself, Mr. Copperfield, are about to examine the desk, the drawers, and other such repositories of the deceased, with the view of sealing up his private papers, and searching for a will. There is no trace of any, elsewhere."

It appeared a wonderful thing to me, but it turned out that there *was* no will. What was scarcely less astonishing to me was, that his affairs were in a most disordered state. In the competition on all points of appearance and gentility then running high in the Commons, he had spent more than his professional income and had reduced his private means to a very low ebb indeed. There was a sale of the furniture and lease at Norwood; and Tiffey told me, little thinking how interested I was in the story, that, paying all the just debts of the deceased, and deducting his share of outstanding bad and doubtful debts due to the firm, he wouldn't give a thousand pounds for all the assets remaining.

This was at the expiration of about six weeks. Miss Mills still reported to me that my broken-hearted little Dora would say nothing, when I was mentioned, but, "Oh, poor papa! oh, dear papa!" Also that she had no other relations than two aunts, maiden sisters of Mr. Spenlow, who lived at Putney, and who had not held any other than chance communication with their brother for many years. Not that they had ever quarreled (Miss Mills informed me); but that having been, on the occasion of Dora's christening, invited to tea when they considered themselves privileged to be invited to dinner, they had expressed their opinion in writing that it was "better for the happiness of all parties" that they should stay away. Since which they had gone their road, and their brother had gone his.

These two ladies now emerged from their retirement, and proposed to take Dora to live at Putney. Dora, clinging to them both and weeping, exclaimed, "Oh, yes, aunts! Please take Julia Mills and me and Jip to Putney." So they went, very soon after the funeral.

MY AUNT, beginning, I imagine, to be made seriously uncomfortable by my prolonged dejection, made a pretense of being anxious that I should go to Dover to see that all was working well at the cottage, which was let; and to conclude an agreement, with the same tenant, for a longer term of occupation. I fell rather willingly into my aunt's pretense, as a means of enabling me to pass a few tranquil hours with Agnes.

I found everything in a satisfactory state at the cottage, and was enabled to gratify my aunt exceedingly by reporting that the tenant inherited her feud, and waged incessant war against donkeys. Having settled the little business I had to transact there, and slept there one night, I walked on to Canterbury early in the morning. It was now winter again, and the fresh, cold, windy day, and the sweeping downland, brightened up my hopes a little.

Arrived at Mr. Wickfield's house, I found, in the little lower room on the ground floor, where Uriah Heep had been of old accustomed to sit, Mr. Micawber plying his pen with great assiduity. He was dressed in a legal-looking suit of black, and loomed burly and large in that small office.

Mr. Micawber was extremely glad to see me. He told me that he had become the tenant of Uriah Heep's old house, and that Mrs. Micawber would be delighted to receive me once more under her own roof.

"It is humble," said Mr. Micawber, "to quote a favorite expression of my friend Heep; but it may prove the stepping-stone to more ambitious domiciliary accommodation."

I asked him whether he had reason, so far, to be satisfied with his friend Heep's treatment of him. He got up to ascertain if the door were close shut, before he replied, in a lower voice,

"My dear Copperfield, a man who labors under the pressure of pecuniary embarrassments is, with the generality of people, at a disadvantage. That disadvantage is not diminished when that pressure necessitates the drawing of stipendiary emoluments before those emoluments are strictly due and payable. All I can say is, that my friend Heep has responded to appeals, to which I need not more particularly refer, in a manner calculated to redound equally to the honor of his head and of his heart."

"I should not have supposed him to be very free with his money either," I observed.

"Pardon me," said Mr. Micawber, with an air of constraint, "I speak of my friend Heep as I have experience."

"I am glad your experience is so favorable," I returned.

"You are very obliging, my dear Copperfield," said Mr. Micawber, and hummed a tune.

"Do you see much of Mr. Wickfield?" I asked, to change the subject.

"Not much," said Mr. Micawber slightingly. "Mr. Wickfield is, I dare say, a man of very excellent intentions; but he is—in short, he is obsolete."

"I am afraid his partner seeks to make him so," said I.

"My dear Copperfield," returned Mr. Micawber, after some uneasy evolutions on his stool, "allow me to offer a remark! I am here in a capacity of confidence. I am here in a position of trust. The discussion of some topics, even with Mrs. Micawber herself (so long the partner of my various vicissitudes, and a woman of a remarkable lucidity of intellect), is, I am led to consider, incompatible with the functions now devolving on me. I would therefore take the liberty of suggesting that in our friendly intercourse—which I trust will never be disturbed—we draw a line. On one side of this line," said Mr. Micawber, representing it on the desk with the office ruler, "is the whole range of the human intellect, with a trifling exception; on the other, *is* that exception—that is to say, the affairs of Messrs Wickfield and Heep, with all belonging and appertaining thereunto. I trust I give no offense to the companion of my youth, in submitting this proposition to his cooler judgment?"

Though I saw an uneasy change in Mr. Micawber, which sat tightly on him, as if his new duties were a misfit, I felt I had no right to be offended. My telling him so appeared to relieve him, and he shook hands with me.

"I am charmed, Copperfield," said Mr. Micawber, "let me assure you, with Miss Wickfield. She is a very superior young lady, of very remarkable attractions, graces, and virtues. Upon my honor," said Mr. Micawber, indefinitely kissing his hand and bowing with his genteelest air, "I do homage to Miss Wickfield! Hem!"

"I am glad of that, at least," said I.

"If you had not assured us, my dear Copperfield, on the occasion of that agreeable afternoon we had the happiness of passing with you, that D. was your favorite letter," said Mr. Micawber, "I should unquestionably have supposed that A. had been so."

We have all some experience of a feeling, that comes over us occasionally, of what we are saying and doing having been said and done before, in a remote time—of our knowing perfectly what will be said next, as if we suddenly remembered it! I never had this mysterious impression more strongly in my life than before he uttered those words.

I looked into the room still belonging to Agnes, and saw her sitting by the fire, at a pretty, old-fashioned desk she had, writing. My darkening the light made her look up. What a pleasure to be the cause of that bright change in her attentive face, and the object of that sweet regard and welcome.

"Ah, Agnes!" said I, when we were sitting together, side by side, "I have missed you so much lately."

"Indeed," she replied. "Again! And so soon?"

I shook my head.

"I don't know how it is, Agnes; I seem to want some faculty of mind that I ought to have. You were so much in the habit of thinking for me, in the happy old days here, and I came so naturally to you for counsel and support, that I really think I have missed acquiring it."

Her head was bent down, looking at the fire.

"It's the old story," said I. "Don't laugh when I say it was always the same in little things as it is in greater ones. My old troubles were nonsense, and now they are serious; but whenever I have gone away from my adopted sister——"

Agnes looked up—with such a heavenly face!—and gave me her hand, which I kissed.

"Whenever I have not had you, Agnes, to advise and approve in the beginning, I have seemed to go wild, and to get into all sorts of difficulty. When I have come to you, at last (as I have always done), I have come to peace and happiness. I come home, now, like a tired traveler, and find such a blessed sense of rest!"

In her placid sisterly manner, with her beaming eyes, with her tender voice, and with that sweet composure which had long ago made the house that held her quite a sacred place to me, she soon led me on to tell all that had happened since our last meeting.

"And there is not another word to tell, Agnes," said I, when I had made an end of my confidence. "Now, my reliance is on you."

"But it must not be on me, Trotwood," returned Agnes, with a pleasant smile. "It must be on someone else."

"On Dora?" said I.

"Assuredly."

I felt so grateful to Agnes, and admired her so! I saw those two together, in a bright perspective, such well-associated friends, each adoring the other so much!

"What ought I to do then, Agnes?" I inquired, after looking at the fire a little while. "What would it be right to do?"

"I think," said Agnes, "that the honorable course to take would be to write to those two ladies. Don't you think that any secret course is an unworthy one?"

"Yes; if *you* think so," said I.

"I am poorly qualified to judge of such matters," replied Agnes, with a modest hesitation, "but I certainly feel that your being secret and clandestine is not being like yourself."

"Like myself, in the too high opinion you have of me, Agnes, I am afraid," said I.

"Like yourself, in the candor of your nature," she returned; "and therefore I would write to those two ladies. I would ask their permission to visit sometimes at their house. Considering that you are young, and striving for a place in life, I think it would be well to say that you would readily abide by any conditions they might impose upon you. I would not be too vehement," said Agnes gently, "or propose too much. I would trust to my fidelity and perseverence —and to Dora."

268

I had no longer any doubt on the subject. With a lightened heart, though with a profound sense of the weighty importance of my task, I devoted the whole afternoon to the composition of the draft of this letter, for which great purpose Agnes relinquished her desk to me. But first I went downstairs to see Mr. Wickfield and Uriah Heep.

I found Uriah in possession of a new, plaster-smelling office, built out in the garden, looking extraordinarily mean, in the midst of a quantity of books and papers. He received me in his usual fawning way, and pretended not to have heard of my arrival from Mr. Micawber—a pretense I took the liberty of disbelieving. He accompanied me into Mr. Wickfield's room, which was the shadow of its former self—having been divested of a variety of conveniences, for the accommodation of the new partner—and stood before the fire, warming his back, and shaving his chin with his bony hand, while Mr. Wickfield and I exchanged greetings.

"You stay with us, Trotwood, while you remain in Canterbury?" said Mr. Wickfield, not without a glance at Uriah for his approval.

"Is there room for me?" said I.

"I am sure, Master Copperfield—I should say Mister, but the other comes so natural," said Uriah—"I would turn out of your old room with pleasure, if it would be agreeable."

"No, no," said Mr. Wickfield. "Why should *you* be inconvenienced? There's another room; there's another room."

"Oh, but you know," returned Uriah, with a grin, "I should really be delighted!"

To cut the matter short, I said I would have the other room, or none at all; so it was settled that I should have the other room, and taking my leave of the firm until dinner, I went upstairs again.

I had hoped to have no other companion than Agnes. But Mrs. Heep had asked permission to bring herself and her knitting near the fire in that room; on pretense of its having an aspect more favorable for her rheumatics. I made a virtue of necessity, and gave her a friendly salutation.

"I'm umbly thankful to you, sir," said Mrs. Heep, in acknowledgment of my inquiries concerning her health, "but I'm only pretty well. I haven't much to boast of. If I could see my Uriah well settled in life, I couldn't expect much more, I think. How do you think my Ury's looking, sir?"

I thought him looking as villainous as ever, and I replied that I saw no change in him.

"Oh, don't you think he's changed?" said Mrs. Heep. "There I must umbly beg to differ from you. Don't you see a thinness in him?"

"Not more than usual," I replied.

"*Don't* you though?" said Mrs. Heep. "But you don't take notice of him with a mother's eye!"

His mother's eye was an evil eye to the rest of the world, I thought as it met mine, howsoever affectionate to him; and I believe she and her son were devoted to one another. It passed me, and went on to Agnes.

"Don't you see a wasting and a wearing in him, Miss Wickfield," inquired Mrs. Heep.

"No," said Agnes, quietly pursuing the work on which she was engaged. "You are too solicitous about him. He is very well."

Mrs. Heep, with a prodigious sniff, resumed her knitting.

She never left off, or left us for a moment. I had arrived early in the day, and we had still three or four hours before dinner; but she sat there, plying her knitting-needles as monotonously as an hourglass might have poured out its sands.

At dinner she maintained her watch, with the same unwinking eyes. After dinner, her son took his turn; and when Mr. Wickfield, himself, and I were left alone together, leered at me, and writhed until I could hardly bear it. In the drawing-room, there was the mother knitting and watching again. It was evident to me that this was the duty assigned to her.

This lasted until bedtime. To have seen the mother and son, like two great bats hanging over the whole house, and darkening it with their ugly forms, made me so uncomfortable, that I would rather have remained downstairs, knitting and all, than gone to bed. I hardly got any sleep. Next day the knitting and watching began again, and lasted all day.

I had not an opportunity of speaking to Agnes for ten minutes. I could barely show her my letter. I proposed to her to walk out with me; but Mrs. Heep repeatedly complaining that she was worse, Agnes charitably remained within, to bear her company. Toward the twilight I went out by myself, musing on what I ought to do, and whether I was justified in withholding from Agnes any longer what Uriah Heep had told me in London, for that began to trouble me again very much.

I had not walked out far enough to be quite clear of the town, upon the Ramsgate Road, where there was a good path, when I was hailed through the dust by somebody behind me. The shambling figure, and the scanty greatcoat, were not to be mistaken. I stopped, and Uriah Heep came up.

"Well?" said I.

"How fast you walk!" said he. "My legs are pretty long, but you've given 'em quite a job."

"Where are you going?" said I.

"I am coming with you, Master Copperfield, if you'll allow me the pleasure of a walk with an old acquaintance." Saying this, with a jerk of his body, which might have been either propitiatory or derisive, he fell into step beside me.

"Uriah!" said I, as civilly as I could, after a silence.

"Master Copperfield!" said Uriah.

"To tell you the truth (at which you will not be offended), I came out to walk alone, because I have had so much company."

He looked at me sideways, and said with his hardest grin, "You mean mother."

"Why, yes, I do," said I.

"Ah! but you know we're so very umble," he returned. "And having such a knowledge of our own umbleness, we must really take care that we're not pushed to the wall by them as isn't umble. All stratagems are fair in love, sir."

Raising his great hands until they touched his chin, he rubbed them softly, and softly chuckled, looking as like a malevolent baboon, I thought, as anything human could look.

"You see," he said, still hugging himself in that unpleasant way, and shaking his head at me, "you're quite a dangerous rival, Master Copperfield. You always was, you know."

"Do you set a watch upon Miss Wickfield, and make her home no home, because of me?" said I.

"Oh! Master Copperfield! Those are very arsh words," he replied.

"Put my meaning into any words you like," said I. "You know what it is, Uriah, as well as I do."

"Oh, no! You must put it into words," he said. "Oh, really! I couldn't myself."

"Do you suppose," said I, constraining myself to be very temperate and quiet with him, on account of Agnes, "that I regard Miss Wickfield otherwise than as a very dear sister?"

"Well, Master Copperfield," he replied, "you perceive I am not bound to answer that question. You may not, you know. But then, you see, you may!"

Anything to equal the low cunning of his visage, and of his shadowless eyes without the ghost of an eyelash, I never saw.

"Come, then!" said I. "For the sake of Miss Wickfield——"

"My Agnes!" he exclaimed, with a sickly, angular contortion of himself. "Would you be so good as call her Agnes, Master Copperfield?"

"For the sake of Agnes Wickfield—Heaven bless her!"—

"Thank you for that blessing, Master Copperfield!" he interposed.

"—I will tell you what I should, under any other circumstances, as soon have thought of telling to—Jack Ketch."

"To who, sir?" said Uriah, stretching out his neck, and shading his ear with his hand.

"To the hangman," I returned. "The most unlikely person I could think of"—though his own face had suggested the allusion quite as a natural sequence. "I am engaged to another young lady. I hope that contents you."

"Upon your soul?" said Uriah.

I was about indignantly to give my assertion the confirmation he required, when he caught hold of my hand and gave it a squeeze.

"Oh, Master Copperfield," he said, "if you had only had the condescension to return my confidence when I poured out the fulness of my art, I never should have doubted you. As it is, I'm sure I'll take off mother directly, and only too appy. I know you'll excuse the precautions of affection, won't you?"

"Before we leave the subject, you ought to understand," said I, "that I believe Agnes Wickfield to be as far above *you*, and as far removed from all *your* aspirations, as that moon herself!"

"Peaceful! ain't she?" said Uriah. "Very! Now confess, Master Copperfield, that you haven't liked me quite as I have liked you. All along you've thought me too umble now, I shouldn't wonder?"

"I am not fond of professions of humility," I returned, "or professions of anything else."

"There now!" said Uriah, looking flabby and lead-colored in the moonlight. "Didn't I know it! But how little you think of the rightful umbleness of a person in my station, Master Copperfield! Father and me was both brought up at a foundation school for boys; and mother, she was likewise brought up at a public, sort of charitable, establishment. They taught us all a deal of umbleness—not much else that I know of, from morning to night. We was to be umble to this person, and umble to that; and to pull off our caps here, and to make bows there; and always to know our place, and abase

272

ourselves before our betters. And we had such a lot of betters! Father got the monitor-medal by being umble. So did I. Father got made a sexton by being umble. He had the character, among the gentlefolks, of being such a well-behaved man, that they were determined to bring him in. 'Be umble, Uriah,' says father to me, 'and you'll get on. It was what was always being dinned into you and me at school: it's what goes down best. Be umble,' says father, 'and you'll do!' And really it ain't done bad! I am very umble to the present moment, Master Copperfield, but I've got a little power!"

He said all this—I knew, as I saw his face in the moonlight—that I might understand he was resolved to recompense himself by using his power. I had never doubted his meanness, his craft, and malice; but I fully comprehended now, for the first time, what a base, unrelenting, and revengeful spirit must have been engendered by this early, and this long, suppression.

Whether his spirits were elevated by the communication I had made to him, or by his having indulged in this retrospect, I don't know; but they were raised by some influence. He talked more at dinner than was usual with him; asked his mother (off duty from the moment of our re-entering the house) whether he was not growing too old for a bachelor; and once looked at Agnes so, that I would have given all I had for leave to knock him down.

When we three males were left alone after dinner, he got into a more adventurous state. He had taken little or no wine; and I presume it was the mere insolence of triumph that was upon him, flushed perhaps by the temptation my presence furnished to its exibition.

I had observed yesterday that he tried to entice Mr. Wickfield to drink; and interpreting the look which Agnes had given me as she went out, had limited myself to one glass, and then proposed that we should follow her. I would have done so again today, but Uriah was too quick for me.

"We seldom see our present visitor, sir," he said, addressing Mr. Wickfield, sitting, such a contrast to him, at the end of the table, "and I should propose to give him welcome in another glass or two of wine, if you have no objections.— Master Copperfield, your elth and appiness!"

I was obliged to make a show of taking the hand he stretched across to me; and then, with very different emotions, I took the hand of the broken gentleman, his partner.

"Come, fellow-partner," said Uriah, "if I may take the liberty—

now, suppose you give us something or another appropriate to Copperfield!"

I pass over Mr. Wickfield's proposing my aunt, his proposing Mr. Dick, his proposing Doctors' Commons, his proposing Uriah, his drinking everything twice; his consciousness of his own weakness, the ineffectual effort that he made against it; it made me sick at heart to see.

"Come, fellow-partner!" said Uriah at last, "I'll give you another one, and I umbly ask for bumpers, seeing I intend to make it the divinest of her sex."

Her father had his empty glass in his hand. I saw him set it down, look at the picture she was so like, put his hand to his forehead, and shrink back in his elbow-chair.

"Agnes," said Uriah, either not regarding him, or not knowing what the nature of his action was, "Agnes Wickfield is, I am safe to say, the divinest of her sex. May I speak out, among friends? To be her father is a proud distinction, but to be her usband——"

Spare me from ever again hearing such a cry as that with which her father rose up from the table!

"What's the matter?" said Uriah, turning of a deadly color. "You are not gone mad, after all, Mr. Wickfield, I hope? If I say I've an ambition to make your Agnes my Agnes, I have as good a right to it as another man. I have a better right to it than any other man!"

I had my arms round Mr. Wickfield, imploring him by everything that I could think of, oftenest of all by his love for Agnes, to calm himself a little. He was mad for the moment, his face all staring and distorted—a frightful spectacle. I besought him to think of Agnes, to recollect how Agnes and I had grown up together, how I honored her and loved her, how she was his pride and joy! I may have effected something, or his wildness may have spent itself; but at length he said, "I know, Trotwood! My darling child and you—I know! But look at him!"

He pointed to Uriah, pale and glowering in a corner, evidently very much out in his calculations, and taken by surprise.

"Look at my torturer," he replied. "Before him I have step by step abandoned name and reputation, peace and quiet, house and home."

"I have kept your name reputation for you, and your peace and quiet, and your house and home too," said Uriah, with a sulky, hurried, defeated air of compromise. "Don't be foolish, Mr. Wickfield. If I have gone a little beyond what you were prepared for, I can go back, I suppose? There's no harm done."

"I looked for single motives in everyone," said Mr. Wickfield, "and I was satisfied I had bound him to me by motives of interest. But see what he is—oh, see what he is!"

"You had better stop him, Copperfield, if you can," cried Uriah, with his long forefinger pointing toward me. "He'll say something presently—mind you!—he'll be sorry to have said afterwards, and you'll be sorry to have heard!"

"I'll say anything!" cried Mr. Wickfield, with a desperate air. "Why should I not be in all the world's power if I am in yours?"

He dropped into a chair, and weakly sobbed. The excitement into which he had been roused was leaving him. Uriah came out of his corner.

"I don't know all I have done in my fatuity," said Mr. Wickfield, putting out his hands as if to deprecate my condemnation. "*He* knows best"—meaning Uriah Heep—"for he has always been at my elbow, whispering me. You see the millstone that he is about my neck. You find him in my house, you find him in my business. You heard him but a little time ago. What need have I to say more?"

"You haven't need to say so much, nor half so much, nor anything at all," observed Uriah, half defiant and half fawning. "You wouldn't have took it up so if it hadn't been for the wine. You'll think better of it tomorrow, sir. If I have said too much, or more than I meant, what of it? I haven't stood by it!"

The door opened, and Agnes, gliding in, without a vestige of color in her face, put her arm round his neck, and steadily said, "Papa, you are not well. Come with me!" He laid his head upon her shoulder, as if he were oppressed with heavy shame, and went out with her. Her eyes met mine for but an instant, yet I saw how much she knew of what had passed.

"I didn't expect he'd cut up so rough, Master Copperfield," said Uriah. "But it's nothing. I'll be friends with him tomorrow. It's for his good. I'm umbly anxious for his good."

I gave him no answer, and went upstairs into the quiet room where Agnes had so often sat beside me at my books. Nobody came near me until late at night. I took up a book and tried to read. I heard the clock strike twelve, and was still reading, without knowing what I read, when Agnes touched me.

"You will be going early in the morning, Trotwood! Let us say good-bye now."

She had been weeping, but her face then was so calm and beautiful!

"Dear Agnes," I said, "it is presumptuous for me, who am so poor in all in which you are so rich—goodness, resolution, all noble qualities—to doubt or direct you; but you know how much I love you, and how much I owe you. You will never sacrifice yourself to a mistaken sense of duty, Agnes?"

More agitated for a moment than I had ever seen her, she took her hand from me, and moved a step back. Oh, long, long afterwards I saw that look subside, as it did now, into the lovely smile with which she told me she had no fear for herself—I need have none for her—and parted from me by the name of Brother, and was gone!

It was dark in the morning when I got upon the coach at the inn door. The day was just breaking when we were about to start; and then, as I sat thinking of her, came struggling up the coach side, through the mingled day and night, Uriah's head.

"Copperfield," said he, in a croaking whisper, as he hung by the iron on the roof, "I thought you'd be glad to hear, before you went off, that there are no squares broke between us. I've been into his room already, and we've made it all smooth. Why, though I'm umble, I'm useful to him, you know; and he understands his interest when he isn't in liquor. What an agreeable man he is after all, Master Copperfield!"

I obliged myself to say that I was glad he had made his apology.

"Oh, to be sure!" said Uriah. "When a person's umble, you know, what's an apology? So easy! I say! I suppose," with a jerk, "you have sometimes plucked a pear before it was ripe, Master Copperfield?"

"I suppose I have," I replied.

"*I* did that last night," said Uriah; "but it'll ripen yet! It only wants attending to. I can wait!"

Profuse in his farewells, he got down again as the coachman got up. For anything I know, he was eating something to keep the raw morning air out; but he made motions with his mouth as if the pear were ripe already, and he were smacking his lips over it.

MY AUNT read my letter to the two old ladies in the morning, and approved of it. I posted it, and had nothing to do then but wait, as patiently as I could, for the reply. I was still in this state of expectation, and had been for nearly a week, when I left the Doctor's one snowy night to walk home.

My shortest way home—and I naturally took the shortest way on such a night—was through St. Martin's Lane. On the steps of the church which gives its name to the lane there was the stooping figure of a man, who had put down some burden on the smooth snow to adjust it. My seeing the face, and my seeing him, were simultaneous. I don't think I had stopped in my surprise; but, in any case, as I went on, he rose, turned, and came down toward me. I stood face to face with Mr. Peggotty!

We shook hands heartily. At first neither of us could speak a word.

"Mas'r Davy," he said, gripping me tight, "it do my 'art good to see you, sir. Well met, well met!"

"Well met, my dear old friend!" said I.

"I had my thowts o' coming to make inquiration for you, sir," he said, "afore going away."

"Again?" said I.

"Yes, sir," he replied, patiently shaking his head, "I'm away to-morrow."

In those days there was a side entrance to the stable-yard of the Golden Cross, and we went across. Two or three public rooms opened out of the stable-yard; and looking into one of them, and finding it empty, and a good fire burning, I took him in there.

When I saw him in the light, I observed, not only that his hair was long and ragged, but that his face was burnt dark by the sun. He was greyer, the lines in his face and forehead were deeper, and he had every appearance of having toiled and wandered through all varieties of weather; but he looked very strong, and like a man upheld by steadfastness of purpose, whom nothing could tire out.

I rang the bell for something hot to drink. He would have nothing stronger than ale; and while it was being brought, and being warmed at the fire, he sat thinking. There was a fine massive gravity in his face I did not venture to disturb.

"When she was a child," he said, lifting up his head soon after we were left alone, "she used to talk to me a deal about the sea, and about them coasts where the sea got to be dark blue, and lay a-shining and a-shining in the sun."

"When she was—lost," said Mr. Peggotty, "I know'd in my mind as he would take her to them countries. I know'd in my mind as he'd have told her wonders of 'em and how she was to be a lady theer. I went across-channel to France, and landed theer, as if I'd fell down from the sky."

I saw the door move, and the snow drift in. I saw it move a little more, and a hand softly interpose to keep it open.

"I found out an English gen'leman as was in authority," said Mr. Peggotty, "and told him I was a-going to seek my niece. He got me them papers as I wanted fur to carry me through—I doen't rightly know how they're called—and he would have give me money, but that I was thankful to have no need on. I thank him kind for all he done, I'm sure, and went away through France."

"Alone, and on foot?" said I.

"Mostly a-foot," he rejoined; "sometimes in carts along with people going to market, sometimes in empty coaches. When I come to any town, I found the inn, and waited about the yard till some-one turned up (someone mostly did) as know'd English. Then they told me what manner of gentlefolks was in the house, and I waited to see any as seemed like her, going in or out. When it warn't Em'ly, I went on agen."

It was Martha at the door, Martha to whom Emily had given the money that night in the kitchen. I saw her haggard, listening face distinctly. My dread was lest he should turn his head and see her too.

"At last I come to the sea. It warn't hard, you may suppose, for a sea-faring man like me to work his way over to Italy. When I got theer, I wandered on as I had done afore. I should have gone from town to town, maybe the country through, but that I got news of her being seen among them Swiss mountains yonder. One as know'd his sarvant see 'em there, all three, and told me how they traveled, and where they was. I made for them mountains, Mas'r Davy, day and night. Ever so fur as I went, ever so fur the mountains seemed to shift away from me. But I come up with 'em, and I crossed 'em."

The listening face, insensible to the inclement night, still drooped at the door, and the hands begged me not to cast it forth.

He stopped and shook his head, and went on with a sigh. "But, Mas'r Davy, it warn't to be—not yet! I was too late, and they was gone. Wheer, I couldn't learn. Some said here, some said theer. I traveled here, and I traveled theer; but I found no Em'ly, and I traveled home."

From some pocket in his breast he took out, with a very careful hand, a small paper bundle containing two or three letters or little packets, which he laid upon the table.

"This fust one come," he said, selecting it from the rest, "afore I had been gone a week—a fifty pound bank-note, in a sheet of paper, directed to me, and put underneath the door in the night. She tried to hide her writing, but she couldn't hide it from me!"

He folded up the note again, with great patience and care, in exactly the same form, and laid it on one side.

"Is that another letter in your hand?" said I.

"It's money, sir," said Mr. Peggotty, unfolding it a little way. "Ten pound, you see. And wrote inside, 'From a true friend,' like the fust. But the fust was put underneath the door, and this come by the post, day afore yesterday. I'm a-going to seek her at the postmark."

He showed it to me. It was a town on the Upper Rhine. He had found out, at Yarmouth, some foreign dealers who knew that country, and they had drawn him a rude map on paper, which he could very well understand.

He gathered up the letters thoughtfully, smoothing them with his hand. The face was gone from the door. I still saw the snow drifting in, but nothing else was there.

"Well!" he said, looking to his bag, "having seen you tonight, Mas'r Davy (and that does me good), I shall away betimes to-morrow morning."

He rose, and I rose too. We grasped each other by the hand again, before going out.

"I'd go ten thousand miles," he said—"I'd go till I dropped dead —to lay that money down afore him. If I do that, and find my Em'ly, I'm content. If I doen't find her, maybe she'll come to hear, sometime, as her loving uncle only ended his search for her when he ended his life; and if I know her, even that will turn her home at last!"

As we went out into the rigorous night, I saw the lonely figure flit away before us. I turned him hastily on some pretense, and held him in conversation until it was gone.

AT LAST an answer came from the two old ladies. They presented their compliments to Mr. Copperfield, and informed him that they had given his letter their best consideration, "with a view to the happiness of both parties." The Misses Spenlow added that they begged to forbear expressing, "through the medium of correspondence," an opinion on the subject of Mr. Copperfield's communication; but that if Mr. Copperfield would do them the favor to call, upon a certain day (accompanied, if he thought proper, by a confidential friend), they would be happy to hold some conversation on the subject.

Mr. Copperfield immediately replied, with his respectful compliments, that he would have the honor of waiting on the Misses Spenlow, at the time appointed; accompanied, in accordance with their kind permission, by his friend, Mr. Thomas Traddles of the Inner Temple. Having dispatched which missive, Mr. Copperfield fell into a condition of strong nervous agitation; and so remained until the day arrived.

It was a great augmentation of my uneasiness to be bereaved, at this eventful crisis, of the inestimable services of Miss Mills. But

Mr. Mills, who was always doing something or other to annoy me—or I felt as if he were, which was the same thing—had brought his conduct to a climax, by taking it into his head that he would go to India, and Julia with him; and Julia went into the country to take leave of her relations.

Excellent fellow as I knew Traddles to be, and warmly attached to him as I was, I could not help wishing, on that delicate occasion, that he had never contracted the habit of brushing his hair so very upright. It gave him a surprised look—not to say a hearth-broomy kind of expression—which, my apprehensions whispered, might be fatal to us. I took the liberty of mentioning it to Traddles as we were walking to Putney, and saying that if he *would* smooth it down a little——

"My dear Copperfield," said Traddles, lifting off his hat, and rubbing his hair all kinds of ways, "nothing would give me greater pleasure. But it won't."

"Won't be smoothed down?" said I.

"No," said Traddles. "Nothing will induce it. I assure you it's quite an old story, my unfortunate hair. It stood very much in my way, too, when I first fell in love with Sophy—very much!"

"Did she object to it?"

"*She* didn't," rejoined Traddles; "but her eldest sister—the one that's the Beauty—quite made game of it, I understand. In fact, all the sisters laugh at it."

"Agreeable!" said I.

"Yes," returned Traddles, with perfect innocence, "it's a joke for us. They pretend that Sophy has a lock of it in her desk, and is obliged to shut it in a clasped book to keep it down. We laugh about it."

His honest face impresses me more in the remembrance than it did in the reality, for I was by this time in a state of such excessive trepidation that Traddles proposed a gentle stimulant in the form of a glass of ale. This having been administered at a neighboring public-house, he conducted me, with tottering steps, to the Misses Spenlow's door.

I had a vague sensation of being, as it were, on view when the maid opened it, and of wavering somehow into a quiet little drawing-room on the ground floor, commanding a neat garden. Also of sitting down here, on a sofa, and seeing Traddles' hair start up, now his hat was removed, like one of those obtrusive little figures made of springs that fly out of fictitious snuff-boxes when the lid is taken off. Also of looking round the room for any sign of Dora, and seeing none. Also of thinking that Jip once barked in the distance, and was instantly choked by somebody. Ultimately I found myself bowing in great confusion to two dry little elderly ladies, dressed in black. There was a disparity of six or eight years between the two sisters; and the younger appeared to be the manager of the conference, inasmuch as she had my letter in her hand.

"Mr. Copperfield, I believe," said the sister who had got my letter, addressing herself to Traddles.

This was a frightful beginning. Traddles had to indicate that I was Mr. Copperfield, and I had to lay claim to myself. To improve it, we all distinctly heard Jip give two short barks, and receive another choke.

"Mr. Copperfield!" said the sister with the letter.

I did something—bowed, I suppose—and was all attention, when the other sister struck in.

"My sister Lavinia," said she, "being conversant with matters of this nature, will state what we consider most calculated to promote the happiness of both parties."

I discovered afterwards that Miss Lavinia was an authority in affairs of the heart, by reason of there having anciently existed a certain Mr. Pidger, who played short whist, and was supposed to have been enamored of her. My private opinion is, that this was entirely a gratuitous assumption, and that Pidger was altogether innocent of any such sentiments—to which he had never given any sort of expression that I could ever hear of. Both Miss Lavinia and Miss Clarissa had a superstition, however, that he would have declared his passion, if he had not been cut short in his youth (at about sixty) by overdrinking his constitution.

"Our niece's position, or supposed position, is much changed by our brother Francis' death," said Miss Lavinia; "and therefore we consider our brother's opinions as regarded her position as being changed too. We have no reason to doubt, Mr. Copperfield, that you are a young gentleman possessed of good qualities and honorable character, or that you have an affection—or are fully persuaded that you have an affection—for our niece."

I replied, as I usually did whenever I had a chance, that nobody had ever loved anybody else as I loved Dora. Traddles came to my assistance with a confirmatory murmur.

Miss Lavinia was going on to make some rejoinder, when Miss Clarissa struck in again.

"If Dora's mamma," she said, "when she married our brother Francis, had at once said that there was not room for the family at the dinner-table, it would have been better for the happiness of all."

"Sister Clarissa," said Miss Lavinia, "perhaps we needn't mind that now."

"Sister Lavinia," said Miss Clarissa, "it belongs to the subject. With your branch of the subject, on which alone you are competent to speak, I should not think of interfering. On this branch of the subject I have a voice and an opinion. It would have been better for the happiness of all parties, if Dora's mamma, when she married our brother Francis, had mentioned plainly what her intentions were. We should then have known what we had to expect. We should have said, 'Pray do not invite us at any time'; and all possibility of misunderstanding would have been avoided."

When Miss Clarissa had shaken her head, Miss Lavinia resumed, again referring to my letter through her eye-glass. They both had little bright round twinkling eyes, by the way, which were like birds' eyes. They were not unlike birds, altogether—having a sharp, brisk, sudden manner, and a little short, spruce way of adjusting themselves, like canaries.

Miss Lavinia, as I have said, resumed,

"You ask permission of my sister Clarissa and myself, Mr. Copperfield, to visit here, as the accepted suitor of our niece."

"If our brother Francis," said Miss Clarissa, breaking out again—if I may call anything so calm a breaking out—"wished to surround himself with an atmosphere of Doctors' Commons, and of Doctors' Commons only, what right or desire had we to object? None, I am sure. We have ever been far from wishing to obtrude ourselves on anyone."

As this appeared to be addressed to Traddles and me, both Traddles and I made some sort of reply. Traddles was inaudible. I think I observed, myself, that it was highly creditable to all concerned. I don't in the least know what I meant.

"Sister Lavinia," said Miss Clarissa, having now relieved her mind, "you can go on, my dear."

"Affection," said Miss Lavinia, glancing at her sister for corroboration, which she gave in the form of a little nod to every clause, "mature affection, homage, devotion, does not easily express itself. Its voice is low. It is modest and retiring; it lies in ambush, waits and waits. Such is the mature fruit. Sometimes a life glides away, and finds it still ripening in the shade."

Of course I did not understand then that this was an allusion to her supposed experience of the stricken Pidger; but I saw, from the gravity with which Miss Clarissa nodded her head, that great weight was attached to these words.

"The light—for I call them, in comparison with such sentiments, the light—inclinations of very young people," pursued Miss Lavinia, "are dust, compared to rocks. It is owing to the difficulty of knowing whether they are likely to endure or have any real foundation, that my sister Clarissa and myself have been very undecided how to act, Mr. Copperfield, and Mr.——"

"Traddles," said my friend, finding himself looked at.

"My sister and myself have been in great doubt, Mr. Traddles, what course we ought to take in reference to the likings, or imaginary likings, of such very young people as your friend Mr. Copperfield and our niece."

"Our brother Francis' child," remarked Miss Clarissa. "If our brother Francis' wife had found it convenient in her lifetime (though she had an unquestionable right to act as she thought best) to invite the family to her dinner-table, we might have known our brother Francis' child better at the present moment. Sister Lavinia, proceed."

Miss Lavinia turned my letter, so as to bring the superscription toward herself, and referred through her eye-glass to some orderly-looking notes she had made on that part of it.

"It seems to us," said she, "prudent, Mr. Traddles, to bring these feelings to the test of our own observation. Therefore we are inclined to admit Mr. Copperfield's visits here."

"I shall never, dear ladies," I exclaimed, relieved of an immense load of apprehension, "forget your kindness!"

"But," pursued Miss Lavinia—"but we would prefer to regard those visits, Mr. Traddles, as made, at present, to us. We must guard ourselves from recognizing any positive engagement between Mr. Copperfield and our niece, until we have had an opportunity——"

"Until you have had an opportunity, sister Lavinia," said Miss Clarissa.

"Be it so," assented Miss Lavinia, with a sigh—"until I have had an opportunity of observing them."

"Copperfield," said Traddles, turning to me, "you feel, I am sure, that nothing could be more reasonable or considerate."

"Nothing!" cried I. "I am deeply sensible of it."

"Sister Clarissa," said Miss Lavinia, "the rest is with you."

Miss Clarissa, unfolding her arms for the first time, took the notes and glanced at them.

"We shall be happy," said Miss Clarissa, "to see Mr. Copperfield to dinner every Sunday, if it should suit his convenience. Our hour is three."

I bowed.

"In the course of the week," said Miss Clarissa, "we shall be happy to see Mr. Copperfield to tea. Our hour is half-past six."

I bowed again.

"Twice in the week," said Miss Clarissa, "but, as a rule, not oftener."

I bowed again.

"Miss Trotwood," said Miss Clarissa, "mentioned in Mr. Copperfield's letter, will perhaps call upon us. When visiting is better for the happiness of all parties, we are glad to receive visits, and return them. When it is better for the happiness of all parties that no visiting should take place (as in the case of our brother Francis, and his establishment), that is quite different."

I intimated that my aunt would be proud and delighted to make their acquaintance—though I must say I was not quite sure of their getting on very satisfactorily together. The conditions being now closed, I expressed my acknowledgments in the warmest manner; and taking the hand, first of Miss Clarissa, and then of Miss Lavinia, pressed it, in each case, to my lips.

Miss Lavinia then arose, and begging Mr. Traddles to excuse us for a minute, requested me to follow her. I obeyed, all in a tremble, and was conducted into another room. There I found my blessed darling stopping her ears behind the door, with her dear little face against the wall; and Jip in the plate-warmer, with his head tied up in a towel.

Oh! how beautiful she was in her black frock, and how she sobbed and cried at first, and wouldn't come out from behind the door! How fond we were of one another, when she did come out at last; and what a state of bliss I was in, when we took Jip out of the plate-warmer, and restored him to the light, sneezing very much, and were all three reunited!

"My dearest Dora! now, indeed, my own forever!"

"Oh, DON'T," pleaded Dora. "Please!"

"Are you not my own forever, Dora?"

"Oh, yes, of course I am!" cried Dora; "but I am so frightened!"

"Frightened, my own?"

"Oh, yes! I don't like him," said Dora. "Why don't he go?"

"Who, my life?"

"Your friend," said Dora. "It isn't any business of his. What a stupid he must be!"

"My love!" (There never was anything so coaxing as her childish ways.) "He is the best creature!"

"Oh, but we don't want any best creatures!" pouted Dora.

"My dear," I argued, "you will soon know him well, and like him of all things. And here is my aunt coming soon; and you'll like her of all things too, when you know her."

"No, please don't bring her!" said Dora, giving me a horrified little kiss, and folding her hands. "Don't. I know she's a naughty, mischief-making old thing! Don't let her come here, Doady!" which was a corruption of David.

Remonstrance was of no use, then; so I laughed, and admired, and was very much in love and very happy; and she showed me Jip's new trick of standing on his hind legs in a corner—which he did for about the space of a flash of lightning, and then fell down— and I don't know how long I should have stayed there, oblivious of Traddles, if Miss Lavinia had not come in to take me away.

I had my hands more full than ever now. My daily journeys to Highgate considered, Putney was a long way off; and I naturally wanted to go there as often as I could. The proposed tea-drinkings being quite impracticable, I compounded with Miss Lavinia for permission to visit every Saturday afternoon, without detriment to my privileged Sundays. So the close of every week was a delicious time for me; and I got through the rest of the week by looking forward to it.

I was wonderfully relieved to find that my aunt and Dora's aunts rubbed on, all things considered, much more smoothly than I could have expected. Dora's aunts soon agreed to regard my aunt as an eccentric and somewhat masculine lady, with a strong understanding; and although my aunt occasionally ruffled the feathers of Dora's aunts, by expressing heretical opinions on various points of ceremony, she loved me too well not to sacrifice some of her little peculiarities to the general harmony.

One thing troubled me much, after we had fallen into this quiet train. It was, that Dora seemed by one consent to be regarded like a pretty toy or plaything. My aunt, with whom she gradually became familiar, always called her Little Blossom; and the pleasure of Miss Lavinia's life was to wait upon her, curl her hair, make ornaments for her, and treat her like a pet child. What Miss Lavinia did, her sister did as a matter of course. It was very odd to me, but they all seemed to treat Dora, in her degree, much as Dora treated Jip in his.

I made up my mind to speak to Dora about this; and one day, when we were out walking (for we were licensed by Miss Lavinia, after a while, to go out walking by ourselves), I said to her that I wished she could get them to behave toward her differently.

"Because you know, my darling," I remonstrated, "you are not a child."

"There!" said Dora. "Now you're going to be cross!"

"Cross, my love?"

"I am sure they're very kind to me," said Dora, "and I am very happy."

"Well! But, my dearest life," said I, "you might be very happy, and yet be treated rationally."

Dora gave me a reproachful look—the prettiest look!—and then began to sob, saying if I didn't like her, why had I ever wanted so much to be engaged to her? And why didn't I go away now, if I couldn't bear her?

What could I do but kiss away her tears, and tell her how I doted on her, after that?

"I am sure I am very affectionate," said Dora; "you oughtn't to be cruel to me, Doady!"

"Cruel, my precious love! As if I would—or could—be cruel to you, for the world!"

"Then don't find fault with me," said Dora, making a rosebud of her mouth, "and I'll be good."

M Y NARRATIVE proceeds to Agnes with a thankful love. She
came with her father on a visit of a fortnight to the Doctor's. I was not much surprised to hear from her that she
had engaged to find a lodging in the neighborhood for Mrs. Heep,
whose rheumatic complaint required change of air, and who would
be charmed to have it in such company. Neither was I surprised
when, on the very next day, Uriah, like a dutiful son, brought his
worthy mother to take possession.

"You see, Master Copperfield," said he, as he forced himself upon
my company for a turn in the Doctor's garden, "where a person
loves, a person is a little jealous—leastways, anxious to keep an eye
on the beloved one."

"Of whom are you jealous now?" said I.

"Thanks to you, Master Copperfield," he returned, "of no one in
particular just at present—no male person, at least."

"Do you mean that you are jealous of a female person?"

He gave me a sidelong glance out of his sinister red eyes, and
laughed.

"Really, Master Copperfield," he said—"I should say Mister, but
I know you'll excuse the abit I've got into—you're so insinuating

that you draw me like a corkscrew! Well, I don't mind telling you"
—putting his fishlike hand on mine—

"I'm not a lady's man in general, sir, and I never was, with Mrs. Strong."

His eyes looked green now, as they watched mine with a rascally cunning.

"What do you mean?" said I.

"Why, though I am a lawyer, Master Copperfield," he replied with a dry grin. "I mean, just at present, what I say."

"And what do you mean by your look?" I retorted quietly.

"By my look? Dear me, Copperfield, that's sharp practice! What do I mean by my look?"

"Yes," said I, "by your look."

He seemed very much amused, and laughed as heartily as it was in his nature to laugh. After some scraping of his chin with his hand, he went on to say, with his eyes cast downward—still scraping, very slowly,

"When I was but an umble clerk, she always looked down upon me. She was forever having my Agnes backwards and forwards at her ouse, and she was forever being a friend to you, Master Copperfield; but I was too far beneath her, myself, to be noticed."

"Well," said I, "suppose you were?"

He left off scraping his chin, and sucked in his cheeks until they seemed to meet inside, keeping his sidelong glance upon me all the while.

"She is one of your lovely women, she is," he pursued, when he had slowly restored his face to its natural form, "and ready to be no friend to such as me, *I* know. She's just the person as would put my Agnes up to higher sort of game. Now, I ain't one of your lady's men, Master Copperfield, but I've had eyes in my ed a pretty long time back. We umble ones have got eyes, mostly speaking, and we look out of 'em."

I endeavored to appear unconscious and not disquieted, but, I saw in his face, with poor success.

"Now, I'm not a-going to let myself be run down, Copperfield," he continued, raising that part of his countenance where his red eyebrows would have been, if he had had any, with malignant triumph, "and I shall do what I can to put a stop to this friendship. I don't approve of it. I don't mind acknowledging to you that I've got rather a grudging disposition, and want to keep off all intruders. I ain't a-going, if I know it, to run the risk of being plotted against."

"You are always plotting, and delude yourself into the belief that everybody else is doing the like, I think," said I.

"Perhaps so, Master Copperfield," he replied; "but I've got a motive, as my fellow-partner used to say, and I go at it tooth and nail. I mustn't be put upon, as an umble person, too much. I can't allow people in my way. Really they must come out of the cart, Master Copperfield!"

"I don't understand you," said I.

"Don't you, though?" he returned, with one of his jerks. "I'm astonished at that, Master Copperfield, you being usually so quick! I'll try to be plainer another time. Is that Mr. Maldon a-norseback, ringing at the gate, sir?"

"It looks like him," I replied as carelessly as I could.

Uriah stopped short, put his hands between his great knobs of knees, and doubled himself up with laughter—with perfectly silent laughter. Not a sound escaped from him. I was so repelled by his odious behavior, particularly by this concluding instance, that I turned away without any ceremony, and left him doubled up in the middle of the garden, like a scarecrow in want of support.

It was not on that evening, but, as I well remember, on the next evening but one, which was a Saturday, that I took Agnes to see Dora. I had arranged the visit beforehand with Miss Lavinia, and Agnes was expected to tea.

She was not in the drawing-room when I presented Agnes to her little aunts, but was shyly keeping out of the way. I knew where to look for her now; and sure enough I found her, stopping her ears again, behind the same dull old door.

At first she wouldn't come at all, and then she pleaded for five minutes by my watch. When at length she put her arm through mine, to be taken to the drawing-room, her charming little face was flushed, and had never been so pretty; but when we went into the room, and it turned pale, she was ten thousand times prettier yet.

Dora was afraid of Agnes. She had told me that she knew Agnes was "too clever." But when she saw her looking at once so cheerful and so earnest, and so thoughtful, and so good, she gave a faint little cry of pleased surprise, and just put her affectionate arms round Agnes' neck, and laid her innocent cheek against her face.

The gentle cheerfulness of Agnes went to all their hearts. Her quiet interest in everything that interested Dora, her manner of making acquaintance with Jip (who responded instantly), her pleasant way when Dora was ashamed to come over to her usual seat by me, her modest grace and ease, eliciting a crowd of blushing little marks of confidence from Dora, seemed to make our circle quite complete.

"I am so glad," said Dora, after tea, "that you like me. I didn't think you would; and I want, more than ever, to be liked, now Julia Mills is gone."

Agnes said she was afraid I must have given her an unpromising character; but Dora corrected that directly.

"Oh, no!" she said, shaking her curls at me; "it was all praise. He thinks so much of your opinion, that I was quite afraid of it."

"My good opinion cannot strengthen his attachment to some people whom he knows," said Agnes, with a smile; "it is not worth their having."

"But please let me have it," said Dora, in her coaxing way, "if you can!"

The short evening flew away on gossamer wings. The time was at hand when the coach was to call for us. I was standing alone before the fire, when Dora came stealing softly in, to give me that usual precious little kiss before I went.

"Don't you think, if I had had her for a friend a long time ago, Doady," said Dora, her bright eyes shining very brightly, and her little right hand idly busying itself with one of the buttons of my coat, "I might have been more clever perhaps?"

"My love!" said I, "what nonsense!"

"Do you think it is nonsense?" returned Dora, without looking at me. "Are you sure it is?"

"Of course I am!"

"I have forgotten," said Dora, still turning the button round and round, "what relation Agnes is to you, you dear bad boy."

"No blood-relation," I replied; "but we were brought up together, like brother and sister."

"I wonder why you ever fell in love with me?" said Dora, beginning on another button of my coat.

"Perhaps because I couldn't see you and not love you, Dora!"

"Suppose you had never seen me at all," said Dora, going to another button.

"Suppose we had never been born!" said I gaily.

I wondered what she was thinking about, as I glanced in admiring silence at the little soft hand traveling up the row of buttons on my coat, and at the clustering hair that lay against my breast, and at the lashes of her downcast eyes, slightly rising as they followed her idle finger. At length her eyes were lifted up to mine, and she stood on tiptoe to give me, more thoughtfully than usual, that precious little kiss—once, twice, three times—and went out of the room.

There was a hurried but affectionate parting between Agnes and herself; and Dora was to write to Agnes (who was not to mind her letters being foolish, she said), and Agnes was to write to Dora; and they had a second parting at the coach-door, and a third when Dora, in spite of the remonstrances of Miss Lavinia, would come running out once more to remind Agnes at the coach-window about writing, and to shake her curls at me on the box.

Never, never had I loved Dora so deeply and truly as I loved her that night. When we had again alighted, and were walking in the starlight along the quiet road that led to the Doctor's house, I told Agnes it was her doing.

"When you were sitting by her," said I, "you seemed to be no less *her* guardian angel than mine; and you seem so now, Agnes."

"A poor angel," she returned, "but faithful."

I glanced at the serene face looking upward, and thought it was the stars that made it seem so noble.

"There has been no change at home," said Agnes, after a few moments.

"No fresh reference," said I, "to—I wouldn't distress you, Agnes, but I cannot help asking—to what we spoke of when we parted last?"

"No, none," she answered.

"I have thought so much about it."

"You must think less about it. Have no apprehensions for me, Trotwood," she added, after a moment; "the step you dread my taking, I shall never take."

We were now within the little courtyard of the Doctor's cottage. It was growing late. There was a light in the window of Mrs. Strong's chamber, and Agnes, pointing to it, bade me good-night.

I had engaged a bed at a decent alehouse close by, and was going out at the gate, when, happening to turn my head, I saw a light in the Doctor's study. A half-reproachful fancy came into my mind that he had been working at the Dictionary without my help. With the view of seeing if this were so, and, in any case, of bidding him good-night, if he were yet sitting among his books, I turned back, and gently opening the door, looked in.

The first person whom I saw, to my surprise, by the sober light of the shaded lamp, was Uriah. He was standing close beside it, with one of his skeleton hands over his mouth, and the other resting on the Doctor's table. The Doctor sat in his study chair, covering his face with his hands. Mr. Wickfield, sorely troubled and distressed, was leaning forward, irresolutely touching the Doctor's arm.

I met Uriah's eye, and saw what was the matter. There was an obtrusive show of compassionate zeal in his voice and manner, more intolerable—at least to me—than any demeanor he could have assumed.

"I have felt it incumbent upon me, Master Copperfield," said Uriah, "to point out to Doctor Strong what you and me have already talked about. It's much against the grain with me, I assure you, Copperfield, to be concerned in anything so unpleasant; but really, as it is, we're all mixing ourselves up with what oughtn't to be. That was what my meaning was, sir, when you didn't understand me."

I gave him a look, but no other answer. I wonder now, when I recall his leer, that I did not collar him and try to shake the breath out of his body.

"I dare say I didn't make myself very clear," he went on, "nor you neither. Naturally, we was both of us inclined to give such a subject a wide berth. Hows'ever, at last I have made up my mind to speak plain, and I have mentioned to Doctor Strong that—did you speak, sir?"

This was to the Doctor, who had moaned. The sound might have touched any heart, I thought, but it had no effect upon Uriah's.

"—mentioned to Doctor Strong," he proceeded, "that anyone may see that Mr. Maldon, and the lovely and agreeable lady as is Doctor Strong's wife, are too sweet on one another. When you come in, sir, I was just putting it to my fellow-partner," toward whom he turned, "to say to Doctor Strong, upon his word and honor, whether he'd ever been of this opinion, or not.—Come, Mr. Wickfield, sir! Would you be so good as tell us? Yes or no, sir? Come, partner!"

"For God's sake, my dear Doctor," said Mr. Wickfield, again laying his irresolute hand upon the Doctor's arm, "don't attach too much weight to any suspicions I may have entertained."

"There!" cried Uriah, shaking his head. "What a melancholy confirmation! ain't it? Him! Such an old friend!"

"My dear Strong," said Mr. Wickfield, in a tremulous voice, "my good friend, I needn't tell you that it has been my vice to look for some one master motive in everybody, and to try all actions by one narrow test. I may have fallen into such doubts as I have had, through this mistake."

"You have had doubts, Wickfield?" said the Doctor, without lifting up his head. "You have had doubts?"

"Speak up, fellow-partner," urged Uriah.

"I had, at one time, certainly," said Mr. Wickfield. "I—God forgive me—I thought *you* had."

"No, no, no!" returned the Doctor, in a tone of most pathetic grief.

"So I found," said Mr. Wickfield. "But I thought that, in a case where there was so much disparity in point of years——"

"That's the way to put it, you see, Master Copperfield!" observed Uriah, with fawning and offensive pity.

"—a lady of such youth and such attractions, however real her respect for you, might have been influenced in marrying by worldly considerations only."

"I married that lady," said the Doctor, "when she was extremely young. I took her to myself when her character was scarcely formed. So far as it was developed, it had been my happiness to form it. I knew her father well. I knew her well. I had taught her what I could, for the love of all her beautiful and virtuous qualities. If I did her wrong—as I fear I did, in taking advantage (but I never meant it) of her gratitude and her affection—I ask pardon of that lady, in my heart!"

For a little while, his eyes kindled, and his voice was firm; for a little while he was again silent. Presently, he proceeded as before,

"It only remains for me to bear the knowledge of the unhappiness I have occasioned as submissively as I can. It is she who should reproach, not I. To save her from misconstruction, cruel misconstruction, that even my friends have not been able to avoid, becomes my duty. The more retired we live, the better I shall discharge it. And when the time comes—may it come soon, if it be His merciful pleasure!—when my death shall release her from constraint, I shall close my eyes upon her honored face with unbounded confidence and love; and leave her, with no sorrow then, to happier and brighter days."

I could not see him for the tears which his earnestness and goodness brought into my eyes. He had moved to the door, when he added,

"Gentlemen, I have shown you my heart. I am sure you will

respect it. What we have said tonight is never to be said more. Wickfield, give me an old friend's arm upstairs!"

Mr. Wickfield hastened to him. Without interchanging a word, they went slowly out of the room together, Uriah looking after them.

"Well, Master Copperfield!" said Uriah, meekly turning to me, "the thing hasn't took quite the turn that might have been expected, for the old Scholar—what an excellent man!—is as blind as a brickbat; but *this* family's out of the cart, I think!"

I needed but the sound of his voice to be so madly enraged as I never was before, and never have been since.

"You villain," said I, "what do you mean by entrapping me into your schemes?"

As we stood, front to front, I saw so plainly, in the stealthy exultation of his face, what I already so plainly knew—I mean, that he forced his confidence upon me expressly to make me miserable, and had set a deliberate trap for me in this very matter—that I couldn't bear it. The whole of his lank cheek was invitingly before me, and I struck it with my open hand with that force that my fingers tingled as if I had burned them.

He caught the hand in his, and we stood in that connection, looking at each other. We stood so, a long time—long enough for me to see the white marks of my fingers die out of the deep red of his cheek, and leave it a deeper red.

"Copperfield," he said at length, in a breathless voice, "have you taken leave of your senses?"

"I have taken leave of you," said I, wresting my hand away. "You dog, I'll know no more of you."

"Won't you?" said he, constrained by the pain of his cheek to put his hand there. "Perhaps you won't be able to help it. Isn't this ungrateful of you, now?"

"I have shown you often enough," said I, "that I despise you. I have shown you now, more plainly, that I do. Why should I dread your doing your worst to all about you? What else do you ever do?"

There was another long pause. His eyes, as he looked at me, seemed to take every shade of color that could make eyes ugly.

"Copperfield," he said, removing his hand from his cheek, "you have always gone against me. I know you always used to be against me at Mr. Wickfield's."

"I'm a very umble person, Master Copperfield."

"You may think what you like," said I, still in a towering rage. "If it is not true, so much the worthier you."

"And yet I always liked you, Copperfield!" he rejoined.

I deigned to make him no reply, and, taking up my hat, was going out to bed, when he came between me and the door.

"Copperfield," he said, "there must be two parties to a quarrel. I won't be one."

"You may go to the devil!" said I.

"Don't say that!" he replied. "I know you'll be sorry afterwards. How can you make yourself so inferior to me as to show such a bad spirit? But I forgive you."

"You forgive me!" I repeated disdainfully.

"I do, and you can't help yourself," replied Uriah. "To think of your going and attacking *me*, that have always been a friend to you! But there can't be a quarrel without two parties, and I won't be one. I will be a friend to you, in spite of you. So now you know what you've got to expect."

The necessity of carrying on this dialogue (his part in which was very slow, mine very quick) in a low tone, that the house might not be disturbed at an unseasonable hour, did not improve my temper, though my passion was cooling down.

"You know, Copperfield," he said, "you're in quite a wrong position"; which I felt to be true, and that made me chafe the more. "You can't make this a brave thing, and you can't help being forgiven. I don't intend to mention it to mother, nor to any living soul. I'm determined to forgive you. I wonder that you should lift your hand against a person that you knew to be so umble!"

I felt only less mean than he. He knew me better than I knew myself. If he had retorted or openly exasperated me, it would have been a relief and a justification; but he had put me on a slow fire, on which I lay tormented half the night.

Agnes and her father had been gone a week before we resumed our usual work. On the day preceding its resumption, the Doctor laid an injunction on me, in a few affectionate words, never to refer to the subject of that evening. I had confided it to my aunt, but to no one else. It was not a subject I could discuss with Agnes, and Agnes certainly had not the least suspicion of what had passed.

Neither, I felt convinced, had Mrs. Strong then. Several weeks elapsed before I saw the least change in her. It came on slowly, like a cloud when there is no wind. Gradually, an unhappy shadow fell upon her beauty, and deepened every day.

CHAPTER 43 ❧ ANOTHER RETROSPECT ✦ ✦ ✦

O NCE again let me pause upon a memorable period of my life. Let me stand aside to see the phantoms of those days go by me, accompanying the shadow of myself, in dim procession. Weeks, months, seasons pass along. I have come legally to man's estate—I have attained the dignity of twenty-one. But this is a sort of dignity that may be thrust upon one. Let me think what I have achieved.

I have tamed that savage stenographic mystery. I make a respectable income by it. I am in high repute for my accomplishment in all pertaining to the art, and am joined with eleven others in reporting the debates in Parliament for a morning newspaper.

I have come out in another way. I have taken, with fear and trembling, to authorship. I wrote a little something in secret, and sent it to a magazine, and it was published in the magazine. Since then I have taken heart to write a good many trifling pieces. Now I am regularly paid for them. Altogether, I am well off. When I tell my income on the fingers of my left hand, I pass the third finger and take in the fourth to the middle joint.

We have removed from Buckingham Street to a pleasant little cottage very near the one I looked at when my enthusiasm first came on. My aunt, however (who has sold the house at Dover to good advantage), is not going to remain here, but intends removing herself to a still more tiny cottage close at hand. What does this portend? My marriage? Yes!

Yes, I am going to be married to Dora! Miss Lavinia and Miss Clarissa have given their consent; and if ever canary birds were in a flutter, they are. Miss Lavinia, self-charged with the superintendence of my darling's wardrobe, is constantly cutting out brown-paper cuirasses, and differing in opinion from a highly respectable young man, with a long bundle, and a yard-measure under his arm.

Miss Clarissa and my aunt roam all over London to find out articles of furniture for Dora and me to look at. It would be better for them to buy the goods at once without this ceremony of inspection; for when we go to see a kitchen fender and meat-screen, Dora sees a Chinese house for Jip and prefers that.

Peggotty comes up to make herself useful, and falls to work immediately. Her department appears to be to clean everything over and over again. She rubs everything that can be rubbed until it shines, like her own honest forehead, with perpetual friction. And now it is that I begin to see her solitary brother passing through the dark streets at night, and looking, as he goes, among the wandering faces. I never speak to him at such an hour. I know too well, as his grave figure passes onward, what he seeks, and what he dreads.

Why does Traddles look so important when he calls upon me this afternoon in the Commons, where I still occasionally attend, for form's sake, when I have time? The realization of my boyish day-dreams is at hand. I am going to take out the license.

"I hope the next time you come here, my dear fellow," I say to Traddles, "it will be on the same errand for yourself. And I hope it will be soon."

"I assure you, my dear boy," says Traddles, "I am almost as pleased as if I were going to be married myself. And really the great friendship and consideration of personally associating Sophy with the joyful occasion, and inviting her to be a bridesmaid in conjunction with Miss Wickfield, demands my warmest thanks."

I hear him, and shake hands with him, and we talk and walk, and dine, and so on; but I don't believe it. Nothing is real.

Sophy arrives at the house of Dora's aunts in due course. She has the most agreeable of faces—not absolutely beautiful, but extraordinarily pleasant—and is one of the most genial, unaffected, frank, engaging creatures I have ever seen. Traddles presents her to us with great pride, and rubs his hands for ten minutes by the clock, with every individual hair upon his head standing on tiptoe, when I congratulate him in a corner on his choice.

I have never seen my aunt in such state. She is dressed in lavender-colored silk, and has a white bonnet on, and is amazing. Janet has dressed her, and is there to look at me. Peggotty is ready to go to church, intending to behold the ceremony from the gallery. Mr. Dick, who is to give my darling to me at the altar, has had his hair curled. Traddles presents a dazzling combination of cream color and light blue; and both he and Mr. Dick have a general effect about them of being all gloves.

The rest is all a more or less incoherent dream.

A dream of their coming in with Dora; of the pew-opener arranging us, like a drill-sergeant, before the altar rails; of the clergyman and clerk appearing; of a few boatmen and some other people strolling in; of an ancient mariner behind me strongly flavoring the church with rum; of the service beginning in a deep voice, and our all being very attentive.

Of Miss Lavinia, who acts as a semi-auxiliary bridesmaid, being the first to cry, and of her doing homage (as I take it) to the memory of Pidger in sobs; of Miss Clarissa applying a smelling-bottle; of Agnes taking care of Dora; of my aunt endeavoring to represent herself as a model of sternness, with tears rolling down her face; of little Dora trembling very much, and making her responses in faint whispers.

Of our kneeling down together, side by side; of Dora's trembling less and less, but always clasping Agnes by the hand; of the service being got through quietly and gravely; of our all looking at each other in an April state of smiles and tears when it is over; of my young wife being hysterical in the vestry, and crying for her poor papa, her dear papa.

Of her soon cheering up again, and our signing the register all round. Of my going into the gallery for Peggotty, to bring *her* to sign it; of Peggotty's hugging me in a corner, and telling me she saw my own dear mother married; of its being over, and our going away.

Of my walking so proudly and lovingly down the aisle with my sweet wife upon my arm, through a mist of half-seen people, pulpits, monuments, pews, fonts, organs, and church-windows, in which there flutter faint airs of association with my childish church at home so long ago.

Of their whispering, as we pass, what a youthful couple we are, and what a pretty little wife she is. Of our all being so merry and talkative in the carriage going back.

Of there being a breakfast, with abundance of things, pretty and substantial, to eat and drink, whereof I partake, as I should do in any other dream, without the least perception of their flavor.

Of my making a speech in the same dreamy fashion, without having an idea of what I want to say, beyond such as may be comprehended in the full conviction that I haven't said it. Of our being very sociably and simply happy (always in a dream though); and of Jip's having wedding cake, and its not agreeing with him afterwards.

Of the pair of hired post-horses being ready, and of Dora's going away to change her dress. Of Dora's making a long series of surprised discoveries that she has forgotten all sorts of little things; and of everybody's running everywhere to fetch them.

Of their all closing about Dora when at last she begins to say good-bye, looking, with their bright colors and ribbons, like a bed of flowers. Of my darling being almost smothered among the flowers, and coming out, laughing and crying both together, to my jealous arms.

Of my wanting to carry Jip (who is to go along with us), and Dora's saying, No, that she must carry him, or else he'll think she don't like him any more now she is married, and will break his heart. Of our going arm in arm, and Dora stopping and looking back, and saying, "If I have ever been cross or ungrateful to anybody, don't remember it!" and bursting into tears.

Of her waving her little hand, and our going away once more. Of her once more stopping and looking back, and hurrying to Agnes, and giving Agnes, above all the others, her last kisses and farewells.

We drive away together, and I awake from the dream. I believe it at last. It is my dear, dear little wife beside me, whom I love so well!

"Are you happy now, you foolish boy?" says Dora, "and sure you don't repent?"

I have stood aside to see the phantoms of those days go by me. They are gone, and I resume the journey of my story.

I T WAS a strange condition of things, the honeymoon being over, and the bridesmaids gone home, when I found myself sitting down in my own small house with Dora.

It seemed such an extraordinary thing to have Dora always there. When I was kept out very late, it seemed so strange to me, as I was walking home, to think that Dora was at home! It was such a wonderful thing at first to have her coming softly down to talk to me as I ate my supper. It was such a stupendous thing to know for certain that she put her hair in papers. It was altogether such an astonishing event to see her do it!

I doubt whether two young birds could have known less about keeping house than I and my pretty Dora did. We had a servant, of course. She kept house for us. I have still a latent belief that she must have been Mrs. Crupp's daughter in disguise, we had such an awful time of it with Mary Anne.

Her name was Paragon. Her nature was represented to us, when we engaged her, as being feebly expressed in her name. She had a written character as large as a proclamation, and, according to this document, could do everything of a domestic nature that ever I heard of, and a great many things that I never did hear of. She was a woman in the prime of life; of a severe countenance; and subject (particularly in the arms) to a sort of perpetual measles or fiery rash.

Our treasure was warranted sober and honest. I am therefore willing to believe that she was in a fit when we found her under the boiler, and that the deficient teaspoons were attributable to the dustman.

But she preyed upon our minds dreadfully. We felt our inexperience, and were unable to help ourselves. We should have been at her mercy, if she had had any; but she was a remorseless woman, and had none. She was the cause of our first little quarrel.

"My dearest life," I said one day to Dora, "do you think Mary Anne has any idea of time?"

"Why, Doady?" inquired Dora, looking up innocently from her drawing.

"My love, because it's five, and we were to have dined at four."

Dora glanced wistfully at the clock, and hinted that she thought it was too fast.

"On the contrary, my love," said I, referring to my watch, "it's a few minutes too slow."

My little wife came and sat upon my knee, to coax me to be quiet, and drew a line with her pencil down the middle of my nose; but I couldn't dine off that, though it was very agreeable.

"Don't you think, my dear," said I, "it would be better for you to remonstrate with Mary Anne?"

"Oh, no, please; I couldn't, Doady!" said Dora.

"Why not, my love?" I gently asked.

"Oh, because I am such a little goose," said Dora, "and she knows I am!"

I thought this sentiment so incompatible with the establishment of any system of check on Mary Anne, that I frowned a little.

"Oh, what ugly wrinkles in my bad boy's forehead!" said Dora; and still being on my knee, she traced them with her pencil, putting it to her rosy lips to make it mark blacker, and working at my forehead with a quaint little mockery of being industrious that quite delighted me in spite of myself.

"There's a good child," said Dora; "it makes its face so much prettier to laugh."

"But, my love," said I.

"No, no, please!" cried Dora, with a kiss, "don't be a naughty Blue Beard! Don't be serious!"

"My precious wife," said I, "we must be serious sometimes. Come;

sit down on this chair, close beside me! Give me the pencil! There! Now let us talk sensibly. You know, dear"—what a little hand it was to hold, and what a tiny wedding-ring it was to see!—"you know, my love, it is not exactly comfortable to have to go out without one's dinner. Now, is it?"

"N—n—no!" replied Dora faintly.

"My love, how you tremble!"

"Because I KNOW you're going to scold me," exclaimed Dora, in a piteous voice.

"My sweet, I am only going to reason."

"Oh, but reasoning is worse than scolding!" exclaimed Dora, in despair. "I didn't marry to be reasoned with. If you meant to reason with such a poor little thing as I am, you ought to have told me so, you cruel boy!"

I tried to pacify Dora, but she turned away her face, and shook her curls from side to side, and said, "You cruel, cruel boy!" so many times, that I really did not exactly know what to do; so I took a few turns up and down the room in my uncertainty, and came back again.

"Dora, my darling!"

"No, I am not your darling. Because you *must* be sorry that you married me, or else you wouldn't reason with me!" returned Dora.

I felt so injured by the inconsequential nature of this charge, that it gave me courage to be grave.

"Now, my own Dora," said I, "you are very childish, and are talking nonsense. You must remember, I am sure, that I was obliged to go out yesterday when dinner was half over; and that, the day before, I was made quite unwell by being obliged to eat underdone veal in a hurry; today, I don't dine at all—and I am afraid to say how long we waited for breakfast—and *then* the water didn't boil. I don't mean to reproach you, my dear, but this is not comfortable."

"Oh, you cruel, cruel boy, to say I am a disagreeable wife!" cried Dora.

"Now, my dear Dora, you must know that I never said that!"

"You said I wasn't comfortable!" said Dora.

"I said the housekeeping was not comfortable."

"It's exactly the same thing!" cried Dora. And she evidently thought so, for she wept most grievously.

I took another turn across the room, full of love for my pretty wife, and distracted by self-accusatory inclinations to knock my head against the door. I sat down again, and said,

"I am not blaming you, Dora. We have both a great deal to learn. I am only trying to show you, my dear, that you must—you really must" (I was resolved not to give this up) "accustom yourself to look after Mary Anne. Likewise to act a little for yourself, and me."

"I wonder, I do, at your making such ungrateful speeches," sobbed Dora, "when you know the other day, when you said you would like a little bit of fish, I went out myself, miles and miles, and ordered it, to surprise you."

"And it was very kind of you, my own darling," said I. "I felt it so much that I wouldn't on any account have even mentioned that you bought a salmon—which was too much for two. Or that it cost one pound six—which was more than we can afford."

"You enjoyed it very much," sobbed Dora. "And you said I was a mouse."

"And I'll say so again, my love," I returned, "a thousand times!"

But I had wounded Dora's soft little heart, and she was not to be comforted. She was so pathetic in her sobbing and bewailing, that I felt as if I had said I don't know what to hurt her. I was obliged to hurry away; I was kept out late; and I felt all night such pangs of remorse as made me miserable. I had the conscience of an assassin, and was haunted by a vague sense of enormous wickedness.

It was two or three hours past midnight when I got home. I found my aunt, in our house, sitting up for me.

"Is anything the matter, aunt?" said I, alarmed.

"Nothing, Trot," she replied. "Sit down, sit down. Little Blossom has been rather out of spirits, and I have been keeping her company—that's all."

I leaned my head upon my hand, and felt more sorry and downcast, as I sat loking at the fire, than I could have supposed possible so soon after the fulfilment of my brightest hopes. As I sat thinking, I happened to meet my aunt's eyes, which were resting on my face. There was an anxious expression in them, but it cleared directly.

"I assure you, aunt," said I, "I have been quite unhappy myself all night, to think of Dora's being so. But I had no other intention than to speak to her tenderly and lovingly about our home-affairs."

My aunt nodded encouragement.

"You must have patience, Trot," said she.

"Of course. Heaven knows I don't mean to be unreasonable, aunt!"

"No, no," said my aunt. "But Little Blossom is a very tender little blossom, and the wind must be gentle with her."

I thanked my good aunt, in my heart, for her tenderness toward my wife; and I was sure that she knew I did.

"Don't you think, aunt," said I, after some further contemplation of the fire, "that you could advise and counsel Dora a little, for our mutual advantage, now and then?"

"Trot," returned my aunt, with some emotion, "no! Don't ask me such a thing."

Her tone was so very earnest that I raised my eyes in surprise.

"I look back on my life, child," said my aunt, "and I think of some who are in their graves, with whom I might have been on kinder terms. If I judged harshly of other people's mistakes in marriage, it may have been because I had bitter reason to judge harshly of my own. Let that pass. I have been a grumpy, frumpy, wayward sort of a woman, a good many years. I am still, and I always shall be. But you and I have done one another some good, Trot—at all events, you have done me good, my dear; and division must not come between us, at this time of day."

"Division between *us!*" cried I.

"Child, child!" said my aunt, smoothing her dress, "how soon it might come between us, or how unhappy I might make our Little Blossom, if I meddled in anything, prophet couldn't say. I want our pet to like me, and be as gay as a butterfly. Remember your own home, in that second marriage, and never do both me and her the injury you have hinted at!"

I comprehended at once that my aunt was right, and I comprehended the full extent of her generous feeling toward my dear wife.

"These are early days, Trot," she pursued, "and Rome was not built in a day, nor in a year. You have chosen freely for yourself"—a cloud passed over her face for a moment, I thought—"and you have chosen a very pretty and a very affectionate creature. It will be your duty, and it will be your pleasure too—of course I know that; I am not delivering a lecture—to estimate her (as you chose her) by the qualities she has, and not by the qualities she may not have. This is marriage, Trot; and Heaven bless you both in it, for a pair of babes in the wood as you are!"

My aunt said this in a sprightly way, and gave me a kiss to ratify the blessing.

"Now," said she, "light my little lantern, and see me into my bandbox by the garden path"; for there was a communication between our cottages in that direction. With this my aunt tied up her head in a handkerchief, and I escorted her home. I was much impressed—for the first time, in reality—by the conviction that Dora and I had indeed to work out our future for ourselves.

Dora came stealing down in her little slippers, to meet me, now that I was alone; and cried upon my shoulder, and said I had been hard-hearted and she had been naughty; and I said much the same thing in effect, I believe; and we made it up, and agreed that our first little difference was to be our last, and that we were never to have another, if we lived a hundred years.

The next domestic trial we went through, was the Ordeal of Servants. Mary Anne went so mildly, on receipt of wages, that I was surprised, until I found out about the teaspoons, and also about the little sums she had borrowed in my name of the tradespeople without authority. After an interval of Mrs. Kidgerbury—the oldest inhabitant of Kentish Town, I believe, who went our charing, but was too feeble to execute her conceptions of that art—we found another treasure, who was one of the most amiable of women, but who generally made a point of falling either up or down the kitchen stairs with the tray, and almost plunged into the parlor, as into a bath, with the tea-things. She was succeeded (with intervals of Mrs. Kidgerbury) by a long line of incapables; terminating in a young person of genteel appearance, who went to Greenwich Fair in Dora's bonnet. After whom I remember nothing but an average equality of failure.

Everybody we had anything to do with seemed to cheat us. Our appearance in a shop was a signal for the damaged goods to be brought out immediately. If we bought a lobster, it was full of water. All our meat turned out to be tough. It appeared to me, on looking over the tradesmen's books, as if we might have kept the basement story paved with butter, such was the extensive scale of our consumption of that article. I don't know whether the Excise returns of the period may have exhibited any increase in the demand for pepper; but if our performances did not affect the market, I should say several families must have left off using it. And the most wonderful fact of all was, that we never had anything in the house.

As to the washerwoman pawning the clothes, and coming in a state of penitent intoxication to apologize, I suppose that might have happened several times to anybody. Also the chimney on fire, the parish engine, and perjury on the part of the beadle. But I apprehend that we were personally unfortunate in engaging a servant with a taste for cordials, who swelled our running account for porter at the public-house by such inexplicable items as "quartern rum shrub (Mrs. C.)"; "Half-quartern gin and cloves (Mrs. C.)"; "Glass rum and peppermint (Mrs. C.)"—the parentheses always referring to Dora, who was supposed, it appeared on explanation, to have imbibed the whole of these refreshments.

One of our first feats in the housekeeping way was a little dinner to Traddles. I met him in town, and asked him to walk out with me that afternoon. He readily consenting, I wrote to Dora, saying I would bring him home. It was pleasant weather, and on the road we made my domestic happiness the theme of conversation. Traddles was very full of it; and said that, picturing himself with such a home, and Sophy waiting and preparing for him, he could think of nothing wanting to complete his bliss.

I could not have wished for a prettier little wife at the opposite end of the table, but I certainly could have wished, when we sat down, for a little more room. I did not know how it was, but though there were only two of us, we were at once always cramped for room, and yet had always room enough to lose everything in. I suspect it may have been because nothing had a place of its own, except Jip's pagoda, which invariably blocked up the main thoroughfare. On the present occasion, Traddles was so hemmed in by the pagoda and the guitar-case, and Dora's flower-painting, and my writing-table, that I had serious doubts of the possibility of his using his knife and fork; but he protested, with his own good-humor, "Oceans of room, Copperfield! I assure you, oceans!"

I could not help wondering in my own mind, as I contemplated the boiled leg of mutton before me, previous to carving it, how it came to pass that our joints of meat were of such extraordinary shapes, and whether our butcher contracted for all the deformed sheep that came into the world; but I kept my reflections to myself. We ate as much of it as was done, and made up with capers. If I had permitted him, I am satisfied that Traddles would have made a perfect savage of himself, and eaten a plateful of raw meat, to express enjoyment of the repast.

My poor little wife was in such affliction when she thought I should be annoyed, and in such a state of joy when she found I was not, that the discomfiture I had subdued very soon vanished, and we passed a happy evening. When Traddles went away, and I came back into the parlor from seeing him out, my wife planted her chair close to mine, and sat down by my side.

"I am very sorry," she said. "Will you try to teach me, Doady?"

"I must teach myself first, Dora," said I. "I am as bad as you, love."

"Ah! but you can learn," she returned; "and you are a clever, clever man!"

"Nonsense, mouse!" said I.

"I wish," resumed my wife, after a long silence, "that I could have gone down into the country for a whole year, and lived with Agnes!"

Her hands were clasped upon my shoulder, and her chin rested on them, and her blue eyes looked quietly into mine.

"Why so?" I asked.

"I think she might have improved me, and I think I might have learned from *her*," said Dora.

"All in good time, my love. Agnes has had her father to take care of for these many years, you should remember. Even when she was quite a child, she was the Agnes whom we know," said I.

"Will you call me a name I want you to call me?" inquired Dora, without moving.

"What is it?" I asked with a smile.

"It's a stupid name," she said, shaking her curls for a moment. "Child-wife."

I laughingly asked my child-wife what her fancy was in desiring to be so called. She answered without moving, otherwise than as the arm I twined about her may have brought her blue eyes nearer to me,

"I don't mean, you silly fellow, that you should use the name instead of Dora. I only mean that you should think of me that way. When you are going to be angry with me, say to yourself, 'It's only my child-wife!' When I am very disappointing, say, 'I knew, a long time ago, that she would make but a child-wife!' When you miss what I should like to be, and I think can never be, say, 'Still my foolish child-wife loves me!' For indeed I do."

I had not been serious with her, having no idea, until now, that she was serious herself. But her affectionate nature was so happy in what I now said to her with my whole heart, that her face became a laughing one before her glittering eyes were dry. She was soon my child-wife indeed—sitting down on the floor outside the Chinese House, ringing all the little bells one after another, to punish Jip for his bad behavior, while Jip lay blinking in the doorway with his head out, even too lazy to be teased.

When my evenings were unoccupied and I was engaged in writing at home, she would sit quietly near me, however late the hour, and be so mute, that I would often think she had dropped asleep. But generally, when I raised my head, I saw her blue eyes looking at me with the quiet attention of which I have already spoken.

"Oh, what a weary boy!" said Dora one night, when I met her eyes as I was shutting up my desk.

"What a weary girl!" said I. "That's more to the purpose. You must go to bed another time, my love. It's far too late for you."

"No, don't send me to bed!" pleaded Dora, coming to my side. "Pray, don't do that."

"Dora!"

To my amazement she was sobbing on my neck.

"Not well, my dear? not happy?"

"Yes! quite well, and very happy!" said Dora. "But say you'll let me stop and see you write."

"Why, what a sight for such bright eyes at midnight!" I replied.

"Are they bright, though?" returned Dora, laughing. "I'm so glad they're bright."

"Little Vanity!" said I.

But it was not vanity; it was only harmless delight in my admiration. I knew that very well, before she told me so.

"If you think them pretty, say I may always stop and see you write!" said Dora. "*Do* you think them pretty?"

"Very pretty."

"Then let me always stop and see you write."

"I am afraid that won't improve their brightness, Dora."

"Yes, it will! Because, you clever boy, you'll not forget me then, while you are full of silent fancies. Will you mind it, if I say something very, very silly?—more than usual?" inquired Dora, peeping over my shoulder into my face.

"What wonderful thing is that?" said I.

"Please let me hold the pens," said Dora. "I want to have something to do with all those many hours when you are so industrious. May I hold the pens?"

The remembrance of her pretty joy when I said Yes brings tears into my eyes. The next time I sat down to write, and regularly afterwards, she sat in her old place, with a spare bundle of pens at her side. Her triumph in this connection with my work, and her delight when I wanted a new pen—which I very often feigned to do —suggested to me a new way of pleasing my child-wife. I occa-

310

sionally made a pretense of wanting a page or two of manuscript copied. Then Dora was in her glory. The preparations she made for this great work, the aprons she put on, the bibs she borrowed from the kitchen to keep off the ink, the time she took, the innumerable stoppages she made to have a laugh with Jip as if he understood it all, her conviction that her work was incomplete unless she signed her name at the end, and the way in which she would bring it to me, like a school-copy, and then, when I praised it, clasp me round the neck, are touching recollections to me, simple as they might appear to other men. She took possession of the keys soon after this, and went jingling about the house with the whole bunch in a little basket, tied to her slender waist. I seldom found that the places to which they belonged were locked, or that they were of any use except as a plaything for Jip; but Dora was pleased, and that pleased me. She was quite satisfied that a good deal was effected by this make-believe of housekeeping, and was as merry as if we had been keeping a baby-house for a joke.

So we went on. Dora was hardly less affectionate to my aunt than to me, and often told her of the time when she was afraid she was "a cross old thing." I never saw my aunt unbend more systematically to anyone. She courted Jip, though Jip never responded; listened, day after day, to the guitar, though I am afraid she had no taste for music; went wonderful distances on foot to purchase, as surprises, any trifles that she found out Dora wanted; and never came in by the garden, and missed her from the room, but she would call out, at the foot of the stairs, in a voice that sounded cheerfully all over the house,

"Where's Little Blossom?"

O NE NIGHT, when I had been married some months, Mr. Dick put his head into the parlor and said, with a significant cough,

"You couldn't speak to me without inconveniencing yourself, Trotwood, I am afraid?"

"Certainly, Mr. Dick," said I; "come in!"

Mr. Dick sat down with greater gravity than usual, and looked at me.

"Now, boy," said Mr. Dick, "I am going to put a question to you."

"As many as you please," said I.

"What do you consider me, sir?" asked Mr. Dick, folding his arms.

"A dear old friend," said I.

"Thank you, Trotwood," returned Mr. Dick, laughing, and reaching across in high glee to shake hands with me. "But I mean, boy," resuming his gravity, "what do you consider me in this respect?" touching his forehead.

I was puzzled how to answer, but he helped me with a word.

"Weak?" said Mr. Dick.

"Well," I replied dubiously, "rather so."

"Exactly!" cried Mr. Dick, who seemed quite enchanted by my reply. "That is, Trotwood, when they took some of the trouble out of you-know-who's head, and put it you know where, there was a——" Mr. Dick made his two hands revolve very fast about each other a great number of times, and then brought them into collision, and rolled them over and over one another, to express confusion. "There was that sort of thing done to me somehow—eh?"

I nodded at him, and he nodded back again.

"Now you are a scholar, Trotwood," said Mr. Dick. "You are a fine scholar. You know what a learned man, what a great man the Doctor is. Not proud in his wisdom. Humble, humble—condescending even to poor Dick, who is simple and knows nothing. And his beautiful wife is a star," said Mr. Dick—"a shining star. I have seen her shine, sir. But," bringing his chair nearer, and laying one hand upon my knee—"clouds, sir—clouds."

I answered the solicitude which his face expressed, by conveying the same expression into my own, and shaking my head.

"Doctor not angry with her, Trotwood?" he said.

"No. Devoted to her."

"Then I have got it, boy!" said Mr. Dick.

The sudden exultation with which he slapped me on the knee, and leaned back in his chair, with his eyebrows lifted up as high as he could possibly lift them, made me think him further out of his wits than ever. He became as suddenly grave again, and leaning forward as before, said—first respectfully taking out his pocket-handkerchief, as if it really did represent my aunt,

"Most wonderful woman in the world, Trotwood. Why has *she* done nothing to set things right?"

"Too delicate and difficult a subject for such interference," I replied.

"Fine scholar," said Mr. Dick, touching me with his finger. "Why has *he* done nothing?"

"For the same reason," I returned.

"Then I have got it, boy!" said Mr. Dick. And he stood up before me, more exultingly than before, nodding his head, and striking himself repeatedly upon the breast, until one might have supposed that he had nearly nodded and struck all the breath out of his body.

"A poor fellow with a craze, sir," said Mr. Dick, "a simpleton, a weak-minded person—present company, you know!" striking him-

313

self again, "may do what wonderful people may not do. I'll bring them together, boy. I'll try. They'll not blame *me*. They'll not object to *me*. They'll not mind what *I* do, if it's wrong. I'm only Mr. Dick. And who minds Dick? Dick's nobody! Whoo!" He blew a slight, contemptuous breath, as if he blew himself away.

To my surprise, I heard no more about it for some two or three weeks, though I was sufficiently interested in the result of his endeavors; descrying a strange gleam of good sense—I say nothing of good feeling, for that he always exhibited—in the conclusion to which he had come. At last I began to believe that, in the flighty and unsettled state of his mind, he had either forgotten his intention or abandoned it.

One fair evening, when Dora was not inclined to go out, my aunt and I strolled up to the Doctor's cottage. It was autumn, when there were no debates to vex the evening air; and I remember how the leaves smelt like our garden at Blunderstone as we trod them under foot, and how the old, unhappy feeling seemed to go by on the sighing wind.

It was twilight when we reached the cottage. I was conscious of Mr. Dick's standing in the shadow of the room. How my aunt and I came to be left together near the door (unless her eyes were quicker than mine, and she held me back), I have forgotten, if I ever knew. But this I know—that we saw the Doctor before he saw us, sitting at his table, among the folio volumes in which he delighted, resting his head calmly on his hand. That, in the same moment, we saw Mrs. Strong glide in, pale and trembling. That Mr. Dick supported her on his arm. That he laid his other hand upon the Doctor's arm, causing him to look up with an abstracted air. That, as the Doctor moved his head, his wife dropped down on one knee at his feet, and, with her hands imploringly lifted, fixed upon his face the memorable look I have never forgotten.

"Doctor!" said Mr. Dick, "what is it that's amiss? Look here!"

"Annie!" cried the Doctor. "Not at my feet, my dear!"

"Yes!" she said. "I beg and pray that no one will leave the room! Oh, my husband and father, break this long silence. Let us both know what it is that has come between us!"

"Annie!" said the Doctor, tenderly taking her in his hands. "My dear! If any unavoidable change has come, in the sequence of time, upon our married life, you are not to blame. The fault is mine, and only mine. There is no change in my affection, admiration, and respect. I wish to make you happy. I truly love and honor you. Rise, Annie, pray!"

But she did not rise. After looking at him for a little while, she sank down closer to him, laid her arm across his knee, and dropping her head upon it, said,

"If I have any friend here who can speak one word for me, or for my husband in this matter; if I have any friend here who has anything within his knowledge, no matter what it is, that may help to mediate between us, I implore that friend to speak!"

There was a profound silence. After a few moments of painful hesitation, I broke the silence.

"Mrs. Strong," I said, "there is something within my knowledge, which I have been earnestly entreated by Doctor Strong to conceal, and have concealed until tonight. But I believe the time has come when it would be mistaken faith to conceal it any longer."

"Our future peace," she said, "may be in your hands. I trust it confidently to your not suppressing anything."

Thus earnestly besought, I made no reference to the Doctor for his permission, but, without any other compromise of the truth than a little softening of the coarseness of Uriah Heep, related plainly what had passed in that same room that night.

When I had finished, Annie remained, for some few moments, silent, with her head bent down as I have described. Then she took the Doctor's hand (he was sitting in the same attitude as when we had entered the room), and pressed it to her breast, and kissed it. Mr. Dick softly raised her; and she stood, when she began to speak, leaning on him, and looking down upon her husband, from whom she never turned her eyes.

"All that has ever been in my mind, since I was married," she said in a low, submissive, tender voice, "I will lay bare before you. I could not live and have one reservation, knowing what I know now."

"Nay, Annie," said the Doctor mildly, "I have never doubted you, my child. There is no need—indeed there is no need, my dear."

"About my cousin Maldon, I had liked him"—she spoke softly, but without any hesitation—"very much. We had been little lovers once. If circumstances had not happened otherwise, I might have come to persuade myself that I really loved him, and might have married him, and been most wretched. There can be no disparity in marriage like unsuitability of mind and purpose."

I pondered on those words, even while I was studiously attending to what followed, as if they had some particular interest, or some strange application that I could not divine. "There can be no disparity in marriage like unsuitability of mind and purpose"—"no disparity in marriage like unsuitability of mind and purpose."

"There is nothing," said Annie, "that we have in common. I have long found that there is nothing. If I were thankful to my husband for no more, instead of for so much, I should be thankful to him for having saved me from the first mistaken impulse of my undisciplined heart."

She stood quite still, before the Doctor, and spoke with an earnestness that thrilled me. Yet her voice was just as quiet as before.

"The cause of the late change in you, which I have seen with so much pain and sorrow, has been made clear tonight; and by an accident I have also come to know, tonight, the full measure of your noble trust in me, even under that mistake. I do not hope that any love and duty I may render in return will ever make me worthy of your priceless confidence; but with all this knowledge fresh upon me, I can lift my eyes to this dear face, revered as a father's, loved as a husband's, and solemnly declare that in my lightest thought I have never wronged you—never wavered in the love and the fidelity I owe you!"

She had her arms around the Doctor's neck, and he leant his head down over her, mingling his grey hair with her dark brown tresses.

In the silence that ensued my aunt walked gravely up to Mr. Dick, without at all hurrying herself, and gave him a hug and a sounding kiss.

"You are a very remarkable man, Dick!" said my aunt, with an air of unqualified approbation; "and never pretend to be anything else, for I know better!"

With that, my aunt pulled him by the sleeve, and nodded to me, and we three stole quietly out of the room, and came away.

CHAPTER 46  INTELLIGENCE • • •

I MUST have been married, if I may trust to my imperfect memory for dates, about a year or so, when one evening, as I was returning from a solitary walk, I came past Mrs. Steerforth's house. I had often passed it before, during my residence in that neighborhood. It had been uniformly gloomy and dull. I do not remember that I ever saw a light in all the house. If I had been a casual passer-by, I should have probably supposed that some childless person lay dead in it.

I fell into a brown study as I walked on, and a voice at my side made me start. I was not long in recollecting Mrs. Steerforth's little parlor-maid.

"If you please, sir, would you have the goodness to walk in and speak to Miss Dartle?"

"Has Miss Dartle sent you for me?" I inquired.

"Not tonight, sir; but it's just the same. Miss Dartle saw you pass a night or two ago; and I was to sit at work on the staircase, and when I saw you pass again, to ask you to step in and speak to her."

I turned back, and inquired of my conductor, as we went along, how Mrs. Steerforth was. She said her lady was but poorly, and kept her own room a good deal.

Miss Dartle saw me as I advanced, and rose for a moment to receive me. I thought her, then, still more colorless and thin than when I had seen her last—the flashing eyes still brighter, and the scar still plainer.

Our meeting was not cordial. We had parted angrily on the last occasion, and there was an air of disdain about her, which she took no pains to conceal.

"I am told you wish to speak to me, Miss Dartle," said I, standing near her, with my hand upon the back of the seat, and declining her gesture of invitation to sit down.

"If you please," said she. "Pray has this girl been found?"

"No."

"And yet she has run away!"

I saw her thin lips working while she looked at me, as if they were eager to load her with reproaches.

"Run away?" I repeated.

"Yes! from him," she said, with a laugh. "If she is not found, perhaps she never will be found. She may be dead!"

The vaunting cruelty with which she met my glance, I never saw expressed in any other face that ever I have seen.

"To wish her dead," said I, "may be the kindest wish that one of her own sex could bestow upon her. I am glad that time has softened you so much, Miss Dartle."

She condescended to make no reply, but, turning on me with another scornful laugh, said,

"The friends of this excellent and much-injured young lady are friends of yours. You are their champion, and assert their rights. Do you wish to know what is known of her?"

"Yes," said I.

She rose with an ill-favored smile, and taking a few steps toward a wall of holly that was near at hand, dividing the lawn from a kitchen-garden, said, in a louder voice, "Come here!"—as if she were calling to some unclean beast.

"You will restrain any demonstrative championship or vengeance in this place, of course, Mr. Copperfield?" said she, looking over her shoulder at me with the same expression.

I inclined my head, without knowing what she meant; and she said, "Come here!" again, and returned, followed by the respectable Mr. Littimer, who, with undiminished respectability, made me a bow, and took up his position behind her. The air of wicked grace, of triumph, in which there was yet something feminine and alluring,

318

with which she reclined upon the seat between us, and looked at me, was worthy of a cruel Princess in a legend.

"Now," said she imperiously, without glancing at him, and touching the old wound as it throbbed—perhaps, in this instance, with pleasure rather than pain—"tell Mr. Copperfield about the flight."

"Mr. James and myself, ma'am——"

"Don't address yourself to me!" she interrupted with a frown.

"Mr. James and myself, sir——"

"Nor to me, if you please," said I.

Mr. Littimer, without being at all discomposed, signified by a slight obeisance that anything that was most agreeable to us was most agreeable to him; and began again,

"Mr. James and myself have been abroad with the young woman, ever since she left Yarmouth under Mr. James's protection. We have been in a variety of places, and seen a deal of foreign country. We have been in France, Switzerland, Italy—in fact, almost all parts."

He looked at the back of the seat, as if he were addressing himself to that, and softly played upon it with his hands, as if he were striking chords upon a dumb piano.

"Mr. James took quite uncommonly to the young woman, and was more settled, for a length of time, than I have known him to be since I have been in his service. The young woman was very improvable, and spoke the languages; and wouldn't have been known for the same country person. I noticed that she was much admired wherever we went."

Miss Dartle put her hand upon her side. I saw him steal a glance at her, and slightly smile to himself.

"The young woman went on in this manner for some time, being occasionally low in her spirits, until I think she began to weary Mr. James by giving way to her low spirits and tempers of that kind, and things were not so comfortable. Mr. James he began to be restless again. The more restless he got, the worse she got; and I must say, for myself, that I had a very difficult time of it indeed between the two. Still matters were patched up here, and made good there, over and over again; and altogether lasted, I am sure, for a longer time than anybody could have expected."

Mr. Littimer, clearing his throat behind his hand with a respectable short cough, went on,

"At last, Mr. James he set off one morning from the neighborhood of Naples, where we had a villa (the young woman being very partial to the sea), and, under pretense of coming back in a day or so, left it in charge with me to break it out that, for the general happiness of all concerned, he was"—here an interruption of the short cough—"gone. But Mr. James, I must say, certainly did behave extremely honorable; for he proposed that the young woman should marry a very respectable person, who was fully prepared to overlook the past, and who was, at least, as good as anybody the young woman could have aspired to in a regular way, her connections being very common."

He changed legs again, and wetted his lips. I was convinced that the scoundrel spoke of himself, and I saw my conviction reflected in Miss Dartle's face.

"The young woman's violence when she came to, after I broke the fact of his departure, was beyond all expectations. She was quite mad, and had to be held by force, or, if she couldn't have got to a knife, or got to the sea, she'd have beaten her head against the marble floor."

Miss Dartle, with a light of exultation in her face, seemed almost to caress the sounds this fellow had uttered.

"But when I came to the second part of what had been entrusted to me," said Mr. Littimer, rubbing his hands uneasily, "which anybody might have supposed would have been, at all events, appreciated as a kind intention, then the young woman came out in her true colors. A more outrageous person I never did see. Her conduct was surprisingly bad. She had no more gratitude, no more feeling, no more patience, no more reason in her, than a stock or a stone. If I hadn't been upon my guard, I am convinced she would have had my blood."

"I think the better of her for it," said I indignantly.

Mr. Littimer bent his head as much as to say, "Indeed, sir? But you're young!" and resumed his narrative.

"It was necessary, in short, for a time, to take away everything nigh her that she could do herself, or anybody else, an injury with, and to shut her up close. Notwithstanding which, she got out in the night, forced the lattice of a window that I had nailed up myself, dropped on a vine that was trailed below, and never has been seen or heard of, to my knowledge, since."

"She is dead, perhaps," said Miss Dartle, with a smile.

"She may have drowned herself, miss," returned Mr. Littimer, catching at an excuse for addressing himself to somebody. "It's very possible. Or she may have had assistance from the boatmen, and the boatmen's wives and children. Being given to low company, she was very much in the habit of talking to them on the beach, Miss Dartle, and sitting by their boats. Mr. James was far from pleased to find out once that she had told the children she was a boatman's daughter."

"Did I tell you not to speak to me?" she said, with stern contempt.

"You spoke to me, miss," he replied. "I beg your pardon. But it's my service to obey."

"Do your service," she returned. "Finish your story, and go!"

"When it was clear," he said, with infinite respectability and an obedient bow, "that she was not to be found, I went to Mr. James and informed him of what had occurred. Words passed between us in consequence, and I felt it due to my character to leave him. Knowing the unfortunate difference between himself and his mother, and what her anxiety of mind was likely to be, I took the liberty of coming home to England, and relating——"

"For money which I paid him," said Miss Dartle to me.

"Just so, ma'am—and relating what I knew. I am not aware," said Mr. Littimer, after a moment's reflection, "that there is anything else. I am at present out of employment, and should be happy to meet with a respectable situation."

Miss Dartle glanced at me, as though she would inquire if there were anything that I desired to ask.

I indicated that I had nothing more to say. "Except," I added, as I saw him moving off, "that I understand this fellow's part in the wicked story, and that, as I shall make it known to the honest man who has been her father from her childhood, I would recommend him to avoid going too much into public."

He had stopped the moment I began, and had listened with his usual repose of manner.

"Thank you, sir. But you'll excuse me if I say, sir, that there are neither slaves or slave-drivers in this country, and that people are not allowed to take the law into their own hands. If they do, it is more to their own peril, I believe, than to other people's. Consequently speaking, I am not at all afraid of going wherever I may wish, sir."

With that, he made a polite bow, and, with another to Miss Dartle, went through the arch in the wall of holly by which he had come.

Reflecting on what had been thus told me, I felt it right that it should be communicated to Mr. Peggotty. On the following evening I went into London in quest of him. He was always wandering about from place to place, with his one object of recovering his

321

niece before him, but was more in London than elsewhere. He kept a lodging over the little chandler's shop in Hungerford Market, which I have had occasion to mention more than once. Hither I directed my walk.

He was sitting reading by a window in which he kept a few plants. The room was very neat and orderly. I saw in a moment that it was always kept prepared for her reception, and that he never went out but he thought it possible he might bring her home. He had not heard my tap at the door, and only raised his eyes when I laid my hand upon his shoulder.

"Mas'r Davy! Thankee, sir! thankee hearty for this visit! Sit ye down. You're kindly welcome, sir!"

"Mr. Peggotty," said I, taking the chair he handed me, "don't expect much! I have heard some news."

"Of Em'ly!"

He put his hand, in a nervous manner, on his mouth, and turned pale, as he fixed his eyes on mine.

"It gives no clue to where she is, but she is not with him."

He sat down, looking intently at me, and listened in profound silence to all I had to tell. When I had done, he shaded his face, and continued silent. I looked out of the window for a little while, and occupied myself with the plants.

"Now, my dear friend——" I began.

"Thankee, thankee, kind sir," he said, grasping my hand in both of his.

"If she should make her way to London, which is likely—for where could she lose herself so readily as in this vast city; and what would she wish to do but lose and hide herself, if she does not go home?"

"And she won't go home," he interposed, shaking his head mournfully.

"If she should come here," said I, "I believe there is one person here more likely to discover her than any other in the world. Do you remember—hear what I say with fortitude; think of your great object!—do you remember Martha?"

"Of our town?"

I needed no other answer than his face.

"Do you know that she is in London?"

"I have seen her in the streets," he answered with a shiver.

"But you don't know," said I, "that Emily was charitable to her, with Ham's help, long before she fled from home; nor that, when we met one night, and spoke together in the room yonder, over the way, she listened at the door."

"Mas'r Davy!" he replied in astonishment. "That night when it snew so hard?"

"That night. I have never seen her since. I went back, after parting from you, to speak to her, but she was gone. I was unwilling to mention her to you then, and I am now; but she is the person of whom I speak, and with whom I think we should communicate. Do you understand?"

"Too well, sir," he replied. We had sunk our voices almost to a whisper, and continued to speak in that tone.

"You say you have seen her. Do you think that you could find her? I could only hope to do so by chance."

"I think, Mas'r Davy, I know wheer to look."

"It is dark. Being together, shall we go out now and try to find her tonight?"

He assented, and prepared to accompany me. Without appearing to observe what he was doing, I saw how carefully he adjusted the little room, put a candle ready and the means of lighting it, arranged the bed, and finally took out of a drawer one of her dresses (I remember to have seen her wear it), neatly folded with some other garments, and a bonnet, which he placed upon a chair. He made no allusion to these clothes, neither did I. There they had been waiting for her, many and many a night, no doubt.

"The time was, Mas'r Davy," he said, as we came downstairs, "when I thowt this girl Martha a'most like the dirt underneath my Em'ly's feet. God forgive me, there's a difference now!"

As we went along, partly to hold him in conversation, and partly to satisfy myself, I asked him about Ham. He said that Ham was just the same—"wearing away his life with kiender no care nohow for 't; but never murmuring, and liked by all."

We had come, through Temple Bar, into the city. We were not far from Blackfriars Bridge, when he turned his head and pointed to a solitary female flitting along the opposite side of the street.

We followed at a distance, never losing sight of her, but never caring to come very near, as she frequently looked about. Once she stopped to listen to a band of music, and then we stopped too. At length she turned into a dull, dark street, where the noise and crowd were lost, and I said, "We may speak to her now"; and, mending our pace, we went after her.

CHAPTER 47 ❧ MARTHA • • •

THE neighborhood was a dreary one at that time—as oppressive, sad, and solitary by night as any about London. There were neither wharves nor houses on the melancholy waste of road near the great blank Prison. A sluggish ditch deposited its mud at the prison walls. Coarse grass and rank weed straggled over all the marshy land in the vicinity. Carcasses of houses, inauspiciously begun and never finished, rotted away.

As if she were a part of the refuse it had cast out, and left to corruption and decay, the girl we had followed strayed down to the river's brink, and stood in the midst of this night-picture, lonely and still, looking at the water. I signed to Mr. Peggotty to remain where he was, and emerged from their shade to speak to her.

I think she was talking to herself. I am sure, although absorbed in gazing at the water, that her shawl was off her shoulders, and that she was muffling her hands in it, in an unsettled and bewildered way, more like the action of a sleep-walker than a waking person. I know, and never can forget, that there was that in her wild manner which gave me no assurance but that she would sink before my eyes, until I had her arm within my grasp.

At the same moment I said, "Martha!"

She uttered a terrified scream, and struggled with me with such strength that I doubt if I could have held her alone. But a stronger hand than mine was laid upon her; and when she raised her frightened eyes, and saw whose it was, she made but one more effort, and dropped down between us. We carried her away from the water to where there were some dry stones, and there laid her down, crying and moaning. In a little while she sat among the stones, holding her wretched head with both her hands.

"Oh, the river!" she cried passionately. "Oh, the river!"

"Hush, hush!" said I. "Calm yourself."

I have never known what despair was, except in the tone of those words.

"I can't keep away from it. I can't forget it. It haunts me day and night. It's the only thing in all the world that I am fit for, or that's fit for me. Oh, the dreadful river!"

The thought passed through my mind that in the face of my companion, as he looked upon her without speech or motion, I might have read his niece's history. A new burst of crying came upon her now, in which she once more hid her face among the stones, and lay before us a prostrate image of humiliation and ruin.

"Martha," said I then, leaning down, and helping her to rise—she seemed to want to rise, as if with the intention of going away; but she was weak, and leaned against a boat—"do you know who this is who is with me?"

She said faintly, "Yes."

"Do you know that we have followed you a long way tonight?"

She shook her head. She looked neither at him nor at me, but stood in a humble attitude, holding her bonnet and shawl in one hand, without appearing conscious of them, and pressing the other, clenched, against her forehead.

"Are you composed enough," said I, "to speak on the subject which so interested you—I hope Heaven may remember it!—that snowy night?"

Her sobs broke out afresh, and she murmured some inarticulate thanks to me for not having driven her away from the door.

"I want to say nothing for myself," she said, after a few moments. "I am bad, I am lost! I have no hope at all! But tell him, sir"—she had shrunk away from him—"if you don't feel too hard to me to do it, that I never was in any way the cause of his misfortune."

"It has never been attributed to you," I returned, earnestly responding to her earnestness.

325

"Martha," said Mr. Peggotty, "God forbid as I should judge you! Forbid as I, of all men, should do that, my girl!"

His influence upon her was complete. She stood, shrinkingly, before him, as if she were afraid to meet his eyes; but her passionate sorrow was quite hushed and mute.

"If you heerd," said Mr. Peggotty, "owt of what passed between Mas'r Davy and me, th' night when it snew so hard, you know as I have been—wheer not—fur to seek my dear niece. My dear niece," he repeated steadily; "fur she's more dear to me now, Martha, than ever she was dear afore."

She put her hands before her face, but otherwise remained quiet.

"According to our reckoning," he proceeded—"Mas'r Davy's here, and mine—she is like, one day, to make her own poor solitary course to London. Help us all you can to find her, and may Heaven reward you!"

She looked at him hastily, and for the first time, as if she were doubtful of what he had said.

"Will you trust me?" she asked, in a low voice of astonishment.

"Full and free!" said Mr. Peggotty.

"To speak to her, if I should ever find her; shelter her, if I have any shelter to divide with her; and then, without her knowledge, come to you, and bring you to her?" she asked hurriedly.

We both replied together, "Yes."

She lifted up her eyes, and solemnly declared that she would devote herself to this task, fervently and faithfully; that she would never waver in it, never be diverted from it, never relinquish it, while there was any chance of hope.

Under a dull lamp in the road, I wrote our two addresses on a leaf of my pocketbook, which I tore out and gave to her, and which she put in her poor bosom. I asked her where she lived herself. She said, after a pause, in no place long. It were better not to know.

Mr. Peggoty suggesting to me, in a whisper, what had already occurred to myself, I took out my purse; but I could not prevail upon her to accept any money, nor could I exact any promise from her that she would do so at another time.

"I could not do what I have promised for money," she replied. "I could not take it, if I was starving. To give me money would be to take away your trust, to take away the object that you have given me, to take away the only certain thing that saves me from the river."

"In the name of the great Judge," said I, "before whom you and all of us must stand at His dread time, dismiss that terrible idea! We can all do some good, if we will."

She repressed the tears that had begun to flow; and putting out her trembling hand, and touching Mr. Peggotty, as if there was some healing virtue in him, went away along the desolate road.

It was midnight when I arrived at home. I had reached my own gate, and was standing listening for the deep bell of St. Paul's, the sound of which I thought had been borne toward me among the multitude of striking clocks, when I was rather surprised to see that the door of my aunt's cottage was open, and that a faint light in the entry was shining out across the road.

Thinking that my aunt might have relapsed into one of her old alarms, and might be watching the progress of some imaginary con-flagration in the distance, I went to speak to her. It was with very great surprise that I saw a man standing in her little garden. The moon was up now, though obscured, and I recognized the man whom I had once supposed to be a delusion of Mr. Dick's, and had once encountered with my aunt in the streets of the city.

The light in the passage was obscured for a moment, and my aunt came out. She was agitated, and tolled some money into his hand. I heard it chink.

"What's the use of this?" he demanded.

"I can spare no more," returned my aunt.

He stood moodily rattling the money, and shaking his head, until at length he said,

"Is this all you mean to give me, then?"

"It is all I *can* give you," said my aunt. "You know I have had losses, and am poorer than I used to be. Having got it, why do you give me the pain of looking at you for another moment, and seeing what you have become?"

"I have become shabby enough, if you mean that," he said. "I lead the life of an owl."

"You stripped me of the greater part of all I ever had," said my aunt. "You closed my heart against the whole world, years and years. You treated me falsely, ungratefully, and cruelly. Go, and repent of it. Don't add new injuries to the long, long list of injuries you have done me!"

"Ay!" he returned. "It's all very fine!—Well, I must do the best I can, for the present, I suppose."

In spite of himself, he appeared abashed by my aunt's indignant tears, and came slouching out of the garden. Taking two or three quick steps, as if I had just come up, I met him at the gate, and went in as he came out. We eyed one another narrowly in passing.

"Aunt," said I hurriedly, "this man alarming you again! Let me speak to him. Who is he?"

"Child," returned my aunt, taking my arm, "come in, and don't speak to me for ten minutes."

We sat down in her little parlor. My aunt retired behind the round green fan of former days, which was screwed on the back of a chair, and occasionally wiped her eyes, for about a quarter of an hour. Then she came out, and took a seat beside me.

"Trot," said my aunt calmly, "it's my husband."

"Your husband, aunt? I thought he had been dead."

"Dead to me," returned my aunt, "but living."

I sat in silent amazement.

"I left him," my aunt proceeded, laying her hand as usual on the back of mine, "generously. I may say at this distance of time, Trot, that I left him generously. He had been so cruel to me that I might have effected a separation on easy terms for myself; but I did not. He soon made ducks and drakes of what I gave him, sank lower and lower, married another woman, I believe, became an adventurer, a gambler, and a cheat. What he is now, you see. But he was a fine-looking man when I married him," said my aunt, with an echo of her old pride and admiration in her tone; "and I believed him—I was a fool!—to be the soul of honor!"

She gave my hand a squeeze, and shook her head.

"He is nothing to me now, Trot—less than nothing. But, sooner than have him punished for his offenses (as he would be if he prowled about in this country), I give him more money than I can afford, at intervals when he reappears, to go away. I was a fool when I married him; and I am so far an incurable fool on that subject, that, for the sake of what I once believed him to be, I wouldn't have even this shadow of my idle fancy hardly dealt with. For I was in earnest, Trot, if ever a woman was."

My aunt dismissed the matter with a sigh, and smoothed her dress.

"There, my dear!" she said. "Now, you know the beginning, middle, and end, and all about it. We won't mention the subject to one another any more; neither, of course, will you mention it to anybody else. This is my grumpy, frumpy story, and we'll keep it to ourselves, Trot!"

I saw the lonely figure flit away before us.

I LABORED hard at my book, without allowing it to interfere with the punctual discharge of my newspaper duties; and it came out, and was very successful. I was not stunned by the praise which sounded in my ears, notwithstanding that I was keenly alive to it, and thought better of my own performance, I have little doubt, than anybody else did.

I had been writing, in the newspaper and elsewhere, so prosperously, that one joyful night I noted down the music of the parliamentary bagpipes for the last time. I had been married, I suppose, about a year and a half. After several varieties of experiment, we had given up the housekeeping as a bad job. The house kept itself, and we kept a page.

This unlucky page, engaged in an evil hour at six pounds ten per annum, was a source of continual trouble to me. He stole Dora's watch, which, like everything else belonging to us, had no particular place of its own. The day after that on which I was obliged to appear against him, he made certain revelations touching a hamper in the cellar, which we believed to be full of wine, but which had nothing in it except bottles and corks. We supposed he had now eased his mind, and told the worst he knew of the cook; but a day or two afterwards his conscience sustained a new twinge, and he disclosed how she had a little girl, who, early every morning, took away our bread, and also how he himself had been suborned to maintain the milkman in coals. In two or three days more, I was informed by the authorities of his having led to the discovery of sirloins of beef among the kitchen-stuff and sheets in the rag-bag. A little while afterwards he broke out in an entirely new direction, and confessed to a knowledge of burglarious intentions as to our premises on the part of the pot-boy, who was immediately taken up. I got to be so ashamed of being such a victim that I would have given him any money to hold his tongue, or would have offered a round bribe for his being permitted to run away.

All this led me into some serious reflections, and presented our mistakes in a new aspect; as I could not help communicating to Dora one evening, in spite of my tenderness for her.

"My love," said I, "it is very painful to me to think that our want of system and management involves not only ourselves (which we have got used to), but other people."

"You have been silent for a long time, and now you are going to be cross!" said Dora.

"No, my dear, indeed! Let me explain to you what I mean."

"I think I don't want to know," said Dora.

"But I want you to know, my love. Put Jip down."

Dora put his nose to mine, and said "Boh!" to drive my seriousness away; but, not suceeding, ordered him into his pagoda, and sat looking at me, with her hands folded, and a most resigned little expression of countenance.

"The fact is, my dear," I began, "there is contagion in us. I begin to be afraid that the fault is not entirely on one side, but that these people all turn out ill because we don't turn out very well ourselves."

"Oh, what an accusation!" exclaimed Dora, opening her eyes wide; "to say that you ever saw me take gold watches! Oh!"

"My dearest," I remonstrated, "don't talk preposterous nonsense! Who has made the least allusion to gold watches?"

"You did," returned Dora. "You know you did. You said I hadn't turned out well, and compared me to him."

"To whom?" I asked.

"To the page," sobbed Dora. "Oh, you cruel fellow! Why didn't you tell me your opinion of me before we were married? Oh, what a dreadful opinion to have of me! Oh, my goodness!"

"My darling girl," I retorted, "I really must entreat you to be reasonable, and listen to what I did say, and do say. My dear Dora, unless we learn to do our duty to those whom we employ, they will never learn to do their duty to us. I am afraid we present opportunities to people to do wrong that never ought to be presented. We are positively corrupting people. We are bound to think of that. I can't help thinking of it, Dora. It is a reflection I am unable to dismiss, and it sometimes makes me very uneasy. There, dear; that's all. Come, now; don't be foolish!"

Dora would not allow me, for a long time, to remove the handkerchief. She sat sobbing and murmuring behind it, that, if I was uneasy, why had I ever been married? Why hadn't I said, even the day before we went to church, that I knew I should be uneasy, and I would rather not? If I couldn't bear her, why didn't I send her away to her aunts at Putney, or to Julia Mills in India? Dora was so afflicted, and so afflicted me by being in that condition, that I felt it was of no use repeating this kind of effort, though never so mildly, and I must take some other course.

What other course was left to take? To "form her mind"? This was a common phrase of words which had a fair and promising sound, and I resolved to form Dora's mind.

I began immediately. When Dora was very childish, and I would have infinitely preferred to humor her, I tried to be grave—and disconcerted her, and myself too. I talked to her on the subjects which occupied my thoughts, and I read Shakespeare to her—and fatigued her to the last degree. I accustomed myself to giving her, as it were quite casually, little scraps of useful information, or sound opinion—and she started from them, when I let them off, as if they had been crackers. No matter how incidentally or naturally I endeavored to form my little wife's mind, I could not help seeing that she always had an instinctive perception of what I was about, and became a prey to the keenest apprehensions. In particular, it was clear to me that she thought Shakespeare a terrible fellow. The formation went on very slowly.

I persevered, even for months. Finding at last, however, that, although I had been all this time a very porcupine or hedgehog, bristling all over with determination, I had effected nothing, it began to occur to me that perhaps Dora's mind was already formed.

On further consideration, this appeared so likely that I abandoned my scheme, resolving henceforth to be satisfied with my child-wife, and to try to change her into nothing else by any process. I was heartily tired of being sagacious and prudent by myself, and of seeing my darling under restraint; so I bought a pretty pair of earrings for her, and a collar for Jip, and went home one day to make myself agreeable.

I sat down by my wife on the sofa, and put the earrings in her ears; and then I told her that I feared we had not been quite as good company lately as we used to be, and that the fault was mine. Which I sincerely felt, and which indeed it was.

"The truth is, Dora, my life," I said, "I have been trying to be wise."

"And to make me wise too," said Dora timidly. "Haven't you, Doady?"

I nodded assent to the pretty inquiry of the raised eyebrows, and kissed the parted lips.

"It's of not a bit of use," said Dora, shaking her head until the earrings rang. "You know what a little thing I am, and what I wanted you to call me from the first. If you can't do so, I am afraid you'll never like me. Are you sure you don't think, sometimes, it would have been better to have——"

"Done what, my dear?" For she made no effort to proceed.

"Nothing!" said Dora.

"Nothing?" I repeated.

She put her arms round my neck, and laughed, and called herself by her favorite name of a goose, and hid her face on my shoulder in such a profusion of curls that it was quite a task to clear them away and see it.

"Don't I think it would have been better to have done nothing than to have tried to form my little wife's mind?" said I, laughing at myself. "Is that the question? Yes, indeed, I do."

"Is that what you have been trying?" cried Dora. "Oh, what a shocking boy!"

"But I shall never try any more," said I. "For I love her dearly as she is."

"Without a story—really?" inquired Dora, creeping closer to me.

"Why should I seek to change," said I, "what has been so precious to me for so long? You never can show better than as your own natural self, my sweet Dora; and we'll try no conceited experiments, but go back to our old way, and be happy."

"And be happy!" returned Dora. "Yes! All day! And you won't mind things going a tiny morsel wrong, sometimes?"

332

"No, no," said I. "We must do the best we can."

"It's better for me to be stupid than uncomfortable, isn't it?" said Dora.

"Better to be naturally Dora than anything else in the world."

"In the world! Ah, Doady, it's a large place!"

She shook her head, turned her delighted bright eyes up to mine, kissed me, broke into a merry laugh, and sprang away to put on Jip's new collar.

So ended my last attempt to make any change in Dora. I had been unhappy in trying it; I could not endure my own solitary wisdom; I could not reconcile it with her former appeal to me as my child-wife. I resolved to do what I could, in a quiet way, to improve our proceedings myself; but I foresaw that my utmost would be very little.

I always loved her. I bore the weight of all our little cares, and all my projects; Dora held the pens; and we both felt that our shares were adjusted as the case required. It made my second year much happier than my first; and, what was better still, made Dora's life all sunshine.

But as that year wore on, Dora was not strong. I had hoped that lighter hands than mine would help to mold her character, and that a baby-smile upon her breast might change my child-wife to a woman. It was not to be. The spirit fluttered for a moment on the threshold of its little prison, and, unconscious of captivity, took wing.

"When I can run about again, as I used to do, aunt," said Dora, "I shall make Jip race. He is getting quite slow and lazy."

"I suspect, my dear," said my aunt, quietly working by her side, "he has a worse disorder than that. Age, Dora."

"Do you think he is old?" said Dora, astonished. "Oh, how strange it seems that Jip should be old!"

"It's a complaint we are all liable to, Little One, as we get on in life," said my aunt cheerfully. "I don't feel more free from it than I used to be, I assure you."

"But Jip," said Dora, looking at him with compassion, "even little Jip! Oh, poor fellow!"

Jip nestled closer to his mistress, and lazily licked her hand.

"You are not so old, Jip, are you, that you'll leave your mistress yet?" said Dora. "We may keep one another company a little longer!"

My pretty Dora! When she came down to dinner on the ensuing

333

Sunday, and was so glad to see old Traddles (who always dined with us on Sunday), we thought she would be "running about as she used to do," in a few days. But they said, wait a few days more; and then, wait a few days more; and still she neither ran nor walked. She looked very pretty, and was very merry; but the little feet that used to be so nimble when they danced round Jip, were dull and motionless.

I began to carry her downstairs every morning, and upstairs every night. She would clasp me round the neck and laugh, the while, as if I did it for a wager. Jip would bark and caper round us, and go on before, and look back on the landing, breathing short, to see that we were coming. My aunt, the best and most cheerful of nurses, would trudge after us, a moving mass of shawls and pillows. Mr. Dick would not have relinquished his post of candle-bearer to anyone alive. Traddles would be often at the bottom of the staircase, looking on, and taking charge of sportive messages from Dora to the dearest girl in the world. We made quite a gay procession of it, and my child-wife was the gayest there.

But sometimes, when I took her up, and felt that she was lighter in my arms, a dead blank feeling came upon me, as if I were approaching to some frozen region, yet unseen, that numbed my life. I avoided the recognition of this feeling by any name, or by any communing with myself; until one night, when it was very strong upon me, and my aunt had left her with a parting cry of "Good-night, Little Blossom," I sat down at my desk alone, and cried to think, Oh, what a fatal name it was, and how the blossom withered in its bloom upon the tree!

CHAPTER 49 ❧ I AM INVOLVED IN MYSTERY ◆ ◆ ◆

I RECEIVED one morning by the post the following letter, dated
Canterbury, and addressed to me at Doctors' Commons, which
I read with some surprise:

"MY DEAR SIR,
    "Circumstances beyond my individual control have, for a
considerable lapse of time, effected a severance of that intimacy
which, in the limited opportunities conceded to me in the midst of
my professional duties, has ever afforded me, as it ever must con-
tinue to afford, gratifying emotions of no common description. This
fact, my dear sir, combined with the distinguished elevation to
which your talents have raised you, deters me from presuming to
aspire to the liberty of addressing the companion of my youth by
the familiar appellation of Copperfield! It is sufficient to know that
the name to which I do myself the honor to refer, will ever be
treasured among the muniments of our house (I allude to the
archives connected with our former lodgers, preserved by Mrs.
Micawber), with sentiments of personal esteem amounting to affection.
    "Without more directly referring to any latent ability that may

possibly exist on my part, of wielding the thunderbolt, or directing the devouring and avenging flame in any quarter, I may be permitted to observe, in passing, that my brightest visions are forever dispelled—that my peace is shattered, and my power of enjoyment destroyed—that my heart is no longer in the right place—and that I no more walk erect before my fellow-man. The canker is in the flower. The cup is bitter to the brim. The worm is at his work, and will soon dispose of his victim. The sooner the better. But I will not disgress.

"Placed in a mental position of peculiar painfulness, beyond the assuaging reach even of Mrs. Micawber's influence, though exercised in the tripartite character of woman, wife, and mother, it is my intention to fly from myself for a short period, and devote a respite of eight-and-forty hours to revisiting some metropolitan scenes of past enjoyment. Among other havens of domestic tranquillity and peace of mind, my feet will naturally tend toward the King's Bench Prison. In stating that I shall be (D.V.) on the outside of the south wall of that place of incarceration on civil process, the day after tomorrow, at seven in the evening precisely, my object in this epistolary communication is accomplished.

"I do not feel warranted in soliciting my former friend Mr. Copperfield, or my former friend Mr. Thomas Traddles of the Inner Temple, if that gentleman is still existent and forthcoming, to condescend to meet me, and renew (so far as may be) our past relations of the olden time. I confine myself to throwing out the observation, that, at the hour and place I have indicated, may be found such ruined vestiges as yet

"Remain,
"Of
"A
"Fallen Tower,
"WILKINS MICAWBER.

"P.S.—It may be advisable to superadd to the above, the statement that Mrs. Micawber is *not* in confidential possession of my intentions."

I read the letter over several times. Making due allowance for Mr. Micawber's lofty style of composition, and for the extraordinary relish with which he sat down and wrote long letters on all possible and impossible occasions, I still believed that something important lay hidden at the bottom of this roundabout communication.

Traddles and I held a long conference, and launched into a number of speculations, which I need not repeat. We took my aunt into our counsels in the afternoon; but our only decided conclusion was, that we would be very punctual in keeping Mr. Micawber's appointment.

Although we appeared at the stipulated place a quarter of an hour before the time, we found Mr. Micawber already there. His manner was something more confused, and something less genteel, than of yore. He had relinquished his legal suit of black for the purposes of this excursion, and wore the old surtout and tights, but not quite with the old air. He gradually picked up more and more of it as we conversed with him; but his very eye-glass seemed to hang less easily, and his shirt collar, though still of the old formidable dimensions, rather drooped.

"Gentlemen!" said Mr. Micawber, after the first salutations, "you are friends in need, and friends indeed. Allow me to offer my inquiries with reference to the physical welfare of Mrs. Copperfield *in esse*, and Mrs. Traddles *in posse*—presuming, that is to say, that my friend Mr. Traddles is not yet united to the object of his affections, for weal and for woe."

We acknowledged his politeness, and made suitable replies. He then directed our attention to the wall, and was beginning, "I assure you, gentlemen," when I ventured to object to that ceremonious form of address, and to beg that he would speak to us in the old way.

"My dear Copperfield," he returned, pressing my hand, "your cordiality overpowers me. This reception of a shattered fragment of the Temple once called Man—if I may be permitted so to express myself—bespeaks a heart that is an honor to our common nature."

"Oh, you are in low spirits, Mr. Micawber," said Traddles.

"I am, sir," interposed Mr. Micawber.

"I hope," said Traddles, "it is not because you have conceived a dislike to the law—for I am a lawyer myself, you know."

Mr. Micawber answered not a word.

"How is our friend Heep, Mr. Micawber?" said I, after a silence.

"My dear Copperfield," returned Mr. Micawber, bursting into a state of much excitement, and turning pale, "if you ask after my employer as *your* friend, I am sorry for it; if you ask after him as *my* friend, I sardonically smile at it. In whatever capacity you ask after my employer, I beg, without offense to you, to limit my reply to this—that whatever his state of health may be, his appearance is foxy, not to say diabolical."

I expressed my regret for having innocently touched upon a theme that roused him so much. "May I ask," said I, "without any hazard of repeating the mistake, how my old friends Mr. and Miss Wickfield are?"

"Miss Wickfield," said Mr. Micawber, now turning red, "is, as

337

she always is, a pattern and a bright example. My dear Copperfield, she is the only starry spot in a miserable existence. My respect for that young lady, my admiration of her character, my devotion to her for her love and truth and goodness!—Take me," said Mr. Micawber, "down a turning, for, upon my soul, in my present state of mind I am not equal to this!"

We wheeled him off into a narrow street, where he took out his pocket-handkerchief, and stood with his back to a wall. We stood by, until he put up his pocket-handkerchief, pulled up his shirt collar, and, to delude any person in the neighborhood who might have been observing him, hummed a tune, with his hat very much on one side. I then mentioned—not knowing what might be lost if we lost sight of him yet—that it would give me great pleasure to introduce him to my aunt, if he would ride out to Highgate, where a bed was at his service.

"You shall make us a glass of your own punch, Mr. Micawber," said I, "and forget whatever you have on your mind, in pleasanter reminiscences."

"Or, if confiding anything to friends will be more likely to relieve you, you shall impart it to us, Mr. Micawber," said Traddles prudently.

"Gentlemen," returned Mr. Micawber, "do with me as you will! I am a straw upon the surface of the deep, and am tossed in all directions by the elephants—I beg your pardon, I should have said the elements."

We went to my aunt's house rather than to mine, because of Dora's not being well. My aunt presented herself on being sent for, and welcomed Mr. Micawber with gracious cordiality. Mr. Micawber kissed her hand, retired to the window, and pulling out his pocket-handkerchief, had a mental wrestle with himself.

Mr. Dick was at home. He was by nature so exceedingly compassionate of any one who seemed to be ill at ease, and was so quick to find any such person out, that he shook hands with Mr. Micawber at least half a dozen times in five minutes. To Mr. Micawber, in his trouble, this warmth, on the part of a stranger, was so extremely touching, that he could only say, on the occasion of each successive shake, "My dear sir, you overpower me!" Which gratified Mr. Dick so much, that he went at it again with greater vigor than before.

"The friendliness of this gentleman," said Mr. Micawber to my aunt, "if you will allow me, ma'am, to cull a figure of speech from the vocabulary of our coarser national sports—floors me."

"My friend Mr. Dick," replied my aunt proudly, "is not a common man."

"That I am convinced of," said Mr. Micawber.—"My dear sir"—for Mr. Dick was shaking hands with him again—"I am deeply sensible of your cordiality."

"How do you find yourself?" said Mr. Dick, with an anxious look.

"Indifferent, my dear sir," returned Mr. Micawber, sighing.

"You must keep up your spirits," said Mr. Dick, "and make yourself as comfortable as possible."

Mr. Micawber was quite overcome by these friendly words, and by finding Mr. Dick's hand again within his own. "It has been my lot," he observed, "to meet, in the diversified panorama of human existence, with an occasional oasis, but never with one so green, so gushing, as the present!"

"You are a very old friend of my nephew's, Mr. Micawber," said my aunt. "I wish I had had the pleasure of seeing you before."

"Madam," returned Mr. Micawber, "I wish I had had the honor of knowing you at an earlier period. I was not always the wreck you at present behold."

"I hope Mrs. Micawber and your family are well, sir," said my aunt.

Mr. Micawber inclined his head. "They are as well, ma'am," he desperately observed after a pause, "as Aliens and Outcasts can ever hope to be!"

"Lord bless you, sir!" exclaimed my aunt in her abrupt way, "what are you talking about?"

"The subsistence of my family, ma'am," returned Mr. Micawber, "trembles in the balance. My employer——"

Here Mr. Micawber provokingly left off, and began to peel the lemons that had been, under my directions, set before him, together with all the other appliances he used in making punch. I saw that a crisis was at hand, and it came. He clattered all his means and implements together, rose from his chair, pulled out his pocket-handkerchief, and burst into tears.

"My dear Copperfield," said Mr. Micawber behind his handkerchief, "this is an occupation, of all others, requiring an untroubled mind and self-respect. I cannot perform it. It is out of the question."

"Mr. Micawber," said I, "what is the matter? Pray speak out. You are among friends."

"Among friends, sir!" repeated Mr. Micawber, and all he had reserved came breaking out of him. "Good heavens, it is principally because I *am* among friends that my state of mind is what it is. What is the matter, gentlemen? What is *not* the matter? Villainy is the matter; baseness is the matter; deception, fraud, conspiracy, are the matter; and the name of the whole atrocious mass is—HEEP!"

I never saw a man so hot in my life. I tried to calm him, that we might come to something rational; but he got hotter and hotter, and wouldn't hear a word.

"I'll put my hand in no man's hand," said Mr. Micawber, gasping, puffing, and sobbing to that degree that he was like a man fighting with cold water, "until I have—blown to fragments—the—a—detestable—serpent—HEEP! I'll partake of no one's hospitality, until I have—a—moved Mount Vesuvius—to eruption—on—a—the abandoned rascal—HEEP! Refreshment—a—underneath this roof—particularly punch—would—a—choke me—unless—I had—previously—choked the eyes—out of the head—a—of—interminable cheat and liar—HEEP! I—a—I'll know nobody—and—a—say nothing—and—a—live nowhere—until I have crushed—to—a—undiscoverable atoms—the—transcendent and immortal hypocrite and perjurer—HEEP!"

He sank into a chair, steaming, and looked at us, with every possible color in his face that had no business there, and an endless procession of lumps following one another in hot haste up his throat, whence they seemed to shoot into his forehead. I would have gone to his assistance, but he waved me off, and wouldn't hear a word.

"No, Copperfield! No communication—a—until—Miss Wickfield—a—redress from wrongs inflicted by consummate scoundrel—HEEP!" (I am quite convinced he could not have uttered three words, but for the amazing energy with which this word inspired him when he felt it coming.) "Inviolable secret—a—from the whole world—a—no exceptions—this day week—a—at breakfast-time—a—everybody present—including aunt—a—and extremely friendly gentleman—to be at the hotel at Canterbury—a—where—Mrs. Micawber and myself—Auld Lang Syne in chorus—and—a—will expose intolerable ruffian—HEEP! No more to say—a—or listen to persuasion—go immediately—not capable—a—bear society—upon the track of devoted and doomed traitor—HEEP!"

With this last repetition of the magic word that had kept him going at all, and in which he surpassed all his previous efforts, Mr. Micawber rushed out of the house, leaving us in a state of excitement, hope, and wonder, that reduced us to a condition little better than his own. But even then his passion for writing letters was too strong to be resisted; for while we were yet in the height of our excitement, hope, and wonder, the following pastoral note was brought to me from a neighboring tavern, at which he had called to write it:

"Most secret and confidential.

"MY DEAR SIR,

"I beg to be allowed to convey, through you, my apologies to your excellent aunt for my late excitement. An explosion of a smouldering volcano long suppressed, was the result of an internal contest more easily conceived than described.

"I trust I rendered tolerably intelligible my appointment for the morning of this day week, at the house of public entertainment at Canterbury, where Mrs. Micawber and myself had once the honor of uniting our voices to yours, in the well-known strain of the Immortal exciseman nurtured beyond the Tweed.

"The duty done, and act of reparation performed, which can alone enable me to contemplate my fellow mortal, I shall be known no more. I shall simply require to be deposited in that place of universal resort, where

'Each in his narrow cell for ever laid,
The rude forefathers of the hamlet sleep'

"—With the plain Inscription,
WILKINS MICAWBER."

I was walking alone in the garden one evening, the second in
Mr. Micawber's week of·suspense. There was a little green
perspective of trellis-work and ivy at the side of our cottage,
through which I could see, from the garden where I was walking,
into the road before the house. I happened to turn my eyes toward
this place, as I was thinking of many things, and I saw a figure beyond, dressed in a plain cloak. It was bending eagerly toward me,
and beckoning.

"Martha!" said I, going to it.

"Can you come with me?" she inquired in an agitated whisper.
"I have been to him, and he is not at home. I wrote down where he
was to come, and left it on his table with my own hand. They said
he would not be out long. I have tidings for him. Can you come
directly?"

My answer was to pass out at the gate immediately. I stopped an
empty coach that was coming by, and we got into it. When I asked
her where the coachman was to drive, she answered, "Anywhere
near Golden Square—and quick!" then shrunk into a corner.

Now much disturbed, and dazzled with conflicting gleams of
hope and dread, I looked at her for some explanation. But, seeing

how strongly she desired to remain quiet, and feeling that it was my own natural inclination too, at such a time, I did not attempt to break the silence. We proceeded without a word being spoken. Sometimes she glanced out of the window, as though she thought we were going slowly, though indeed we were going fast; but otherwise remained exactly as at first.

We alighted at one of the entrances to the Square she had mentioned, where I directed the coach to wait, not knowing but that we might have some occasion for it. She laid her hand on my arm, and hurried me on to one of the somber streets, of which there are several in that part, where the houses were once fair dwellings in the occupation of single families, but had long degenerated into poor lodgings let off in rooms. Entering at the open door of one of these, and releasing my arm, she beckoned me to follow her up the common staircase, which was like a tributary channel to the street.

The house swarmed with inmates. As we went up, doors of rooms were opened and people's heads put out; and we passed other people on the stairs, who were coming down. In glancing up from the outside, before we entered, I had seen women and children lolling at the windows over flowerpots; and we seemed to have attracted their curiosity, for these were principally the observers who looked out of their doors. It was a broad paneled staircase, with massive balustrades of some dark wood; cornices above the doors, ornamented with carved fruit and flowers; and broad seats in the windows. But all these tokens of past grandeur were miserably decayed and dirty; rot, damp, and age had weakened the flooring, which in many places was unsound and even unsafe. Some attempts had been made, I noticed, to infuse new blood into this dwindling frame, by repairing the costly old woodwork here and there with common deal; but it was like the marriage of a reduced old noble to a plebeian pauper, and each party to the ill-assorted union shrunk away from the other. Several of the back windows on the staircase had been darkened or wholly blocked up. In those that remained there was scarcely any glass; and through the crumbling frames by which the bad air seemed always to come in, and never to go out, I saw, through other glassless windows, into other houses in a similar condition, and looked giddily down into a wretched yard, which was the common dust-heap of the mansion.

We proceeded to the top story of the house. Two or three times, by the way, I thought I observed, in the indistinct light, the skirts of a female figure going up before us. As we turned to ascend the

343

last flight of stairs between us and the roof, we caught a full view of this figure pausing for a moment at a door. Then it turned the handle, and went in.

"What's this?" said Martha, in a whisper. "She has gone into my room. I don't know her!"

I knew her. I had recognized her with amazement for Miss Dartle.

I said something to the effect that it was a lady whom I had seen before, in a few words, to my conductress; and had scarcely done so, when we heard her voice in the room, though not, from where we stood, what she was saying. Martha, with an astonished look, softly led me up the stairs, and then into a small empty garret with a low sloping roof, little better than a cupboard. Between this, and the room she had called hers, there was a small door of communication, standing partly open. I could not see Miss Dartle, or the person whom we had heard her address.

A dead silence prevailed for some moments. Martha kept one hand on my lips, and raised the other in a listening attitude.

"It matters little to me her not being at home," said Rosa Dartle haughtily; "I know nothing of her. It is you I come to see."

"Me?" replied a soft voice. At the sound of it a thrill went through my frame; for it was Emily's!

"Yes," returned Miss Dartle; "I have come to look at you. What? You are not ashamed of the face that has done so much?"

The resolute and unrelenting hatred of her tone, its cold stern sharpness, and its mastered rage, presented her before me, as if I had seen her standing in the light. I saw the flashing black eyes, and the passion-wasted figure; and I saw the scar, with its white track cutting through her lips, quivering and throbbing as she spoke.

"I have come to see," she said, "James Steerforth's fancy; the girl who ran away with him, and is the town talk of the commonest people of her native place; the bold, flaunting, practiced companion of persons like James Steerforth. I want to know what such a thing is like."

There was a rustle, as if the unhappy girl, on whom she heaped these taunts, ran toward the door, and the speaker swiftly interposed herself before it. It was succeeded by a moment's pause.

When Miss Dartle spoke again, it was through her set teeth, and with a stamp upon the ground.

"Stay there!" she said, "or I'll proclaim you to the house and the whole street! If you try to evade *me*, I'll stop you, if it's by the hair, and raise the very stones against you!"

A frightened murmur was the only reply that reached my ears. A silence succeeded. I did not know what to do. Much as I desired to put an end to the interview, I felt that I had no right to present myself; that it was for Mr. Peggotty alone to see her and recover her.

"So!" said Rosa Dartle, with a contemptuous laugh, "I see her at last! Why, he was a poor creature to be taken by that delicate mock-modesty, and that hanging head!"

"Oh, for Heaven's sake, spare me!" exclaimed Emily. "Whoever you are, you know my pitiable story; and, for Heaven's sake, spare me, if you would be spared yourself!"

"If *I* would be spared!" returned the other fiercely. "What is there in common between *us*, do you think?"

"Nothing but our sex," said Emily, with a burst of tears.

"And that," said Rosa Dartle, "is so strong a claim, preferred by one so infamous, that if I had any feeling in my breast but scorn and abhorrence of you, it would freeze it up. Our sex! You are an honor to our sex!"

Miss Dartle placed herself in a chair, within view of the door, and looked downward, as if Emily were crouching on the floor before her. Being now between me and the light, I could see her curled lip, and her cruel eyes intently fixed on one place, with a greedy triumph.

"Oh, have some mercy on me!" cried Emily. "Show me some compassion, or I shall die mad!"

"It would be no great penance," said Rosa Dartle, "for your crimes. Do you know what you have done? Do you ever think of the home you have laid waste?"

"Oh, is there ever night or day when I don't think of it!" cried Emily; and now I could just see her, on her knees, with her head thrown back, her pale face looking upward, her hands wildly clasped and held out, and her hair streaming about her. "Has there ever been a single minute, waking or sleeping, when it hasn't been before me, just as it used to be! Oh, home, home! I have none, none, no comfort upon earth!" She dropped on her face, before the imperious figure in the chair, with an imploring effort to clasp the skirt of her dress.

Rosa Dartle sat looking down upon her, as inflexible as a figure of brass. Her lips were tightly compressed, as if she knew that she must keep a strong constraint upon herself—I write what I sincerely believe—or she would be tempted to strike the beautiful form with her foot. I saw her distinctly, and the whole power of her face and character seemed forced into that expression.—Would he never come?

"The miserable vanity of these earth-worms!" she said, when she had so far controlled the angry heavings of her breast that she could trust herself to speak. "*Your* home! Do you imagine that I bestow a thought on it, or suppose you could do any harm to that low place which money would not pay for, and handsomely? *Your* home! You were a part of the trade of your home, and were bought and sold like any other vendible thing your people dealt in."

"Oh, not that!" cried Emily. "Say anything of me; but don't visit my disgrace and shame, more than I have done, on folks who are as honorable as you! Have some respect for them, as you are a lady, if you have no mercy for me."

"I speak," she said, not deigning to take any heed of this appeal, and drawing away her dress from the contamination of Emily's touch, "I speak of *his* home—where I live. Here," she said, stretching out her hand with her contemptuous laugh, and looking down upon the prostrate girl, "is a worthy cause of division between lady mother and gentleman son; of grief in a house where she wouldn't have been admitted as a kitchen-girl; of anger, and repining, and reproach. This piece of pollution, picked up from the waterside, to be made much of for an hour, and then tossed back!"

"No! no!" cried Emily, clasping her hands together. "When he first came into my way—that the day had never dawned upon me, and he had met me being carried to my grave!—I had been brought up as virtuous as you or any lady, and was going to be the wife of as good a man as you or any lady in the world can ever marry. If you live in his home, and know him, you know, perhaps, what his power with a weak, vain girl might be. I don't defend myself, but I know well, and he knows well—or he will know when he comes to die, and his mind is troubled with it—that he used all his power to deceive me; and that I believed him, trusted him, and loved him!"

Rosa Dartle sprang up from her seat, recoiled, and in recoiling struck at her, with a face of such malignity, so darkened and disfigured by passion, that I had almost thrown myself between them. The blow, which had no aim, fell upon the air. As she now stood panting, looking at her with the utmost detestation, and trembling from head to foot with rage and scorn, I thought I had never seen such a sight, and never could see such another.

"*You* love him? *You?*" she cried, with her clenched hand, quivering as if it only wanted a weapon to stab the object of her wrath.

Emily had shrunk out of my view. There was no reply.

"And tell that to *me*," she added, "with your shameful lips? Why don't they whip these creatures? If I could order it to be done, I would have this girl whipped to death."

And so she would, I have no doubt. I would not have trusted her with the rack itself while that furious look lasted.

She slowly, very slowly, broke into a laugh, and pointed at Emily with her hand, as if she were a sight of shame for gods and men.

"*She* love!" she said. "That carrion! And he ever cared for her, she'd tell me. Ha, ha! The liars that these traders are!"

Her mockery was worse than her undisguised rage. Of the two, I would have much preferred to be the object of the latter. But when she suffered it to break loose, it was only for a moment. She had chained it up again, and however it might tear her within, she subdued it to herself.

"I came here, you pure fountain of love," she said, "to see—as I began by telling you—what such a thing as you was like. I was curious. I am satisfied. Also to tell you, that you had best seek that home of yours with all speed, and hide your head among those excellent people who are expecting you, and whom your money will console. When it's all gone, you can believe, and trust and love again, you know!—I have something more to say. Attend to it; for what I say I'll do. Do you hear me, you fairy spirit? What I say, I mean to do!"

Her rage got the better of her again, for a moment; but it passed over her face like a spasm, and left her smiling.

"Hide yourself," she pursued, "if not at home, somewhere. Let it be somewhere beyond reach; in some obscure life—or, better still, in some obscure death. I wonder, if your loving heart will not break, you have found no way of helping it to be still! I have heard of such means sometimes. I believe they may be easily found."

A low crying, on the part of Emily, interrupted her here. She stopped, and listened to it as if it were music.

"I am of a strange nature, perhaps," Rosa Dartle went on; "but I can't breathe freely in the air you breathe. I find it sickly. Therefore, I will have it cleared—I will have it purified of you. If you live here tomorrow, I'll have your story and your character proclaimed on the common stair. There are decent women in the house, I am told; and it is a pity such a light as you should be among them, and concealed. If, leaving here, you seek any refuge in this town in any character but your true one (which you are welcome to bear, without molestation from me), the same service shall be done you, if I hear of your retreat."

Would he never, never come? How long was I to bear this? How long could I bear it?

"Oh me, oh me!" exclaimed the wretched Emily, in a tone that might have touched the hardest heart, I should have thought; but there was no relenting in Rosa Dartle's smile. "What, what shall I do?"

"Do?" returned the other. "Live happy in your own reflections! Consecrate your existence to the recollection of James Steerforth's tenderness—he would have made you his serving-man's wife, would he not?—or to feeling grateful to the upright and deserving creature who would have taken you as his gift. Or, if those proud remembrances, and the consciousness of your own virtues, and the honorable position to which they have raised you in the eyes of everything that wears the human shape, will not sustain you, marry that good man, and be happy in his condescension. If this will not do either, die! There are doorways and dust-heaps for such deaths and such despair: find one, and take your flight to heaven!"

I heard a distant foot upon the stairs. I knew it, I was certain. It was his, thank God! She moved slowly from before the door when she said this, and passed out of my sight.

"But mark," she added, slowly and sternly, opening the other door to go away, "I am resolved, for reasons that I have and hatreds that I entertain, to cast you out, unless you withdraw from my reach altogether, or drop your pretty mask. This is what I had to say; and what I say, I mean to do!"

The foot upon the stairs came nearer—nearer—passed her as she went down—rushed into the room!

"Uncle!"

A fearful cry followed the word. I paused a moment, and, looking in, saw him supporting her insensible figure in his arms. He gazed for a few seconds in the face, then stooped to kiss it—oh, how tenderly!—and drew a handkerchief before it.

"Mas'r Davy," he said, in a low, tremulous voice, when it was covered, "I thank my Heav'nly Father as my dream's come true! I thank Him hearty for having guided of me, in His own ways, to my darling!"

With those words he took her up in his arms, and, with the veiled face lying on his bosom, and addressed toward his own, carried her, motionless and unconscious, down the stairs.

348

CHAPTER 51 🥀 THE BEGINNING OF A
LONGER JOURNEY • • •

IT WAS yet early in the morning of the following day, when, as I
was walking in my garden with my aunt (who took little other
exercise now, being so much in attendance on my dear Dora),
I was told that Mr. Peggotty desired to speak with me. He came into
the garden to meet me half-way.

"I'll go in now, Trot," said my aunt, "and look after Little
Blossom, who will be getting up presently."

"Not along of my being here, ma'am, I hope?" said Mr. Peggotty.
"Unless my wits is gone a bahd's-neezing"—by which Mr. Peggotty
meant to say bird's-nesting—"this morning, 'tis along of me as you're
a-going to quit us?"

"You have something to say, my good friend," returned my aunt,
"and will do better without me."

"By your leave, ma'am," returned Mr. Peggotty, "I should take
it kind, pervising you doen't mind my clicketen, if you'd bide here."

"Would you?" said my aunt, with short good-nature. "Then I
am sure I will!"

So she drew her arm through Mr. Peggotty's, and walked with him
to a leafy little summer-house there was at the bottom of the garden,
where she sat down on a bench, and I beside her. There was a seat

for Mr. Peggotty too, but he preferred to stand, leaning his hand on the small rustic table. As he stood, looking at his cap for a little while before beginning to speak, I could not help observing what power and force of character his sinewy hand expressed, and what a good and trusty companion it was to his honest brow and iron-grey hair.

"I took my dear child away last night," Mr. Peggotty began, as he raised his eyes to ours, "to my lodging, wheer I have a long time been expecting of her and preparing fur her. It was hours afore she knowed me right; and when she did, she kneeled down at my feet, and kiender said to me, as if it was her prayers, how it all come to be. You may believe me, when I heerd her voice, as I had heerd at home so playful—and see her humbled, as it might be in the dust our Saviour wrote in with His blessed hand—I felt a wownd go to my 'art in the midst of all its thankfulness."

He drew his sleeve across his face, without any pretense of concealing why, and then cleared his voice.

"All night long," said Mr. Peggotty, "we have been together, Em'ly and me. 'Tis little (considering the time) as she has said, in wureds, through them broken-hearted tears; 'tis less as I have seen of her dear face, as grow'd into a woman's at my hearth. But all night long her arms has been about my neck, and her head has laid here; and we knows full well as we can put our trust in one another evermore."

He ceased to speak, and his hand upon the table rested there in perfect repose, with a resolution in it that might have conquered lions.

"You have quite made up your mind," said I to Mr. Peggotty, "as to the future, good friend? I need scarcely ask you."

"Quite, Mas'r Davy," he returned; "and told Em'ly. Theer's mighty countries fur from here. Our future life lays over the sea."

"They will emigrate together, aunt," said I.

"Yes!" said Mr. Peggotty, with a hopeful smile. "No one can't reproach my darling in Australia. We will begin a new life over theer!"

I asked him if he yet proposed to himself any time for going away.

"I was down at the Docks early this morning, sir," he returned, "to get information concerning of them ships. In about six weeks or two months from now there'll be one sailing—I see her this morning—went aboard—and we shall take our passage in her."

"Quite alone?" I asked.

"Ay, Mas'r Davy!" he returned. "My sister, you see, she's that fond of you and yourn, and that accustomed to think on'y of her own country, that it wouldn't be hardly fair to let her go. Besides which, theer's one she has in charge, Mas'r Davy, as doen't ought to be forgot."

"Poor Ham!" said I.

"My good sister takes care of his house, you see, ma'am, and he takes kindly to her," Mr. Peggotty explained, for my aunt's better information.

"And Mrs. Gummidge?" said I.

"Well, I've had a mort of con-sideration, I do tell you," returned Mr. Peggotty, with a perplexed look which gradually cleared as he went on, "concerning of Missis Gummidge. Betwixt you and me, Mas'r Davy—and you, ma'am—when Missis Gummidge takes to wimicking,"—our old county word for crying,—"she's liable to be considered to be, by them as didn't know the old 'un, peevish-like. Wheerby," said Mr. Peggotty, "my sister might—I doen't say she would, but might—find Missis Gummidge give her a leetle trouble now and again. Theerfur 'tan't my intentions to moor Missis Gummidge 'long with them, but to find a beein' fur her wheer she can fisherate fur herself." (A beein' signifies, in that dialect, a home; and to fisherate, is to provide.) "Fur which purpose," said Mr. Peggotty, "I means to make her a 'lowance afore I go, as'll leave her pretty comfort'ble."

He forgot nobody. He thought of everybody's claims and striv-ings but his own.

"Theer's one thing furder, Mas'r Davy," said he, putting his hand in his breast-pocket, and gravely taking out the little paper bundle I had seen before, which he unrolled on the table. "Theer's these here bank-notes—fifty-pound, and ten. To them I wish to add the money as she come away with. I've asked her about that (but not saying why), and have added of it up. I an't a scholar; would you be so kind as see how 'tis?"

He handed me, apologetically for his scholarship, a piece of paper, and observed me while I looked it over. It was quite right.

"Thankee, sir," he said, taking it back. "This money, if you doen't see objections, Mas'r Davy, I shall put up jest afore I go, in a cover d'rected to him; and put that up in another, d'rected to his mother. I shall tell her, in no more wureds than I speak to you, what it's the price on; and that I'm gone, and past receiving of it back."

I told him that I thought it would be right to do so—that I was

351

thoroughly convinced it would be, since he felt it to be right.

"I said that theer was on'y one thing furder," he proceeded, with a grave smile, when he had made up his little bundle again, and put it in his pocket, "but theer was two. I warn't sure in my mind, when I come out this morning, as I could go and break to Ham, of my own self, what had so thankfully happened. So I writ a letter while I was out, and put it in the post-office, telling of 'em how all was as 'tis, and that I should come down tomorrow to unload my mind of what little needs a-doing of down theer, and, most-like, take my farewell leave of Yarmouth."

"And do you wish me to go with you?" said I, seeing that he left something unsaid.

"If you could do me that kind favor, Mas'r Davy," he replied, "I know the sight on you would cheer 'em up a bit."

My little Dora being in good spirits, and very desirous that I should go—as I found on talking it over with her—I readily pledged myself to accompany him in accordance with his wish. Next morning, consequently, we were on the Yarmouth coach, and again traveling over the old ground.

That night, for the first time in all those many nights, the candle was taken out of the window, Mr. Peggotty swung in his old hammock in the old boat, and the wind murmured with the old sound round his head.

All next day he was occupied in disposing of his fishing-boat and tackle; in packing up, and sending to London by wagon, such of his little domestic possessions as he thought would be useful to him; and in parting with the rest, or bestowing them on Mrs. Gummidge. She was with him all day. As I had a sorrowful wish to see the old place once more, before it was locked up, I engaged to meet them there in the evening.

The door of the boat-house stood open when I approached, and, on entering, I found it emptied of all its furniture, saving one of the old lockers, on which Mrs. Gummidge, with a basket on her knee, was seated, looking at Mr. Peggotty. He leaned his elbow on the rough chimney-piece, and gazed upon a few expiring embers in the grate; but he raised his head hopefully, on my coming in, and spoke in a cheery manner.

"Come, according to promise, to bid farewell to't, eh, Mas'r Davy?" he said, taking up the candle. "Bare enough, now, an't it?"

"Indeed you have made good use of the time," said I.

"Why, we have not been idle, sir. Missis Gummidge has worked

352

like a—I doen't know what Missis Gummidge an't worked like," said Mr. Peggotty, looking at her, at a loss for a sufficiently approving simile.

"Dan'l," said Mrs. Gummidge, suddenly deserting her basket, and clinging to his arm, "my dear Dan'l, the parting words I speak in this house is, I mustn't be left behind. Doen't ye think of leaving me behind, Dan'l! Oh, doen't ye ever do it!"

Mr. Peggotty, taken aback, looked from Mrs. Gummidge to me, and from me to Mrs. Gummidge, as if he had been awakened from a sleep.

"Doen't ye, dearest Dan'l, doen't ye!" cried Mrs. Gummidge fervently. "Take me 'long with you, Dan'l; take me 'long with you and Em'ly! I'll be your servant, constant and true. If there's slaves in them parts where you're a-going, I'll be bound to you for one, and happy; but doen't ye leave me behind, Dan'l, that's a deary dear!"

"My good soul," said Mr. Peggotty, shaking his head, "you doen't know what a long voyage and what a hard life 'tis!"

"Yes, I do, Dan'l! I can guess!" cried Mrs. Gummidge. "But my parting words under this roof is, I shall go into the House and die, if I am not took. I can dig, Dan'l. I can work. I can live hard. I can be loving and patient now—more than you think, Dan'l, if you'll on'y try me. I wouldn't touch the 'lowance, not if I was dying of want, Dan'l Peggotty; but I'll go with you and Em'ly, if you'll on'y let me, to the world's end! I know how 'tis; I know you think that I am lone and lorn; but, deary love, 'tan't so no more! I ain't sat here so long, a-watching, and a-thinking of your trials, without some good being done me.—Mas'r Davy, speak to him for me! I knows his ways, and Em'ly's, and I knows their sorrows, and can be a comfort to 'em, some odd times, and labor for 'em allus! Dan'l, deary Dan'l, let me go 'long with you!"

And Mrs. Gummidge took his hand, and kissed it with a homely pathos and affection, in a homely rapture of devotion and gratitude, that he well deserved.

We brought the locker out, extinguished the candle, fastened the door on the outside, and left the old boat close shut up, a dark speck in the cloudy night. Next day, when we were returning to London outside the coach, Mrs Gummidge and her basket were on the seat behind, and Mrs Gummidge was happy.

CHAPTER 52  I ASSIST AT AN EXPLOSION • • •

WHEN the time Mr. Micawber had appointed so mysteriously was within four-and-twenty hours of being come, my aunt was very unwilling to leave Dora, Ah! how easily I carried Dora up and down stairs now!

We were disposed to arrange that she should stay at home, and be represented by Mr. Dick and me, when Dora unsettled us by declaring that she never would forgive herself, and never would forgive her bad boy, if my aunt remained behind, on any pretense.

"I won't speak to you," said Dora, shaking her curls at my aunt. "I'll be disagreeable! I'll make Jip bark at you all day. I shall be sure that you really are a cross old thing, if you don't go!"

"Tut, Blossom!" laughed my aunt. "You know you can't do without me!"

"Yes, I can," said Dora. "You are no use to me at all. You never run up and down stairs for me, all day long. You never sit and tell me stories about Doady, when his shoes were worn out, and he was covered with dust—oh, what a poor little mite of a fellow! You never do anything at all to please me, do you, dear?" Dora made haste to kiss my aunt, and say, "Yes, you do! I'm only joking!"— lest my aunt should think she really meant it.

354

"Besides," said Dora, putting back her hair, and looking wonderingly at my aunt and me, "why shouldn't you both go? I am not very ill indeed—am I?"

"Why, what a question!" cried my aunt.

"What a fancy!" said I.

"Yes! I know I am a silly little thing!" said Dora, slowly looking from one of us to the other, and then putting up her pretty lips to kiss us as she lay upon her couch. "Well, then, you must both go, or I shall not believe you; and then I shall cry!"

We agreed, without any more consultation, that we would both go, and that Dora was a little impostor, who feigned to be rather unwell because she liked to be petted. She was greatly pleased, and very merry; and we four—that is to say, my aunt, Mr. Dick, Traddles, and I—went down to Canterbury by the Dover mail that night.

At the hotel where Mr. Micawber had requested us to await him I found a letter, importing that he would appear in the morning punctually at half-past nine. At the first chime of the half-hour he appeared.

"Gentlemen, and madam," said Mr Micawber, "good-morning! My dear sir," to Mr. Dick, who shook hands with him violently, "you are extremely good."

"Have you breakfasted?" said Mr. Dick. "Have a chop!"

"Not for the world, my good sir!" cried Mr. Micawber, stopping him on his way to the bell; "appetite and myself, Mr. Dixon, have long been strangers."

Mr. Dixon was so well pleased with his new name, and appeared to think it so very obliging in Mr. Micawber to confer it upon him, that he shook hands with him again, and laughed rather childishly.

"Dick," said my aunt, "attention!"

Mr. Dick recovered himself, with a blush.

"Now, sir," said my aunt to Mr. Micawber, as she put on her gloves, "we are ready for Mount Vesuvius, or anything else, as soon as *you* please."

"Madam," returned Mr. Micawber, "I trust you will shortly witness an eruption. Mr. Traddles, I have your permission, I believe, to mention here that we have been in communication together?"

"It is undoubtedly the fact, Copperfield," said Traddles, to whom I looked in surprise. "Mr. Micawber has consulted me in reference to what he has in contemplation, and I have advised him to the best of my judgment."

355

"Perhaps, under such circumstances, madam and gentlemen," said Mr. Micawber, "you will do me the favor to submit yourselves, for the moment, to the direction of one who, however unworthy to be regarded in any other light but as a Waif and Stray upon the shore of human nature, is still your fellow-man."

"We have perfect confidence in you, Mr. Micawber," said I, "and will do what you please."

"Mr. Copperfield," returned Mr. Micawber, "your confidence is not, at the existing juncture, ill-bestowed. I would beg to be allowed a start of five minutes by the clock; and then to receive the present company, inquiring for Miss Wickfield, at the office of Wickfield and Heep, whose stipendiary I am."

My aunt and I looked at Traddles, who nodded his approval.

"I have no more," observed Mr. Micawber, "to say at present."

With which, to my infinite surprise, he included us all in a comprehensive bow, and disappeared; his manner being extremely distant, and his face extremely pale.

Traddles only smiled, and shook his head (with his hair standing upright on the top of it), when I looked to him for an explanation; so we all went out together to the old house, without saying one word on the way.

We found Mr. Micawber at his desk. The large office-ruler was stuck into his waistcoat, and was not so well concealed but that a foot or more of that instrument protruded from his bosom, like a new kind of shirt-frill. As it appeared to me that I was expected to speak, I said aloud,

"How do you do, Mr. Micawber?"

"Mr. Copperfield," said Mr. Micawber gravely, "I hope I see you well."

"Is Miss Wickfield at home?" said I.

"Mr. Wickfield is unwell in bed, sir, of a rheumatic fever," he returned; "but Miss Wickfield, I have no doubt, will be happy to see old friends. Will you walk in, sir?"

He preceded us to the dining-room—the first room I had entered in that house—and flinging open the door of Mr. Wickfield's former office, said, in a sonorous voice,

"Miss Trotwood, Mr. David Copperfield, Mr. Thomas Traddles, and Mr. Dixon!"

I had not seen Uriah Heep since the time of the blow. Our visit astonished him, evidently. He did not gather his eyebrows together, for he had none worth mentioning; but he frowned to that degree that he almost closed his small eyes, while the hurried raising of his gristly hand to his chin betrayed some trepidation or surprise. This was only when we were in the act of entering his room. A moment afterwards he was as fawning and as humble as ever.

"Well, I am sure," he said, "this is indeed an unexpected pleasure! Mr. Copperfield, I hope I see you well—if I may umbly express self so—friendly toward them as is ever your friends, whether or not."

I felt ashamed to let him take my hand, but I did not know yet what else to do.

Agnes, now ushered in by Mr. Micawber, was not quite so self-possessed as usual, I thought, and had evidently undergone anxiety and fatigue. But her earnest cordiality and her quiet beauty shone with the gentler luster for it. I saw Uriah watch her while she greeted us; and he reminded me of an ugly and rebellious genie watching a good spirit. In the meanwhile some slight sign passed between Mr. Micawber and Traddles; and Traddles, unobserved except by me, went out.

"Don't wait, Micawber," said Uriah.

Mr. Micawber, with his hand upon the ruler in his breast, stood erect before the door, most unmistakably contemplating one of his fellow-men, and that man his employer.

"What are you waiting for?" said Uriah. "Micawber! did you hear me tell you not to wait?"

"Yes!" replied the immovable Mr. Micawber.

"Then why *do* you wait?" said Uriah.

"Because I—in short, choose," replied Mr. Micawber, with a burst.

Uriah's cheeks lost color, and an unwholesome paleness, still faintly tinged by his pervading red, overspread them. He looked at Mr. Micawber attentively, with his whole face breathing short and quick in every feature.

"You are a dissipated fellow, as all the world knows," he said, with an effort at a smile, "and I am afraid you'll oblige me to get rid of you. Go along! I'll talk to you presently."

"If there is a scoundrel on this earth," said Mr. Micawber, suddenly breaking out again with the utmost vehemence, "with whom I have already talked too much, that scoundrel's name is—HEEP!"

Uriah fell back, as if he had been struck or stung. Looking slowly round upon us, with the darkest and wickedest expression that his face could wear, he said, in a lower voice,

"Oho! This is a conspiracy! You have met here by appointment!

You are playing Booty with my clerk, are you, Copperfield? Now, take care. You'll make nothing of this. We understand each other, you and me. There's no love between us. You were always a puppy with a proud stomach from your first coming here; and you envy me my rise, do you? None of your plots against me; I'll counterplot you! Micawber, you be off. I'll talk to you presently."

"Mr. Micawber," said I, "there is a sudden change in this fellow, in more respects than the extraordinary one of his speaking the truth in one particular, which assures me that he is brought to bay. Deal with him as he deserves!"

"You are a precious set of people, ain't you?" said Uriah, in the same low voice and breaking out into a clammy heat, which he wiped from his forehead with his long lean hand, "to buy over my clerk, who is the very scum of society—as you yourself were, Copperfield, you know it, before anyone had charity on you—to defame me with his lies? Miss Trotwood, you had better stop this, or I'll stop your husband shorter than will be pleasant to you. I won't know your story professionally for nothing, old lady! Miss Wickfield, if you have any love for your father, you had better not join that gang. I'll ruin him, if you do. Now, come! I have got some of you under the harrow. Think twice, before it goes over you. Think twice, you, Micawber, if you don't want to be crushed. I recommend you to take yourself off, and be talked to presently, you fool, while there's time to retreat. Where's mother?" he said, suddenly appearing to notice with alarm the absence of Traddles, and pulling down the bell-rope. "Fine doings in a person's own house!"

"Mrs. Heep is here, sir," said Traddles, returning with that worthy mother of a worthy son. "I have taken the liberty of making myself known to her."

"Who are you to make yourself known?" retorted Uriah. "And what do you want here?"

"I am the agent and friend of Mr. Wickfield, sir," said Traddles, in a composed, business-like way. "And I have a power of attorney from him in my pocket, to act for him in all matters."

"The old ass has drunk himself into a state of dotage," said Uriah, turning uglier than before, "and it has been got from him by fraud!"

"Something has been got from him by fraud, I know," returned Traddles quietly; "and so do you, Mr. Heep. We will refer that question, if you please, to Mr. Micawber."

"Ury——" Mrs. Heep began, with an anxious gesture.

358

"You hold your tongue, mother," he returned; "least said, soonest mended."

"But, my Ury——"

"Will you hold your tongue, mother, and leave it to me?"

Though I had long known that his servility was false, and all his pretenses knavish and hollow, I had had no adequate conception of the extent of his hypocrisy, until I now saw him with his mask off. The suddenness with which he dropped it when he perceived that it was useless to him; the malice, insolence, and hatred he revealed; the leer with which he exulted, even at this moment, in the evil he had done, at first took even me by surprise.

After some rubbing of the lower part of his face, and some looking at us with those bad eyes, over his gristly fingers, he made one more address to me, half whining and half abusive.

"You think it justifiable, do you, Copperfield, you who pride yourself so much on your honor and all the rest of it, to sneak about my place, eavesdropping with my clerk? If it had been *me*, I shouldn't have wondered—for I don't make myself out a gentleman (though I never was in the streets either, as you were, according to Micawber)—but being *you!* And you're not afraid of doing this, either? You don't think at all of what I shall do in return; or of getting yourself into trouble for conspiracy and so forth? Very well. We shall see! Mr. What's-your-name, you were going to refer some question to Micawber. There's your referee. Why don't you make him speak? He has learnt his lesson, I see."

Seeing that what he said had no effect on me, or any of us, he sat on the edge of his table with his hands in his pockets, and one of his splay feet twisted round the other leg, waiting doggedly for what might follow.

Mr. Micawber, whose impetuosity I had restrained thus far with the greatest difficulty, and who had repeatedly interposed with the first syllable of Scoun-drel! without getting to the second, now burst forward, drew the ruler from his breast (apparently as a defensive weapon), and produced from his pocket a foolscap document, folded in the form of a large letter. Opening this packet, with his old flourish, and glancing at the contents, as if he cherished an artistic admiration of their style of composition, he began to read as follows:

" 'Dear Miss Trotwood and gentlemen——' "

"Bless and save the man!" exclaimed my aunt in a low voice, "he'd write letters by the ream, if it was a capital offense!"

Mr. Micawber, without hearing her, went on.

" 'In appearing before you to denounce probably the most consummate Villain that has ever existed' "—Mr. Micawber, without looking off the letter, pointed the ruler, like a ghostly truncheon, at Uriah Heep—" 'I ask no consideration for myself. The victim, from my cradle, of pecuniary liabilities to which I have been unable to respond, I have ever been the sport and toy of debasing circumstances. Ignominy, Want, Despair, and Madness have, collectively or separately, been the attendants of my career.' "

The relish with which Mr. Micawber described himself as a prey to these dismal calamities was only to be equaled by the emphasis with which he read his letter, and the kind of homage he rendered to it with a roll of his head, when he thought he had hit a sentence very hard indeed.

" 'In an accumulation of Ignominy, Want, Despair, and Madness, I entered the office—or, as our lively neighbor the Gaul would term it, the Bureau—of the Firm, nominally conducted under the appellation of Wickfield and—Heep, but, in reality, wielded by—Heep alone. Heep, and only Heep, is the mainspring of that machine. Heep, and only Heep, is the Forger and the Cheat.' "

Uriah, more blue than white at these words, made a dart at the letter, as if to tear it in pieces. Mr. Micawber, with a perfect miracle of dexterity or luck, caught his advancing knuckles with the ruler, and disabled his right hand. It dropped at the wrist, as if it were broken. The blow sounded as if it had fallen on wood.

"The devil take you!" said Uriah, writhing in a new way with pain. "I'll be even with you."

"Approach me again, you—you—you Heep of infamy," gasped Mr. Micawber, "and if your head is human, I'll break it. Come on, come on!"

I think I never saw anything more ridiculous—I was sensible of it, even at the time—than Mr. Micawber making broadsword guards with the ruler, and crying, "Come on!" while Traddles and I pushed him back into a corner, from which, as often as we got him into it, he persisted in emerging again.

His enemy, muttering to himself, after wringing his wounded hand for some time, slowly drew off his neckerchief and bound it up; then held it in his other hand, and sat upon his table with his sullen face looking down.

Mr. Micawber, when he was sufficiently cool, proceeded with his letter:

" 'The stipendiary emoluments in consideration of which I entered into the service of—HEEP' "—always pausing before that word, and uttering it with astonishing vigor—" 'were not defined, beyond the pittance of twenty-two shillings and six per week. Need I say that it soon became necessary for me to solicit from—HEEP—pecuniary advances toward the support of Mrs. Micawber and our blighted but rising family? Need I say that this necessity had been foreseen by—HEEP? And that I thus became immeshed in the web he had spun for my reception?' "

Mr. Micawber's enjoyment of his epistolary powers, in describing this unfortunate state of things, really seemed to outweigh any pain or anxiety that the reality could have caused him. He read on:—

" 'Then it was that—HEEP began to favor me with just so much of his confidence as was necessary to the discharge of his infernal business. I found that my services were constantly called into requisition for the falsification of business, and the mystification of an individual whom I will designate as Mr. W.; that Mr. W. was imposed upon, kept in ignorance, and deluded, in every possible way.

" 'My charges against—HEEP,' " he read on, glancing at him, and drawing the ruler into a convenient position under his left arm, in case of need, " 'are as follows.' "

We all held our breath, I think. I am sure Uriah held his.

" 'First,' " said Mr. Micawber. " 'When Mr. W.'s faculties and memory for business became, through causes into which it is not necessary or expedient for me to enter, weakened and confused—HEEP designedly perplexed and complicated the whole of the official transactions. He obtained Mr. W.'s signature under such circumstances to documents of importance, representing them to be other documents of no importance. He induced Mr W. to empower him to draw out thus one particular sum of trust-money, amounting to twelve six fourteen, two, and nine, and employed it to meet pretended business charges and deficiencies which were either already provided for, or had never really existed. He gave this proceeding, throughout, the appearance of having originated in Mr. W.'s own dishonest intention, and of having been accomplished by Mr. W.'s own dishonest act; and has used it ever since to torture and constrain him.' "

"You shall prove this, you, Copperfield!" said Uriah, with a threatening shake of the head. "All in good time!"

"Ask—HEEP, Mr. Traddles, who lived in his house after him," said Mr. Micawber, breaking off from the letter; "will you?"

"The fool himself; and lives there now," said Uriah disdainfully.

"Ask—Heep if he ever kept a pocket-book in that house," said Mr. Micawber; "will you?"

I saw Uriah's lank hand stop, involuntarily, in the scraping of his chin.

"Or ask him," said Mr. Micawber, "if he ever burnt one there. If he says Yes, and asks you where the ashes are, refer him to Wilkins Micawber, and he will hear of something not at all to his advantage!"

The triumphant flourish with which Mr. Micawber delivered himself of these words, had a powerful effect in alarming the mother, who cried out in much agitation,

"Ury, Ury! be umble, and make terms, my dear!"

"Mother!" he retorted, "will you keep quiet? You're in a fright, and don't know what you say or mean. Umble!" he repeated, looking at me with a snarl; "I've umbled some of 'em for a pretty long time back, umble as I was!"

Mr. Micawber, genteelly adjusting his chin in his cravat, presently proceeded with his composition:

" 'Second. Heep has, on several occasions, to the best of my knowledge, information, and belief, systematically forged, to various entries, books, and documents, the signature of Mr. W.; and has distinctly done so in one instance, capable of proof by me. To wit, in manner following, that is to say.' "

Mr. Micawber had a relish in this formal piling up of words, which, however ludicrously displayed in his case, was, I must say, not at all peculiar to him. We talk about the tyranny of words, but we like to tyrannize over them too. We are fond of having a large superfluous establishment of words to wait upon us on great occasions; we think it looks important, and sounds well. Mr. Micawber read on, almost smacking his lips:

" 'To wit, in manner following, that is to say: Heep deemed it expedient to have a bond ready by him, as from Mr. W., for the before-mentioned sum of twelve six fourteen, two, and nine, with interest, stated therein to have been advanced by—Heep to Mr. W. to save Mr. W. from dishonor; though really the sum was never advanced by him, and has long been replaced. The signatures to this instrument, purporting to be executed by Mr. W. and attested by Wilkins Micawber, are forgeries by—Heep. I have in my possession, in his hand and pocket-book, several similar imitations of Mr. W.'s signature, here and there defaced by fire, but legible to anyone.

I never attested any such document. And I have the document itself in my possession.' "

Uriah Heep, with a start, took out of his pocket a bunch of keys, and opened a certain drawer; then suddenly bethought himself of what he was about, and turned again toward us, without looking in it.

" 'And I have the document,' " Mr. Micawber read again, looking about as if it were the text of a sermon, " 'in my possession,'—that is to say, I had, early this morning, when this was written, but have since relinquished it to Mr. Traddles."

"It is quite true," assented Traddles.

"Ury, Ury!" cried the mother, "be umble, and make terms. I know my son will be umble, gentlemen, if you'll give him time to think. Mr. Copperfield, I'm sure you know that he was always very umble, sir!"

It was singular to see how the mother still held to the old trick, when the son had abandoned it as useless.

"Mother," he said, with an impatient bite at the handkerchief in which his hand was wrapped, "you had better take and fire a loaded gun at me."

"But I love you, Ury!" cried Mrs. Heep. And I have no doubt she did; or that he loved her, however strange it may appear— though, to be sure, they were a congenial couple. "And I can't bear to hear you provoking the gentleman, and endangering of yourself more. I told the gentleman at first, when he told me upstairs it was come to light, that I would answer for your being umble, and making amends.—Oh, see how umble *I* am, gentlemen, and don't mind him!"

"Why, there's Copperfield, mother," he angrily retorted, pointing his lean finger at me, against whom all his animosity was leveled, as the prime mover in the discovery—and I did not undeceive him— "there's Copperfield would have given you a hundred pound to say less than you've blurted out!"

"I can't help it, Ury," cried his mother. "I can't see you running into danger, through carrying your head so high. Better be umble, as you always was."

He remained for a little biting the handkerchief, and then said to me with a scowl,

"What more have you got to bring forward? If anything, go on with it. What do you look at me for?"

363

Mr. Micawber promptly resumed his letter, glad to revert to a performance with which he was so highly satisfied:

" 'Third. And last. I am now in a condition to show, by—HEEP's false books, and—HEEP's real memoranda, beginning with the partially destroyed pocket-book, that Mr. W. has been for years deluded and plundered in every conceivable manner, to the pecuniary aggrandizement of the avaricious, false, and grasping—HEEP. That his last act, completed but a few months since, was to induce Mr. W. to execute a relinquishment of his share in the partnership, and even a bill of sale on the very furniture of his house, in consideration of a certain annuity, to be well and truly paid by—HEEP on the four common quarter-days in each and every year. That these meshes— beginning with alarming and falsified accounts of the estate of which Mr. W. is the receiver, going on with pretended borrowings of money at enormous interest, really coming from—HEEP and by —HEEP fraudulently obtained or withheld from Mr. W. himself— gradually thickened, until the unhappy Mr. W. could see no world beyond. Bankrupt, as he believed, alike in circumstances, in all other hope, and in honor, his sole reliance was upon the monster in the garb of man' "—Mr. Micawber made a good deal of this, as a new turn of expression—" 'who, by making himself necessary to him, had achieved his destruction. All this I undertake to show—probably much more!' "

There was, as I had noticed on my first visit long ago, an iron safe in the room. The key was in it. A hasty suspicion seemed to strike Uriah; and, with a glance at Mr. Micawber, he went to it, and threw the doors clanking open. It was empty.

"Where are the books?" he cried, with a frightful face. "Some thief has stolen the books!"

Mr. Micawber tapped himself with the ruler. "*I* did, when I got the key from you as usual—but a little earlier—and opened it this morning."

"Don't be uneasy," said Traddles. "They have come into my possession. I will take care of them, under the authority I mentioned."

"You receive stolen goods, do you?" cried Uriah.

"Under such circumstances," answered Traddles, "yes."

What was my astonishment when I beheld my aunt, who had been profoundly quiet and attentive, make a dart at Uriah Heep, and seize him by the collar with both hands!

"You know what *I* want?" said my aunt.

"A strait-waistcoat," said he.

"No. My property!" returned my aunt.—"Agnes, my dear, as long as I believed it had been really made away with by your father, I wouldn't—and, my dear, I didn't, even to Trot, as he knows—breathe a syllable of its having been placed here for investment. But, now, I know this fellow's answerable for it, and I'll have it!—Trot, come and take it away from him!"

Whether my aunt supposed, for the moment, that he kept her property in his neckerchief, I am sure I don't know, but she certainly pulled at it as if she thought so. I hastened to put myself between them, and to assure her that we would all take care that he should make the utmost restitution of everything he had wrongly got. This, and a few moments' reflection, pacified her; but she was not at all disconcerted by what she had done (though I cannot say as much for her bonnet), and resumed her seat composedly.

During the last few minutes, Mrs. Heep had been clamoring to her son to be "umble," and had been going down on her knees to all of us in succession, and making the wildest promises. Her son sat her down in his chair, and, standing sulkily by her, holding her arm with his hand, but not rudely, said to me, with a ferocious look,

"What do you want done?"

"I will tell you what must be done," said Traddles.

"Has that Copperfield no tongue?" muttered Uriah. "I would do a good deal for you if you could tell me, without lying, that somebody had cut it out."

"My Uriah means to be umble!" cried his mother. "Don't mind what he says, good gentlemen!"

"What must be done," said Traddles, "is this. First, the deed of relinquishment, that we have heard of, must be given over to me now—here."

"Suppose I haven't got it," he interrupted.

"But you have," said Traddles; "therefore, you know, we won't suppose so." And I cannot help avowing that this was the first occasion on which I really did justice to the clear head, and the plain, patient, practical good sense, of my old schoolfellow. "Then," said Traddles, "you must prepare to make restoration to the last farthing. All the partnership books and papers must remain in our possession; all your books and papers; all money accounts and securities, of both kinds. In short, everything here."

"Must it? I don't know that," said Uriah. "I must have time to think about that."

"Certainly," replied Traddles; "but, in the meanwhile, and until everything is done to our satisfaction, we shall maintain possession of these things, and beg you—in short, compel you—to keep your own room, and hold no communication with anyone."

"I won't do it!" said Uriah, with an oath.

"Maidstone Jail is a safer place of detention," observed Traddles; "and though the law may be longer in righting us, and may not be able to right us so completely as you can, there is no doubt of its punishing *you*. Dear me, you know that quite as well as I!—Copperfield, will you go round to the Guildhall and bring a couple of officers?"

Here Mrs. Heep broke out again, crying on her knees to Agnes to interfere in their behalf, exclaiming that he was very humble, and it was all true, and if he didn't do what we wanted, she would, and much more to the same purpose, being half frantic with fears for her darling. To inquire what he might have done, if he had had any boldness, would be like inquiring what a mongrel cur might do, if it had the spirit of a tiger. He was a coward, from head to foot; and showed his dastardly nature through his sullenness and mortification, as much as at any time of his mean life.

"Stop!" he growled to me, and wiped his hot face with his hand. "Mother, hold your noise. Well, let 'em have that deed. Go and fetch it!"

"Do you help her, Mr. Dick," said Traddles, "if you please."

Proud of his commission, and understanding it, Mr. Dick accompanied her as a shepherd's dog might accompany a sheep. But Mrs. Heep gave him little trouble; for she not only returned with the deed, but with the box in which it was, where we found a banker's book and some other papers that were afterwards serviceable.

"Good!" said Traddles, when this was brought. "Now, Mr. Heep, you can retire to think."

It was necessary for Agnes to return to her father, and for someone else to hold Uriah in safe keeping. So Traddles remained for the latter purpose, to be presently relieved by Mr. Dick; and Mr. Dick, my aunt, and I, went home with Mr. Micawber.

His house was not far off; and as the street door opened into the sitting-room, and he bolted in with a precipitation quite his own, we found ourselves at once in the bosom of the family. Mr. Micawber exclaiming, "Emma! my life!" rushed into Mrs. Micawber's arms. Mrs. Micawber shrieked, and folded Mr. Micawber in her embrace.

"Emma!" said Mr. Micawber, "the cloud is passed from my mind. Mutual confidence, so long preserved between us once, is restored, to know no further interruption. Now, welcome poverty!" cried Mr. Micawber, shedding tears. "Welcome misery, welcome houselessness, welcome hunger, rags, tempest, and beggary! Mutual confidence will sustain us to the end!"

My aunt mused a little while, and then said,

"Mr. Micawber, I wonder you have never turned your thoughts to emigration."

"Madam," returned Mr. Micawber, "it was the dream of my youth, and the fallacious aspiration of my riper years." I am thoroughly persuaded, by-the-by, that he had never thought of it in his life.

"Ay?" said my aunt, with a glance at me. "Why, what a thing it would be for yourselves and your family, Mr. and Mrs. Micawber, if you were to emigrate now."

"Capital, madam, capital," urged Mr. Micawber gloomily.

"That is the principal, I may say the only difficulty, my dear Mr. Copperfield," assented his wife.

"Capital?" cried my aunt. "But you are doing us a great service —have done us a great service, I may say, for surely much will come out of the fire—and what could we do for you, that would be half so good, as to find the capital?"

"I could not receive it as a gift," said Mr. Micawber, full of fire and animation; "but if a sufficient sum could be advanced, say at five per cent interest per annum, upon my personal liability—say my notes of hand, at twelve, eighteen, and twenty-four months, respectively, to allow time for something to turn up——"

"Could be? Can be and shall be, on your own terms," returned my aunt, "if you say the word. Think of this now, both of you. Here are some people David knows going out to Australia shortly. If you decide to go, why shouldn't you go in the same ship? You may help each other. Think of this now, Mr. and Mrs. Micawber. Take your time, and weigh it well."

"There is but one question, my dear ma'am, I could wish to ask," said Mrs. Micawber. "The climate, I believe, is healthy?"

"Finest in the world!" said my aunt.

"Just so," returned Mrs. Micawber. "Then my question arises. Now, *are* the circumstances of the country such that a man of Mr. Micawber's abilities would have a fair chance of rising in the social scale? I will not say, at present, might he aspire to be Governor, or anything of that sort; but would there be a reasonable opening for his talents to develop themselves—that would be amply sufficient—and find their own expansion?"

"No better opening anywhere," said my aunt, "for a man who conducts himself well, and is industrious."

"For a man who conducts himself well," repeated Mrs. Micawber, with her clearest business manner, "and is industrious. Precisely. It is evident to me that Australia is the legitimate sphere of action for Mr. Micawber!"

"I entertain the conviction, my dear madam," said Mr. Micawber, "that it is, under existing circumstances, the land, the only land, for myself and family; and that something of an extraordinary nature will turn up on that shore. It is no distance—comparatively speaking; and though consideration is due to the kindness of your proposal, I assure you that is a mere matter of form."

Shall I ever forget how, in a moment, he was the most sanguine of men, looking on to fortune; or how Mrs. Micawber presently discoursed about the habits of the kangaroo? Shall I ever recall that street of Canterbury on a market-day, without recalling him, as he walked back with us—expressing, in the hardy roving manner he assumed, the unsettled habit of a temporary sojourner in the land, and looking at the bullocks, as they came by, with the eye of an Australian farmer!

I MUST pause yet once again. Oh, my child-wife, there is a figure in the moving crowd before my memory, quiet and still, saying in its innocent love and childish beauty, Stop to think of me—turn to look upon the Little Blossom, as it flutters to the ground!

I do. All else grows dim, and fades away. I am again with Dora, in our cottage. I do not know how long she has been ill. I am so used to it in feeling, that I cannot count the time. It is not really long, in weeks or months; but, in my usage and experience, it is a weary, weary while.

They have left off telling me to "wait a few days more." I have begun to fear, remotely, that the day may never shine when I shall see my child-wife running in the sunlight with her old friend Jip.

He is, as it were suddenly, grown very old. It may be that he misses in his mistress something that enlivened him and made him younger; but he mopes, and his sight is weak, and his limbs are feeble, and my aunt is sorry that he objects to her no more, but creeps near her as he lies on Dora's bed—she sitting at the bedside—and mildly licks her hand.

Dora lies smiling on us, and is beautiful, and utters no hasty or complaining word. She says that we are very good to her; that her

369

dear old careful boy is tiring himself out, she knows; that my aunt has no sleep, yet is always wakeful, active, and kind. Sometimes, the little birdlike ladies come to see her; and then we talk about our wedding-day, and all that happy time.

What a strange rest and pause in my life there seems to be—and in all life, within doors and without—when I sit in the quiet, shaded, orderly room, with the blue eyes of my child-wife turned toward me, and her little fingers twining round my hand! Many and many an hour I sit thus; but, of all those times, three times come the freshest on my mind.

It is morning; and Dora, made so trim by my aunt's hands, shows me how her pretty hair *will* curl upon the pillow yet, and how long and bright it is.

"Not that I am vain of it now, you mocking boy," she says, when I smile; "but because you used to say you thought it so beautiful, and because, when I first began to think about you, I used to peep in the glass, and wonder whether you would like very much to have a lock of it. Oh, what a foolish fellow you were, Doady, when I gave you one!"

"That was on the day when you were painting the flowers I had given you, Dora, and when I told you how much in love I was."

"Ah! but I didn't like to tell *you*," says Dora, "*then*, how I had cried over them, because I believed you really liked me! When I can run about again as I used to do, Doady, let us go and see those places where we were such a silly couple, shall we? And take some of the old walks? And not forget poor papa?"

"Yes, we will, and have some happy days. So you must make haste to get well, my dear."

"Oh, I shall soon do that! I am so much better, you don't know!"

It is evening; and I sit in the same chair, by the same bed, with the same face turned toward me. We have been silent, and there is a smile upon her face. I have ceased to carry my light burden up and down stairs now. She lies here all the day.

"Doady!"

"My dear Dora!"

"You won't think what I am going to say unreasonable, after what you told me, such a little while ago, of Mr. Wickfield's not being well? I want to see Agnes. Very much I want to see her."

370

"I will write to her, my dear."

"Will you?"

"Directly."

"What a good, kind boy! Doady, take me on your arm. Indeed, my dear, it's not a whim. It's not a foolish fancy. I want, very much indeed, to see her!"

"I am certain of it. I have only to tell her so, and she is sure to come."

"You are very lonely when you go downstairs now?" Dora whispers, with her arm about my neck.

"How can I be otherwise, my own love, when I see your empty chair?"

"My empty chair!" She clings to me for a little while in silence. "And you really miss me, Doady?" looking up, and brightly smiling. "Even poor, giddy, stupid me?"

"My heart, who is there upon earth that I could miss so much?"

"Oh, husband! I am so glad, yet so sorry!" creeping closer to me, and folding me in both her arms. She laughs and sobs, and then is quiet and quite happy.

"Quite!" she says. "Only give Agnes my dear love, and tell her that I want very, very much to see her; and I have nothing left to wish for."

"Except to get well again, Dora."

"Ah, Doady! Sometimes I think—you know I always was a silly little thing!—that that will never be!"

"Don't say so, Dora! Dearest love, don't think so!"

"I won't, if I can help it, Doady. But I am very happy; though my dear boy is so lonely, before his child-wife's empty chair!"

It is night; and I am with her still. Agnes has arrived—has been among us for a whole day and an evening. She, my aunt, and I have sat with Dora since the morning, all together. We have not talked much, but Dora has been perfectly contented and cheerful. We are now alone.

Do I know now that my child-wife will soon leave me? They have told me so; they have told me nothing new to my thoughts; but I am far from sure that I have taken that truth to heart. I cannot master it. I have withdrawn by myself, many times today, to weep. I have remembered Who wept for a parting between the living and the dead. I have tried to resign myself, and to console myself; and that, I hope, I may have done imperfectly; but what I cannot firmly settle in my mind is, that the end will absolutely come. I hold her hand in mine; I hold her heart in mine; I see her love for me, alive in all its strength. I cannot shut out a pale lingering shadow of belief that she will be spared.

"I am going to speak to you, Doady. I am going to say something I have often thought of saying lately. You won't mind?" with a gentle look.

"Mind, my darling?"

"Because I don't know what you will think, or what you may have thought sometimes. Perhaps you have often thought the same. Doady, dear, I am afraid I was too young."

I lay my face upon the pillow by her, and she looks into my eyes, and speaks very softly. Gradually, as she goes on, I feel, with a stricken heart, that she is speaking of herself as past.

"I am afraid, dear, I was too young. I don't mean in years only, but in experience, and thoughts, and everything. I was such a silly little creature! I am afraid it would have been better, if we had only loved each other as a boy and girl, and forgotten it. I have begun to think I was not fit to be a wife."

I try to stay my tears, and to reply, "Oh, Dora, love, as fit as I to be a husband!"

"I don't know," with the old shake of her curls. "Perhaps! But, if I had been more fit to be married, I might have made you more so, too. Besides, you are very clever, and I never was."

"We have been very happy, my sweet Dora."

"I was very happy, very. But, as years went on, my dear boy would have wearied of his child-wife. She would have been less and less a companion for him. He would have been more and more sensible of what was wanting in his home. She wouldn't have improved. It is better as it is."

"Oh, Dora, dearest, dearest, do not speak to me so. Every word seems a reproach!"

"No, not a syllable!" she answers, kissing me. "Oh, my dear, you never deserved it; and I loved you far too well to say a reproachful word to you, in earnest. It was all the merit I had, except being pretty—or you thought me so. Is it lonely downstairs, Doady?"

"Very! very!"

"Don't cry! Is my chair there?"

"In its old place."

"Oh, how my poor boy cries! Hush! hush! Now, make me one promise. I want to speak to Agnes. When you go downstairs, tell

372

Agnes so, and send her up to me; and while I speak to her, let no one come—not even aunt. I want to speak to Agnes by herself. I want to speak to Agnes, quite alone."

I promise that she shall, immediately; but I cannot leave her for my grief.

"I said that it was better as it is!" she whispers, as she holds me in her arms. "Oh, Doady, after more years, you never could have loved your child-wife better than you do; and, after more years, she would so have tried and disappointed you, that you might not have been able to love her half so well!"

Agnes is downstairs when I go into the parlor, and I give her the message. She disappears, leaving me alone with Jip.

His Chinese house is by the fire, and he lies within it, on his bed of flannel, querulously trying to sleep. The bright moon is high and clear. As I look out on the night, my tears fall fast, and my undisciplined heart is chastened heavily—heavily.

I sit down by the fire, thinking with a blind remorse of all those secret feelings I have nourished since my marriage. I think of every little trifle between me and Dora, and feel the truth, that trifles make the sum of life. Ever rising from the sea of my remembrance is the image of the dear child as I knew her first, graced by my young love, and by her own, with every fascination wherein such love is rich. Would it, indeed, have been better if we had loved each other as a boy and girl, and forgotten it? Undisciplined heart, reply!

How the time wears, I know not, until I am recalled by my child-wife's old companion. More restless than he was, he crawls out of his house, and looks at me, and wanders to the door, and whines to go upstairs.

"Not tonight, Jip! Not tonight!"

He comes very slowly back to me, licks my hand, and lifts his dim eyes to my face.

"Oh, Jip! it may be never again!"

He lies down at my feet, stretches himself out as if to sleep, and, with a plaintive cry, is dead.

"Oh, Agnes! look, look here!" That face, so full of pity and of grief, that rain of tears, that awful mute appeal to me, that solemn hand upraised toward Heaven!

"Agnes?"

It is over. Darkness comes before my eyes, and, for a time, all things are blotted out of my remembrance.

CHAPTER 54 ⚜ MR. MICAWBER'S TRANSACTIONS ◆ ◆ ◆

THIS is not the time at which I am to enter on the state of my mind beneath its load of sorrow. I was to go abroad. That seemed to have been determined among us from the first. The ground now covering all that could perish of my departed wife, I waited only for what Mr. Micawber called the "final pulverization of Heep," and for the departure of the emigrants.

At the request of Traddles, most affectionate and devoted of friends in my trouble, we returned to Canterbury—I mean my aunt, Agnes, and I. We proceeded by appointment straight to Mr. Micawber's house.

"Well, Mr. and Mrs. Micawber," was my aunt's first salutation, after we were seated. "Pray, have you thought about that emigration proposal of mine?"

"My dear madam," returned Mr. Micawber, "perhaps I cannot better express the conclusion at which Mrs. Micawber, your humble servant, and I may add our children, have jointly and severally arrived, than by borrowing the language of an illustrious poet, to reply that our Boat is on the shore, and our Bark is on the sea."

"That's right," said my aunt. "I augur all sorts of good from your sensible decision."

"In reference to our domestic preparations, madam," said Mr. Micawber, with some pride, "for meeting the destiny to which we are now understood to be self-devoted, I beg to report them. My eldest daughter attends at five every morning in a neighboring establishment, to acquire the process—if process it may be called—of milking cows. My younger children are instructed to observe, as closely as circumstances will permit, the habits of the pigs and poultry maintained in the poorer parts of this city—a pursuit from which they have, on two occasions, been brought home, within an inch of being run over. I have myself directed some attention, during the past week, to the art of baking; and my son Wilkins has issued forth with a walking-stick and driven cattle, when permitted by the rugged hirelings who had them in charge."

"All very right indeed," said my aunt encouragingly.

Mr. Micawber gave Mrs. Micawber his arm, and glancing at the heap of books and papers lying before Traddles on the table, said they would leave us to ourselves, which they ceremoniously did.

"I must do Mr. Micawber the justice to say," Traddles began, "that although he would appear not to have worked to any good account for himself, he is a most untiring man when he works for other people. The heat into which he has been continually putting himself, and the distracted and impetuous manner in which he has been diving, day and night, among papers and books—to say nothing of the immense number of letters he has written me often across the table when he has been sitting opposite, and might much more easily have spoken—is quite extraordinary."

"Letters!" cried my aunt. "I believe he dreams in letters!"

"Now, let me see," said Traddles, looking among the papers on the table. "Having counted our funds, we take it to be clear that Mr. Wickfield might now wind up his business, and his agency trust, and exhibit no deficiency or defalcation whatever."

"Oh, thank Heaven!" cried Agnes fervently.

"But," said Traddles, "the surplus that would be left as his means of support—and I suppose the house to be sold, even in saying this —would be so small, not exceeding in all probability some hundreds of pounds, that perhaps, Miss Wickfield, it would be best to consider whether he might not retain his agency of the estate to which he has so long been receiver. His friends might advise him, you know, now he is free. You yourself—Copperfield—I——"

"I have considered it, Trotwood," said Agnes, looking to me, "and I feel that it ought not to be, and must not be, even on the recommendation of a friend to whom I am so grateful, and owe so much. Our wants are not many. If I rent the dear old house, and keep a school, I shall be useful and happy."

The calm fervor of her cheerful voice brought back so vividly, first the dear old house itself, and then my solitary home, that my heart was too full for speech. Traddles pretended for a little while to be busily looking among the papers.

"Next, Miss Trotwood," said Traddles, "that property of yours."

"Well, sir," sighed my aunt, "all I have got to say about it is, that if it's gone, I can bear it; and if it's not gone, I shall be glad to get it back."

"It was originally, I think, eight thousand pounds, Consols?" said Traddles.

"Right!" replied my aunt.

"I can't account for more than five," said Traddles, with an air of perplexity.

"—thousand, do you mean?" inquired my aunt, with uncommon composure, "or pounds?"

"Five thousand pounds," said Traddles.

"It was all there was," returned my aunt. "I sold three myself. One, I paid for your articles, Trot, my dear; and the other two I have by me. When I lost the rest, I thought it wise to say nothing about that sum, but to keep it secretly for a rainy day. I wanted to see how you would come out of the trial, Trot; and you came out nobly—persevering, self-reliant, self-denying! So did Dick.—Don't speak to me, for I find my nerves a little shaken!"

Nobody would have thought so, to see her sitting upright, with her arms folded; but she had wonderful self-command.

"Then I am delighted to say," cried Traddles, beaming with joy, "that we have recovered the whole money!"

"Don't congratulate me, anybody!" exclaimed my aunt. "How so, sir?"

"You believed it had been misappropriated by Mr. Wickfield?" said Traddles.

"Of course I did," said my aunt, "and was therefore easily silenced.—Agnes, not a word!"

"And indeed," said Traddles, "it was sold, by virtue of the power of management he held from you; but I needn't say by whom sold, or on whose actual signature. A most remarkable circumstance is, that I really don't think he grasped this sum even so much for the gratification of his avarice, which was inordinate, as in the hatred

376

he felt for Copperfield. He said so to me, plainly. He said he would even have spent as much to balk or injure Copperfield."

"Ha!" said my aunt, knitting her brows thoughtfully, and glancing at Agnes. "And what's become of him?"

"I don't know. He left here," said Traddles, "with his mother, who had been clamoring, and beseeching, and disclosing the whole time. They went away by one of the London night-coaches, and I know no more about him."

"Do you suppose he has any money, Traddles?" I asked.

"Oh dear, yes, I should think so," he replied, shaking his head seriously. "I should say he must have pocketed a good deal, in one way or other. But I think you would find, Copperfield, if you had an opportunity of observing his course, that money would never keep that man out of mischief. He is such an incarnate hypocrite, that whatever object he pursues he must pursue crookedly."

"He is a monster of meanness!" said my aunt.

"Really I don't know about that," observed Traddles thoughtfully. "Many people can be very mean, when they give their minds to it."

"And now, touching Mr. Micawber," said my aunt. "What would you give him?"

"Oh! before you come to that," said Traddles, a little disconcerted, "I am afraid those I. O. U.'s, and so forth, which Mr. Micawber gave him for the advances he had——"

"Well, they must be paid," said my aunt.

"Yes; but I don't know when they may be proceeded on, or where they are," rejoined Traddles, opening his eyes, "and I anticipate that, between this time and his departure, Mr. Micawber will be constantly arrested, or taken in execution."

"Then he must be constantly set free again, and taken out of execution," said my aunt. "What's the amount altogether?"

"Why, Mr. Micawber has entered the transactions—he calls them transactions—with great form, in a book," rejoined Traddles, smiling; "and he makes the amount a hundred and three pounds, five."

"Now, what shall we give him, that sum included?" said my aunt. "Agnes, my dear, you and I can talk about division of it afterwards. What should it be? Five hundred pounds?"

Upon this, Traddles and I both struck in at once. We both recommended a small sum in money, and the payment, without stipulation to Mr. Micawber, of the Uriah claims as they come in. We proposed that the family should have their passage and their outfit, and a hundred pounds; and that Mr. Micawber's arrangement for the repayment of the advances should be gravely entered into, as it might be wholesome for him to suppose himself under that responsibility. To this I added the suggestion, that I should give some explanation of his character and history to Mr. Peggotty, who I knew could be relied on; and that to Mr. Peggotty should be quietly entrusted the discretion of advancing another hundred. We all entered warmly into these views; and I may mention at once, that the principals themselves did so, shortly afterwards, with perfect goodwill and harmony.

"Well, Mr. and Mrs. Micawber," said my aunt, when they entered, "we have been discussing your emigration, with many apologies to you for keeping you out of the room so long, and I'll tell you what arrangements we propose."

Mr. Micawber could not be dissuaded from immediately rushing out, in the highest spirits, to buy the stamps for his notes of hand. But his joy received a sudden check, for within five minutes he returned in the custody of a sheriff's officer, informing us, in a flood of tears, that all was lost. We, being quite prepared for this event, which was, of course, a proceeding of Uriah Heep's, soon paid the money; and in five minutes more Mr. Micawber was seated at the table, filling up the stamps with an expression of perfect joy.

We went back next day to my aunt's house—not to mine; and when she and I sat alone, as of old, before going to bed, she said,

"Trot, do you wish to know what I have had upon my mind lately?"

"Indeed I do, aunt. If there ever was a time when I felt unwilling that you should have a sorrow or anxiety which I could not share, it is now."

"You have had sorrow enough, child," said my aunt affectionately, "without the addition of *my* little miseries. I could have no other motive, Trot, in keeping anything from you."

"I know that well," said I. "But tell me now."

"Would you ride with me a little way tomorrow morning?" asked my aunt.

"Of course."

"At nine," said she. "I'll tell you then, my dear."

At nine, accordingly, we went out in a little chariot, and drove to London. We drove a long way through the streets, until we came to one of the large hospitals. Standing hard by the building was a plain hearse. The driver recognized my aunt, and in obedience to a motion of her hand at the window, drove slowly off, we following.

"You understand it now, Trot?" said my aunt. "He is gone."

We followed the plain coffin to a corner I remember well, where the service was read consigning it to the dust.

"Six-and-thirty years ago, this day, my dear," said my aunt, as we walked back to the chariot, "I was married. God forgive us all!"

We took our seats in silence; and so she sat beside me for a long time, holding my hand. At length she suddenly burst into tears, and said,

"He was a fine-looking man when I married him, Trot—and he was sadly changed!"

It did not last long. After the relief of tears, she soon became composed, and even cheerful. Her nerves were a little shaken, she said, or she would not have given way to it. God forgive us all!

So we rode back to her little cottage at Highgate, where we found the following short note, which had arrived by that morning's post from Mr. Micawber:

"CANTERBURY, *Friday*.

"MY DEAR MADAM AND COPPERFIELD,

"The fair land of promise lately looming on the horizon is again enveloped in impenetrable mists, and forever withdrawn from the eyes of a drifting wretch whose Doom is sealed!

"Another writ has been issued (in His Majesty's High Court of King's Bench at Westminster), in another cause of HEEP *v.* MICAWBER.

> " 'Now's the day and now's the hour,
> See the front of battle lower,
> See approach proud EDWARD's power—
> Chains and slavery!'

Consigned to which, and to a speedy end (for mental torture is not supportable beyond a certain point, and that point I feel I have attained), my course is run. Bless you, bless you! Some future traveler, visiting, from motives of curiosity, not unmingled, let us hope, with sympathy, the place of confinement allotted to debtors in this city, may, and I trust will, Ponder, as he traces on its wall, inscribed with a rusty nail,

"The obscure initials
"W. M.

"P.S.—I reopen this to say that our common friend, Mr. Thomas Traddles (who has not yet left us, and is looking extremely well), has paid the debt and costs, in the noble name of Miss Trotwood, and that myself and family are at the height of earthly bliss."

CHAPTER 55 🐚 TEMPEST ✦ ✦ ✦

I NOW approach an event in my life, so indelible, so awful, so bound by an infinite variety of ties to all that has preceded it in these pages, that, from the beginning of my narrative, I have seen it growing larger and larger as I advanced, and throwing its forecast shadow even on the incidents of my childish days.

For years after it occurred I dreamed of it often. I have started up so vividly impressed by it, that its fury has yet seemed raging in my quiet room, in the still night. I dream of it sometimes, though at lengthened and uncertain intervals, to this hour. I have an association between it and a stormy wind, or the lightest mention of a sea-shore, as strong as any of which my mind is conscious. As plainly as I behold what happened, I will try to write it down. I do not recall it, but see it done; for it happens again before me.

The time drawing on rapidly for the sailing of the emigrant ship, my good old nurse (almost broken-hearted for me, when we first met) came up to London. I was constantly with her, and her brother, and the Micawbers (they being very much together); but Emily I never saw. She might desire, I thought, to send some parting word by me to her unhappy lover. I ought to give her the opportunity. I therefore sat down in my room, before going to bed, and wrote to her.

380

I was weaker than I knew then; and not falling asleep until the sun was up, lay late, and unrefreshed, next day. I was roused by the silent presence of my aunt at my bedside. I felt it in my sleep, as I suppose we all do feel such things.

"Trot, my dear," she said, when I opened my eyes, "I couldn't make up my mind to disturb you. Mr. Peggotty is here; shall he come up?"

I replied yes, and he soon appeared.

"Mas'r Davy," he said, when we had shaken hands, "I giv Em'ly your letter, sir, and she writ this here; and begged of me fur to ask you to read it, and if you see no hurt in't, to be so kind as take charge on't."

"Have you read it?" said I.

He nodded sorrowfully. I opened it, and read as follows:

"Oh, what can I write, to thank you for your good and blessed kindness to me! I have prayed, oh, I have prayed so much! When I find what you are, and what uncle is, I think what God must be, and can cry to Him.

"Good-bye forever. Now, my dear, my friend, good-bye forever in this world. In another world, if I am forgiven, I may wake a child and come to you. All thanks and blessings. Farewell, evermore."

This, blotted with tears, was the letter.

"I am thinking," said I, "that I'll go down again to Yarmouth. There's time and to spare for me to go and come back before the ship sails. My mind is constantly running on him, in his solitude. To put this letter of her writing in his hand at this time, and to enable you to tell her, in the moment of parting, that he has got it, will be a kindness to both of them."

Though he anxiously endeavored to dissuade me, I saw that he was of my mind; and this, if I had required to be confirmed in my intention, would have had the effect. He went round to the coach-office, at my request, and took the box-seat for me on the mail. In the evening I started, by that conveyance, down the road I had traversed under so many vicissitudes.

"Don't you think that," I asked the coachman, in the first stage out of London, "a very remarkable sky? I don't remember to have seen one like it."

"Nor I—not equal to it," he replied. "That's wind, sir. There'll be mischief done at sea, I expect, before long."

381

It was a murky confusion—here and there blotted with a color like the color of the smoke from damp fuel—of flying clouds tossed up into most remarkable heaps. There had been a wind all day; and it was rising then, with an extraordinary great sound. In another hour it had much increased, and the sky was more overcast, and it blew hard.

But as the night advanced, the clouds closing in and densely over-spreading the whole sky, then very dark, it came on to blow harder and harder. It still increased, until our horses could scarcely face the wind, and we were often in serious apprehension that the coach would be blown over. Sweeping gusts of rain came up before this storm, like showers of steel.

When the day broke, it blew harder and harder. I had been in Yarmouth when the seamen said it blew great guns; but I had never known the like of this, or anything approaching to it. Long before we saw the sea, its spray was on our lips, and showered salt rain upon us. The water was out, over miles and miles of the flat country adjacent to Yarmouth; and every sheet and puddle lashed its banks, and had its stress of little breakers setting heavily toward us. When we came within sight of the sea, the waves on the horizon, caught at intervals above the rolling abyss, where like glimpses of another shore with towers and buildings. When at last we got into the town, the people came out to their doors, all aslant, and with streaming hair, making a wonder of the mail that had come through such a night.

I put up at the old inn, and went down to look at the sea; stag-gering along the street, which was strewn with sand and seaweed, and with flying blotches of sea-foam; afraid of falling slates and tiles; and holding by people I met, at angry corners. Coming near the beach, I saw, not only the boatmen, but half the people of the town, lurking behind buildings; some now and then braving the fury of the storm to look away to sea, and blown sheer out of their course in trying to get zigzag back.

The tremendous sea itself, when I could find sufficient pause to look at it, in the agitation of the blinding wind, the flying stones and sand, and the awful noise, confounded me. As the high watery walls came rolling in, and, at their highest, tumbled into surf, they looked as if the least would engulf the town. As the receding wave swept back with a hoarse roar, it seemed to scoop out deep caves in the beach, as if its purpose were to undermine the earth.

Not finding Ham among the people whom this memorable wind

—for it is still remembered down there, as the greatest ever known to blow upon that coast—had brought together, I made my way to his house. It was shut; and as no one answered to my knocking, I went, by back ways and by-lanes, to the yard where he worked. I learned there that he had gone to Lowestoft, to meet some sudden exigency of ship-repairing in which his skill was required, but that he would be back tomorrow morning, in good time.

I went back to the inn; and when I had washed and dressed, and tried to sleep, but in vain, it was five o'clock in the afternoon. I had not sat five minutes by the coffee-room fire, when the waiter coming to stir it, as an excuse for talking, told me that two colliers had gone down, with all hands, a few miles away; and that some other ships had been seen laboring hard in the roads, and trying, in great distress, to keep off shore. Mercy on them, and on all poor sailors, said he, if we had another night like the last!

My dinner went away almost untasted, and I tried to refresh myself with a glass or two of wine. In vain. I fell into a dull slumber before the fire, without losing my consciousness, either of the up-roar out of doors or of the place in which I was. Both became over-shadowed by a new and indefinable horror; and when I awoke—or rather when I shook off the lethargy that bound me in my chair—my whole frame thrilled with objectless and unintelligible fear. At length, the steady ticking of the undisturbed clock on the wall tormented me to that degree that I resolved to go to bed.

For hours I lay there, listening to the wind and water—imagining, now, that I heard shrieks out at sea; now, that I distinctly heard the firing of signal guns; and now, the fall of houses in the town.

At length my restlessness attained to such a pitch that I hurried on my clothes, and went downstairs. In the large kitchen, where I dimly saw bacon and ropes of onions hanging from the beams, the watchers were clustered together, in various attitudes. I remained there, I dare say, two hours. Once, I opened the yard gate, and looked into the empty street. The sand, the seaweed, and the flakes of foam were driving by, and I was obliged to call for assistance before I could shut the gate again, and make it fast against the wind.

There was a dark gloom in my solitary chamber when I at length returned to it; but I was tired now, and, getting into bed again, fell—off a tower and down a precipice—into the depths of sleep until I made a great exertion, and awoke. It was broad day—eight or nine o'clock; the storm raging, and someone knocking and calling at my door.

"What is the matter?" I cried.

"A wreck! Close by!"

I sprung out of bed, and asked, what wreck?

"A schooner, from Spain or Portugal, laden with fruit and wine. Make haste, sir, if you want to see her! It's thought, down on the beach, she'll go to pieces every moment."

The excited voice went clamoring along the staircase; and I wrapped myself in my clothes as quickly as I could, and ran into the street.

Numbers of people were there before me, all running in one direction—to the beach. I ran the same way, outstripping a good many, and soon came facing the wild sea.

The wind might by this time have lulled a little, but the sea, having upon it the additional agitation of the whole night, was infinitely more terrific than when I had seen it last. The height to which the breakers rose, bore one another down, and rolled in, in interminable hosts, was most appalling. I looked out to sea for the wreck, and saw nothing but the foaming heads of the great waves. A half-dressed boatman, standing next me, pointed with his bare arm (a tattooed arrow on it, pointing in the same direction) to the left. Then, O great Heaven, I saw it, close in upon us!

One mast was broken short off, six or eight feet from the deck, and lay over the side, entangled in a maze of sail and rigging; and all that ruin, as the ship rolled and beat—which she did without a moment's pause, and with a violence quite inconceivable—beat the side as if it would stave it in. Some efforts were even then being made to cut this portion of the wreck away; for I plainly descried her people at work with axes. But a great cry, which was audible even above the wind and water, rose from the shore at this moment: the sea, sweeping over the rolling wreck, made a clean breach, and carried men, spars, casks, planks, bulwarks, heaps of such toys, into the boiling surge.

The second mast was yet standing, with the rags of a rent sail and a wild confusion of broken cordage flapping to and fro. The ship had struck once, the same boatman hoarsely said in my ear, and then lifted in and struck again. As he spoke, there was another great cry of pity from the beach: four men arose with the wreck out of the deep, clinging to the rigging of the remaining mast. Again we lost her, and again she rose. Two men were gone. The agony on shore increased. Some ran wildly up and down along the beach, crying for help where no help could be. I found myself one

384

of these, frantically imploring a knot of sailors whom I knew not to let those two lost creatures perish before our eyes.

They were making out to me, in an agitated way, that the lifeboat had been bravely manned an hour ago, and could do nothing; and that as no man would be so desperate as to attempt to wade off with a rope, and establish a communication with the shore, there was nothing left to try; when I noticed that some new sensation moved the people on the beach, and saw them part, and Ham come breaking through them to the front.

The determination in his face, and his look out to sea, awoke me to a knowledge of his danger. I held him back with both arms, and implored the men with whom I had been speaking not to listen to him, not to do murder, not to let him stir from off that sand!

Another cry arose on shore; and looking to the wreck, we saw the cruel sail, with blow on blow, beat off the lower of the two men, and fly up in triumph round the active figure left alone upon the mast.

Against such a sight, and against such determination as that of the calmly-desperate man who was already accustomed to lead half the people present, I might as hopefully have entreated the wind. "Mas'r Davy," he said, cheerily grasping me by both hands, "if my time is come, 'tis come. If 't an't, I'll bide it. Lord above bless you, and bless all! Mates, make me ready; I'm a-going off!"

I was swept away, but not unkindly, to some distance. I saw men running with ropes from a capstan that was there, and penetrating into a circle of figures that hid him from me. Then I saw him standing alone in a seaman's frock and trousers, a rope in his hand, or slung to his wrist, another round his body; and several of the best men holding, at a little distance, to the latter, which he laid out himself, slack upon the shore, at his feet.

The wreck, even to my unpracticed eye, was breaking up. I saw that she was parting in the middle, and that the life of the solitary man upon the mast hung by a thread. Still, he clung to it. He had a singular red cap on—not like a sailor's cap, but of a finer color; and as the few yielding planks between him and destruction rolled and bulged, he was seen by all of us to wave it. I saw him do it now, and thought I was going distracted when his action brought an old remembrance to my mind of a once dear friend.

Ham watched the sea, standing alone, with the silence of suspended breath behind him, and the storm before, until there was a great retiring wave, when, with a backward glance at those who

385

held the rope which was made fast round his body, he dashed in after it, and in a moment was buffeting with the water—rising with the hills, falling with the valleys, lost beneath the foam, then drawn again to land. They hauled in hastily.

He was hurt. I saw blood on his face, from where I stood; but he took no thought of that. He seemed hurriedly to give them some directions for leaving him more free—or so I judged from the motion of his arm—and was gone as before.

And now he made for the wreck, rising with the hills, falling with the valleys, lost beneath the rugged foam, borne in toward the shore, borne on toward the ship, striving hard and valiantly. The distance was nothing, but the power of the sea and wind made the strife deadly. At length he neared the wreck. He was so near that with one more of his vigorous strokes he would be clinging to it—when a high, green, vast hillside of water moving on shoreward from beyond the ship, he seemed to leap up into it with a mighty bound, and the ship was gone!

Some eddying fragments I saw in the sea, as if a mere cask had been broken, in running to the spot where they were hauling in. Consternation was in every face. They drew him to my very feet —insensible—dead. He was carried to the nearest house, but he had been beaten to death by the great wave.

As I sat beside the bed, when hope was abandoned and all was done, a fisherman, who had known me when Emily and I were children, and ever since, whispered my name at the door.

"Sir," said he, with tears starting to his weather-beaten face, which, with his trembling lips, was ashy pale, "will you come over yonder?"

The old remembrance that had been recalled to me was in his look. I asked him, terror-stricken, leaning on the arm he held out to support me,

"Has a body come ashore?"

He said, "Yes."

"Do I know it?" I asked then.

He answered nothing.

But he led me to the shore. And on that part of it where she and I had looked for shells, two children—on that part of it where some lighter fragments of the old boat, blown down last night, had been scattered by the wind—among the ruins of the home he had wronged—I saw him lying with his head upon his arm, as I had often seen him lie at school.

386

CHAPTER 56  THE NEW WOUND,
AND THE OLD ✦ ✦ ✦

WE WENT into the town, and took our burden to the inn.
So soon as I could at all collect my thoughts, I sent for
Joram, and begged him to provide me a conveyance in
which it could be got to London in the night. I knew that the care
of it, and the hard duty of preparing his mother to receive it, could
only rest with me.

Upon a mellow autumn day, about noon, when the ground was
perfumed by fallen leaves, and many more, in beautiful tints of
yellow, red, and brown, yet hung upon the trees, through which
the sun was shining, I arrived at Highgate. I walked the last mile,
and left the carriage that had followed me all through the night,
awaiting orders to advance.

I had not at first the courage to ring at the gate; and when I
did ring, my errand seemed to me to be expressed in the very sound
of the bell. The little parlor-maid came out, with the key in her
hand, and looking earnestly at me as she unlocked the gate, said,

"Is anything the matter, sir? Mr. James——"

"Hush!" said I. "Yes, something has happened that I have to
break to Mrs. Steerforth. She is at home?"

387

The girl anxiously replied that her mistress was very seldom out now, even in a carriage; that she kept her room; that she saw no company, but would see me.

Giving her a strict charge to be careful of her manner, and only to carry in my card and say I waited, I sat down in the drawing-room (which we had now reached) until she should come back. Its former pleasant air of occupation was gone, and the shutters were half closed. The harp had not been used for many and many a day. His picture as a boy was there. The cabinet in which his mother had kept his letters was there. I wondered if she ever read them now; if she would ever read them more!

The house was so still, that I heard the girl's light step upstairs. On her return, she brought a message to the effect that Mrs. Steerforth was an invalid, and could not come down; but that, if I would excuse her being in her chamber, she would be glad to see me. In a few moments I stood before her. At her chair, as usual, was Rosa Dartle.

"I am sorry to observe you are in mourning, sir," said Mrs. Steerforth:

"I am unhappily a widower," said I.

"You are very young to know so great a loss," she returned. "I am grieved to hear it. I am grieved to hear it. I hope Time will be good to you."

"I hope Time," said I, looking at her, "will be good to all of us. Dear Mrs. Steerforth, we must all trust to that in our heaviest misfortunes."

The earnestness of my manner, and the tears in my eyes, alarmed her. She said with enforced calmness,

"My son is ill."

"Very ill."

"You have seen him?"

"I have."

"Are you reconciled?"

I could not say Yes, I could not say No.

"When I was last here," I faltered, "Miss Dartle told me he was sailing here and there. The night before last was a dreadful one at sea. If he were at sea that night, and near a dangerous coast, as it is said he was, and if the vessel that was seen should really be the ship which——"

"Rosa!" said Mrs. Steerforth, "come to me!"

She came, but with no sympathy or gentleness. Her eyes gleamed like fire as she confronted his mother, and broke into a frightful laugh.

"Now," she said, "is your pride appeased, you madwoman? *Now* has he made atonement to you——with his life! Do you hear?—His life!"

Mrs. Steerforth, fallen back stiffly in her chair, and making no sound but a moan, cast her eyes upon her with a wide stare.

"Ay!" cried Rosa, smiting herself passionately on the breast, "look at me! Moan, and groan, and look at me! Look here," striking the scar, "at your dead child's handiwork!"

"Miss Dartle," I entreated her, "for Heaven's sake——"

She clenched her hand, and trembled through her spare worn figure, as if her passion were killing her by inches.

"You, resent his self-will!" she exclaimed. "You, injured by his haughty temper! You, who opposed to both, when your hair was grey, the qualities which made both when you gave him birth! You, who from his cradle reared him to be what he was, and stunted what he should have been! Are you rewarded *now* for your years of trouble?"

"Oh, Miss Dartle, shame! Oh, cruel!"

"I tell you," she returned, "I *will* speak to her. Have I been silent all these years, and shall I not speak now? I loved him better than you ever loved him!" turning on her fiercely. "I could have loved him, and asked no return. If I had been his wife, I could have been the slave of his caprices for a word of love a year. I should have been. Who knows it better than I? You were exacting, proud, punctilious, selfish. My love would have been devoted—would have trod your paltry whimpering under foot!"

With flashing eyes, she stamped upon the ground as if she actually did it.

"Miss Dartle," said I, "if you can be so obdurate as not to feel for this afflicted mother——"

"Who feels for me?" she sharply retorted. "She has sown this. Let her moan for the harvest that she reaps today!"

"And if his faults——" I began.

"Faults!" she cried, bursting into passionate tears. "Who dares malign him? He had a soul worth millions of the friends to whom he stooped!"

All this time the figure was unchanged, and looked unchangeable —motionless, rigid, staring; moaning in the same dumb way from time to time, but giving no other sign of life. Miss Dartle suddenly kneeled down before it, and began to loosen the dress.

"A curse upon you!" she said, looking round at me, with a mingled expression of rage and grief. "It was in an evil hour that you ever came here! A curse upon you! Go!"

After passing out of the room, I hurried back to ring the bell, the sooner to alarm the servants. She had then taken the impassive figure in her arms, and, still upon her knees, was weeping over it, kissing it, calling to it, rocking it to and fro upon her bosom like a child, and trying every tender means to rouse the dormant senses. No longer afraid of leaving her, I noiselessly turned back again, and alarmed the house as I went out.

ONE thing more I had to do before yielding myself to the shock of these emotions. It was, to conceal what had occurred from those who were going away, and to dismiss them on their voyage in happy ignorance. In this no time was to be lost.

I took Mr. Micawber aside that same night, and confided to him the task of standing between Mr. Peggotty and intelligence of the late catastrophe. He zealously undertook to do so, and to intercept any newspaper through which it might, without such precautions, reach him.

"If it penetrates to him, sir," said Mr. Micawber, striking himself on the breast, "it shall first pass through this body!"

Mr. Micawber, I must observe, in his adaptation of himself to a new state of society, had acquired a bold buccaneering air, not absolutely lawless, but defensive and prompt. One might have supposed him a child of the wilderness, long accustomed to live out of the confines of civilization, and about to return to his native wilds.

He had provided himself, among other things, with a complete suit of oilskin, and a straw hat with a very low crown, pitched or calked on the outside. In this rough clothing, with a common mariner's telescope under his arm, and a shrewd trick of casting up his eyes at the sky as looking out for dirty weather, he was far more nautical, after his manner, than Mr. Peggotty.

I had told Traddles of the terrible event, and he had come to help me in this last service. The Micawber family were lodged in a little, dirty, tumble-down public-house, whose protruding wooden rooms overhung the river. My aunt and Agnes were there, busily making some little extra comforts, in the way of dress, for the children. Peggotty was quietly assisting with the old insensible work-box, yard-measure, and bit of wax candle before her, that had now outlived so much.

"And when does the ship sail, Mr. Micawber?" asked my aunt.

Mr. Micawber considered it necessary to prepare either my aunt or his wife by degrees, and said, sooner than he had expected yesterday.

"The boat brought you word, I suppose?" said my aunt.

"It did, ma'am," he returned.

"Well?" said my aunt. "And she sails——"

"Madam," he replied, "I am informed that we must positively be on board before seven tomorrow morning."

"Heyday!" said my aunt, "that's soon. Is it a sea-going fact, Mr. Peggotty?"

"'Tis so, ma'am. She'll drop down the river with that theer tide. If Mas'r Davy and my sister comes aboard at Gravesen', arternoon o' next day, they'll see the last on us."

"And that we shall do," said I, "be sure!"

Here a boy came in to say that Mr. Micawber was wanted downstairs. Mr. Micawber withdrew, and was absent some little time. At length, the same boy reappeared, and presented me with a note written in pencil, and headed, in a legal manner, "Heep v. Micawber." From this document I learned that Mr. Micawber, being again arrested, was in a final paroxysm of despair; and that he begged me to send him his knife and pint pot, by bearer, as they might prove serviceable during the brief remainder of his existence in jail. He also requested, as a last act of friendship, that I would see his family to the Parish Workhouse, and forget that such a Being ever lived.

Of course, I answered this note by going down with the boy to pay the money, where I found Mr. Micawber sitting in a corner, looking darkly at the sheriff's officer who had effected the capture. On his release, he embraced me with the utmost fervor, and made an entry of the transaction in his pocket-book, being very particular, I recollect, about a half-penny I inadvertently omitted from my statement of the total.

"If you have any opportunity of sending letters home, on your passage, Mrs. Micawber," said my aunt, "you must let us hear from you, you know."

"Please Heaven, there will be many such opportunities," said Mr. Micawber. "The ocean, in these times, is a perfect fleet of ships, and we can hardly fail to encounter many in running over. It is merely crossing," said Mr. Micawber, trifling with his eyeglass, "merely crossing. The distance is quite imaginary."

I think, now, how odd it was, but how wonderfully like Mr. Micawber, that when he went from London to Canterbury he should have talked as if he were going to the farthest limits of the earth, and when he went from England to Australia as if he were going for a little trip across the Channel.

"What *I* chiefly hope, my dear Mr. Copperfield," said Mrs. Micawber, "is, that in some branches of our family we may live again in the old country. When our race attains to eminence and fortune, I own I should wish that fortune to flow into the coffers of Britannia."

"My dear," said Mr. Micawber, "Britannia must take her chance. I am bound to say that she has never done much for me, and that I have no particular wish upon the subject."

"Micawber," returned Mrs. Micawber, "there you are wrong. You do not know your power, Micawber. It is that which will strengthen, even in this step you are about to take, the connection between yourself and Albion."

Mr. Micawber sat in his elbow-chair, with his eyebrows raised, half receiving and half repudiating Mrs. Micawber's views as they were stated.

"My dear Mr. Copperfield," said Mrs. Micawber, "I wish Mr. Micawber to feel his position. It appears to me highly important that Mr. Micawber should, from the hour of his embarkation, feel his position."

"My love," he observed, "perhaps you will allow me to remark that it is barely possible that I *do* feel my position at the present moment."

"I think not, Micawber," she rejoined. "Not fully.—My dear Mr. Copperfield, Mr. Micawber's is not a common case. Mr. Micawber is going to a distant country expressly in order that he may be fully understood and appreciated for the first time. I wish Mr. Micawber to take his stand upon that vessel's prow and firmly say: 'This country I am come to conquer! Have you honors? have you riches? have you posts of profitable pecuniary emolument? Let them be brought forward! they are mine!'"

Mr. Micawber, glancing at us all, seemed to think there was a good deal in this idea.

"I wish Mr. Micawber, if I make myself understood," said Mrs. Micawber, in her argumentative tone, "to be the Cæsar of his own fortunes. That, my dear Mr. Copperfield, appears to me to be his true position. From the first moment of this voyage, I wish Mr. Micawber to stand upon that vessel's prow, and say: 'Enough of delay! enough of disappointment! enough of limited means! That was in the old country; this is the new! Produce your reparation! bring it forward!'"

Mr. Micawber folded his arms in a resolute manner, as if he were then stationed on the figure-head.

"And therefore it is," said Mrs. Micawber, "that I the more wish that, at a future period, we may live again on the parent soil. Mr. Micawber may be—I cannot disguise from myself that the probability is Mr. Micawber will be—a page of History; and he ought, then, to be represented in the country which gave him birth, and did *not* give him employment!"

"My love," observed Mr. Micawber, "it is impossible for me not to be touched by your affection. I am always willing to defer to your good sense. What will be will be. Heaven forbid that I should grudge my native country any portion of the wealth that may be accumulated by our descendants!"

In the afternoon of the next day my old nurse and I went down to Gravesend. We found the ship in the river, surrounded by a crowd of boats; a favorable wind blowing; the signal for sailing at her masthead. I hired a boat directly, and we put off to her, and, getting through the little vortex of confusion of which she was the center, went on board.

Among the great beams, bulks, and ringbolts of the ship, and the emigrant berths, and chests, and bundles, and barrels, and heaps of miscellaneous baggage—lighted up here and there by dangling lanterns, and elsewhere by the yellow daylight straying down a windsail or a hatchway—were crowded groups of people, making new friendships, taking leave of one another, talking, laughing, crying, eating and drinking; some already settled down into the possession of their few feet of space, with their little households arranged, and tiny children established on stools or in dwarf elbow-chairs; others despairing of a resting-place, and wandering disconsolately. From babies who had but a week or two of life behind them, to crooked old men and women who seemed to have but a week or two of life before them; and from plowmen, bodily carrying out soil of England on their boots, to smiths taking away samples of its soot and smoke upon their skins,—every age and occupation appeared to be crammed into the narrow compass of the 'tween decks.

As my eye glanced round this place, I thought I saw, sitting by an open port, with one of the Micawber children near her, a figure like Emily's. It first attracted my attention by another figure parting from it with a kiss, and, as it glided calmly away through the disorder, reminding me of—Agnes! But in the rapid motion and confusion, and in the unsettlement of my own thoughts, I lost it again, and only knew that the time was come when all visitors were being warned to leave the ship; that my nurse was crying on a chest beside me; and that Mrs. Gummidge, assisted by some younger stooping woman in black, was busily arranging Mr. Peggotty's goods.

"Is there any last wured, Mas'r Davy?" said he. "Is there anyone forgotten thing afore we parts?"

"One thing!" said I. "Martha?"

He touched the younger woman I have mentioned on the shoulder, and Martha stood before me.

"Heaven bless you, you good man!" cried I. "You take her with you?"

She answered for him with a burst of tears. I could speak no more at that time, but I wrung his hand, and if ever I have loved and honored any man, I loved and honored that man in my soul.

The time was come. I embraced him, took my weeping nurse upon my arm, and hurried away. On deck, I took leave of poor Mrs. Micawber. She was looking distractedly about for her family, even then, and her last words to me were that she never would desert Mr. Micawber.

We went over the side into our boat, and lay at a little distance to see the ship wafted on her course. As the sails rose to the wind, and the ship began to move, there broke from all the boats three resounding cheers, which those on board took up and echoed back, and which were echoed and re-echoed.

I WENT away from England, not knowing, even then, how great the shock was that I had to bear. I left all who were dear to me, and went away; and believed that I had borne it, and it was past. As a man upon a field of battle will receive a mortal hurt and scarcely know that he is struck, so I, when I was left alone with my undisciplined heart, had no conception of the wound with which it had to strive.

The knowledge came upon me, not quickly, but little by little, and grain by grain. The desolate feeling with which I went abroad deepened and widened hourly. At first it was a heavy sense of loss and sorrow, wherein I could distinguish little else. By imperceptible degrees it became a hopeless consciousness of all that I had lost—love, friendship, interest; of all that had been shattered—my first trust, my first affection, the whole airy castle of my life; of all that remained—a ruined blank and waste, lying wide around me, unbroken, to the dark horizon.

When this despondency was at its worst, I believed that I should die. Sometimes, I thought that I would like to die at home, and actually turned back on my road that I might get there soon. At other times I proceeded restlessly from place to place, stopping nowhere; sometimes, I lingered long in one spot. I had had no purpose, no sustaining soul within me, anywhere.

I was in Switzerland. I had come out of Italy, over one of the great passes of the Alps, and had since wandered with a guide among the by-ways of the mountains. If those awful solitudes had spoken to my heart, I did not know it. I had found sublimity and wonder in the dread heights and precipices, in the roaring torrents, and the wastes of ice and snow; but as yet they had taught me nothing else.

I came, one evening before sunset, down into a valley, where I was to rest. In the course of my descent to it, by the winding track along the mountain-side, from which I saw it shining far below, I think some long unwonted sense of beauty and tranquillity, some softening influence awakened by its peace, moved faintly in my breast. I remember pausing once, with a kind of sorrow that was not all oppressive, not quite despairing. I remember almost hoping that some better change was possible within me.

I had found a packet of letters awaiting me but a few minutes before, and had strolled out of the village to read them while my supper was making ready. Other packets had missed me, and I had received none for a long time. Beyond a line or two, to say that I was well, and had arrived at such a place, I had not had fortitude or constancy to write a letter since I left home.

The packet was in my hand. I opened it, and read the writing of Agnes.

She was happy and useful; was prospering as she had hoped. That was all she told me of herself. The rest referred to me.

She gave me no advice; she urged no duty on me; she only told me, in her own fervent manner, what her trust in me was. She knew, she said, how such a nature as mine would turn affliction to good. She knew how trial and emotion would exalt and strengthen it. She, who so gloried in my fame, and so looked forward to its augmentation, well knew that I would labor on; and in her sisterly affection cherished me always, and was always at my side go where I would—proud of what I had done, but infinitely prouder yet of what I was reserved to do.

I read her letter many times. I wrote to her before I slept. I told her that I had been in sore need of her help; that without her I was not, and I never had been, what she thought me; but that she inspired me to be that, and I would try.

I did try. I worked early and late, patiently and hard. I wrote a story, and sent it to Traddles, and he arranged for its publication very advantageously for me; and the tidings of my growing reputation began to reach me from travelers whom I encountered by chance. After some rest and change, I fell to work, in my old ardent way, on a new fancy which took strong possession of me. As I advanced in the execution of this task, I felt it more and more, and roused my utmost energies to do it well. This was my third work of fiction. It was not half written, when, in an interval of rest, I thought of returning home.

For a long time, though studying and working patiently, I had accustomed myself to robust exercise. My health, severely impaired when I left England, was quite restored. I had seen much. I had been in many countries, and I hope I had improved my store of knowledge.

I have now recalled all that I think it needful to recall here of this term of absence—with one reservation. I have desired to keep the most secret current of my mind apart, and to the last. I enter on it now.

I cannot so completely penetrate the mystery of my own heart as to know when I began to think that I might have set its earliest and brightest hopes on Agnes. I cannot say at what stage of my grief it first became associated with the reflection that, in my wayward boyhood, I have thrown away the treasure of her love. But the thought came into my mind as a new reproach and new regret, when I was left so sad and lonely in the world.

If, at that time, I had been much with her, I should, in the weakness of my desolation, have betrayed this. It was what I remotely dreaded when I was first impelled to stay away from England. I could not have borne to lose the smallest portion of her sisterly affection; yet, in that betrayal, I should have set a constraint between us hitherto unknown.

I could not forget that the feeling with which she now regarded me had grown up in my own free choice and course; that if she had ever loved me with another love—and I sometimes thought the time was when she might have done so—I had cast it away. I did glance, through some indefinite probation, to a period when I might possibly hope to cancel the mistaken past, and to be so blessed as to marry her. But, as time wore on, this shadowy prospect faded and departed from me. If she had ever loved me, then, I should hold her the more sacred, remembering the sacrifice she must have made to be my friend and sister, and the victory she had won. If she had never loved me, could I believe that she would love me now?

These, with their perplexities and inconsistencies, were the shifting quicksands of my mind, from the time of my departure to the time of my return home, three years afterwards. Three years. Long in the aggregate, though short as they went by. And home was very dear to me, and Agnes too. But she was not mine—she was never to be mine. She might have been, but that war past!

I LANDED in London on a wintry autumn evening. It was dark and raining, and I saw more fog and mud in a minute than I had seen in a year. I walked from the Custom House to the Monument before I found a coach; and although the very house fronts, looking on the swollen gutters, were like old friends to me, I could not but admit that they were very dingy friends.

For some changes in the fortunes of my friends I was prepared. My aunt had long been re-established at Dover; and Traddles had begun to get into some little practice at the Bar, in the very first term after my departure. He had chambers in Gray's Inn now; and had told me, in his last letters, that he was not without hopes of being soon united to the dearest girl in the world.

They expected me home before Christmas, but had no idea of my returning so soon. I had purposely misled them, that I might have the pleasure of taking them by surprise. And yet I was perverse enough to feel a chill and disappointment in receiving no welcome, and rattling, alone and silent, through the misty streets. The well-known shops, however, with their cheerful lights, did something for me, and when I alighted at the door of the Gray's Inn Coffee-house I had recovered my spirits.

"Do you know where Mr. Traddles lives in the Inn?" I asked the waiter, as I warmed myself by the coffee-room fire.

"Holborn Court, sir. Number two."

"Mr. Traddles has a rising reputation among the lawyers, I believe?" said I.

"Well, sir," returned the waiter, "probably he has, sir, but I am not aware of it myself."

Being very anxious to see the dear old fellow I dispatched my dinner in a manner not at all calculated to raise me in the opinion of the waiter, and hurried out by the back way. Number two in the Court was soon reached; and an inscription on the doorpost informing me that Mr. Traddles occupied a set of chambers on the top story, I ascended the staircase. A crazy old staircase I found it to be, feebly lighted on each landing by a club-headed little oil wick, dying away in a little dungeon of dirty glass.

In the course of my stumbling upstairs I fancied I heard a pleasant sound of laughter; and not the laughter of an attorney or barrister, or attorney's clerk or barrister's clerk, but of two or three merry girls. My heart beat high when I found the outer door, which had MR. TRADDLES painted on it, open. I knocked. A considerable scuffling within ensued, but nothing else. I therefore knocked again.

A small sharp-looking lad, half-footboy and half-clerk, who was very much out of breath, but who looked at me as if he defied me to prove it legally, presented himself.

"Is Mr. Traddles within?" I said.

"Yes, sir; but he's engaged."

"I want to see him."

After a moment's survey of me, the sharp-looking lad decided to let me in; and opening the door wider for that purpose, admitted me, first, into a little closet of a hall, and next into a little sitting-room, where I came into the presence of my old friend (also out of breath) seated at a table, and bending over papers.

"Good God!" cried Traddles, looking up, "it's Copperfield!" and rushed into my arms, where I held him tight.

"All well, my dear Traddles?"

"All well, my dear, dear Copperfield, and nothing but good news!"

We cried with pleasure, both of us.

"My dear fellow," said Traddles, rumpling his hair in his excitement, which was a most unnecessary operation. "My dearest Copperfield, my long-lost and most welcome friend, how glad I am to see you! How brown you are! How glad I am! Upon my life and honor, I never was so rejoiced, my beloved Copperfield, never!"

I was equally at a loss to express my emotions. I was quite unable to speak at first.

"To think," said Traddles, "that you should have been so nearly coming home as you must have been, my dear old boy, and not at the ceremony."

"What ceremony, my dear Traddles?"

"Good gracious me!" cried Traddles, opening his eyes in his old way. "Didn't you get my last letter?"

"Certainly not, if it referred to any ceremony."

"Why, my dear Copperfield," said Traddles, sticking his hair upright with both hands, and then putting his hands on my knees, "I am married!"

"Married!" I cried joyfully.

"Lord bless me, yes!" said Traddles—"Why, my dear boy, she's behind the window curtain! Look here!"

To my amazement, the dearest girl in the world came at that same instant, laughing and blushing, from her place of concealment. And a more cheerful, amiable, honest, happy, bright-looking bride, I believe (as I could not help saying on the spot) the world never saw. I kissed her as an old acquaintance should, and wished them joy with all my might of heart.

"We are all as happy as possible!" said Traddles. "Even the girls are happy. Dear me, I declare I forgot them!"

"Forgot?" said I.

"The girls," said Traddles—"Sophy's sisters. They are staying with us. They have come to have a peep at London. The fact is, I was romping with the girls. In point of fact, we were playing at Puss in the Corner. But as that wouldn't do in Westminster Hall, and as it wouldn't look quite professional if they were seen by a client, they decamped."

"I am sorry," said I, laughing, "to have occasioned such a dispersion."

"Upon my word," rejoined Traddles, greatly delighted, "if you had seen them running away, and running back again, after you had knocked, to pick up the combs they had dropped out of their hair, and going on in the maddest manner, you wouldn't have said so.—My love, will you fetch the girls?"

Sophy tripped away, and we heard her received in the adjoining room with a peal of laughter.

"But then," said Traddles, "our domestic arrangements are, to say the truth, quite unprofessional altogether, my dear Copperfield. Even Sophy's being here is unprofessional. And we have no other place of abode. We have put to sea in a cockboat, but we are quite prepared to rough it. And Sophy's an extraordinary manager! You'll be surprised how those girls are stowed away. I am sure I hardly know how it's done."

"Are many of the young ladies with you?" I inquired.

"The eldest, the Beauty, is here," said Traddles, in a low, confidential voice, "Caroline. And Sarah's here—the one I mentioned to you as having something the matter with her spine, you know. Immensely better! And the two youngest that Sophy educated are with us. And Louisa's here."

"Indeed!" cried I.

"Yes," said Traddles. "Now the whole set—I mean the chambers —is only three rooms; but Sophy arranges for the girls in the most wonderful way, and they sleep as comfortably as possible. Three in that room," said Traddles, pointing; "two in that."

I could not help glancing round in search of the accommodation remaining for Mr. and Mrs. Traddles. Traddles understood me.

"Well!" said Traddles, "we are prepared to rough it, as I said just now, and we *did* improvise a bed last week upon the floor here. But there's a little room in the roof—a very nice room when you're up there—which Sophy papered herself, to surprise me; and that's our room at present. It's a capital little gipsy sort of place. There's quite a view from it."

"And you are happily married at last, my dear Traddles!" said I. "How rejoiced I am!"

"Thank you, my dear Copperfield," said Traddles, as we shook hands once more. "But, indeed, I am in a most enviable state. I work hard, and read law insatiably. I get up at five every morning, and don't mind it at all. I hide the girls in the daytime, and make merry with them in the evening. And I assure you I am quite sorry that they are going home on Tuesday, which is the day before the first day of Michaelmas Term. But here," said Traddles, breaking off in his confidence, and speaking aloud, "*are* the girls! Mr. Copperfield, Miss Crewler—Miss Sarah—Miss Louisa—Margaret and Lucy!"

They were a perfect nest of roses, they looked so wholesome and fresh. They were all pretty, and Miss Caroline was very handsome; but there was a loving, cheerful, fireside quality in Sophy's bright looks, which was better than that, and which assured me that my friend had chosen well.

Neither could they do anything without Sophy. Somebody's hair fell down, and nobody but Sophy could put it up. Somebody forgot how a particular tune went, and nobody but Sophy could hum that tune right. Somebody wanted to recall the name of a place in Devonshire, and only Sophy knew it. Something was wanted to be written home, and Sophy alone could be trusted to write before breakfast in the morning. Somebody broke down in a piece of knitting, and no one but Sophy was able to put the defaulter in the right direction. They were entire mistresses of the place, and Sophy and Traddles waited on them. The best of all was that, in the midst of their exactions, all the sisters had a great tenderness and respect both for Sophy and Traddles. I am sure, when I took my leave, and Traddles was coming out to walk with me to the coffee-house, I thought I had never seen an obstinate head of hair, or any other head of hair, rolling about in such a shower of kisses.

Thoroughly tired, I went to bed; passed the next day on the Dover coach; burst safe and sound into my aunt's old parlor while she was at tea (she wore spectacles now); and was received by her, and Mr. Dick, and dear old Peggotty, who acted as housekeeper, with open arms and tears of joy.

ᴀɴᴅ when, Trot," said my aunt, patting the back of my hand, as we sat in our old way before the fire—"when are you going over to Canterbury?"

"I shall get a horse and ride over tomorrow morning, aunt—unless you will go with me?"

"No!" said my aunt, in her short, abrupt way. "I mean to stay where I am."

Then I should ride, I said. I could not have come through Canterbury today without stopping, if I had been coming to anyone but her.

She was pleased, but answered, "Tut, Trot; *my* old bones would have kept till tomorrow!" and softly patted my hand again as I sat looking thoughtfully at the fire.

We both kept silence for some minutes. When I raised my eyes, I found that she was steadily observant of me.

"Has Agnes any——" I was thinking aloud, rather than speaking.

"Well? Hey? Any what?" said my aunt sharply.

"Any lover?" said I.

"A score!" cried my aunt, with a kind of indignant pride. "She

405

might have married twenty times, my dear, since you have been gone!"

"No doubt," said I; "no doubt. But has she any lover who is worthy of her? Agnes could care for no other."

My aunt sat musing for a little while, with her chin upon her hand. Slowly raising her eyes to mine, she said,

"I suspect she has an attachment, Trot."

"A prosperous one?" said I.

"Trot," returned my aunt gravely, "I can't say. I have no right to tell you even so much. She has never confided it to me, but I suspect it."

She looked so attentively and anxiously at me (I even saw her tremble), that I felt that she had followed my late thoughts. I summoned all the resolutions I had made, in all those many days and nights, and all those many conflicts of my heart.

"If it should be so," I began, "and I hope it is——"

"I don't know that it is," said my aunt curtly. "You must not be ruled by my suspicions. You must keep them secret. They are very slight, perhaps. I have no right to speak."

"If it should be so," I repeated, "Agnes will tell me at her own good time. A sister to whom I have confided so much, aunt, will not be reluctant to confide in me."

My aunt withdrew her eyes from mine, as slowly as she had turned them upon me, and covered them thoughtfully with her hand. By-and-by she put her other hand on my shoulder; and so we both sat, looking into the past, without saying another word until we parted for the night.

I rode away early in the morning for the scene of my old school-days. The well-remembered ground was soon traversed, and I came into the quiet streets, where every stone was a boy's book to me. The staid old house was, as to its cleanliness and order, still just as it had been when I first saw it. I requested the new maid who admitted me to tell Miss Wickfield that a gentleman, who waited on her from a friend abroad, was there; and I was shown up the grave old stair-case (cautioned of the steps I knew so well) into the unchanged drawing-room. The books that Agnes and I had read together were on their shelves, and the desk where I had labored at my lessons many a night stood yet at the same old corner of the table. All the little changes that had crept in when the Heeps were there were changed again. Everything was as it used to be in the happy time.

The opening of the little door in the paneled wall made me start and turn. Her beautiful serene eyes met mine as she came toward me. She stopped, and laid her hand upon her bosom, and I caught her in my arms.

"Agnes! my dear girl! I have come too suddenly upon you."

"No, no! I am so rejoiced to see you, Trotwood!"

"Dear Agnes, the happiness it is to me to see you once again!"

I folded her to my heart, and for a little while we were both silent. Presently we sat down, side by side, and her angel face was turned upon me with the welcome I had dreamed of, waking and sleeping, for whole years.

She was so true, she was so beautiful, she was so good—I owed her so much gratitude, she was so dear to me, that I could find no utterance for what I felt. I tried to bless her, tried to thank her, tried to tell her (as I had often done in letters) what an influence she had upon me; but all my efforts were in vain. My love and joy were dumb.

With her own sweet tranquillity she calmed my agitation; led me back to the time of our parting; touched the chords of my memory so softly and harmoniously that not one jarred within me.

"And you, Agnes," I said, by-and-by. "Tell me of yourself. You have hardly ever told me of your own life, in all this lapse of time!"

"What should I tell?" she answered, with her radiant smile. "Papa is well. You see us here, quiet in our own home; our anxieties set at rest, our home restored to us. And knowing that, dear Trotwood, you know all."

"All, Agnes?" said I.

She looked at me, with some fluttering wonder in her face.

"Is there nothing else, sister?" I said.

Her color, which had just now faded, returned, and faded again. She smiled—with a quiet sadness, I thought—and shook her head.

I had sought to lead her to what my aunt had hinted at; for, sharply painful to me as it must be to receive that confidence, I was to discipline my heart, and do my duty to her. I saw, however, that she was uneasy, and I let it pass.

I walked through the streets, and, once more seeing my old adversary the butcher—now a constable, with his staff hanging up in the shop—went down to look at the place where I had fought him; and there meditated on Miss Shepherd and the eldest Miss Larkins, and all the idle loves and likings and dislikings of that time. Nothing seemed to have survived that time but Agnes; and she, ever a star above me, was brighter and higher.

When I returned, Mr. Wickfield had come home from a garden he had, a couple of miles or so out of town, where he now employed himself almost every day. The tranquillity and peace belonging, of old, to that quiet ground in my memory, pervaded it again. After tea we three sat together, talking of the bygone days.

"Have you any intention of going away again?" Agnes asked me.

"What does my sister say to that?"

"I hope not."

"Then I have no such intention, Agnes."

"I think you ought not, Trotwood, since you ask me," she said mildly. "Your growing reputation and success enlarge your power of doing good; and if *I* could spare my brother," with her eyes upon me, "perhaps the time could not."

"What I am you have made me, Agnes. You should know best."

She only shook her head; through her tears I saw the same sad, quiet smile.

"And I am so grateful to you for it, Agnes, so bound to you, that there is no name for the affection of my heart. I want you to know, yet don't know how to tell you, that all my life long I shall look up to you, and be guided by you, as I have been through the darkness that is past. You will always be my solace and resource, as you have always been. Until I die, my dearest sister, I shall see you always before me, pointing upward!"

She put her hand in mine, and told me she was proud of me, and of what I said, although I praised her very far beyond her worth.

"Will you laugh at my cherishing such fancies, Agnes?"

"Oh, no! Oh, no!"

For an instant a distressful shadow crossed her face; but, even in the start it gave me, it was gone, and she was playing on, and looking at me with her own calm smile.

As I rode back in the lonely night, the wind going by me like a restless memory, I thought of this, and feared she was not happy. *I* was not happy; but, thus far, I had faithfully set the seal upon the Past, and, thinking of her pointing upward, thought of her as pointing to that sky above me, where, in the mystery to come, I might yet love her with a love unknown on earth, and tell her what the strife had been within me when I loved her here.

OR a time—at all events until my book should be completed,
which would be the work of several months—I took up my
abode in my aunt's house at Dover; and there, sitting in the
window from which I had looked out at the moon upon the sea
when that roof first gave me shelter, I quietly pursued my task.

Occasionally I went to London—to lose myself in the swarm of
life there, or to consult with Traddles on some business point. He
had managed for me, in my absence, with the soundest judgment,
and my worldly affairs were prospering. As my notoriety began to
bring upon me an enormous quantity of letters from people of
whom I had no knowledge—chiefly about nothing, and extremely
difficult to answer—I agreed with Traddles to have my name painted
up on his door. There the devoted postman on that beat delivered
bushels of letters for me; and there, at intervals, I labored through
them, like a Home Secretary of State, without the salary.

I wondered, at first, why I so often found Sophy writing in a
copy-book, and why she always shut it up when I appeared, and
hurried it into the table-drawer. But the secret soon came out. One

day, Traddles (who had just come home through the drizzling sleet from Court) took a paper out of his desk, and asked me what I thought of that handwriting?

"Oh, *don't*, Tom!" cried Sophy, who was warming his slippers before the fire.

"My dear," returned Tom, in a delighted state, "why not?—What do you say to that writing, Copperfield?"

"It's extraordinarily legal and formal," said I. "I don't think I ever saw such a stiff hand."

"Not like a lady's hand, is it?" said Traddles.

"A lady's!" I repeated. "Bricks and mortar are more like a lady's hand!"

Traddles broke into a rapturous laugh, and informed me that it was Sophy's writing; that Sophy had vowed and declared he would need a copying-clerk soon, and she would be that clerk; that she had acquired this hand from a pattern; and that she could throw off—I forget how many folios an hour. Sophy was very much confused by my being told all this, and said that when "Tom" was made a judge he wouldn't be so ready to proclaim it. Which "Tom" denied, averring that he should always be equally proud of it, under all circumstances.

The year came round to Christmas-time, and I had been at home above two months. I had seen Agnes frequently. At least once a week, and sometimes oftener, I rode over there, and passed the evening.

This Christmas-time being come, and Agnes having reposed no new confidence in me, a doubt that had several times arisen in my mind—whether she could have that perception of the true state of my breast, which restrained her with the apprehension of giving me pain—began to oppress me heavily. I resolved to set this right beyond all doubt; if such a barrier were between us, to break it down at once with a determined hand.

It was—what lasting reason have I to remember it!—a cold, harsh, winter day. There had been snow some hours before, and it lay, not deep, but hard-frozen on the ground. Out at sea, beyond my window, the wind blew ruggedly from the north.

"Riding today, Trot?" said my aunt, putting her head in at the door.

"Yes," said I; "I am going over to Canterbury. It's a good day for a ride."

"I hope your horse may think so too," said my aunt; "but at

present he is holding down his head and his ears, standing before the door there as if he thought his stable preferable."

My aunt, I may observe, allowed my horse on the forbidden ground, but had not at all relented toward the donkeys.

"He will be fresh enough presently," said I.

"The ride will do his master good, at all events," observed my aunt, glancing at the papers on my table. "Ah, child, you pass a good many hours here! I never thought, when I used to read books, what work it was to write them."

"It's work enough to read them sometimes," I returned. "As to the writing, it has its own charms, aunt."

"Ah, I see!" said my aunt: "Ambition, love of approbation, sympathy, and much more, I suppose? Well, go along with you!"

"Do you know anything more," said I, standing composedly before her—she had patted me on the shoulder, and sat down in my chair—"of that attachment of Agnes?"

She looked up in my face a little while before replying,

"I think I do, Trot."

"Are you confirmed in your impression?" I inquired.

"I think I am, Trot."

She looked so steadfastly at me, with a kind of doubt, or pity, or suspense in her affection, that I summoned the stronger determination to show her a perfectly cheerful face.

"And what is more, Trot——" said my aunt.

"Yes!"

"I think Agnes is going to be married."

"God bless her!" said I cheerfully.

"God bless her," said my aunt, "and her husband too!"

I echoed it, parted from my aunt, went lightly downstairs, mounted, and rode away. There was greater reason than before to do what I had resolved to do.

I found Agnes alone by the fire, reading. She put down her book on seeing me come in; and having welcomed me as usual, took her work-basket, and sat in one of the old-fashioned windows.

I sat beside her on the window-seat, and we talked of what I was doing, and when it would be done, and of the progress I had made since my last visit. Agnes was very cheerful, and laughingly predicted that I should soon become too famous to be talked to on such subjects.

"So I make the most of the present time, you see," said Agnes, "and talk to you while I may."

As I looked at her beautiful face, observant of her work, she raised her mild clear eyes, and saw that I was looking at her.

"You are thoughtful today, Trotwood!"

"Agnes, shall I tell you what about? I came to tell you."

She put aside her work, as she was used to do when we were seriously discussing anything, and gave me her whole attention.

"My dear Agnes, do you doubt my being true to you?"

"No!" she answered, with a look of astonishment.

"Do you remember that I tried to tell you, when I came home, what a debt of gratitude I owed you, dearest Agnes, and how fervently I felt toward you?"

"I remember it," she said gently, "very well."

"You have a secret," said I. "Let me share it, Agnes."

She cast down her eyes, and trembled.

"I could hardly fail to know, even if I had not heard—but from other lips than yours, Agnes, which seems strange—that there is someone upon whom you have bestowed the treasure of your love. Do not shut me out of what concerns your happiness so nearly! If you can trust me as you say you can, and as I know you may, let me be your friend, your brother, in this matter, of all others!"

With an appealing, almost a reproachful, glance, she rose from the window, and hurrying across the room as if without knowing where, put her hands before her face, and burst into such tears as smote me to the heart.

And yet they awakened something in me bringing promise to my heart. Without my knowing why, these tears allied themselves with the quietly sad smile which was so fixed in my remembrance, and shook me more with hope than fear or sorrow.

"Agnes! sister! dearest! What have I done?"

"Let me go away, Trotwood. I am not well. I am not myself. I will speak to you by-and-by—another time. I will write to you. Don't speak to me now. Don't! don't!"

"I must say more. I must speak plainly. If you have any lingering thought that I could envy the happiness you will confer; that I could not resign you to a dearer protector, of your own choosing; that I could not, from my removed place, be a contented witness of your joy—dismiss it, for I don't deserve it!"

She was quiet now. In a little time she turned her pale face toward me, and said in a low voice, broken here and there, but very clear,

"I owe it to your pure friendship for me, Trotwood—which, indeed, I do not doubt—to tell you, you are mistaken. If I have any secret, it is—no new one, and is—not what you suppose. I cannot reveal it, or divide it. It has long been mine, and must remain mine."

"Agnes! Stay! A moment!"

She was going away, but I detained her. I clasped my arm about her waist. "It is not a new one!" New thoughts and hopes were whirling through my mind, and all the colors of my life were changing.

"Dearest Agnes! whom I so respect and honor—whom I so devotedly love!—when I came here today, I thought that nothing could have wrested this confession from me. But, Agnes, if I have indeed any new-born hope that I may ever call you something more than sister, widely different from sister!——"

Her tears fell fast, but they were not like those she had lately shed. Still weeping, but not sadly—joyfully! And clasped in my arms as she had never been, as I had thought she never was to be!

"When I loved Dora—fondly, Agnes, as you know——"

"Yes!" she cried earnestly. "I am glad to know it!"

"When I loved her—even then, my love would have been incomplete without your sympathy. I had it, and it was perfected. And when I lost her, Agnes, what should I have been without you still?"

Closer in my arms, nearer to my heart, her trembling hand upon my shoulder, her sweet eyes shining through her tears, on mine!

"I went away, dear Agnes, loving you. I stayed away, loving you. I returned home, loving you!"

And now I tried to tell her of the struggle I had had, and the conclusion I had come to. If she did so love me, I said, that she could take me for her husband, she could do so on no deserving of mine, except upon the truth of my love for her.

"I am so blest, Trotwood—my heart is so overcharged—but there is one thing I must say."

"Dearest, what?"

She laid her gentle hands upon my shoulders, and looked calmly in my face.

"Do you know yet what it is?"

"I am afraid to speculate on what it is. Tell me, my dear."

"I have loved you all my life!"

Oh, we were happy, we were happy! Our tears were not for the trials (hers so much the greater) through which we had come to be thus, but for the rapture of being thus, never to be divided more!

We walked, that winter evening, in the fields together, and the blessed calm within us seemed to be partaken by the frosty air. The early stars began to shine while we were lingering on, and looking up to them, we thanked our GOD for having guided us to this tranquillity.

We stood together in the same old-fashioned window at night, when the moon was shining—Agnes with her quiet eyes raised up to it; I followed her glance. Long miles of road then opened out before my mind; and, toiling on, I saw a ragged, way-worn boy, forsaken and neglected, who should come to call even the heart now beating against mine, his own.

It was nearly dinner-time next day when we appeared before my aunt. She was up in my study, Peggotty said—which it was her pride to keep in readiness and order for me. We found her, in her spectacles, sitting by the fire.

"Goodness me!" said my aunt, peering through the dusk, "who's this you're bringing home?"

"Agnes," said I.

As we had arranged to say nothing at first, my aunt was not a little discomfited. She darted a hopeful glance at me when I said "Agnes"; but seeing that I looked as usual, she took off her spectacles in despair, and rubbed her nose with them.

She greeted Agnes heartily, nevertheless, and we were soon in the lighted parlor downstairs, at dinner. My aunt put on her spectacles twice or thrice to take another look at me, but as often took them off again, disappointed, and rubbed her nose with them—much to the discomfiture of Mr. Dick, who knew this to be a bad symptom.

"By-the-by, aunt," said I, after dinner. "I have been speaking to Agnes about what you told me."

"Then, Trot," said my aunt, turning scarlet, "you did wrong, and broke your promise."

"You are not angry, aunt, I trust? I am sure you won't be when you learn that Agnes is not unhappy in any attachment."

"Stuff and nonsense!" said my aunt.

As my aunt appeared to be annoyed, I thought the best way was to cut her annoyance short. I took Agnes in my arm to the back of her chair, and we both leaned over her. My aunt, with one clap of her hands, and one look through her spectacles, immediately went into hysterics, for the first and only time in all my knowledge of her.

The hysterics called up Peggotty. The moment my aunt was

restored she flew at Peggotty, and calling her a silly old creature, hugged her with all her might. After that she hugged Mr. Dick (who was highly honored, but a good deal surprised); and after that told them why. Then we were all happy together.

I could not discover whether my aunt, in her last short conversation with me, had fallen on a pious fraud, or had really mistaken the state of my mind. It was quite enough, she said, that she had told me Agnes was going to be married, and that I now knew better than anyone how true it was.

We were married within a fortnight. Traddles and Sophy, and Doctor and Mrs. Strong, were the only guests at our quiet wedding. We left them full of joy, and drove away together. Clasped in my embrace, I held the source of every worthy aspiration I had ever had—the center of myself, the circle of my life, my own, my wife— my love of whom was founded on a rock!

"Dearest husband!" said Agnes—"now that I may call you by that name—I have one thing more to tell you."

"Let me hear it, love."

"It grows out of the night when Dora died. She sent you for me."

"She did."

"She told me that she left me something. Can you think what it was?"

I believed I could. I drew the wife who had so long loved me closer to my side.

"She told me that she made a last request to me, and left me a last charge."

"And it was——"

"That only I would occupy this vacant place."

And Agnes laid her head upon my breast, and wept; and I wept with her, though we were so happy.

CHAPTER 62  A VISITOR ♦ ♦ ♦

WHAT I have purposed to record is nearly finished; but there
is yet an incident conspicuous in my memory, on which it
often rests with delight, and without which one thread in
the web I have spun would have a raveled end.

I had advanced in fame and fortune; my domestic joy was perfect;
I had been married ten happy years. Agnes and I were sitting by the
fire, in our house in London, one night in spring, and three of our
children were playing in the room, when I was told that a stranger
wished to see me.

He had been asked if he came on business, and had answered No;
he had come for the pleasure of seeing me, and had come a long
way. He was an old man, my servant said, and looked like a farmer.

As this sounded mysterious to the children, and moreover was
like the beginning of a favorite story Agnes used to tell them, intro-
ductory to the arrival of a wicked old Fairy in a cloak who hated
everybody, it produced some commotion. One of our boys laid his
head in his mother's lap to be out of harm's way, and little Agnes
(our eldest child) left her doll in a chair to represent her, and thrust
out her little heap of golden curls from between the window-
curtains, to see what happened next.

"Let him come in here!" said I.

There soon appeared, pausing in the dark doorway as he entered, a hale, grey-haired old man. Little Agnes, attracted by his looks, had run to bring him in, and I had not yet clearly seen his face, when my wife, starting up, cried out to me, in a pleased and agitated voice, that it was Mr. Peggotty!

It *was* Mr. Peggotty. An old man now, but in a ruddy, hearty, strong old age. When our first emotion was over, and he sat before the fire with the children on his knees, and the blaze shining on his face, he looked to me as vigorous and robust, withal as handsome, an old man, as ever I had seen.

"Mas'r Davy," said he—and the old name in the old tone fell so naturally on my ear!—"Mas'r Davy, 'tis a joyful hour as I see you, once more, 'long with your own true wife!"

"A joyful hour indeed, old friend!" cried I.

"And these here pretty ones," said Mr. Peggotty. "To look at these here flowers! Why, Mas'r Davy, you was but the heighth of the littlest of these when I first see you! When Em'ly warn't no bigger, and our poor lad were *but* a lad!"

"Time has changed me more than it has changed you since then," said I. "But let these dear rogues go to bed; and as no house in England but this must hold you, tell me where to send for your luggage"—(is the old black bag among it, that went so far, I wonder?)—"and then, over a glass of Yarmouth grog, we will have the tidings of ten years!"

We sat him between us, not knowing how to give him welcome enough; and as I began to listen to his old familiar voice, I could have fancied he was still pursuing his long journey in search of his darling niece.

"And now tell us," said I, "everything relating to your fortunes."

"Our fortuns, Mas'r Davy," he rejoined, "is soon told. We haven't fared nohows but fared to thrive. We've allus thrived. We've worked as we ought to 't, and maybe we lived a leetle hard at first or so; but we have allus thrived. What with sheep-farming, and what with stock-farming, and what with one thing and what with t'other, we are as well to do as well could be. Theer's been kiender a blessing fell upon us," said Mr. Peggotty, reverentially inclining his head, "and we've done nowt but prosper. That is, in the long run. If not yesterday, why then today. If not today, why then to-morrow."

"And Emily?" said Agnes and I, both together.

417

"Some thinks," he said, "as her affection was ill-bestowed; some, as her marriage was broke off by death. No one knows how 'tis. She might have married well a mort of times, 'But, uncle,' she says to me, 'that's gone forever.' Cheerful along with me; retired when others is by; fond of going any distance fur to teach a child, or fur to tend a sick person, or fur to do some kindness tow'rd a young girl's wedding (and she's done a many, but has never seen one); fondly loving of her uncle; patient; liked by young and old; sowt out by all that has any trouble—that's Em'ly!"

He drew his hand across his face, and with a half-suppressed sigh looked up from the fire.

"Is Martha with you yet?" I asked.

"Martha," he replied, "got married, Mas'r Davy, in the second year. A young man, a farm-laborer, as come by us on his way to market with his mas'r's drays—a journey of over five hundred mile, theer and back—made offers fur to take her fur his wife (wives is very scarce theer), and then to set up fur their two selves in the Bush. She spoke to me fur to tell him her true story. I did. They was married, and they live fower hundred mile away from any voices but their own and the singing birds."

"Mrs. Gummidge?" I suggested.

It was a pleasant key to touch, for Mr. Peggotty suddenly burst into a roar of laughter, and rubbed his hands up and down his legs, as he had been accustomed to do when he enjoyed himself in the long-shipwrecked boat.

"Would you believe it?" he said. "Why, someun even made offers fur to marry *her!* If a ship's cook that was turning settler, Mas'r Davy, didn't make offers fur to marry Missis Gummidge, I'm gormed—and I can't say no fairer than that!"

I never saw Agnes laugh so. This sudden ecstasy on the part of Mr. Peggotty was so delightful to her, that she could not leave off laughing; and the more she laughed the more she made me laugh, and the greater Mr. Peggotty's ecstasy became, and the more he rubbed his legs.

"And what did Mrs. Gummidge say?" I asked, when I was grave enough.

"If you'll believe me," returned Mr. Peggotty, "Missis Gummidge, 'stead of saying, 'Thank you, I'm much obleeged to you; I ain't a-going fur to change my condition at my time of life,' up'd with a bucket as was standing by, and laid it over that theer ship's cook's head 'til he sung out fur help, and I went in and reskied of him."

Mr. Peggotty burst into a great roar of laughter, and Agnes and I both kept him company.

"Now, last, not least, Mr. Micawber," said I. "He has paid off every obligation he incurred here—even to Traddles's bill, you remember, my dear Agnes—and therefore we may take it for granted that he is doing well. But what is the latest news of him?"

Mr. Peggotty, with a smile, put his hand in his breast-pocket, and produced a flat-folded paper parcel, from which he took out, with much care, a little odd-looking newspaper.

"You are to unnerstan', Mas'r Davy," said he, "as we have left the Bush now, being so well to do, and have gone right away round to Port Middlebay Harbour, wheer theer's what *we* call a town."

"Mr. Micawber was in the Bush near you?" said I.

"Bless you, yes," said Mr. Peggotty, "and turned to with a will. I never wish to meet a better gen'l'man for turning to with a will. I've seen that theer bald head of his a-perspiring in the sun, Mas'r Davy, 'til I a'most thowt it would have melted away. And now he's a Magistrate."

"A Magistrate, eh?" said I.

Mr. Peggotty pointed to a certain paragraph in the newspaper, where I read aloud as follows, from the *Port Middlebay Times*:

"☞ The public dinner to our distinguished fellow-colonist and townsman, WILKINS MICAWBER, ESQUIRE, Port Middlebay District Magistrate, came off yesterday in the large room of the Hotel, which was crowded to suffocation. It is estimated that not fewer than forty-seven persons must have been accommodated with dinner at one time, exclusive of the company in the passage and on the stairs. The beauty, fashion, and exclusiveness of Port Middlebay flocked to do honor to one so deservedly esteemed, so highly talented, and so widely popular. Dr. Mell (of Colonial Salem-House Grammar School, Port Middlebay) presided, and on his right sat the distinguished guest. After the removal of the cloth, and the singing of Non Nobis (beautifully executed, and in which we were at no loss to distinguish the bell-like notes of that gifted amateur, WILKINS MICAWBER, ESQUIRE, JUNIOR), the usual loyal and patriotic toasts were severally given and rapturously received. Dr. Mell, in a speech replete with feeling, then proposed 'Our distinguished Guest, the ornament of our town. May he never leave us but to better himself, and may his success among us be such as to render his bettering himself impossible!' The cheering with which the toast was received defies description. Again and again it rose and fell, like the waves of ocean. At length all was hushed, and WILKINS MICAWBER, ESQUIRE, presented himself to return thanks. Far be it from us, in the present comparatively imperfect state of the resources of our establishment, to endeavor to follow our distinguished townsman through the smoothly-flowing periods of his polished and highly-ornate address! Suffice it to observe, that it was a masterpiece of eloquence; and that those passages in which he more particularly traced his own successful career to its source, and warned the younger portion of his auditory from the shoals of ever incurring pecuniary liabilities which they were unable to liquidate, brought a tear to the manliest eye present. The remaining toasts were DOCTOR MELL; MRS. MICAWBER (who gracefully bowed her acknowledgments from the side-door, where a galaxy of beauty was elevated on chairs, at once to witness and adorn the gratifying scene); MRS. RIDGER BEGS (late Miss Micawber); MRS. MELL; WILKINS MICAWBER, ESQUIRE, JUNIOR (who convulsed the assembly by humorously remarking that he found himself unable to return thanks in a speech, but would do so, with their permission, in a song); MRS. MICAWBER'S FAMILY (well-known, it is needless to remark, in the mother country), etc., etc., etc. At the conclusion of the proceedings the tables were cleared as if by art-magic for dancing. Among the votaries of TERPSICHORE, who disported themselves until Sol gave warning for departure, Wilkins Micawber, Esquire, Junior, and the lovely and accomplished Miss Helena, fourth daughter of Doctor Mell, were particularly remarkable."

I was looking back to the name of Doctor Mell, pleased to have discovered, in these happier circumstances, Mr. Mell, formerly poor pinched usher to my Middlesex magistrate, when I found, on glancing at the remaining contents of the newspaper, that Mr. Micawber was a diligent and esteemed correspondent of that Journal. There was a letter from him in the same paper, touching a bridge; there was an advertisement of a collection of similar letters by him, to be shortly republished, in a neat volume, "with considerable additions"; and, unless I am very much mistaken, the Leading Article was his also.

We talked much of Mr. Micawber, on many other evenings while Mr. Peggotty remained with us. He lived with us during the whole term of his stay—which, I think, was something less than a month—and his sister and my aunt came to London to see him. Agnes and I parted from him aboard ship when he sailed; and we shall never part from him more, on earth.

But before he left, he went with me to Yarmouth, to see a little tablet I had put up in the churchyard to the memory of Ham. While I was copying the plain inscription for him, I saw him stoop and gather a tuft of grass from the grave, and a little earth. "For Em'ly," he said, as he put it in his breast. "I promised, Mas'r Davy."

And now my written story ends. I look back, once more—for the last time—before I close these leaves.

I see myself, with Agnes at my side, journeying along the road of life. I see our children and our friends around us; and I hear the roar of many voices, not indifferent to me as I travel on.

What faces are the most distinct to me in the fleeting crowd? Lo, these! all turning to me as I ask my thoughts the question.

Here is my aunt, in stronger spectacles, an old woman of four-score years and more, but upright yet, and a steady walker of six miles at a stretch in winter weather. Always with her, here comes Peggotty, my good old nurse.

The cheeks and arms of Peggotty, so hard and red in my childish days, when I wondered why the birds didn't peck her in preference to apples, are shriveled now; and her eyes, that used to darken their whole neighborhood in her face, are fainter (though they glitter still); but her rough forefinger, which I once associated with a pocket nutmeg-grater, is just the same, and when I see my least child catching at it as it totters from my aunt to her, I think of our little parlor at home, when I could scarcely walk. My aunt's old disappointment is set right now. She is godmother to a real living

421

Betsey Trotwood; and Dora (the next in order) says she spoils her.

Among my boys, this summer holiday time, I see an old man making giant kites, and gazing at them in the air, with a delight for which there are no words. He greets me rapturously, and whispers, with many nods and winks, "Trotwood, you will be glad to hear that I shall finish the Memorial when I have nothing else to do, and that your aunt's the most extraordinary woman in the world, sir."

Who is this bent lady, supporting herself by a stick, and showing me a countenance in which there are some traces of old pride and beauty, feebly contending with a querulous, imbecile, fretful wandering of the mind? She is in a garden; and near her stands a sharp, dark, withered woman, with a white scar on her lip. Let me hear what they say.

"Rosa, I have forgotten this gentleman's name."

Rosa bends over her, and calls to her, "Mr. Copperfield."

"I am glad to see you, sir. I am sorry to observe you are in mourning. I hope Time will be good to you."

Her impatient attendant scolds her, tells her I am not in mourning, bids her look again, tries to rouse her.

"You have seen my son, sir," says the elder lady. "Are you reconciled?"

Looking fixedly at me, she puts her hand to her forehead, and moans. Suddenly she cries, in a terrible voice, "Rosa, come to me. He is dead!" Rosa, kneeling at her feet, by turns caresses her, and quarrels with her; now fiercely telling her, "I loved him better than you ever did!"—now soothing her to sleep on her breast, like a sick child. Thus I leave them; thus I always find them; thus they wear their time away, from year to year.

What ship comes sailing home from India, and what English lady is this, married to a growling old Scotch Crœsus, with great flaps of ears? Can this be Julia Mills?

Indeed it is Julia Mills, peevish and fine, with a black man to carry cards and letters to her on a golden salver, and a copper-colored woman in linen, with a bright handkerchief round her head, to serve her tiffin in her dressing-room. Julia is steeped in money to the throat, and talks and thinks of nothing else. I liked her better in the Desert of Sahara.

And lo, the Doctor, always our good friend, laboring at his Dictionary (somewhere about the letter D), and happy in his home and wife.

Working at his chambers in the Temple, with a busy aspect, and his hair (where he is not bald) made more rebellious than ever by the constant friction of his lawyer's wig, I come, in a later time, upon my dear old Traddles. His table is covered with thick piles of papers, and I say, as I look around me,

"If Sophy were your clerk now, Traddles, she would have enough to do!"

"You may say that, my dear Copperfield. But those were capital days, too, in Holborn Court! Were they not?"

"When she told you you would be a Judge? But it was not the town talk *then!*"

"At all events," says Traddles, "if I ever am one——"

"Why, you know you will be."

"Well, my dear Copperfield, *when* I am one, I shall tell the story, as I said I would."

And now, as I close my task, subduing my desire to linger yet, these faces fade away. But one face, shining on me like a Heavenly light by which I see all other objects, is above them and beyond them all. And that remains.

I turn my head, and see it, in its beautiful serenity, beside me. My lamp burns low, and I have written far into the night; but the dear presence, without which I were nothing, bears me company.

O Agnes, O my soul! so may thy face be by me when I close my life indeed; so may I, when realities are melting from me like the shadows which I now dismiss, still find thee near me, pointing upward!